PRAISE FOR
ROBERT MAGARIAN

Praise for *72 Hours*

"I was compelled to carry *72 Hours* around with me. It's a blend of trouble both personal and political, with an evil that will stop at nothing and a CDC that may—or may not—have found the only salvation. Here, also, is a family in pain. Suspenseful, timely, and breath-catching."
—Carolyn Wall, author of *Sweeping Up Glass*

Praise for *The Watchman*

"*The Watchman* came to life for me, because it is so well written and instills a sense of caution as you read. I am delighted to have had the pleasure of discovering Robert Magarian and his talent."
—Bea Kunz, Amazon reviewer

Praise for *You'll Never See Me Again*

"I absolutely loved this book, I couldn't put it down. The details and thought put into this book by Dr. Magarian are absolutely amazing. I felt as if I was in the book myself."
—Brooke, Amazon reviewer

"Loved the book. It kept my attention, kept me guessing and kept me reading. I didn't want to put it down. Highly recommend it."
—Nancy Loyd, Amazon reviewer

Praise for *Follow Your Dream*

"In *Follow Your Dream*, Robert Magarian provides a template for turning a dream into reality, step-by-step. In 1987 Magarian created the first annual Norman Community Christmas Dinner, serving a free meal to individuals and family who would have been alone on Christmas Day. In the years hence, the event has grown to serve 1,600 people, with 200 volunteers. This is a remarkable story of what one person can do with a dream and how that dream can change many lives."
—Robert L. Ferrier, Amazon reviewer

ALSO BY ROBERT MAGARIAN

Fiction

The Watchman

You'll Never See Me Again: A Crime to Remember

Essays

Follow Your Dream

A Journey into Faith

72 HOURS

A Novel

By

ROBERT MAGARIAN

Publisher's Note. This is a work of fiction. Names, characters, places, and incidents either are the product of the author's imagination or are used fictitiously. Any resemblance to persons, living or dead is entirely coincidental.

Author Photo: "shevyvision"
shevaun williams & associates, Norman, OK
www.shevaunwilliams.com

Editing: Nancy Hancock

Print Formatting: By Your Side Self-Publishing
www.ByYourSideSelfPub.com

DEDICATION

To my father and mother,
the greatest love a son could have

PROLOGUE

Twenty-six years earlier: 1966.

The clouds look mean. Susan watches the road from the passenger side of Daddy's Cadillac. Her twin Sabrina is in the back with six-year-old Michael, who is snoring. Daddy wheels into the lot of St. Mary's Hospital.

"We're here, Susan," he says.

Sabrina starts to cry as they clamber out. Daddy lifts Michael. The back door of a red and white ambulance is open, parked under the canopy. The glass doors hiss and the Prescotts hurry into a room with leather chairs and couches. Every seat is taken. A young woman holds up a hand wrapped in a bloody towel. A man mops the floor. His sign says CAUTION. The water smells strong, like the janitor's pail at school.

When the elevator opens on the fourth floor, they step out. Michael is asleep on Daddy's shoulder.

"The doctors have done all they can," Daddy tells us.

That's what grownups always say.

Poor Daddy, Susan thinks. He looks so tired, but he doesn't close his eyes at night. In room 4010, Daddy reaches for Mommy's hand and kisses it. She's as white as the sheet. The chairs in this room are yellow. A painting shows Jesus among his sheep. A nurse with shiny brown hair and red lips arrives. She does something to Mommy's IV and smiles at us.

Sabrina asks Daddy, "Isn't Mommy going to wake up?"

Susan knows better.

"She's talking with God," Daddy says. He shifts Michael to his other shoulder.

1

"Wake up, Mommy," says Sabrina. She climbs in bed and snuggles next to her.

Mommy's gone. Who will make us do our homework and tie bows in our hair and read to Michael? Not Daddy. He's too busy keeping people out of jail. The doctor touches Daddy on the shoulder. Twelve-year-old Susan has never seen him cry, but now he wipes his tears with a tissue from the nightstand. Susan takes Mommy's hand.

Michael wakes up and rubs his eyes. He cries, calling for mommy, reaching out for her.

"It's time to say goodbye," Daddy tells us.

"No," Susan says.

And it isn't goodbye: The next morning Mommy's standing in Susan's bedroom doorway. She's smiling. Susan jumps out of bed and slams the door shut. When she carefully opens it, Mommy is gone. She can't be here, according to Daddy. God has her doing something in Heaven.

Twelve years later: 1978. Sabrina goes to be with Mom. Susan, Michael, and Dad are devastated and filled with rage. Another part of Susan is gone.

CHAPTER ONE

November 1992.

Elevator doors open in the circular lobby of the D.C. Marriott Hotel, and Susan Prescott is about to charge out against a wall of people blocking her exit. "Damn you," she mutters to herself, pushing her way through the throng. Sane persons usually stand aside when the elevator doors open. Many in the wall of eager people are wearing badges like hers, indicating they are attending the same meeting as she—the 1992 International Infectious Disease Conference. You'd think these experts would know better, but she singles out their behavior as being no different than that of other non-thinking Homo sapiens. Susan isn't in the habit of criticizing people, but when they do stupid things, it bugs her. She learned at an early age, after her mother died, that when you did stupid stuff, you heard about it from good ole Dad. She must have learned it from him.

She hurries through the brightly lighted rotunda with white walls trimmed in gold, shiny Italian marble floors, and a humongous Waterford crystal chandelier in the center. She continues down one of the four corridors that lead away from the lobby and steps into Starbucks coffee shop. Free-standing tables occupy most of the space, with a counter around the periphery. The place is packed with coffee drinkers eating unhealthy snacks. A woman at a table close to the door is talking and gesturing to a guy who is paying more attention to one of those new laptop computers than to her. Must be his wife, she thinks.

Susan gets in line for coffee, sets her book and purse on the counter, and can barely see the clerk behind the large black coffee urns. Since she hasn't had breakfast, the aroma of hazelnut and French vanilla coffees and the sight of warm blueberry muffins make her stomach growl. She likes blueberries, but the muffins aren't on her list of healthy foods. She orders a light latte. Several years ago, she decided to avoid eating at fast-food joints and follow the Mediterranean diet, going heavy on fruit and vegetables and whole grains. Actually, she's been thinking about becoming a vegetarian. Susan takes several drinks from her hazelnut coffee before picking up her stuff, hurries out and pivots to her left, padding across the ankle-deep red carpet. A series of glass chandeliers hang in a straight line down the center of the hallway as far as she can see, reflecting light off the vertical, four-inch gold stripes on taupe walls. Maneuvering her way through crowds thronged in front of a string of large oak doors, waiting for the meeting rooms to open, Susan stops in front of rooms E & F at the end of the hall. An exit door opens and three people enter, followed by a cloud of smoke, and stand behind Susan. The harsh smell of tobacco turns her stomach. *Will they ever learn?* She takes a swallow of her coffee and checks her watch. Two minutes to nine.

She glances around. Some of the scientists are dressed in suits, but most are in casual attire—open-collared shirts with slacks; blouses or sweaters with skirts. They are clutching green zipper-bags that have the name of the conference—24th Annual International Infectious Disease Meeting, the date—November 1992—and the site—Washington D.C.—printed on them. These goody bags were handed out at registration, but Susan left hers in the room. It contained too much junk—notepads, pens, maps, places to eat and shop in D.C., coupons, a list of the pre-registrants, and a copy of the latest issue of the Infectious Disease Journal—to lug around. She only brought the book of abstracts for the four-day conference with her, which lists the titles of the papers, authors' names, synopses, and the times and meeting room numbers of those making a presentation. Scores of people are shaking hands and laughing, as if they hadn't seen each other since last year's meeting.

The doors open and the noisy crowd moves in like rowdy children. The dividers between rooms E & F have been pulled back into the wall so that the room could be filled with over two hundred chairs arranged in theatre style. Inside, everyone rushes to find a place to sit. Susan dashes down the center aisle to the second row and plops her abstract book and purse on an aisle seat facing the podium. She sighs, takes several sips of her coffee, and looks around, spotting an old friend, Hal Woolrich, at the far side. She'll catch up with him later.

An elevated platform covers the entire front of the room, with a huge screen center stage. The lights are bright and a tall, broad-shouldered blonde man wearing black trousers and matching turtleneck sweater under a dark sport coat stands at the lectern making sure his slides are in proper order. Interestingly, some speakers think they can dazzle their audiences with fancy slides to cover up the omission of data in their experiments, but in most cases it doesn't work—it's an obvious ploy.

Vladimir Sokolov is the first speaker, and Susan's certain that's he on the stage. His sea-blue eyes scan the room and lock on hers. He smiles. *Was that a wink?* Susan feels a little warmth around her neck. She glances at her black loafers and tugs at her collar. *Wow! He's hot.*

Susan looks around again and checks her watch. Five minutes have gone by. All seats have been taken, and now people are standing along the walls and in the back. *Let's get this show on the road.* She's eager to hear about Sokolov's cancer research, especially since reading his journal articles and researching him on the Internet. He may have discovered the holy grail of cancer cures and she has to get to him before the pharmaceutical vultures sink their teeth into him.

The noise abates when a tall brunette with short hair comes from behind the curtain, dressed in a dark blue suit with heels that click as she strolls across the stage. Click. Click. Click. Stopping next to the speaker, she says something to the big man and taps the microphone, asking if she can be heard in the back. Several people standing back there yell that they can hear her.

"My name is Dr. Natalie Hamil," the slender lady with the smooth tan says. She adjusts her dark glasses and continues. *She'd be sexy without those glasses,* Susan thinks. "I'll be introducing our speaker for this first session, Dr. Vladimir Sokolov, a renowned geneticist who will be speaking to us on *Re-engineered Viruses in the Treatment of Cancer.*" She glances at the sheets in front of her and begins reading from what is probably Sokolov's curriculum vita, emphasizing his education and institutions where he had conducted his research, adding his latest scientific discoveries, and giving a litany of his publications ad nauseam. *Get on with it.* After Hamil finishes, there's a thunderous applause welcoming Dr. Sokolov. *Maybe everyone's clapping because they're glad Hamil finally shuts up.*

Sokolov thanks Dr. Hamil, who turns and leaves the stage. He pushes a button on the podium to bring up his first slide, which flashes on the screen behind him. Listed are the title of his talk, his name and those of his co-workers, and below is a picture of his research group at the State Research Center for Applied Microbiology in Obolensk, Russia. During his presentation, a dozen people are snapping pictures, capturing the information from Sokolov's slides.

Susan knows they are from the pharmaceutical companies and what they are doing, as does everyone else in the room. They'll carry this information back to their respective drug companies where researches will examine Sokolov's work and look for ways to beat him to market, or if not, they can develop a "Me-Too" drug. Me-Too drugs are common among pharmaceutical companies. It's a practice that involves making structural variations in the molecule of a competitor's new drug, and if found effective after going through their testing methods, they patent it as *their* new drug. This way they capture part of the market. But developing a Me-Too could be tricky in this case, since Sokolov's product is a re-engineered virus, and he's deliberately left out several subtle steps as a ploy to keep others from duplicating his work. Nevertheless, that won't stop the Me-Too people from trying. Sokolov is now standing in the shadows, posturing like a movie star, smiling as flashing lights inundate his gorgeous face. *It's like he's giving them the finger.*

When he finishes his presentation, Dr. Hamil returns to the stage and opens the floor for questions. Twenty minutes later, she cuts off the questioning and allows a fifteen-minute break before the start of the second session. The room empties and Susan jumps up, rushes to the front and grabs Sokolov's arm as he comes down the steps, carrying his briefcase under one arm.

"Dr. Sokolov, can we meet? I'd like to discuss your work." She quickly hands him her business card and introduces herself. "How about lunch?" she asks. His blue eyes smile as he reads her card. "The CDC?" he says in a tone that leads Susan to believe he's impressed. He's much taller and broader than he appeared on the stage.

"Yes," she says, following alongside, heading toward the back of the room. "I have a lunch engagement," he says, slipping her card into his coat pocket, but not slowing his pace as they reach the door. "Dinner?" he says. "I'll call your room, Dr. Prescott."

"I'd like that." Outside the door he's mobbed by a crowd in the hall. *In the nick of time.*

Susan spots Hal Woolrich talking to a guy in front of meeting room C. Hal has been a good friend since their days at Harvard. He went to Sloan-Kettering Cancer Center in New York City after leaving Cambridge.

She waves. He nods that he sees her, and seconds later the two men part and Hal comes over to her. They hug and kiss each other on the cheek.

"How'd you like Sokolov's talk?" she asks as they stroll through the hallway.

"Excellent work, but I kinda waited for the part he left out."

"That was deliberate!" she says with conviction. "The guy's too damn smart to let these pharmaceutical junkies steal his ideas." She pauses. "Actually, I'm surprised no one asked him about it."

Hal smiled and winked. "I thought you would," he says.

"No way. I want him all to myself. We're having dinner tonight."

"Good for you," he says, taking her arm as he escorts her into the lobby. "I haven't had breakfast. Are you hungry?"

"I could eat a small horse."

"Oh, we'd better hurry then," he says. "I don't want you to faint on me." They laugh as they pass a bank of elevators and step into the Downtown Café. Inside, Susan is surprised to find that she's back in time. Elvis Presley is crooning "Don't Be Cruel" on the jukebox, and pictures of the superstars of the '50s are in the alcoves: Charlton Heston, Grace Kelly, Marlo Brando, and Elizabeth Taylor.

A slender brunette in her mid-twenties, wearing a white uniform and a big smile, grabs two menus from the trunk of a miniature 1957 Corvette *Fuelie* and motions for them to follow her, escorting them past a long black Formica counter with black leather stools, where two guys in uniforms and paper hats, looking like soda jerks, are serving customers pancakes, eggs, and bacon with buttered toast. Susan shudders. Passing several booths, the waitress seats Susan and Hal at a table near a window with a view of the street. The sun is behind the clouds and the street traffic is heavy. Scores of people are walking past, carrying laptops, gym bags, and brief cases.

"Do you have one of those laptops?" Susan asks as she adjusts herself in the seat. "I hear they're the thing today."

"Got one back at the lab, but haven't gotten used to carrying it around yet."

"I've been thinking about getting one." The waitress hands them menus and takes their drink orders. A picture of Marilyn Monroe is on the back wall. The place is packed with the conferees talking above each other, and on each table are the green goody-bags. Elvis stops singing and Sinatra takes over.

"Were you serious when you said you were going to meet with Sokolov?" Hal asks, reaching for his water and taking several swallows.

Susan nods. "I'm very interested in his work. He's on to something."

Hal glances over the menu, "Still searching for the holy grail, huh?"

"You betcha. It's important to me," she says, moving her water glass to one side as the waitress comes with their drinks. Hal's coffee is set in front of him and the second one is placed next to Susan's plate. "The cream is on the table," she says. "So is the sugar."

"Thank you," Susan and Hal say in unison.

"Are you ready to order?" she asks.

"I believe so," Susan says.

"Good. What can I get you folks?" she says, pulling a pad from her apron and a pencil from a lower pocket. Susan nods for Hal to begin.

He orders scrambled eggs, buttered whole wheat toast, and three buttermilk pancakes with butter and hot maple syrup. Susan selects fat-free yogurt, a bowl of unsweetened blueberries, and a toasted multi-grain bagel, no butter.

"Still eating healthy, I see," Hal says as he places Susan's menu on top of his and hands them to the brunette, who smiles and leaves. "Don't you know all that healthy stuff will kill you some day?"

"That's what everyone tells me," she says.

They laugh.

"Getting back to Sokolov, don't be surprised if he's brusque with you," Hal says, looking across the room. "Russkies don't play by our rules, especially since the fall of the Soviet Union. The KGB and the Mafia are into everything."

"You think he's—"

"KGB? Naw. But I did read where the scientists were treated badly. Very badly. Some went back to their home states." He reaches for his coffee. "I wouldn't be surprised if some slipped into the Mafia."

"I'm sensing you don't trust their scientists."

"All I'm saying is... be careful, and make sure his motives are clear."

She nods, feeling a little scared now. She flashes on KGB officers she's seen on TV clipping off fingers.

Dammit. Now he's got me worried. She takes a couple of sips of her coffee.

"Speaking of the devil, there he is," Hal says, pointing. "Over there at the table in the corner with some bruiser."

Susan sets her coffee cup in the saucer and glances across the room at the two men. "The guy with him certainly doesn't look like any pharmaceutical rep," Susan says. "He looks more like a skin-head."

"I wouldn't want to meet him in any dark place. That's for sure," Hal says.

Maybe they are KGB. Golly, what am I thinking? I can't let my emotions get the best of me.

The waitress returns with their orders, balancing plates of food on both arms as well as in her hands, and sets them one-by-one on the table. "Can I get you anything else?"

Wow! She's pretty damn good. "I think we're fine for now," Susan says. "Thank you."

Hal nods his approval, picks up his knife and spreads grape jelly on his buttered toast, takes a bite, and digs a fork into his eggs.

"They're gone," Susan says. She reaches for the bowl of berries and dumps them into the yogurt.

"Who's gone?" Hal asks with a mouth full of food.

"Sokolov and his mobster friend."

"Mobster?" He laughs. "That's probably a stretch."

"Hey, you brought it up," she says, swallowing a spoonful of blueberry yogurt.

"I'm probably a little paranoid. Sorry," he says.

Dammit. Thanks a lot. Through the rest of the meal, Susan battles her fear of losing the holy grail and wonders now if she can trust Sokolov.

When they finish eating, Hal checks his watch. "The last session this morning is in fifteen minutes. You game?"

"Naw. I got in around two this morning, and feel exhausted. My plane was held up because of bad weather. Gotta check in with my people at the lab and finish this article I'm working on. The publisher's on my back. Then I think I'll hit the sack for a while."

CHAPTER TWO

Startled out of a deep sleep to the sound of the phone, Susan feels disoriented for a moment, staring at the ceiling until she realizes she's in her hotel room. The last thing Susan remembers is leaving Hal at the elevator bank, coming to her room to work for a few hours on her paper, and falling asleep on the bed. She raises herself on her elbows, checks the clock on the nightstand: 5:30 p.m. She hadn't realized how tired she was from working so late in the lab the evening before coming to this meeting. The phone rings a third time.

She grabs the receiver and says hello. Vladimir Sokolov is on the other end. He's made dinner reservations for seven-thirty at the Capitol Hill Club on the first floor in the hotel, and would she join him for a drink at seven? After accepting his invitation and hanging up the phone, she sheds the comforter. Still in her street clothes, she slides her feet into her shoes next to the bed and walks to the window, pulls the drapes apart, opens the sliding glass doors to step out on the balcony and inhales the frigid November air. She can see her breath, but doesn't mind the wintry sting.

Susan books hotel rooms no higher than the second floor. Being close to street level gives her a sense of confidence that in any emergency she can get to safety. The street lights are on and there's a haze around the lamps. Below, the town is alive, bustling with commuters, and streams of vehicles—some idling at the stoplight—belch white clouds of exhaust that hang in the mist. Flashing flames of orange light off the buildings and the street noise make her feel alive... like being in Vegas.

Moving back into the room, she ambles into the bathroom and flips on the shower. Forty minutes later, she returns in red panties and bra, pulls on the black dress she had packed, knowing she would somehow finagle Sokolov to have dinner with her. She parks herself at the dressing table. In the middle of applying makeup she frowns, wondering if Hal was trying to be helpful or to scare the pants off her when he told her to watch out for the Russians. *Does he know something she doesn't? Does he really think Sokolov is KGB or in the Mob? Surely not; Sokolov's a scientist, for criminy sakes.* She finishes her makeup, snaps a diamond locket around her neck, and fastens matching earrings. Her dark eyes and shoulder-length hair glisten against the black dress. *Not bad.* She stands and checks out her slim figure with a tight butt, then glides her feet into red shoes, grabs her purse and flips off the light, slamming the door behind her.

At the elevators, Susan pushes the down button and waits. Checking her watch, she has five minutes, and is left with her reflection in the shiny metal door. Never late for her appointments, she considers taking the stairs. The bell tolls and the doors open. Her eyes must have widened as she wonders how in the hell she's going to fit into this sardine-packed car. Should she get in? Decides against it, and says "I'll take the stairs."

"No," a tall, chivalrous man in his sixties, facing her and smiling, says as he moves to one side, "There's room for one more." Some people in the back groan.

Aw, shut up. Susan enters sideways and holds her breath. The door closes. The air is filled with an array of colognes that are on the strong side. Two women behind her are gabbing about how waiting on Susan could now make them miss their friends and the buses waiting in front of the hotel to take them to Aster's annual reception. Aster Pharmaceuticals is not only famous for its research in the infectious disease area, but also for its amazing parties. Humongous amounts of food and drinks are served, and hundreds of gift boxes of expensive watches, purses, handbags, and pens are handed out. Susan has attended a few of these receptions, but lost interest in them because, in her opinion, most of the guests are scavengers—stuffing their faces, sopping up the booze, and acting like frantic Christmas shoppers, shoving each other aside when the gifts are handed out. Few care about Aster's latest scientific discoveries, expressed in their literature distributed from a special exhibitor's booth during the party. At one gathering, only she and one other person were in the exhibit area.

When the elevator doors open on the street level, Susan shoots out to keep from being crushed by the stampede. She continues down one of the corridors that lead from the circular lobby like spokes on a wheel, glancing at the shops on the way to the Club, wondering who could afford the stuff in the showcases. She stops at the ornate black marquee with its flashing lights above the Capitol Club's entrance, yanks on the glass door and enters. Recessed wall lights give the place inviting warmth.

Behind the bar is a large mural of the white marble-domed building of the U.S. Congress, and along the walls are pictures of D.C. lawmakers smiling and shaking hands with Club patrons, which give Susan the impression that this place is one of their favorites.

The dining area has sleek enclaves of dark mahogany, spacious red leather booths, and side-arm chairs pushed under tables dressed in white tablecloths and formal place settings. A piano player wearing a tux and bow tie is in the back keying in "The Way We Were." Barbra Streisand made it famous, Susan remembers.

Sokolov is the only one seated at the mahogany bar, perched on a high-back chair talking to the gal pouring drinks. The bartender, probably in her early thirties, with red hair pulled back into a pony tail, is wearing a low-cut white blouse exposing enough flesh to make men drool. She's smiling at the hunk of a man in front of her while mixing his drink.

Sokolov's in a pin-striped dark suit and tie that make his blonde hair and deep blue eyes striking. *Wow. He's handsome.* Susan's heart is beating a little fast as she walks towards him, thinking how he would look naked. Muscular and sexy, of course. He spots her, stands. Wide-eyed, he tells Susan how beautiful she looks as he moves the chair next to him away from the bar. He's two heads taller and three times her size. Maybe four. Susan thanks him, sets her purse on the bar, slides on the seat and settles in. A hint of Sokolov's cologne reaches her, but she can't make it out. She likes it, and struggles to block the romantic images flashing through her mind.

Not now, she reminds herself.

"What'll you have?" the smiling redhead with glistening teeth asks.

"White wine."

"Sure thing." She reaches for a goblet, places it on the bar in front of Susan, and fills it half-full with Chablis. Susan reaches for her drink and in the process notices her face in the polished surface of the bar. *I'd say not bad.* She laughs to herself.

Susan is surprised Sokolov is wearing cologne. She thought Russian's liked body soap fragrance more. Maybe he's worldlier than his comrades. Susan reaches for her drink and swallows a little, then raises it in the air when he glances her way as she says "Thank you."

"You like very dry wine," he says more as a statement than a question. Susan nods. "Me, I like vodka." He eases his glass forward for a refill. It doesn't take him long to empty it and to ask for another. "After the first one, it doesn't burn as much," he says.

They laugh.

It's true. Russians do like their vodka. Glad he doesn't have to drive tonight.

"Now, down to business," he says, turning to her. "Tell me what it is that you want from me?"

Oh, don't go there. I'd need a couple more drinks before I can answer that. She takes another swallow of her Chablis and says, "Your work on re-engineered viruses… especially their effect on cancer, excites me."

Sokolov doesn't say a word. Instead, he gestures for a refill, and for a few moments becomes fixed on the mural facing him. The bartender fills his glass. Sokolov's jaw muscles tighten and he snorts almost imperceptibly, as his eyes seem to lock onto the Capitol Dome.

What's that all about? Susan wonders as she drinks more wine.

Finally, he says, "My work is only preliminary," his gaze still glued to the mural.

Susan takes a long breath and blows it out slowly. "Dr. Sokolov—"

"Vladimir, please," he says, turning to her. "Not so formal."

She decides he's lying about his work and changes her approach to get to the truth. The Russians respect boldness, so it's time to get aggressive. She'd do anything to get his drug. Well, maybe not anything. "Vladimir. Let's not play games. You deliberately omitted steps in your talk to make it seem your work is preliminary. Yet you and I know better, and so does a cancer researcher friend of mine who was at your talk. You couldn't have reached that last step in your work without those intermediates you omitted."

He turns away, swallows the last of his drink and slams the glass on the bar, checks his watch, and raises his hand, signaling to the bartender that he's had enough. Turning back to Susan, his eyes lock on hers. "You and your friend are badly mistaken."

"I don't think so." She realizes she's holding her breath, wondering if she's gone too far, but presses on. "I have a hunch you've discovered the holy grail of cancer drugs," she says as she searches his eyes for the answer. They say that the eyes are the gateway to the soul, and she wants through. "You're not being honest with me for some reason," she says, still locked on his gaze. "I'm thinking maybe you're holding out for the highest bidder." He turns away.

He's not answering me. Maybe one of those pharmaceutical junkies has gotten to him? Have I turned him off with my aggressiveness? Russians probably don't like aggressive women. She covers her glass to stop the bartender from filling it. "You know those pharmaceutical companies could beat you to the market, don't you?" Actually, she's stretching the truth. If he patents his invention first, there'd be no way. Vladimir smiles, but still doesn't say a word. She thinks he's got something up his sleeve.

A nice-looking waiter in his early forties dressed in a white shirt, bow tie and black jacket, steps behind Vladimir, and says, "Sir, your table is ready."

Vladimir nods, hands the redhead behind the bar several large bills, and reaches for Susan's arm. "Come," he says. "We can talk over dinner."

The waiter guides them down three steps, past several tables occupied by well-dressed diners, some drinking and laughing, others simply enjoying their food. The waiter stops at a booth in the back near the piano, pulls out the table. Susan and Vladimir slide in behind it and he pushes it back. "My name is Elgin," he says, handing Vladimir the wine list. "I will be your head waiter this evening."

"Thank you, Elgin," Vladimir says, as he slides a finger down the list and orders an expensive French wine. He chooses white Bordeaux.

"Excellent choice, sir," the waiter says.

When Elgin leaves, Susan asks, "Was your lab closed after the fall of Communism?"

Vladimir's generous mouth turns down, and his eyes give way to sadness. "One month later. It was hell." He pauses as another waiter fills Susan's water goblet next to the red and white wine glasses, then reaches for Vladimir's.

The head waiter brings an ice bucket, sets it beside the table, opens a bottle of Domaine de Chevalier Blanc and pours a little in a glass, handing it to Vladimir, who twirls the glass, sniffs it and swishes a little around in his mouth. "Very good," he says. *What would the waiter do if Vladimir didn't like it? Choose another?*

The waiter nods, removes the red wine goblets, and fills their white wine glasses halfway.

Susan takes a drink. Not bad. She frowns. Where is he getting his money? My per diem wouldn't even cover this glass of wine.

Vladimir reaches for his menu and the waiter hands one to Susan. A younger man dressed like Elgin, but without the jacket, brings a basket of assorted breads wrapped in a white cloth napkin and sets it on the table between them, followed by pats of butter that he places on their bread plates.

"Were you able to finish your work before the lab closed?" Susan asks, wondering if she has worded the question in the right way to get the answer she wants.

Vladimir reaches for a roll, butters it, seemingly taking his time to answer, and sets it on the plate.

Come on, dammit. Open up.

Vladimir asks Susan if she would like him to order for her. Preferring to select for herself, she glances down the menu until she comes to the vegetarian section and orders the Chef's choice seasonal vegetable plate.

"Hors d'oeuvre, Madame?"

"None."

"Soup?" he asks with disdain in his eyes.

"No." *You jerk.*

"As you wish," he says, reaching for her menu. "Thank you," he says and turns to Vladimir. "And you, sir?"

Vladimir selects for his hors d'oeuvre: baked onion soup with melted Gruyere cheese; for his salad: a classic Caesar salad with Reggiano cheese, anchovy and egg yolk, to be prepared at the table; and for his entrée, roasted Muscovy duck breast with fresh grapes, baby turnips and parsnips.

"Excellent choices, sir," the waiter says, glancing at Susan.

Up yours, monsieur. "Now, Vladimir. You haven't answered my question." *You've had enough time to cook up an answer, let's hear it.*

"What was that?"

Where in hell have you been? Mars? "I asked you if you had found the cancer drug before your lab closed."

He takes a bite of bread roll. "Almost," he says, reaching for his wine.

"So, you have more work to do," she says, more as a statement than a question.

He nods, swallows some wine, and sets the glass down.

"But how will you finish it?" *Dammit.* Tired of pulling everything out of him, she feels like stabbing her dinner knife into his hand. "I thought you said we were going to talk at dinner. So far you've done nothing but dodge my questions."

He waits until the waiter refills his wine glass. "I must confess," he says. "I did get something."

Susan bolts upright. "You did?"

He laughs one of those belly laughs. "Gotcha. Isn't that what you Americans say?"

"You... you've been playing with me?" *Watch your words,* she tells herself.

He nods. "Only because I wanted to see how far you would push me. I like your determination."

Determined I am. "Does this mean you don't have anything?"

Elgin arrives with Vladimir's onion soup. He turns to Susan and asks, "Does madam wish her vegetable plate when I bring the gentleman's entrée, or does she prefer it now?"

What is it with this guy? He sounds like he's talking about some old woman seated next to me. "That'll be fine. Bring it with his duck," Susan says. She's more interested in what Vladimir has to say at the moment than eating.

"Tell me what you have, Vladimir, and don't hold back."

The head waiter's assistant places a cart next to the table. Elgin returns and begins mixing the Caesar salad, removes Vladimir's soup bowl, and replaces it with the salad.

"What I meant earlier, about my work being preliminary... I meant additional testing is needed."

"On the cancer agent, right?" Susan says interrupting. She couldn't contain her excitement. "I can help with that."

He takes a bite of his salad and nods. "Since we met this morning, I've been thinking about you. Someone as pushy as you would make a good associate."

Pushy? I'm more than pushy. "I would?" she says, surprised that he has been thinking about her at all.

"I have the data with me. And a sample."

She feels faint. *The holy grail with him.* "You... you... can't mean you have a sample with you. Here?"

He gazes at her and smiles. "I do, I do."

This is too good to be true. Susan's heart is about to burst out of her chest. This isn't really happening. Finally, she says, "Of course, I would be thrilled to work with you."

Their entrees arrive. Vladimir reaches for his wine glass, finishes it off, and gestures for a refill.

Susan looks at her vegetable plate. *Who can eat at a time like this?*

"Tell me one thing," Susan says. "Why didn't you go with one of the pharmaceutical companies? They're really interested in your work."

"Earlier, you were correct when you said I was planning to sell it to highest bidder."

I knew it.

"But not for the reason you're thinking. I need lots of money to open a new laboratory. I wanted to work with them, but they wanted my drug for nothing."

"So, you've met with them?"

He nods. "Only to test them. They think: he's Russian. What does he know?" Now Vladimir has a mean look on his face. "They wanted to screw me." He slams his fist on the table. "They insulted me."

For once Susan doesn't know what to say. All she can think of is: "They're vultures." *Am I a vulture?*

He nods. "That they are." He pauses to swallow some wine. "I need an American associate I can trust to test my drug further, and to help me sell it to a company. You can be that person."

Susan immediately thinks about Kraft Pharmaceuticals back in Atlanta, owned by Karl Gerber's wife and her brother Harry Wentworth. "I know a company that would be very interested, but your drug must prove worthy," she says.

"I assure you that my data are promising, but you will determine that on your own when you repeat the work on Tican."

"Tican?"

"Yes, that's its name." He frowns as he sips his wine. "But how can you take a cancer drug into the CDC?" he says. "You are an infectious disease expert."

He's done his homework. She couldn't tell him that they have been testing biologicals from his country ever since she's been with the CDC. But the samples were given to them by the CIA. "You're right in a way, but with a sound plan of action, it's doable. I only have to convince my boss, Karl Gerber, the director of the Infectious Disease Center. He's a tough nut to crack, but he can be reasonable."

"I like your confidence."

"I have an advantage," Susan says. "His wife, Eva, has colon cancer. That makes Karl easier to persuade, especially if you give me some convincing data to show him. He would do anything for his wife." That's Susan's plan for now. "When can I see the data?"

"When we finish here."

CHAPTER THREE

American Airlines flight 332 from D.C. has landed and Susan is charging out of the jetway into the terminal. Glad to be back in Atlanta, she can't wait to tell Alec about Vladimir and the prize she has in her possession. She rushes through the terminal, following the green arrows to ground transportation. A few feet from the doors, this big guy with no hair, wearing a black overcoat, comes out of nowhere and slams into her, knocking the wind out of her. *What the hell?* The asshole doesn't say a word, just grunts and whips away. She takes a moment to get her breath before heading to the doors. She'd like to kill the bastard.

She frowns. Something about him makes her skin crawl.

The electronic glass doors hiss open as she steps out into the cold November air and stops by the curb, shifting the leather bag to the other shoulder and breathing in the cool air. The sky is clear and the sun is out. Maybe it will warm up today, she thinks. Several taxis slow at the curb, but she waves them on. The shuttle approaches and she boards it.

The driver drops her off behind her Caddy and Susan steps out with her bags, throws them into the trunk and slips in behind the wheel. She drops the leather bag on the passenger seat, sighs in relief. *I'm home.* She doesn't turn the ignition key just yet. Instead, she sits quietly thinking about what has happened the last two days. Was it luck—being at the right place at the right time—or maybe something like a miracle, that she was the only person destined to work with Vladimir Sokolov? The past fourteen years, she's hidden her fear pretty well from everyone, even her own father, but now she's less afraid, more peaceful, as she touches the bag next to her. *I have my cure, Sabrina.*

She starts the engine and drives out of the airport, heads north on I-85 for ten minutes, exits and drives north to Briarcliff Road. Her boss, Karl

Gerber, won't be too enthusiastic about her bringing a Russian drug into the Center without prior approval, even though her lab has been testing their biologicals for years. During that time Karl had come to distrust the Soviets. But this is different. She has exciting data to back her up. She turns right on Clifton Road and follows it to the Centers for Disease Control, situated in the middle of a wooded area in Clifton, a suburb of Atlanta. She swings around the island with a fifty-foot flag pole and pulls up to the entrance of what could be mistaken for a maximum security facility, with its high walls topped with razor wire. She lowers her window as the guard approaches.

"Welcome back, Dr. Prescott," he says. "How'd the meeting go?"

She beams at him. "Better than expected. I see the place is still here."

"'Fraid so," he says, smiling.

The gate rises and she drives to the National Center for Infectious Diseases and wheels into her space marked "Chief," next to Special Path Building 15. She grabs the bag from the seat and rushes round to the front, colliding with security guard Phil Corben.

"Whoa! Dr. Prescott?"

"Sorry," she says.

He's slender and tall, has a long narrow face with a head of thinning gray hair, but looks sharp in his starched uniform.

"Whatever's got you wound up, you seem happy about it."

She smiles. *If only you knew.* "No time to explain. Have a good day."

"You, too," he says and motors on past her.

She enters the code in the keypad and steps into the long narrow corridor with its white cinder-block walls, twelve-inch white floor tiles, a series of doors, and her lab at the far end. The mechanical handlers that remove air from the Level-3 and Level-4 labs rumble throughout the building. She's eager to get to Level-3 and really doesn't want to stop at her office, used for her position as Chief of the Special Pathogens Branch—a Branch in the National Center for Infectious Diseases. *But there will be messages.* Her group's mission is the control and prevention of infection from the most pathogenic of all viruses. She opens the door and closes it behind her, drops the bag on the desk and checks her phone.

The walls are covered with her university degrees and framed pictures of coworkers. Science books fill shelves next to the desk. A photo of her mother and Susan's twin, Sabrina, is next to the phone. Behind it is one of Susan with her father and brother after the death of her mother and sister.

The light on the recorder is blinking. She presses the button. Two messages. One is from Karl Gerber, Director for Center of Infectious Diseases, asking her to come to his office upon her return. She glances at her bag wondering if Karl will believe her story. He has to.

The second message is from her father. He sounds distressed.

It has to be about Michael. Damn him. Her brother might be thirty-two, but he acts nineteen—has sleazy friends, drinks too much, never graduated from college, and hasn't held a job. She glances at her mother's picture. *What are we going to do about Michael?*

Reaching for the phone, she dials her father's office in New Haven.

"Your brother's at it again," he says. "Michael won't listen, and now he's moved out. Can you talk to him?"

"Dad, we've been through this—"

"But Sue, he's living with those punks."

Sue? Was that a slip? She hasn't heard that name since Sabrina passed. When they were toddlers, Sabrina couldn't say *Susan*, and the name *Sue* stuck. But no other family member ever called her that. *Dad must really be hurting.*

Susan stares at the family picture. What's wrong with you, Michael? You've been a shit ever since Mom died.

"Are you there?" her father asks.

"Yes, I'm here."

"Maybe he'll listen to you, if you come," he says. She hears him sigh. "Or he's going to end up in jail again."

An edge of impatience creeps into Susan's voice. "Dad, I'm very busy right now. Maybe I can come for Thanksgiving."

Click.

Dammit, Dad, chill out. I've got more pressing things on my mind.

Susan scampers out of the office with the shoulder bag and goes into the locker room a couple doors down the hall to change into a surgical gown, cap and gloves. She heads to the thick glass door at the end of the hall, yanks it open and steps into a laboratory brightly lit from overhead fluorescent bulbs and filled with work benches. Around the perimeter are offices for her staff and rooms for instruments and conferences. The place is neat and clean. Wooden cabinets above the counters contain glassware. Beakers, flasks, rotary evaporators, and centrifuges line the counters. In one corner are a white refrigerator and a freezer chest. Two small desks loaded with stacks of paper and computers are situated in the opposite corner.

Tech Robin McCulley is at the microscope looking through the eyepiece and isn't aware that Susan has entered. One of Susan's research associates is in her office working at the computer. Tony Seymour, the other tech, comes out of the instrument room. "Oh, Dr. Prescott, welcome back." Both techs are dressed in blue scrubs.

"Thank you. Where's Dr. Sutherland?"

Robin looks up and smiles. "Hi, sweetie." *God, I hate it when she calls me that.* "He's in level Three."

"Good," Susan says as she makes her way past them to the back wall. She shifts her shoulder bag to the other side and grabs a mask from the box on a bench, then goes up three metal steps, swipes her ID and pulls on the heavy door labeled: *Level-3—the biosafety lab-3*. Roaring air flows around her as she enters due to negative pressure, which prevents pathogens from leaking out the door or cracks. Microbes handled in this lab are transmitted by the respiratory route and if they escape or are breathed or carelessly handled could cause serious infections. She sets her bag on the bench inside by the door.

There are twelve-inch white tiles on the walls and floor. Alec is seated at the binocular microscope with his back to the biosafety cabinet, its heavy glass door down and the area inside illuminated by a yellow light. He's holding a T-25 flask—used to isolate viruses—up to the bright light in the room. The canopied walkway outside can be seen through a large thick-plate window. Alec's dressed in booties and a blue surgical scrub suit, with white gloves taped at the wrist. He appears surprised to see her. "Welcome back, stranger," he says, and sets the flask on the tray with six others.

"Glad to be back," she says.

After finishing her medical education at Yale, Susan worked on her doctorate in microbiology and genetics at Harvard. There, she met this tall muscular guy with short black hair and handsome face behind dark stubble. They dated a few times, but nothing serious had come of it. Two years later she ran into Alec at a cell biology meeting in Boston and offered him a research position in her lab, and he accepted.

"Hey, what went on in D.C.?" His tone is suspicious. "Your face is glowing."

"I'm excited—"

"I can see that." He gets up and goes to her. "Me, too."

"Not that way—"

"It's been a week," he says.

"Don't get horny on me. I need to tell you something."

He eases back onto the stool and crosses his legs. "Let's have it."

"First, I hope you've finished with Ebola Zaire," she says. *He better be.*

Hundreds of frozen ampoules of sera and blood collected years earlier from people around Yambuku in northern Zaire are now stored at the CDC in another lab, the Level-4, biosafety level-4. Alec had tested them for Ebola antibodies, but none were found. "Entered all the data this morning," he says.

"Karl wanted those last week," she says. "That's the second time he's asked. Better get them to him fast."

Alec has this thing about recording experimental results in his lab journal before transferring all data to the computer, which slows him down. He nods. "Okay already." He looks over at the desk. "You got an urgent memo from the boss about training more researchers for Lab Four."

She waves it off. "That can wait."

He shrugs. "You're the boss."

"Now, I'm glad you're sitting down because what I'm about to tell you will blow your socks off." His eyes narrow, causing her fists to ball up. "I've brought *the* cancer cure back with me."

He recoils. "Cure? Whattayu been sniffing?"

"I'm serious. This Russian—Vladimir Sokolov—presented his work, and listen to this: he's re-engineered a virus that wipes out *all* cancer cells."

His head tilts. "You gotta be kidding."

"Yeah, I know. I couldn't believe it either."

"Wait a minute. It's not like you to be this naive."

Ouch. "I wasn't the only one. The pharmaceutics people were really after him."

"Well, there you go. That makes him legit."

"Don't be cynical." She feels her pulse rising. "I've looked over his data. I'm telling you, he's got the cure. Even Hal thinks so."

"Hal Woolrich?"

"Yeah. One and the same."

He eyed her with suspicion. "What did Hal say?"

"Said the guy's a genius and he's onto something. I've brought several copies of Vladimir's data." The look on Alec's face is making her blood pressure rise. She hurries to the bench near the door where she had deposited the bag, pulls out a copy of Vladimir's data and a taped box. She rushes back and throws the fifty page document at Alec.

He catches it and frowns. Pursing his lips, he begins flipping through the pages.

"Regardless," Alec says, "a cure for cancer? You know the literature. No one's even close."

"Vladimir is," she says, stamping her foot. "He wants us to test it and help him sell it."

"Sell it. Yeah, that's what I thought."

She shoots back, "You've never met him. He's a scientist who wants to cure cancer. That's all."

Alec becomes quiet as he continues reading.

"Dammit. Think for a minute," she says. "If this drug proves worthy, we could help revolutionize cancer therapy. No more chemo, radiation, or surgery. It would empty the oncology wards across the country. Don't you want to be part of that?"

He looks up. "It's been a year since the Soviet Union fell apart, and they're still in a mess." He returns to reading the manuscript.

"He only wants the money to build his own lab in Russia. That's his motive. And I believe him."

Susan removes the tape from around the box and lifts out a small refrigerated canister, carries it to the freezer, and releases the pressure seal on the cylinder. She grips the vial half-full of pale liquid, sets it on the rack and closes the freezer lid. She glances over at Alec. Her stomach is in knots, wondering why he's so concerned about what happened to the former Soviet Union. She moves over to him. "Vladimir didn't work in a biological lab," she says. Alec pays her no mind.

Okay, you shit, be stubborn. "Another thing in Vladimir's favor," she says, pointing a finger at the document in Alec's hand. "He worked years on Tican in secret and hid it from his superiors when they closed his lab." Now that's a solid justification, she thinks, in Vladimir's favor. She's beginning to feel her confidence rise.

Alec doesn't say a word. He's studying the pages in deep concentration. Finally, he says, "Susan, when their laboratories crumbled, these guys were selling radioactive materials out of their labs like M & M candies to the highest bidder. The U.S. stepped in and paid their salaries to keep them honest." He scowls at her. "So, how in the hell can your Russian friend be trusted?"

What the hell am I doing? I'm Alec's boss. I hired him. I don't need his approval. I must be out of my mind.

"That's it," she says. "I'm done arguing. We'll find out if Tican's any good when we test it!"

Alec throws up his hands. "Okay, okay. The data look good."

She heads to the door with the shoulder bag. "While I'm gone, have the techs culture Tican. The sample is in the freezer. And you separate out two test samples for the box. We're going into Four when I get back." She doesn't wait for him to answer and pushes through the door, grabs her coat from the locker and steps out into the cold, trudging between bare elms to the brown brick structure, Building 16, as she thinks about her pitch to Karl Gerber. He could be more difficult than Alec. But she's ready.

Inside, Karl is in the hall outside his office, talking with Susan's technician, Robin McCulley, a tall, supple redhead with fair skin and a slim figure. She entices men with heavy makeup, dangling earrings, and red curls. Susan is eleven years older than she, making the technician twenty-seven. Susan dislikes her fake disposition; especially when Robin calls her "sweetie." In the lab, Robin is required to wear green scrubs, a cap, and no jewelry. In there, she cooperates.

Karl glances at Susan as she heads through the corridor toward them. He whispers something to the leggy redhead, who hurries away. He's at it again, Susan thinks. Robin's life outside the lab is none of her business, but she's sure Robin and Gerber are having an affair. Robin often goes into this building during her lunch hour. Susan looks at her watch. 12: 45 p.m.

"I got your message," Susan says to her boss.

"How was the meeting?" he asks as he directs her into his office.

"Exciting."

She feels anxious as she follows him into the room. Inside, the walls are lined with bookcases; two chairs bracket a coffee table in front of a leather couch. Gerber gestures to the couch as he ambles over to his desk near the window and shoves a magazine in the drawer. He reaches for his sport coat on the hall tree behind his desk and slips it on.

Karl is six-foot, slender, sandy hair, and has a tan that makes him look younger than mid-fifty. Women like to hang on to this hazel-eyed Lothario, but Susan isn't one of them. At times his eyes undress her and she feels like socking him.

She glances at the leather couch and wonders how many women he's laid on it. *Robin is one, for sure.* She flashes on them lying on the couch naked, then shakes the image from her mind and sits. Karl rounds his desk and takes a seat at the opposite end.

During her five-minute presentation, Susan chooses her words carefully as she tells Karl about Vladimir Sokolov and his remarkable cancer cure. When she finishes Karl is staring at her. Susan realizes she's holding her breath waiting for him to say something, but feels confident she's sold him on Tican.

"You've reviewed his data thoroughly?" Karl asks.

"I have and they are impressive," she says, reaching into the leather bag. "I brought copies."

She hands him a folder. He lays it on his lap and locks on her gaze. "Can we trust him?"

What's going on? Doesn't anyone trust the Russians? "I'm sold on him."

"He must want a ton of money for it."

"It's the holy grail."

"That good?"

"Better than good. There's nothing like it," she says. "It's the answer to the prayers of millions of sufferers around the world. It could clear the hospitals of all cancer patients."

He crosses his legs and the folder slides onto the couch. "I see you're really sold on this drug."

"Very much, and Vladimir only wants our help if it proves worthy," she says. "You know about what happened when the Soviet Union fell apart?"

He nods. "I read about it in *Time*."

"His lab was closed," Susan says, "and since he hid Tican from his superiors, he feared going to prison. Vladimir wants money to build a lab of his own back home. I thought maybe Kraft Pharmaceuticals would jump at this, if we can verify Vladimir's data." She waits for his reaction. *Is he buying it?*

He jumps up and moves to the window, stares for a minute at a blue jay perched on a bare limb.

"Are you okay, Karl?"

He doesn't answer. Instead he turns in the direction of an eight by ten photo on his desk. Susan has seen it before—his wife Eva in an elegant evening gown.

"Eva," he says. "Her colon cancer... it's bad. I'm losing her."

"I'm so sorry, Karl."

Eva's a tall brunette with a slender body, who loves jewelry. The Gerbers are prominent in the arts, support charities, and donate one million dollars annually to Emory University. The Performing Arts building is named the *Eva Wentworth Gerber Building*. Karl had once told Susan how much he detested his wife's parties, haunted by politicians, educators, philanthropists, and ass-kissing money grubbers.

Gerber takes his seat. His eyes become gray. "My poor Eva is so frail."

Now's my chance. Push hard. "Tican is the answer to your prayers, Karl. It's a definite cure for Eva."

His sigh is one of frustration. "But Harry would never agree to the amount of money Sokolov would want."

"Vladimir never mentioned how much," she says, "but what does it matter? Tican is *the* wonder drug, and Kraft stands to make millions, even billions."

A thin smile crosses Gerber's face. "That's right. Viewed in that way, Harry would definitely go for it."

Yes, he would. Come on, Karl. Go for it.

Kraft Pharmaceuticals, currently a leader in the discovery, development, and manufacture of biotherapeutic drugs, recently turned its focus to non-Hodgkin's lymphoma and other cancers. Surely Harry Wentworth would want it for his sister, Eva.

"I know you'll be excited as I am, Karl, once you review these data," she says, pointing to the folder on the couch next to her.

"We'll see," he says with doubt in his voice. "Eva has taught me to be guarded. Learned it from her father. She saved the company on several occasions when Harry's impulsiveness nearly bankrupted the company."

"Karl? I think we should begin testing Tican immediately. I'd like to move it into Four. Whattayu think?" Susan asks, holding her breath, again.

His eyes are fixed on the folder.

Come on, Karl. Come on. Is that a smile I see?

He nods. "Okay, go ahead, but do it in Four until we know what it is."

She jumps up. Adrenaline is flowing through her veins. "Think about this, Karl: If Tican is what I think it is... no more cancer."

Gerber takes the folder to his desk. "We can't have any other company getting wind of this. Move fast, Susan."

Now, that's what I want to hear. She slips the bag over her shoulder and rushes to the door. "We're on it."

"Keep me informed," he says, opening the folder. "If I like what I see, I'll need you in a meeting with Harry."

"Maybe we can get Vladimir to meet with us, too."

He nods. "With you there, Harry may commit," Gerber says. "You're a heck of a salesman. Oh, I guess I should say salesperson."

She doesn't care what he calls her, she's excited as hell.

CHAPTER FOUR

Susan steps out of Building 16 into the bright afternoon with clear skies and strides briskly down the walk to the Path Building. Her pulse is climbing. Gerber has granted her wish. She's clutching Vladimir's manuscript against her chest and whispers, "My miracle drug."

Something else is running through her mind: she's wondering what it would be like to live in a world free from cancer. Every year there are so many deaths—hundreds of thousands of men and women. But now she has something that will empty the hospital beds. It's almost as if destiny is calling her, guiding her, ensuring her success.

It's true, isn't it, Mother?

Susan enters her building and hustles to the Level-3, almost out of breath. Robin McCulley approaches the front, reaches in the incubator for a stack of culture flasks, and hauls them back to Tony Seymour who is standing at the biosafety cabinet next to Alec, swabbing Petri dishes. There's a continuous hum of laboratory equipment and a smell of media used in the Petri dishes.

"Dr. Sutherland and I are going into Four, Robin," Susan says. "We'll need more flasks and tissue plates."

"I'm working on them, *sweetie*," Robin says.

Susan rolls her eyes at the sound of that word. Alec pulls his arms out of the rubber gloves attached to the cabinet. "I'm done here."

"You're smiling. Karl must have given you the green light."

"He did."

"Tican samples are in the box ready to go," he says.

"Let's do it," she says as she leads the way.

Susan strides out of the lab and down the metal steps. Alec follows, carrying the leak-proof box equipped with a gasket-sealed lid.

27

They round the corner and continue through a bright corridor with yellow cement block walls, tile floor, and the roar of air handlers

"I've been thinking," she says. "If Tican is a scam, we'll eventually find out, so why would Vladimir take that chance?" She shakes her head. "No, he wouldn't. I think it's real and he's in it for the money."

"He could have gone with the pharmaceutical companies, but instead he chose you."

"Because he wants control of his drug. You know how those companies work."

"I'm just wondering," Alec says. "That's all."

Always the cynic.

They reach an electronic steel door surrounded by thick black rubber. Susan enters numbers in the keypad. A red light above the door turns green and it slides open, then closes behind them.

The most dangerous pathogens on the planet—including the genetically engineered microbes that pose the highest risks—are studied in the Level-4 lab, also called the Hot Zone. No vaccines or treatments are available for these microorganisms, and workers are required to wear the full-body biosafety suit, sometimes called the blue suit.

Ahead is a large staging area, decon shower and the Hot Zone, sealed off by locked doors and negative air pressure to prevent the escape of deadly pathogens. Filtered air is pumped into each room, and air from the Hot Zone is circulated through an incinerator before being cooled and returned.

The staging area contains lockers and wooden benches. Blue suits hang on the opposite wall, and cabinets are in the back. Susan and Alec undress in separate areas, store their clothes in lockers. After showering and drying off, she slips into a sterile scrub, without undergarments, to allow for easy movement in the suit. She pulls on socks and a cloth cap over her hair and snaps on three pairs of latex gloves, taping them at the wrist.

Alec appears and slips into his blue suit. After zipping up, they do a careful inspection of each other. Susan remembers the first time she'd worn the full-body biosafety suit; it weighed a ton and was bulky, and the air took some getting used to. She has an intercom installed in the helmet and a button on the left arm. When the button is depressed, she can communicate with her workers. At a nearby cabinet they choose a pair of thick black gloves, tug them over their elastic gloves, again sealing them at the wrist with tape.

"I'll go first," she says.

He nods.

Susan pulls the plastic helmet over her head. The Plexiglas faceplate is large enough for her to see on either side of her. She enters the decon shower, locks the door, and engages the handle. Disinfectant spews over her. After seven minutes, blowers engage and dry her off. She unlatches the steel door emblazoned with the international biohazard symbol, steps into the Level-4, and reaches for one of the air hoses suspended from the ceiling, locking it into her suit. She inhales the cool air that flows over and around her. Minutes later, Alec appears carrying the box and hooks up to an air hose. They shuffle through the corridor like astronauts on the moon, passing several labs. Another corridor leads at right angle to the animal room. Ceiling cameras swivel in all areas. Because of the limited amount of air in their suits, they have to reconnect every ten yards. They stop at the entrance to the main lab and hook up to new hoses.

A team member is seated by the scanning electron microscope, another is standing at a biosafety cabinet, and a third is sitting at a computer. Dressed in the blue suits, they look like invaders from Mars.

Susan presses the intercom button on her arm, and says, "Hello, everyone. Are you ready?"

They wave and she can hear their responses inside her helmet. "Ready," they say in unison. The room is filled with equipment: Incubators, freezers, autoclaves, and a G.C.-mass spectrometer, computers, DNA sequencers and a PCR.

Alec sets the container on the center table and opens it.

Sokolov's data indicate that Tican has three single-strands of RNA encased in a circular lipid envelope. Susan removes a sample, takes it to Ellen at the electron microscope, and asks her to prepare a sample to run in it

"Let's see what images we get."

Ellen nods.

Alec carries another sample to the counter across the room and requests that Stuart perform genetic analysis on the sample using RT-PCR (reverse transcriptase polymerase chain reaction).

Susan's in a buoyant mood, but she can't get too excited just yet; there's much too do. Alec moves out and heads to the animal room.

Eight hours later, the electron micrographs are transmitting to the main computers in the Level-3. Susan and Alec shuffle back through the corridor to the chamber door, taking turns in decontamination and removing their biosafety suits in the locker room. They slip into fresh scrubs and head out.

Tican's electron micrograph appears on the screen, an image of RNA squeezed into a bunch of circular casings. Susan opens the files on the genetic analysis from the PCR run.

"Look at this," she says.

The printouts have identified genome segments of three hemorrhagic RNA viruses: Lassa Fever, Hantavirus, and Rift Valley Fever.

"Wow!" she says. "It's definitely an engineered virus."
Alec has an astounded look on his face.
"What?" she asks.
"Your Russian's either a genius or a crazy man," he says.

———— ◆ ————

That evening Susan lies back in a tub of bubble bath, closes her eyes to the music of Eric Clapton's "Tears in Heaven." She wonders why millions of people liked this gentle ballad about the death of Clapton's young son. Maybe it's because they were hit with tragedy, too, and the song reminds them that they aren't alone. It's like a support group out there. They know your pain. You never get over it. Your past becomes a part of you and you do the best you can to deal with it. *Mamma, Sabrina, I miss you both very much.*

An hour later, Susan slips into a black negligee and silk robe and saunters into the dining area, where Alec is pouring red wine. He has showered and dressed in a T-shirt and shorts. She follows him into the den and sits on the white bearskin rug in front of the fireplace. The fire crackles. He hands her a glass and nestles in beside her.

"So, what do you think we're dealing with?" Susan asks, staring at the fire. "I mean, do you really think we have the miracle drug?"

He takes a drink of his wine.

"I know it's too early, but what's your gut feeling?"

"Tican's too good to be true," he says. "And you know the rest."

He rises, stokes the fire, throws in a log, and then sits back down. "It may not prove worthy in the end."

Susan swallows her drink and thinks about their relationship as she concentrates on the dancing flames. She's thirty-eight, living in an apartment with a guy in his early forties who can't commit to marriage because it would make him feel trapped. Freedom, that's what these guys want today. Or is it an excuse? *We gals make it too easy for them.* She has urged Alec to explore his feelings, but he won't. They are growing apart, and she is mad at herself for settling the last two years on an imaginary relationship. She wants a family, a granddaughter for her father. She'd name her Sabrina. She imagines Alec will leave her like the others, and she'll end up as before, spending nights curled in a ball, staring at the picture on the nightstand and missing her mother.

Still, her life is good. At work all is going well. She loves being a microbe hunter, and while she doesn't have the kind of relationship with Alec she'd like, they work well together. They even agree on a few issues: Both dislike sloppy work and are turned off by politics in the Center.

Alec's touch stirs her out of her reverie. "Sorry I hammered you today," he says. "Sometimes I can be a jerk."

More like an ass.

"Forget it," she says, not meaning a word of it. She finishes off her wine.

He plants a kiss on her lips and makes his move.

CHAPTER FIVE

The black Mercedes SL 600 travels north on Druid Hills Road. In the rear, Dmitry Belofsky watches the rain pelt his window. Stanislavski is behind the wheel, traveling at the speed limit, watching the cars around them. He pulls in front of Leopold's Lounge and stops, scans the area, and hops out.

Heavily armed and wearing a long black coat, Stanislavski opens the back door and holds an umbrella for the Mafioso. Belofsky steps out, glances around for a few seconds. No sign of any New Jersey Mafia. Belofsky and his driver hurry into the bar.

Inside, the lighting is subdued, cigarette smoke is thick and the place smells of stale beer. No one is sitting at the dozen tables. Only three people are at the bar, blowing clouds of smoke above their heads, watching a football game on the TV. The owner, Gino Morelli, wearing a white apron around his thick waist, rubbing the sweat from his bald head with tobacco-stained fingers, is behind the bar. A Camel cigarette is burning in the ashtray at the edge of the bar. He looks up, nods at Belofsky as he lifts the glass in front of the only woman in the place, and continues to wipe down the bar. Belofsky follows his bodyguard to a table in the back.

Thirty minutes later, Vladimir Sokolov, the Bear, appears with two bodyguards, Nevasheva and Petrovich. The blonde-headed Mafia boss with sea-blue eyes is wearing a black leather coat that covers his knees and a white scarf around his neck. His shoulders are as wide as those of two men. He unbuckles his coat, moseys over to the bar. Morelli's eyes widen. A woman in her early thirties, with her elbow on the bar, holding a cigarette close to her face, turns, reaches for her glass and raises it to acknowledge the big man. The Bear smiles and nods. He asks Morelli for

32

three fingers of vodka, reaches for it, gulps down the drink, and slams the glass on the bar. Another measure of vodka appears. The big man stops for a second to gaze at the woman, but says nothing and carries his drink to the back. Stanislavski jumps up and greets Nevasheva and Petrovich: "*Privyet*," he says. They respond in unison, "*Privyet*," and the three men move to the bar.

The Bear sets his drink on the table, removes his coat and scarf, and throws them on a chair. "Dmitry," he says, arms extended, "*Kak dyela?*"

"*Khorosho*," Belofsky says. "*Au vas?*"

"*Nyeplakho*," Sokolov says. They grab each other by the shoulders and kiss on one cheek and then the other.

Months of weight-lifting, steroids, and protein drinks have worked for Sokolov. He downs his vodka and sits. Belofsky lifts his hand to the bartender and sits facing his boss. Morelli dashes over with another drink. "Bring the bottle, and another glass," Belofsky says.

In 1974, Vladimir Sokolov had joined Biopreparat, the Soviet State Pharmaceutical Agency, which had engineered the largest covert biological program in the world and produced the most dangerous viruses, toxins and bacteria for weapons of mass murder. Life had been good. He earned a good salary, loved his wife and two boys.

In December, 1991, all that changed. The Soviet Union collapsed and the economy hit rock bottom. The Communist Party, KGB and Ministry of Defense were in chaos. Sokolov and his colleagues suffered fifty percent salary cuts, and most were forced to return to their home states. He began drinking. The loving husband and father transformed into a drunk who abused his family. His wife fled with their sons to her parents. Sokolov partied with the Solntsevskaya Brotherhood—the largest gang in all of Russia. After the KGB infiltrated the Mafia, he joined forces with them, rising to *Big Boss*, with the nickname, *Bear*. He then selected their most ruthless sociopath, Dmitry Belofsky, to be his side-kick.

Bear glances around the room, and turns back and locks eyes with his subordinate. "So, this place, you like it?"

He nods. "That's Morelli over there," he says, pointing to the chubby man behind the bar. "He's okay. Keeps his mouth shut."

Sokolov doesn't seem interested. "You got the darts I sent?"

"Got 'em," Belofsky says. The TV above the bar blares. The Bear finishes his drink. Morelli rushes over with another glass, fills both, and sets the bottle on the table.

"How's the investigation going?" Sokolov asks.

"I know the building where the Prescott woman works, and her people." Belofsky could hear his own strong accent.

"So, have you been tracking her?" Bear asks, swallowing his drink.

"Yeah, ever since she returned from D.C." If Sokolov knew Belofsky was spending more time dogging women than watching Dr. Prescott, he would lose a finger or an ear. It's Russian custom to inflict pain. Lots of it. Belofsky empties his glass and refills it.

"Good," Sokolov says.

The TV is blaring and the patrons aren't paying attention to the Russians.

The Bear's eyes narrow. "You *must* find a way to get into Prescott's building and steal our microbe," he says.

"Can do," Belofsky says, not knowing how just yet.

"You must get rid of her before she finds out."

Belofsky pats the .38 caliber Russian military Makarov PM in the shoulder holster under his suit coat. "That would be my pleasure. Consider it done," he says, smiling as he fills the Bear's glass.

"Now," Sokolov says. He turns, reaches into his coat for a notebook, opens it, and sets it on the table. "Listen good," he says. For the next two hours he explains to Belofsky the plan, as he lists the steps in their operation.

When he finishes, the Bear says, "You understand?"

"Of course."

Sokolov closes the notebook and slips it into his coat. "Your part must be completed by the time I return to D.C. in December with the girls."

"Don't worry," Belofsky says. "I'll be there."

The Mafia Boss smiles smoothly, and stands. He finishes off his drink.

Belofsky rises. They hug and kiss again.

"*Do svidaniya*," Sokolov says.

Belofsky nods. "*Do svidaniya.*"

Nevasheva and Petrovich jump to their feet and rush over.

The Bear reaches for his coat and scarf and leaves with his bodyguards.

CHAPTER SIX

The sun is peering through the clouds this November morning and the air is chilly, but the weather isn't what's on Susan's mind. Fourteen years ago, Susan promised Sabrina that she'd find the cure for their familial disease. That's why she went to Harvard to study under the Nobel Laureate Max Spengler, geneticist. Through his charisma, however, he lured her away from cancer to study the HIV virus, and at the end of her doctoral studies she was introduced to Karl Gerber, who wasted no time in recruiting her. But now she's back on the road to keeping her promise to her deceased twin sister.

Susan is driving Gerber and Vladimir Sokolov to Kraft Pharmaceuticals, where they arrive ten minutes before their eight o'clock meeting, scheduled early because Vladimir has a plane to catch.

Kraft covers 200 acres with brick buildings, interlocking glass corridors, and a multistory parking garage about five miles east of the CDC on Clifton Road. Harry Wentworth, President and CEO, along with his co-owner sister, Eva Gerber, have offices on the top floor of the administration building.

They enter the central building at the north entrance and ride the elevator to the tenth floor. When the doors open, they step out. An attractive woman in her late thirties, dressed in a black skirt that is a size too small and a white blouse that exposes cleavage, introduces herself as Ms. Archer, Mr. Wentworth's administrative assistant. Archer and Gerber exchange smiles. She leads them down the hall, her spiked heels clicking on the concrete floor, hips swaying. Gerber walks at her side with his hand on her back. Susan wonders if his hand is going to slide down to her butt. They pass a suite of offices, moving into a conference room with large windows, a huge walnut

35

table and twelve red leather chairs.

Coffee and a fruit tray are on a small table next to the wall, and yellow pads and pens are arranged around the walnut table. A leather folder is at the head. Archer pulls the half-drawn drapes completely open. The visitors fill their cups. Susan and Gerber move to chairs by the door, and Vladimir sits facing them, his back to the window.

Gerber's eyes are fixed on Archer's tight rear as she places a bottle of water next to the folder.

"Mr. Wentworth will be with you momentarily," she says.

Archer touches Karl's shoulder and smiles on the way out. *She has to be one of his conquests.*

Harry Wentworth steps into the room a few minutes later and moves behind Susan and Karl and takes his place at the head of the table. He's about six feet tall, dressed in a blue suit and vest that go well with his dark hair, graying at the temples, and a red tie.

Sexy, Susan thinks.

"I see you have coffee," he says. "I hope I haven't kept you waiting too long." No one says anything, so Susan speaks up. "We're just getting situated, sir."

Harry glances at his brother-in-law. That's Gerber's cue to get on with it. He rises to introduce Dr. Vladimir Sokolov. Harry's brown eyes widen as the Russian stands up to shake his hand. He's twice his size and half-a-head taller than Harry's six feet.

"Welcome to America and Kraft Pharmaceuticals," Harry says.

Vladimir nods. "Thank you for seeing me, Mr. Wentworth."

Harry sits, adjusts his suit coat, and opens the folder in front of him, and Vladimir takes his seat.

Susan rubs her wet palms together. *Please, God, be on my side.*

"Karl," he says as he examines the pages in the folder, "I see that you and Dr. Prescott have reviewed Dr. Sokolov's data on his drug, Tican."

Gerber nods. "We have."

Flipping to the back of the report, Harry says, "And the CDC also has preliminary findings."

"That's correct."

"Please summarize your work."

Gerber glances at Susan, and she nods for him to speak first. "Dr. Prescott can back me up on this," he says. "Dr. Sokolov's data are impressive, and from our preliminary data, we find that the virus does, indeed, have great potential against cancer." He sighs and glances at Susan.

I'm with you, Karl.

"We recommend that a confidentiality agreement be made."

Susan waits for the shoe to drop.

"And of course," Gerber continues, "there should be some upfront money to bind the agreement until we finish our work." He turns to Susan. "Does that sum it up, Dr. Prescott?"

She nods. "All I can add is that Dr. Sutherland has already injected rabbits with the drug, but we won't know the results for three weeks."

Vladimir's azure eyes smile at Susan. *Is he flirting with me, again?* He turns to Wentworth and says in a smooth voice, "Would it be possible for you to reach a decision in fourteen days? I must build my lab as soon as possible."

Susan's heart races. *Buy it. Ohhhh, please.*

Harry frowns. "Dr. Sokolov, it's our policy to offer upfront money and in return you allow us to test your drug for one year before we commit to purchase."

Vladimir leans forward. "Mr. Wentworth, let's not beat around the bush, as you Americans say. I know of several companies interested in making millions off my drug, but because of my relationship with Dr. Prescott, I feel obligated to give you first option."

Smooth, really smooth.

Harry momentarily glances at his brother-in-law and then at her. The wrinkles in his face are more prominent than ever.

Come on, Mr. Wentworth.

"Can we get enough data in fourteen days, Dr. Prescott?"

Susan fears that her hopes for finding a cancer cure are about to vanish. "I'm afraid not, Mr. Wentworth." She turns to Vladimir. "Maybe Dr. Sokolov would agree to thirty days."

His eyes sparkle. "Maybe I should look—"

She interrupts. "I'm sure Mr. Wentworth is eager to work with you, Vladimir."

Harry frowns at Susan, then turns back to the Russian. "How much money would it take to buy Tican?"

Here it comes. Please, Lord. Millions of cancer patients are counting on this drug.

Vladimir rubs his chin and takes his time answering. "I would entertain an offer."

He's playing with us. Damn, he's good.

Susan's pager goes off. It's her brother. *Dammit, Michael. I'm busy.*

"Dr. Prescott, are there any other quick tests that could help us decide?" Harry asks.

She shakes her head. "We've completed all those, sir. The animal testing is what's left."

Harry is known for his stinginess, but surely he won't let this drug slip through his hands? Think of the millions Kraft would make.

Susan's pager bleeps again. "Excuse me," she says. She goes down the hall to use the secretary's phone. "What do you want, Michael? I'm in a meeting."

"Sis, I'm in jail," he says. "I need money to get out."

"Didn't we say this would happen?" she says, frustrated. "I can't do anything from here. Call Dad."

"He's not answering his phone."

No surprise there. "Well, keep trying." She hands the phone back to the secretary.

When Susan returns to the conference room, Gerber is signaling Harry to make another offer.

Harry's face tightens. "Forty thousand."

Vladimir leans forward. "I'm thinking seven figures."

"Seven figures?" Harry questions with a scowl.

Susan is afraid Harry's going to fold.

Although it's customary for pharmaceutical companies to offer up to fifty thousand dollars, most strive to dole out very little. Attorneys for the inventors make certain that their clients aren't screwed out of what's coming to them. In return, companies demand that they have the option to buy the rights to the drug.

"You must realize, Dr. Sokolov," Harry says. "We're taking a risk here. Tican could flop after we've spent millions testing it." He pauses to swallow some water, but doesn't take his eyes off the Russian. "One hundred thousand."

"One million."

Oh, shit. There goes my cancer drug. Wentworth will never pay a million without rigorous testing. Could she blame him? No, but she was hoping.

Staring at the papers in the folder, Harry runs a hand through his hair. A minute later he gets up. "I'd like to see Dr. Gerber and Dr. Prescott in the hall. Would you excuse us, Dr. Sokolov?"

"Of course."

"Help yourself to the fruit," Harry says.

In the hall, Harry turns to Susan. "Dr. Prescott, before I sink a million dollars in Tican, I need to know if there's anything about this drug that bothers you."

He's putting her on the spot. She likes what data she has now, but if he buys Tican for one million and it fails, he's going to blame her. She can't take that risk, not on prelim data.

"Mr. Wentworth. There's a lot of money at stake here. A decision based on my current findings would be unfair to you. I can only tell you that it has great promise, but as to affirming that it will positively kill cancers, I can't do that without further testing."

"So, what would you do, if you were me?"

"Please, don't—"

"I'd go for it," Gerber interrupts.

Susan is shocked. Her eyes must be as wide as saucers. Her boss isn't known for taking risks, at least not in the Infectious Disease Center. Maybe it's because he won't be dishing out the money.

Harry's brow shoots up in surprise. "You would?"

Gerber shrugs as if he made this kind of decision every day. "It's business. If Tican fails, I'm sure you'd find a way to write most of it off, and if it's successful, you stand to make billions. Billions with a B." He emphasizes the B.

Susan wonders where Karl got all his courage.

"Let's get back in there," Harry says. "I've made my decision."

When they return, Harry makes his way to the front and Susan and Karl take their seats. Vladimir is eating pineapple, looking out the window. He turns and slithers into his chair.

"Dr. Sokolov, I believe we have a deal. Do you have a bank in mind?"

Thanks for big favors.

"I do." Sokolov takes a card from his pocket and pushes it across the table.

Wentworth scribbles entries on the sheets in front of him, slides them to the Russian and hands him a pen. "If you'll sign on the bottom line of all three pages that I had my attorneys draw up, I'll have my secretary get them notarized and your copy will be ready as you leave."

Harry pauses at the door, and says, "It'll take thirty minutes to make the transfer." Then he leaves.

Vladimir rises. A wry smile crosses his face. Gerber rushes round the table and grabs his hand, congratulating him.

Vladimir approaches Susan. "Want to thank you for your support and believing in my drug. I look forward to working with you." He reaches for her hand, kisses it. His sexy eyes penetrate her soul.

CHAPTER SEVEN

Early the next morning, Susan drives through Starbucks, stops at the pickup window to get her skinny latte, takes a drink before heading round the building and out the parking lot. The adrenaline still flows when she thinks about the meeting at Kraft yesterday, which went better than she imagined. She has to admit, though, there was one point when Harry scared her, wondering if he was going to bail out, but he didn't. *Thank God for miracles.* Now, she's eager to finish her work with Tican, while Alec continues his rabbit studies.

She rests one hand on the steering wheel as she drives along, holding her coffee cup in the other and taking several drinks. Several miles down Interstate 85, her gaze falls on the rearview mirror. Her pulse begins to rise. The front of a dark sedan is coming up behind her fast. Too fast. *It's going to ram me.* She speeds up. Susan wouldn't have noticed the sedan but for the speed. It's too close for comfort. Her gaze locks on two giant skinheads dressed in black in the front seat. She doesn't believe her eyes. The guy in the passenger seat is pointing something. It looks like a gun. No, it couldn't be. She's not completely awake, hasn't finished her coffee, yet. But she saw what she saw. It is a gun. *I'm going to pee in my pants.* She barrels forward, passing several cars. The Mercedes chases after her. She hears several pops. Pop. Pop. Pop. The back window blows out. *Holy mackerel! These guys mean business. This isn't happening. I'm going to wake up and find it's all a dream.* Another pop brings her back to reality. She swerves from side to side, thinking she can avoid the bullets, almost side-swiping the car in front of her. They're closing in on her. A hand claps her chest. *Oh, my, god. They want me dead. Be calm, be calm.* Pop. A shot whizzes past her ear and cracks the front window. She struggles to see the road through the spider web fracture lines spreading across the window.

She's doing 90 in the inner lane. She never drives this fast, but who cares at a time like this. Maybe the cops will catch her speeding. *Hell, they're never around when you need them.*

She thinks about calling Alec. He left before her and should be in the lab by now. She reaches for the car phone, sets it against her thigh, and punches in the number, holding one hand on the steering wheel. Raises it to her ear. It's ringing. *Come on, come on, Alec.* "Answer the damn phone," she shouts. No answer. Another shot hits metal, somewhere. She tries Alec's office. No answer. *Damn, damn, damn.* She glances in the rearview mirror. They're still there. *Of course, they're still there. A shot just hit the damn car.* She slams the phone in its slot, races off the next exit, and the Mercedes powers after her. She barrels on toward the Center, hits the brakes, and swings into the entrance, stopping at the gate. She turns around and looks over her shoulder. The Mercedes eases past. They're gawking at her. *You bastards.*

The guard raises the gate and she pulls through and races to her building, jumps out and darts inside, almost out of breath. The adrenaline's buzzing her ears. She feels faint, leans up against the wall and inhales three deep breaths, something she'd learned in a yoga class while at Yale. *Breathe in slowly and clear the mind.* But it's not working. She closes her eyes and focuses on her breathing. Sweat pours out of her pores. She bends over with her hands on her knees, still laboring to catch her breath and at the same time struggling to understand what had just happened.

"What's wrong," Alec said, coming down the hallway. "Man, you look like you've just finished a marathon."

She raises a hand but says nothing.

"Sue!" He grabs her arm. Let me help you into my office."

Sue? I've told him no one outside of my family calls me that. "Susan to you," she says.

"You're correcting me at a time like this?" He guides her to the chair next to his desk and reaches in the mini-fridge for a bottle of water. The room smells of stale coffee. He rarely uses the place. She reaches for the water, and drinks half of it, and then says, "Someone tried to kill me. Two bruisers in a black Mercedes shot up my car, blew out the back window. Can you believe that?" She takes another swallow of water.

"Wow! Who in the world...?" but he doesn't finish the sentence. He only frowns. "Why you?"

"I *don't* know," she says with emphasis on don't. She shakes her head. "All I know is I could have been killed."

"But you weren't."

"What should I do?"

"Only thing to do. Call the cops."

CHAPTER EIGHT

An hour later, Susan waits in her office at her desk for the police, rubbing her temples. The headache has left and her anger is subsiding. She's now thinking more clearly. She glances at her mother's picture. *There was a moment during the chase when I thought I was going to join you and Sabrina, Mom.* She inhales a deep breath. *Guess it wasn't my time or you didn't want me to come.*

Alec opens the door and enters with two men in dark suits. The taller guy smiles and moves to Susan. She recognizes him immediately. *It's Nick Hunter.*

"Hello, Dr. Prescott," he says. "Remember me? Nick Hunter, Atlanta PD, Homicide. We worked together on a case about a year ago."

She stands and comes round the desk. "Of course, I remember," she says, "the E. coli child at the fast food restaurant."

He smiles. "That's right. You've got a good memory." He turns to the other man. "This is my partner, Detective A. Jaye Chandler."

A. Jaye is heavier than Hunter, has a stout chest, large shoulders, and is wearing a wide brim hat. She flashes on him drawing his gun, like in those mobster movies.

She nods. "Detective."

He smiles, tips his hat. "Ma'am."

Susan returns to her chair behind the desk, and gestures. "Have a seat, gentlemen."

They sit in the two chairs facing her.

Alec asks, "Can I get you anything? Coffee, water?"

They decline his offer. "Then, I'll be in the lab, if you need me," he says.

"Good enough," Hunter says. He turns to Susan. "Looks like your Caddy has seen its better days."

"Why are homicide detectives interested in a car chase?" Susan asks. "As you can see, I'm very much alive... maybe pretty shaken, but now much better." She pauses for a moment, glancing at her mother's picture again and back to Hunter. "Isn't this incident one for uniform officers?"

"Normally, yes, but the CDC is special," he says. "The department likes to think they are in charge of the place when anything unusual happens here. Meaning, we like to step in and nip it before anything drastic happens "

"That's comforting," Susan says.

Hunter continues, "And that means the more experienced officers are assigned. That's us." He looks at A. Jaye. They smile.

"Could be some terrorist nut," A. Jaye adds, turning to Susan, "and that could open a can of worms."

Her body jerks. "You suspect terrorists? I never..."

"Just saying, ma'am," A. Jaye says. "Never know till we get into our investigation."

"I guess I should be flattered to have the attention of the homicide division," she says, feeling a little better now that detectives are with her.

Hunter pulls out a notebook and opens it. "Now, tell me about that black Mercedes."

Susan begins the story about the chase, the shots, the condition of her car, and how she made it to the Center, barely. She finishes with: "I don't know who in the hell they are, and why they want me dead. I wish I did, but I don't." Susan finds herself shaking with controlled anger. Never before has she faced death, and she doesn't want to again.

"Did you piss someone off lately?" Hunter asks.

She doesn't like that question. She never pisses anyone off. Well, maybe Alec, sometimes. "I can't think of anyone."

"Has there been a change in your life, your work, or your intimates?"

"No."

"Something's changed," A. Jaye says. "You can bet on it."

"I don't know what that could be," she says.

Hunter closes his notebook and slips it into his coat pocket. "This is going to be a tough one," he says, looking at his partner, who is nodding. Hunter turns back to Susan.

"We'll go over your car and maybe it'll tell us a thing or two. Guess you were too busy to get a read on the Mercedes' plate."

"You're joking, right?"

He smiles. "Just asking," he says. "Would make our job easier." He slides something across the desk. "Here's my card, page me if you see that Mercedes again."

She picks it up, fixes on Hunter's gaze. "I know what you both are thinking. I don't have any enemies. I really don't."

"You do now," A. Jaye says.

CHAPTER NINE

Belofsky's alcoholic mother had beaten him so many times he couldn't remember when it started. In his teens, he joined the Solntsevskaya Brotherhood—an organized crime group—named after the Solntsevo neighborhood in Moscow. His initiation required that he kill someone to earn his tattoos.

He learned early on that it was Russian custom to inflict pain before killing. He had chosen his mother as his victim—breaking the redhead's arms and ribs and clipping off her fingers at the second joint while she was still alive. He silenced her screams by jabbing a specially made ice pick up her nostril, twirling the tip to sever the brain arteries, and threw her body into a river. No one cried for her. No one missed her. Belofsky was pleased with himself. Later, in the mob, he gained notoriety for the horrible way he raped and killed his women.

Some men search the chat rooms or bulletin boards for fun, but Belofsky does it to get victims. Now at his desk, Belofsky has found one. He likes redheads under the age of fifty—those without families are his easiest targets—and he never meets them at their homes. He flirts with them until a relationship develops. Then he strikes.

Belofsky is eager to meet his eight o'clock date this Saturday evening. She invited him to meet her at the Lion's Den. She's a forty-nine-year-old instructor at a health club. He steps into the kitchen, reaches into the cabinet for the vodka, removes a glass, fills it half full, and takes a long draft of his drink. "G-o-o-d," he says as he sets the glass on the counter. He grabs his black leather coat and heads out the back of his basement apartment. On his way round the building, three black men are waiting for him. When he pushes between them, the tall one grabs his arm and says, "Where you goin', fucker?" Belofsky yanks his arm free from the guy's grasp, draws the .38 Makarov PM from its shoulder holster, and slams it into the man's face, breaking his nose.

"Shit!" Blood squirts down the man's coat.

"You want somethin'?" Belofsky says, shoving the cold barrel against the man's temple.

The other two men take off running. The wounded man throws his hands in the air and cries out, "No problem, man! No problem!" He darts across the street where he meets the other two. They disappear into the playground.

Belofsky makes his way along the dim street in this southwest part of Atlanta. He chose this area because cops never come here, and he needs time away from the business. He walks past two men arguing over drugs and approaches a prostitute leaning against a pole. His erection is strong. He twists the shaft of the pick in his pocket. She'll fight him the way he likes it when he sticks it to her.

"Howya doin', baby," says the woman in a fake fur coat and dangling, circular earrings.

"Okay," he says, pushing her into the shadows between the buildings, away from the street light.

"Take it easy, baby," she says. "You'll get it."

Belofsky forces her up against the building, pulls out the instrument, presses the button and out shoots a six-inch pick. He holds it against his leg while he grinds his body against hers, kissing her on the neck.

"You're a hot one," she says. "Wee, you are a big one."

"You're gonna love it," Belofsky says, jamming the pick up her nose.

"Jesus," is the last word out of her mouth before she falls to the ground.

Minutes later, Belofsky appears out of the shadows, zipping up his pants. A shot rings out. He continues for another block, turns on Rhode Island Street, and opens the door of the '89 Buick Century he bought off a used car lot with a fake ID. He slips in behind the wheel, removes the gun still in the holster and throws them into the glove compartment.

At Lion's Den he wheels in the back, hops out and hurries to the entrance. He passes a man arguing with his woman about her flirting with some guy.

Knock her on her ass.

Inside, hordes of coeds are on the dance floor, shaking their asses to blasting music. There's a redhead. Must be her. A little guy sitting on the stool next to her jumps up and flutters away like a nervous butterfly when he sees Belofsky.

When Belofsky wants a woman, it's easy for him to smile. He moves onto the stool and orders vodka.

"You Sharon?"

She nods.

"Are you Dmitry?

"Yeah." He had given her his name. It doesn't matter. He's going to kill her anyway.

She's in a white blouse with a heart necklace that hangs in her cleavage. Her hair is off her neck in a pony tail. She has on fishnet stockings under a short black skirt. Belofsky wants to take her right there.

"You're a big man," she says.

"You like big men?"

She smiled. "I like all men."

"Need a drink?" he asks.

"Sure, honey." She motions to the bartender and shoves the glass across the bar, hitches her head, "On my friend here."

Belofsky rubs her muscular thigh. She is going to be a good one.

"Where you from, big guy?" she says, not paying attention to his hand.

"Where do you think," he says.

She studies him. "You're foreign. That much I know... I'd say, German."

He shakes his head. "Russian."

She reaches for the fresh glass of scotch. "What are you doing in Atlanta?"

Belofsky's muscles tense. The music is so loud he has to lean in to her. "I work for a cable company."

"You look very strong. I like strong men."

He glances at her athletic body. He wants this one more than anything. "You ready?" he asks.

"Where we goin'?" She downs her drink.

"Surprise."

Outside, they hurry to his car. He drives out of the parking lot with one hand under her skirt. Ten miles later, he turns into the woods and parks under an oak tree.

He grabs her and kisses her on the lips, neck and sucks the lobe of her ear. She moans and kisses him hard, cupping his face in her hands. "I want you, big guy."

He pushes her down, spreads her legs. When he's in her, he reaches into his pocket, pulls out the pick.

"Holy crap! What's that?"

"For you," he says.

She screams, clutches his wrists.

"I like good fighters."

With a quick jab, the pick penetrates upward in her nostril at an angle. Twirling it, he holds on, riding the bronco.

CHAPTER TEN

Parked in his Buick Century near the entrance of the CDC this Friday evening, Belofsky waits. When he toured the place two days earlier, he realized it would be impossible to get past the guard at the main gate or over the fence that surrounds the Center. An elaborate security system protects the buildings. The Center is sealed tighter than the White House. The tour guide told him Dr. Prescott would have to pre-approve his visit and then meet him at the entrance. He couldn't do that, she had seen his face in the airport. Instead, he was able to get a list of the names of those in Prescott's laboratory and looked up their addresses in the city directory. Breaking into their homes while they were at work was easy.

He glances at his watch. Five-thirty. Seconds later, coming out of one of the buildings, is the redhead he saw in a picture in her apartment. She drives out, and Belofsky flows in behind her Honda Civic. Several miles down the interstate, she exits. A reddish-orange glare streaming from the horizon nearly blinds him as he follows her off the ramp. Within minutes, he guides his car to the curb in front of her apartment. She wheels in near her building, gets out and bounds up the stairs to the second floor. Belofsky watches and thinks about the time he had broken into her apartment, saw pictures of her with some guys taken at a Pub called O'Leary's.

Twenty minutes later, Robin appears wearing a short gray overcoat, climbs into her car, and drives out of the parking lot. Belofsky checks his watch, again. Six-thirty. He takes off after her and ends up where he figured she was going. O'Leary's. This is one woman he won't be killing. At least not now. He has to play it cool and turn on the charm to get her to do what he has in mind.

He crosses the street, dodging several cars, and goes inside the dimly lit room. People are seated at tables and in booths eating corn beef and cabbage, drinking beer from tall glasses. A waitress moves past him carrying a tray of drinks as he heads to the bar. The noise rages. He edges his way between Robin and the guy next to her. She's talking to the bartender. A large picture of an Irish countryside is next to a mirror that runs across the back wall. Belofsky's shiny head is visible in the mirror, and his scar looks smaller. He touches Robin's arm. "Can I buy you a drink?"

She turns, abruptly. Her dangling earring hoops swing against her cheeks. "Sure, honey. What's your name?"

"Belofsky."

"I'm Robin. This is Jim," she says, pointing to the bartender.

Belofsky doesn't take his eyes off her. "What do you drink?"

She orders a Bud on tap, and Belofsky has his usual. When the drinks slide across the bar, he carries them away from the crowd and sets them on a table near the front. Robin follows. He removes her coat and hangs it on the wall hook. She's wearing a yellow sweater and pearls. Her green skirt slides above her knees when she sits.

"Aren't you cold in just that sweater?" Robin asks.

"I like cold weather. I'm Russian."

"Russian, huh? I figured as much, with that accent."

"Yeah."

Her long fingers with bright red nails circle the beer glass. An imprint of her equally red lips is left on the rim. Belofsky thinks she's too thin. He likes his women with more meat, like Russian women, big and strong, but she'll do. She smiles at him as he stares at her legs.

Belofsky glances around and says, "Noisy place?"

She nods. "I don't mind. You get used to it after awhile, and I have a lot of friends here."

"You sleep with that bartender?"

Her hand went to her chest. "Oh, no, his wife's a nurse, and he's in med school. In South Carolina, where I come from, I wouldn't sleep with a married man unless he's lonely."

Belofsky wonders how many men have laid her. "You speak funny," he says.

Her earrings sway again, as she laughs. "You're one to talk."

Rage builds. That's the second time she's made fun of him. No one gets away with it, especially, women. He controls his anger and fakes a smile, reaching for his drink.

Her eyes widen. "You have tattoos on every finger."

"When I was young and drunk."

"I knew guys who got tattoos of the devil on their arms when they were spaced-out on drugs."

Wait until she sees my body.

"How'd you get that scar on your face?" she asks.

Belofsky rubs it with a thumb. "Bad fight. Long ago."

"Oh," she says in a way that sounds like it's no big deal. She drinks some of her beer. "My people are farmers," she says. "What about yours?"

"When a young man, I worked the farms," he says, lying. "Didn't like it. Where do you work?"

"CDC."

"You a scientist?"

"Oh, no, just a technician."

"Who do you work for?" he asks, as if he doesn't know.

O'Leary's is packed now with more partiers, and the noise is hurting Belofsky's ears.

Robin leans in to the table, and says, "My boss is Dr. Susan Prescott. She's the chief of infectious disease section, and very smart."

"What do you do there?" He's wondering if she'll mention the microbe.

"Working on a cancer drug. Dr. Prescott thinks it's going to be great." Robin finishes her drink. A good-looking man in his thirties stops for a minute to talk with her. Belofsky's hands clench. The guy glances at him but says nothing, then goes to the next table and sits with three other guys.

Turning back, she asks, "What were we talking about? Oh, the cancer drug. Even our director, Dr. Berger, is counting on it being good. His poor wife has colon cancer, you know."

"I didn't know."

"Oh, I didn't mean..." She laughs. "His wife is very sick."

Belofsky wolfs down his drink and slams the glass on the table. "Would you like to go to my place for a treat?"

"Treat?"

"I have Russian sweets."

"Never had Russian sweets. Guess that would be okay."

Belofsky rises, reaches for her coat and they leave.

Outside, it is cold. "I hate winter," Robin says. "You're going to freeze without a coat."

"I'm strong."

————— ◆ —————

When they arrive in the back of the building, at his basement apartment, Belofsky hops out and opens Robin's door. Inside, he removes her coat and hangs it in a small closet, leads her through the short hallway and round an open kitchen and into the living room with only a couch, chair and a TV tray. Nothing on the walls, and no windows.

Robin thinks his job must not pay very much. The bare walls are off-white. A washing machine or dryer is vibrating in the next apartment. The room is cold. She wishes she had kept her coat.

A few minutes later, Belofsky returns with napkins and a plate of pastry.

"You will like," he says.

She reaches for a crescent-shaped piece and a napkin. He sets the plate on a TV tray and heads back into the kitchen. He seems nice, but she has this uneasy feeling about him. He returns with two cups of coffee.

Footsteps are loud in the apartment above.

She reaches for a cup and he sits next to her, taking a couple of drinks from his coffee. "Are you okay?" she asks. "You seem edgy."

He doesn't answer her right away; instead, he swallows more coffee. When he does speak, he says with excitement in his voice, "I know of a way we can make a million dollars."

She nearly chokes on her coffee. "You gotta be kidding. A m-i-l-l-i-o-n? How?"

"No kidding. Very serious."

"I wouldn't know how to act if I had that kind of money," she says. "I've been poor all my life. My folks never gave me a penny. Made me go to work at fourteen. Quit school two years later."

"You have tears in your eyes," he says. "Don't be sad. I will make you feel good again." He pauses while she wipes her eyes with her napkin.

"I'm tired of being poor." She's also tired of sleeping around for extra cash.

"You need money?"

"Who in the hell doesn't? Of course, I need money. Doesn't everyone?" She finishes her coffee. He reaches for her empty cup and places it on the tray. "I have a way for us to make lots and lots of money."

"You're not into drugs, are you?" she says.

"No, no."

Robin looks around, taking pity on him living in a place like this. *He's no better off than I am.* No wonder he wants money. She moves forward in her seat. "Tell me how we can make a million."

"Later."

He pulls her up on her feet and holds her close, kissing her. She feels his male hardness against her. He leads her into the bedroom.

———◆———

Eleven-thirty the next morning, Robin emerges from her bedroom, steps into the kitchen, opens the fridge and removes a bottle of orange juice, fills a glass and drinks half of it. She looks out the window, rubbing her arms and licking her lips. Last night Dmitry treated her pretty rough during sex. And what do those tattoos on his neck and shoulders mean? She had never seen anything like them. She drinks the rest of her juice. What has she gotten herself into?

She jumps when the phone rings. A rat is chewing at her stomach, and her hand shakes as she lifts the receiver. It's him. He talks about enjoying her last night, and wants to know what she thought about his plan.

The thought sends chills through her. She doesn't know if she can do it.

Dr. Prescott's been so good to me.

"Think money, baby. Think money."

"We need to talk," she says.

"Good. I'll bring pizza."

Click.

She sits, wondering if she can trust him. The money would mean no more shacking up with Dr. Gerber, and she could have nice things and maybe help her mother, who lives in a dilapidated shack with her widowed sister, now that her mother's lecherous husband has kicked her out.

Close to one p.m., Dmitry arrives with the smell of liquor on his breath. He moves past her, carrying a pizza box and a bottle of wine. She brings wine glasses. They sit. He opens the box and pours their drinks. "Time to celebrate," he says, holding the wine bottle above his head for a few seconds. His glistening eyes stare at her while he chews on a slice of pizza and takes a drink.

"You're not eating."

"I'm not hungry," she says, adrenaline racing through her veins. *He's staring a hole through me. Those dark eyes are scary.* On TV, she's seen those same eyes in animals before they tear their prey to pieces.

He grunts and slams his fist on the table. "Do you want money, or not? I must know now."

She jerks. "You're drunk. You scare me." Robin bounds from her chair and races into the bedroom, slams the door and locks it.

———◆———

Dmitry stares at his half-eaten slice of pizza. Robin has to get those samples for him, or the Bear will see that he ends up dead. He swallows his glass of wine, jumps up, and shuffles to the bedroom door. *I can talk the pants off any woman.*

"Robin? Think what all that money can do for us," he says in the warmest voice he could fake. "We can go to another country, maybe south of France, buy diamonds, and you'll live like queen." He pauses with his ear at the door. "Think about fancy clothes, cars. How about a red Jaguar? I'll buy you a mansion on the seashore. We'll live the life you deserve."

The knob turns slowly, and the door inches open. Her red eyes peer through the crack. "You'd do all that for me? Really?"

"Sure, my darling. All for you."

The bedroom door swings open, and Robin falls into his arms.

"Oh, Dmitry, I want all those things."

CHAPTER ELEVEN

In the kitchen, Robin McCulley reaches into the gym bag on the chair for the .38 Special Smith and Wesson that Dmitry showed her how to shoot. She shot a rifle back home, but never a handgun. She likes the way it feels as she aims it at the wall, thinking about the times her stepdad raped her. If she had this gun, she would have emptied it into him. Imagining him against the wall, she aims it at his heart and acts like she's firing off three rounds. "Bang, bang, bang! Gotcha, you son-of-a-bitch!" She returns the .38 to the bag and calls work to report that she's feeling better and will be in after lunch.

———— ♦ ————

Robin enters the Level-3 close to one in the afternoon. Susan Prescott yanks her arms out of the rubber gloves at the biosafety cabinet. "Are you okay, Robin?" she asks. "You look pale."

"This flu has drained me. I'll be okay."

"I've been there. No fun," Susan says. "You should have stayed home. Tony could have filled in for you."

Robin shakes her head. "I'm better."

"Look at this," Alec says.

"What is it?" Susan says, making her way to him.

He's shuffling through a stack of cell culture plates. "Tican has killed off the cancer cells. The protein it produces is doing the job."

"That's wonderful," she says.

"Don't get your hopes up just yet," he says.

Susan remembers how smooth the blonde-haired Vladimir was in

54

the Kraft meeting. She is drawn to him and thinks he's gorgeous. "So now, you'd have to say that it looks promising, wouldn't you," Susan says.

"We'll know for sure later today when the rabbit experiment is done," he says.

"Have it your way. I'm out of here," she says.

"Don't wait on me for dinner. I'll be late," Alec says.

She turns to Robin. "Take tomorrow off and get some rest."

Robin smiles. "Thank you, sweetie."

Susan cringes.

———————◆———————

Robin shoves flasks into the incubator and glances at the wall clock. It is nearly nine, time for her Friday night rendezvous. She heads to the door. A few feet away, Dr. Sutherland rises from the desk. He glances her way. "Going home?"

"Naw. Got lots more to do. I'm just taking a break."

He nods and turns, facing the biosafety cabinet.

She pushes through the door, heads to her locker and reaches in for her coat. Outside, she pulls the hood over her head and treks to Gerber's building, against blowing snow that has descended on Atlanta. She plans to stay with him until Phil Corben has finished making his rounds before going off duty. Maybe Dr. Sutherland will be gone by then, too, and she won't have to use the gun.

Robin steps into Building 16, taps on the Director's door.

He opens it, smiling, wearing a blue silk robe, tied loosely, hinting that there's a naked body underneath. She smells Armani cologne. She eases past him, removes her coat and hangs it on the hall tree. He grabs her and pulls her to him and plants a five-second kiss on her lips. She feels his stiffness against her. Candles on a table illuminate the room, and a bottle of champagne and two flutes are in the center. Gerber fills the glasses, hands her one, and takes a drink of his. He's undressing her with his eyes.

Robin is the first to speak. She begins by embellishing Tican's ability to kill cancer cells as she drinks her wine. Dmitry would be proud of her performance.

Gerber doesn't seem impressed. He empties his wine and refills the glass.

"Dr. Sutherland found something exciting today," she says, downing her drink, and motioning for a refill. "Tican killed different cancers, and Dr. Prescott is really excited."

Gerber refills her glass. "Dr. Sokolov's data do look promising," he says. "I've been hopeful from the beginning. I guess you know why?"

You bet I know.

He sips his wine, but says nothing for several minutes. He's staring into space.

"What's wrong, honey?" she asks, moving in close to him. "A few minutes ago, you were ready to hop me." She pushes her body up against his. "Don't you want me?"

He finishes his wine. "My wife—she's not doing well," he says. "I'm losing her."

You bastard. You're screwing me and every gal in the Center and now you're thinking about your wife because the poor thing is dying? You must love her money. Robin blinks, and wonders what the hell she's thinking? He's weak now. It's just what she wants.

"Tican can help her," she says softly, wiggling her body against him, while holding her glass in one hand.

He puts his arm around her and kisses her ear. "You... you could get me a vial," he whispers.

Robin drinks from her glass. "Dr. Prescott would never—"

He cuts her off. "I didn't mean...."

Robin has Gerber where she wants him. She knew he'd never ask Dr. Prescott. Last evening, Dmitry went over his plan until she couldn't keep her eyes open. Now it's paying off.

"You mean steal it?" she says, jerking backwards, faking surprise.

"You're sneaky," he says, rubbing her shoulder. "Would money motivate you?"

She shakes her head. "Dr. Sutherland's always there."

He frowns. "What's one vial? They'd never miss it. Would a thousand dollars convince you?"

"I don't know."

The phone on his desk rings. Gerber ignores it. After six rings, it stops. *Probably his wife,* Robin thinks.

He kisses her ear, again. "Just slip a vial into your pocket. It's that easy."

She doesn't respond.

"Two thousand," he says in a soft, alluring voice.

Gerber can be charming when he wants special favors. Dmitry would laugh at his measly two thousand dollars. "When do you want it?"

"Tomorrow?"

"That soon?"

"Eva is dying."

"I'll call you when I have it."

Belofsky can get more money out of him, lots more, she thinks. Her pulse races as she thinks about the millions people would pay for a cancer cure. This is easier than she thought. It will be the last time Gerber'll have her, but she has to do her part for Belofsky.

Robin taunts Gerber like a stripper, wiggling her rear as she removes the top of her scrubs and lets the bottoms fall to the floor. She presses her naked body against him, rubbing him and licking her lips. He guides her to the couch, drops his robe. He's ready. "You devil," he says as he eases into her. She looks up into his eyes, rubs a hand through his hair. *We gotcha, money bags.*

————— ◆ —————

Robin leaves Gerber's office close to midnight, stops at her locker, removes her coat and pulls out the blue bag. She unzips it and looks inside. It's all there.

Thank God the ceiling cameras aren't working.

When she steps into the lab her heart sinks. Dr. Sutherland is still at the biosafety cabinet with his back to the desk. *Shit! Why in the hell is he still here? Now I'll have to kill him. Damn, damn, damn.* Sweat trickles down between her breasts. She grips the .38 Special, her heart is pounding, hands shaking. She grips the weapon tighter, and aims it at the imaginary bull's eye on Sutherland's back, just the way Belofsky taught her, and fires.

Twice.

CHAPTER TWELVE

During the early morning hours, Susan's outstretched arm lands into the empty space next to her. She bolts up, wipes her eyes and glances at the clock on the nightstand. Four o'clock. She grabs the phone and calls the lab. Six rings. No answer. Alec's voice mail turns on.

He's never this late. He could be dead on the side of the road. Stop it! You've been watching too many late night mysteries.

She inhales a deep breath and dials Phil Corben.

"Do you know what time it is?" he says.

"Sorry to wake you, Mr. Corben. This is Susan Prescott. It's important."

"Oh, Dr. Prescott, sorry."

"Dr. Sutherland hasn't come home, and he's not answering his phone."

"He was there when I made my rounds around midnight. I wouldn't worry, Dr. Prescott. He's in another world in that lab."

Blood pounds in her throat. "He should have called me by now. He's never this late." She closes the phone, jumps out of bed, dons her running suit and leaves the apartment.

Before starting the Ford Explorer she bought with some of the insurance money from when her Caddy got shot up, Susan inhales a deep breath to relax the knot in her stomach. Adrenaline is soaring through her veins. She starts the SUV, races to the Center and brakes at the main gate.

"Did you see Dr. Sutherland leave?" she asks the guard.

"No ma'am. I came on at eleven and haven't seen him."

After he raises the gate, she barrels through, stops in front of her building and jumps out. She enters the code at the door, yanks it open, and races down the corridor and throws her things into her locker. Once in scrubs, she hurries through the general lab and at the top of the stairs in the back, she swipes her ID, pulls on the Level-3 door and rushes in.

———— • ————

Robin McCulley zips past several cars, but makes sure she isn't more than five miles over the speed limit. Her heart is pounding so hard she is having a hard time concentrating on the road.

I can't believe I did it. I aimed the .38 and fired and Dr. Sutherland went down.

"It was terrible, all that blood—poor, Dr. Sutherland. He never hurt anyone." She was shaking. "Ohmigod! Girl, what have you done?"

She glances at the gym bag on the seat next to her, filled with canisters of Tican. She wonders if Dmitry is going to screw her out of her share of the money. *I can kill him too, if he tries it.*

It takes Robin twenty minutes to get to her apartment parking space, and just a few seconds to rush up the stairs to the second level. Inside her apartment, she places the bag on the kitchen table. Exhausted, she flops in a chair and sighs. Images of Dr. Sutherland's body are haunting her. She blinks them away, jumps up and unzips the bag, removes one of the cold canisters and releases the top. Her hands shake as she takes a vial to the sink and wipes off the condensation. *It doesn't look like much, just a pale liquid. But it's pure gold—her ticket out of poverty.*

The phone rings. Her body jerks and the vial slips from her hand, strikes the sink, and shatters into pieces on the floor. "God have mercy!" She takes a deep breath. "Girl, you're a clumsy fool!" Dmitry will kill her if he finds out.

She reaches for the phone. "It's done," she says, staring at the wet spot and the shards of glass on the floor. She slams the phone on its base, stoops and yanks open the door under the sink, grabs a rag and a bottle of bleach, and kneels. "Ouch!" she shouts and rolls over. A piece of glass sticks in her knee and blood trickles down her leg.

After treating her knee, she wipes up the floor and sits staring at the bag. *Good thing there are many more in there.*

CHAPTER THIRTEEN

In the Level-3 lab, Susan spots Alec's body on the floor a few feet from her in a pool of blood. Red splatter is all over the biosafety cabinet. The sweet odor turns Susan's stomach and the room begins to spin. She collapses to her knees and lands on her back. When she awakes, she is staring at the ceiling. She inhales several breaths, sits up and remembers what has happened. She doesn't look at Alec's body as she gets up, steadies herself against the bench and reaches for the phone. She places a call to security and rouses Gerber from a sound sleep.

Thirty minutes later, Karl Gerber shows up dressed in scrubs. His hair is uncombed and he hasn't shaved. He glances at Alec's body and begins pacing the room like a lion in its cage. He stops, gazes at Susan sitting on a stool next to the bench. He asks her if she's touched anything.

Susan shakes her head. "I'm not thinking straight, but I don't think so."

"Do you feel up to checking around before the police get here?" he asks, reaching for her arm. "They'll want to know what's missing, if anything."

She inches her way to the freezer and hesitates before laying a hand on the lid. She barely has enough energy to raise it. "Oh my God!"

"What... what?" Gerber asks, as he peers inside.

"The vials are gone!" she says, then turns and hurries to the incubator, yanks on the door. "Shit!" she says, slamming it. "Someone's taken all our samples."

"Son-of-a-bitch," Gerber says. "So that's what they were after."

"It looks like it," she says.

Gerber is trembling. "Are you okay?" Susan asks.

"Tican was supposed to be Eva's miracle drug."

"I'm so sorry, Karl, really sorry."

"Who would have done this?" he asks.

"How did they slip past the guards?" Susan says. "That's what I would like to know."

He shrugs, but doesn't answer. Instead, he escorts Susan past security to her Center office.

While waiting for the Atlanta police, Gerber taps Susan's shoulder and says, "I'm sorry, too, about Dr. Sutherland. I know you two were very close." He shakes his head. "This is all so tragic."

The Atlanta PD officers arrive around five-thirty and secure the area. The Crime Scene Unit and the medical examiner follow soon after.

Susan's at her desk and Gerber is pacing when Nick Hunter and A. Jaye Chandler show up dressed in white disposable gowns.

Hunter nods. "Dr. Prescott? We're seeing a lot of each other lately."

A. Jaye tips his hat, and smiles.

"'Fraid so," she says.

"Who's the victim?" Hunter asks.

"Dr. Alec Sutherland, my research associate," Susan says as she gets up and moves round her desk and introduces Gerber. "This is Dr. Karl Gerber," she says. "He's the Director of the Infectious Disease Center."

Gerber greets them with a thin smile and a handshake. "We'll cooperate to the fullest," he says. "Dr. Prescott found the body... I mean she found Dr. Sutherland."

Gerber never cared much for Alec, but now he seems sympathetic.

"You look pale," Nick says to Susan, moving in closer. "Do you need anything?"

She shakes her head "I'm okay. Thank you."

"Do you feel up to visiting the scene and answering a few questions?" he asks.

Susan hesitates, not knowing if she's ready, or not. "I think so."

Gerber follows them into the corridor, looking gaunt and weak with fatigue. He never was good at handling problems in the department, and tried hard to avoid them or push them on to someone else. Alec's death has shaken up his Center, and he's overly anxious.

Gerber says "If I'm not needed, detectives, I'd like to go to my office. That is, if it's all right."

"I'll go with you and take your statement," A. Jaye says.

"We'll need to coordinate our investigation with your office and CDC Security," Hunter says. "And we may need some things from you. Any problem with that?"

"None, detective."

"Good. Dr. Prescott and I will go to the crime scene."

As they move down the corridor toward the lab at the end, Susan's thoughts turn to the time when she and Alec began their relationship.

In Starbucks, over coffee, they probed each other about their backgrounds. He asked where she was born. What she did growing up. Did she have buck teeth? Why did she go to Yale and Harvard, and why did she come to the CDC instead of some research institute? Were her mother and father scientists? Did she have any siblings? They laughed, but at one point she became sensitive to the questions about her parents, especially about her mother and sister.

She remembered feeling guilty that she had been raised in a wealthy family, but didn't know why. She had lots of friends growing up. Her father is a successful attorney in New Haven. Her mother and twin sister and both sets of grandparents are dead, but she has a brother, Michael. She went to Yale to be close to home, but went to Harvard for special training. Only her father lives in the homestead in Mystic, and sometimes her brother, when he isn't living with his drinking buddies. Coming to the CDC had seemed like the right thing for her to do.

Now it was her turn to ask the questions. She learned he was raised in Jackson, Mississippi, had only one friend when he was young, never hung out in a group, and she had determined he was short on social skills. Susan felt sad for Alec when he told her he only had one friend growing up. His father and mother are physicians and his mother teaches at the Ole Miss medical school. Alec was influenced mostly by his maternal grandmother, who read to him at an early age and took him every Saturday to the library. He once met Eudora Welty in the supermarket.

Susan is shaken from her reverie when they reach the metal stairs at the Level-3.

"Sorry about Dr. Sutherland," Phil Corben says. "We'll miss him." He opens the door and holds it.

Susan forces a smile. "Thank you."

Inside, behind the yellow tape, a technician from the CSU is snapping pictures. The man she calls Doc is examining the body. The badge that hangs from his neck reads *Medical Examiner*.

"Whatta we got, Doc?" Hunter asks.

"White male, in his early to mid-forties, been dead, oh... about five to seven hours," he says, "Two shots: one below the left shoulder blade that exited the nipple area here." He points. "And the other went through the neck. The bullet that exited the chest probably got him, but won't know until we get him into the pit. The neck wound didn't contribute as much, at least not at first."

Susan backs up to the bench and leans against it. *That's Alec's body he's turning over. Poor Alec.* The room is swirling around her.

"I'm done here, Doc," the CSU tech says, and steps to the wall. She digs something out with a probe. "Found it. Looks like a thirty-eight." She bags it. "Now where's the other one?"

Doc grunts and rubs his knees as he gets up. "That's all I can do here. Can we take him?"

Hunter nods. "We'll be down later."

"Here's the other bullet," CSU tech calls out. "Same caliber. No surprise."

Doc signals to the men waiting near the wall. They roll the stretcher to the body, remove a black body bag, and kneel. Susan's stomach flip-flops when they cart Alec away like one of her dead lab animals.

Hunter points to a stool, chooses the one next to her. "Do you need a few minutes?"

"I'll be okay."

He reaches for his notebook and opens it.

"I'll need Dr. Sutherland's file."

"Gerber's office can get it for you."

"How long did Sutherland work here?"

"Almost six years."

"Anything special about what he did?"

"Viral research that involved this lab and another one called Level Four." She glanced over at Doc, who is standing where Alec had lain.

"You okay?" Hunter asks.

Seeing Alec's blood on the floor close to Doc's feet sends chills through her body. She focuses her eyes on Nick's notebook. She nods.

"What's the difference between the two labs?" he asks.

"Biosafety Labs are categorized 1 through 4. Dangerous microbes are handled in this Level Three, and the most dangerous ones in Level Four."

Hunter makes a few notations in his notebook. "So, Dr. Sutherland worked in both?"

"He did. Is that important?"

"Don't know yet. Did he argue with anyone here recently?"

"No."

The CSU tech and co-worker wave as they pass on their way out.

"Have any enemies?" Hunter asks.

"None."

"Hate his boss?"

"I'm... I mean, I was his boss."

"Did he have any dealings with Gerber?"

"Very little."

He pauses to make a few notes. "How about a wife? Children?"

She shakes her head. "No on both accounts. He never married."

"Did he always work late?"

"Most of the time."

"Did he live close to the Center?"

"About ten miles away."

"Alone?"

She hesitated. She would be telling on herself. So what? Even though her dad doesn't approve of her living with Alec, it is her life.

"Is that important?" she says.

"Never know."

"We lived together."

He looks up with raised brows. "Dr. Sutherland was your lover?"

He's judging me. She doesn't like his attitude. "You're very blunt," she says.

"Excuse the cliché, but I'm doing my job. You guys have any arguments lately?"

She stands. "What are you insinuating?"

"Have to ask."

She sits down.

"Did you touch the body when you found it?"

"No!"

"Know anyone who'd like to see him dead?"

"Didn't we discuss that under enemies?"

"How about a jealous friend?"

"I'm his only friend."

Two uniformed policeman interrupt Hunter to tell him that they have finished and are leaving. He nods.

"Anything missing from the lab?" he asks.

"All of our Tican samples."

"What's that?"

"A drug we were testing."

"Looks like someone killed the doc for it," Hunter says.

She tells him about Vladimir Sokolov, and about his cancer drug Tican.

He continues writing. "How do you spell that?"

She tells him and adds: "We were able to confirm Sokolov's findings in our cancer cell lines."

Hunter frowns. "I thought the CDC only dealt in hunting down killer bugs."

"This was an unusual situation. We also began testing Tican as a biological."

His brow forms a straight line, again. "Biological? You lost me. I thought it was a drug."

"Biologicals are weapons of mass destruction. Generally, they're viruses that have been re-engineered genetically to kill."

"That's messing with DNA, right?"

"You got it."

Hunter's face takes on a hunted look. "First you tell me this Tican is better than M&Ms, and now you're saying it could wipe out millions of people. Which is it?"

"Since the Soviet Union fell apart, the Center has been testing their unknown microorganisms as biologicals. In this case, the virus Tican is also treated as a biological. But more tests are needed to confirm that it isn't a deadly substance."

"So, there is danger?"

"I didn't say that. What I am saying is: our tests show its effectiveness in treating cancers, but to be sure it isn't a biological, we need several more weeks for our experiment to play out."

"How can it be good for cancer and yet be a biological?"

My God, if I only had more sleep.

"Because a virus can mutate, and if it does, it will do so after three weeks. We agreed to test it for six weeks, but were just half-way when..." Her voice drops off.

Hunter takes more notes. He gets up and paces in front of her. He stops and aims his pen at her. "So, you *don't* really know anything about this Tican?"

Susan senses a difference in Hunter's demeanor.

"Detective! I thought I explained it all pretty well."

"Nick. I like to be called Nick," he says, sitting down.

She sighs. "*Nick.* Let me explain again. I cannot say for sure if it's a biological."

"Okay, okay," he says, gesturing. "Don't get your dander up." He pauses, looking at his notes. "Let's assume for the moment that it cures cancer," he says. "Someone had to know. Who knew about it?"

Sokolov's name pops into her mind.

"Your Russian friend," he says. Then he looks at his notes, again. "Vladimir Sokolov. He would know."

She wonders if Nick has read her mind. "He can't be involved."

"Why not?"

"Because I helped him get an agreement with Kraft, and he stands to make millions. He wants to use the money to build a lab back home."

"For the moment, I'll rule him out. What about Harry Wentworth, the CEO of Kraft? Maybe he doesn't want to pay those millions."

"That's ridiculous. He was going to get a sample from us. He had no need to steal it."

"I guess Dr. Gerber is out, too," Nick says.

She thinks about Eva, but he wouldn't jeopardize his position at the Center. Besides, it's logical to assume he'd only need one vial, not all of them, if he did.

"You were slow to answer. Is there something I should know about him?"

"His wife is dying of colon cancer, but he'd never get involved with anyone that did this."

Nick jots something in his notebook. "I'll be the one to determine that."

"Dr. Gerber is very supportive of my work, obviously hoping that Tican will prove to be a cancer drug for his wife."

"Desperate men do desperate things," he says.

"Detective. Oh, I'm sorry, *Nick*," she says with irritation in her voice. "Eva probably would have died before we finished the work on Tican."

"All the more reason for him to steal it," he says. "Gerber will still remain a person of interest. Now, what about your techs?"

"Robin McCulley and Tony Seymour?" she says. "What motive would they have?"

Nick doesn't look up from his notebook. "Money, it's always about money," he says. "Need to talk to them. Can you get me their files?"

"I can arrange that."

"Am I a suspect, too?" she asks.

His doesn't look up. "Especially you. Spouses and lovers are always prime suspects in murder cases. We investigate all those closest to the victim and then move outward to others he knew." Nick looks up. "Where were you last night?"

She jumps up. "You can't be serious?"

"Sorry."

"I don't believe this."

He breaks a thin smile. "Police work."

"I was home all evening. Woke up around four and realized Alec hadn't come home. I immediately called Phil Corben, the security guard. He can vouch for me."

Nick stands. "Sure you and Dr. Sutherland were hitting it off okay? No lovers' quarrel or anything like that? After all, you were his boss, too."

"I find that offensive. Alec and I were the best of friends."

Nick turns a page in his notebook. "Friends fight sometimes." He pauses and looks up. "You own a .38?"

"No. I've never owned a gun, rifle or even a water pistol. I could never shoot anyone."

"Anything else you'd like to tell me?"

She pauses in thought. "I haven't seen the two men again in that black Mercedes, the ones who tried to kill me."

"I figured as much since I didn't hear from you. For now, we know that the .38 that killed Dr. Sutherland wasn't used in the attack on your old Cadillac. They were rounds from an AK-47."

"Isn't that a Russian weapon?" she asks.

His eyes widened. "So, you know something about weapons after all'

She shook her head. "Learned about the AK from TV."

"I see. We'll we're still searching for the Mercedes. There are hundreds of them in Atlanta."

What Hal Woolrich had said in D.C. about the Russian Mafia and KGB crossed her mind. "Would it be presumptuous of me to think that those goons are Russian?"

Nick smiles. "I'd say you were on the right track." He takes her arm. "Let's go to your office."

"Well?"

"Well, what?"

"Have you been checking on any Russian criminals here in Atlanta?" she asks.

"Police work is unbecoming to you. Let us handle it."

On the way he changes the subject. "Help me here. What if you found Tican to be a biological? What next?"

He pushes open the door and they head down the stairs, through the large lab. Nick removes his gown and throws it on the lab bench, and they exit into the corridor.

"Protocol requires that I report our findings to the Director of my division. That would be Gerber. He would then report the findings to the Director of CDC. If, after a thorough review, the Director determines the agent to be a threat to the public, he would immediately notify the authorities."

Nick's eyes widen.

"Why the worried look?" she asks.

"That's what I do. It's my job."

"Don't fret. I'm almost positive Tican isn't a biological."

"Either way, someone has it… and it's for sale," Nick says.

———◆———

When Nick steps out of the Path building, he spots A. Jaye strolling toward him. He waits and they head to the front gate. "What's bothering you?" Nick asks.

"Did you know these folks are working on a cancer drug?" A. Jaye says.

"Yeah."

"I didn't know they do that kind of stuff here."

"It's a special thing. We'll talk about it when we get to the station."

At the patrol car, Nick opens the driver's door and his partner goes to the passenger side. They slip in the patrol car and snap on seat belts.

"That Doc Gerber is weird," A. Jaye says.

"In what way?"

"When I drilled him about Ms. McCulley, he became as nervous as a kitten in a room full of rocking chairs. He's hiding something."

"We'll find out eventually what that is," Nick says as they drive off.

"And that Dr. Prescott," A. Jaye says. "She's some classy chick. Good looking legs, too."

"You said that the last time we were here."

"Can't help it, man, she's sexy."

"Too aggressive for my money," Nick says. "Don't like pushy women."

"Whoa," A. Jaye says, leaning back in his seat. "There you go again, thinking about the wife."

"Ex," Nick says. "Ex-wife."

His partner throws up his hands. "I know. She's a bitch."

"That bitch took every penny I had, and my son."

"Sorry, boss, didn't mean to bring up old baggage."

"Why you calling me *boss*?"

"Hey, you the man... big D.C. detective." He laughs.

"Ex! Ex-D.C. detective. *Partner*."

CHAPTER FOURTEEN

Robin's flesh crawls as she waits for Dmitry.

"Get hold of yourself, girl," she mutters. "Everything's okay. He won't know."

There's a pounding on the door. Her heart races and she's afraid to open it. When she does, Dmitry crashes in, knocking the wind out of her.

"Where are the samples?" he asks. "I want to see them."

Robin inhales deeply. "Calm down. Calm down," she says, pointing. "They're in the blue bag over there on the kitchen table."

Dmitry grabs the bag, opens it, counts the canisters, reaches in and pulls out a vial. "Good. Good," he says. "People pay lots of money for cancer drug."

He's smiling, but it doesn't ease Robin's tension. "Call your friend Gerber now!" he says.

She goes to the counter, carries the phone to the table, and dials the number. Her hand is shaking. "It's ringing," she says.

He grabs the phone and seconds later says into it, "I read in the paper your wife has cancer. I have a cancer drug for sale. You interested?"

Silence.

Robin crosses her fingers.

"Yes," he says. "It's Tican. I have a vial."

There is silence and Robin wonders what Gerber is saying to him.

"Doesn't matter where I got it. Do you want it or not?"

Will Gerber connect her to Dmitry? How could he? She just met him a few days ago.

Dmitry's face hardens. "I didn't kill him."

Robin flops in a chair. The thought hadn't crossed her mind until now. Will Gerber connect her to Dr. Sutherland's murder, since Dmitry couldn't have gotten into the lab? Would Gerber figure out it was an inside job?

Berger must have asked how much, because Dmitry says, "Two hundred thousand."

Robin holds her breath.

"Two hundred!" the Russian demands. "Tomorrow, you come to Leopold's Lounge at two o'clock."

Another pause.

Robin is feeling better. If Gerber buys Tican, he won't go to the cops. Or will he? He could turn Dmitry in after he gets the drug. *Naw, he's scared of his own shadow.*

"Wear a yellow shirt, no tie," the Russian says.

CHAPTER FIFTEEN

Nick arrives at the medical examiner's building around ten o'clock that morning instead of nine. He doesn't want to enter the pit before Doc begins. Nick has seen enough autopsies to last him the rest of his life. He's now only interested in getting the facts. Inside the building, classical music is playing through the intercom—a favorite of Doc McCormick. Nick walks past Doc's secretary in the reception area, she smiles and waves as he descends to the lower level and pushes through the door of the dressing room.

There are four lockers, a bench, and boxes of gowns, latex gloves, caps and masks on a large table. The place smells of Lysol. Nick removes his overcoat and suit coat, places them in the locker. At the table he reaches for a gown and slips into it, pulls on a cap, reaches in his coat for cologne and sprays a few squirts in the mask, and heads out. Nick adjusts his mask before pushing through the door. He would rather smell the cologne than that shit in the pit—formalin, blood and human organs.

Inside, a bright overhead light blazes over the body on the table.

Doc McCormick is gowned and caped, arched over the body. Classical music is piped into the room. Alec has been opened with a Y-incision—a cut from each shoulder meeting at the sternum and down the front of the abdomen to the pubis. The rib cage and all organs from top to bottom have been removed. Marty, the thirty-something assistant, has finished removing the brain, and Sutherland's scalp has been pulled down over his face.

Doc's piercing eyes gaze at Nick over glasses set on the tip of his nose. "We got started on time. Glad you were able to make it."

"Thanks, Doc," Nick says, ignoring the sarcasm. *Doc's okay, he just likes to feel important.* Nick is glad they had finished with removing the

71

brain. Watching them cut through the scalp and pulling it down over the face churns his stomach. Not to mention the saw buzzing its way through the skull.

"Why do you always remove the brain last?" Nick asks.

"To permit the blood to drain before we remove it," Doc says. "Makes the examination easier."

Doc's a large man. He has gray hair and a salt-and-pepper beard. He walks away with a limp, carrying a tray of organs and jars of tissue in formalin to a table against the wall. When he returns, Nick bends forward, fixing his eyes on the two holes in Alec's body. "Exit wounds?" Nick asks, pointing at the hole in the left nipple area and then to the one in the neck.

"The bullet that entered the back below the left shoulder blade tore through his heart and aorta and exited here next to the nipple," Doc says. "It's the one that killed him." He points to the neck wound. "The bullet that exited here didn't do that much damage, missed the carotid."

"Anything else?" Nick asks.

"Clean under his nails, no defensive marks on his arms. That's about it."

Marty added, "No struggle. He didn't know what hit him."

"When are you releasing the body, Doc?"

"This afternoon."

CHAPTER SIXTEEN

Susan doesn't know if Alec wanted to be cremated or interred. They never talked about it. Why would they? Death was far from their minds and he wasn't her husband, only her lover. She is so thankful that Karl Gerber takes charge and helps her with the funeral arrangements.

The November wind whips the sides of the canopy covering Alec Sutherland's casket. Susan is holding Karl's arm as they make their way to the front row of chairs. She's wearing a black dress, wide-brimmed hat, and black coat. Karl told her earlier that she reminded him of Jacqueline Kennedy Onassis.

The aroma of the flowers brings back memories. She and Sabrina are twelve; their mother passes away. They are standing next to the casket at the end of the service, rubbing it, hugging it, their tears streaming down it, purifying their mother. They hold on to the casket ever so tightly, not wanting it to fall in the hole below, losing Mama forever. Twelve years later, at twenty four, Susan stands next to another coffin. It is Sabrina's. Rage fills Susan's heart as she tells her sister goodbye, but promises her, someday she'd find the cure.

Now tears are trickling down Susan's cheeks again, grieving for another person.

Why did Alec have to die such a violent death? He never hurt anyone.

When the minister arrives, he stops briefly to speak with Susan and then goes to the head of the casket. Nick Hunter arrives and moves in under the canopy. Robin McCulley and Tony Seymour step around the fresh chunks of dirt, making their way next to the detective. Dr. Ryan Jordan, the Director of the CDC, and Phil Corben, Security Guard, are seated on the other side of Gerber.

Susan wonders why Detective Hunter has come. During the eulogy, Robin McCulley begins sobbing so violently that Nick leads her away.

The minister throws dirt on the casket, and intones: "From dust you have come and to dust you shall return." At the end of the ceremony, Gerber guides Susan to the casket where she places a red rose, lowers her head and prays that Alec is now in a better place. She is a believer, but not much of a churchgoer.

Gerber leads her to the limousine parked thirty yards away at the top of a hill. He opens the back door, Susan eases in and he settles in beside her. Gerber is about to close the door when a hand grasps it and holds it open.

Detective Hunter sticks his head in. "Dr. Prescott. Sorry to bother you at this time, but I'd like to know if Ms. McCulley and Dr. Sutherland were involved."

He knows damn well they weren't, she thinks. What the hell is he attempting to prove? "Why would you ask such a thing?"

"You must have heard Ms. McCulley's wailing. For her to be that distressed, she had to be very close to the deceased, don't you think?" He inches closer to Gerber. "I had to take her to the car."

"I heard her!" Susan shouts. "But they were never intimate as you are suggesting, and I take offense—"

"Sorry," Nick says as his hands shoot up in the air, "very sorry to upset you."

Susan leans across the front of Gerber to make sure Nick hears her loud and clear. "Alec didn't like her, never did! He even called her *Hussy* behind her back."

Nick shakes his head. "Odd, very odd." And he slams the door shut.

———————— ◆ ————————

After the limousine driver lets him out at his home, Gerber quickly changes into a yellow shirt and takes off in his silver Infinity. He parks in front of Leopold's and hurries in for his two o'clock appointment, carrying a leather satchel. Inside, he pauses to look around. It has been a decade since he'd stepped into this place. He smiles, thinking about the good times he'd had with the easy women that came here. The place hasn't changed much, though, the bar has been refinished and several TVs have been added.

A guy with a glass of beer in front of him is at the bar, watching a football game, eating pretzels. Two women are three seats down from him, and several couples are at the tables. A muscular giant dressed in a dark suit with white shirt open at the collar is at the end, and Gino Morelli is wiping up the wet spots in front of him. Morelli glances Gerber's way, but doesn't address him.

Gerber wonders if Morelli remembers him. *Nah, it's been too long.*

Gerber glances in the back. A bald guy, three times Gerber's size, wearing a yellow shirt with no tie, is waving at him. Gerber hurries over to the booth.

"Your name?" says the man in a thick accent. The giant in the suit springs over from the stool and stands next to the booth.

"Karl Gerber. And yours?"

"Belofsky. Have a seat," he says, gesturing.

Gerber moves in. The skinhead has a five-inch scar running down his right cheek and the open collar reveals the inked edge of a tattoo. Gerber places the leather satchel on the seat next to him and eyes the gray bag on the table.

Is that my miracle drug?

"You have it?" Gerber says with a cotton mouth, as he glances at the bodyguard. Sweat is trickling from his underarms.

Belofsky unzips the bag, takes out a small canister, and sets it on the table. Gerber touches it. The big guy in the suit grabs his hand and nearly breaks it at the wrist.

"Son-of-a-bitch!" Gerber shouts. "What's—?"

Belofsky interrupts. "First, see the money."

A couple at the bar screams. Must have been a touchdown, Gerber thinks.

He shakes the circulation back into his hand, reaches for his satchel, and spreads it open for the bastard to peer in.

Gerber's eyes lock on Belofsky, who pushes the canister across the table. "Money," Belofsky says.

Gerber hands the bag off and grabs the canister. Belofsky dumps the money into the sack next to him. Each man takes a few moments to treasure his prize without saying a word.

What's with this guy? He has tattoos on the back of each finger, too.

"It's all there in hundred-dollar bills," Gerber says, pushing the button on the refrigerated canister and the lid flies open.

Belofsky is busy with his hands in the bag counting the money.

Gerber lifts out the cold vial and stares at the pale liquid in the light.

"It's good," the Russian says. The bodyguard ambles over to the back wall.

"I hope so, for my wife's sake," Gerber says, slipping the vial back into the container and then into the bag.

The idea that this foreigner has him by the balls upsets Gerber, but there's nothing he can do about it, if he wants to cure Eva. He squirms in his seat, thinking Detective Hunter probably knows more than he revealed at Sutherland's funeral—that maybe someone in the Center killed Sutherland. Robin seemed interested in the money he offered her for a vial. She had the means and opportunity, and probably this mobster is helping her. He couldn't have gotten into the Center. Gerber is damn sure their motive is money.

Gerber stares at the boar in front of him, zipping up the bag of money.

"What if I need more?" Gerber asks.

"Call Morelli," he says, hitching his bald head toward the bar. He gets up and signals to his companion. Gerber jumps up, blocking Belofsky's path. Gerber has to know who gave this pig his name.

"Who told you I needed—?" The bodyguard slams a fist into Gerber's stomach, knocking him into his seat before he can finish his question.

Belofsky grunts and smirks as he passes. The mobsters make their way to the front and disappear.

Gerber waits until he can breathe again and heads to the door.

"Don't be a stranger," Morelli says. He smiles.

The bastard remembers.

CHAPTER SEVENTEEN

Gerber is faced with a challenge: how is he going to convince Eva to let him inject her with Tican? He had pitched other drugs as being miracles and they didn't work. She had told him no more experimental drugs. He's ready for a fight.

He steps into the dining room and strolls past his wife, takes a seat at the other end of the table. Eva is pushing salad around on her plate. The maid, Isabella, dressed in a cotton dress and apron, steps in from the kitchen and asks if he wants something to eat. He orders coffee and dessert. Eva looks up, staring hard at him.

"Where did you go?"

She isn't in the habit of asking him to account for his whereabouts, particularly since she moved out of their bedroom two years ago, and told him she was no longer interested in him or his boring life.

"Is there something you want to say to me, sweet?" he says.

Isabella returns with a silver coffee urn, sets it on the buffet, and cuts a slab of New York cheese cake, Gerber's favorite.

"I'm getting worse." Eva sighs. "And I'm ready."

"Ready for what?"

Isabella sets the coffee and cake in front of him. He smiles at her and she leaves.

"You know what. Don't play the innocent husband. It doesn't suit you."

"Sorry, dear." *This is my chance to bring it up.* "There's this new drug... much different from the others and very effective in treating colon cancer. I would like to use it on you." He took a drink of coffee. "What do you think?

"You've said that many times before," she says in a whisper. "And

77

nothing worked."

"I just learned about this one," he says, disappointed in her fatalistic attitude. He stares at her pale face over the rim of his cup. She could be mean whenever she doesn't get her way, and delights in using him as her punching bag.

"I don't want any more of your false hope," she says, squirming in her chair. "Stop lying to me."

"Eva, please. I'm not lying. This is the drug for you. I've checked it out thoroughly. Remember, we talked about beating this thing together." He takes a bite of dessert.

Isabella pushes through the door.

"This's really good cake. Want some?" he says.

Eva shakes her head. "I've been thinking about something. St. Michael's," she says, pausing long enough to lock on his gaze. "I see the surprise in your eyes. You think that's funny, don't you?"

"Why would I? We used to go to church often when we were first married. I don't know why we quit." He finishes his coffee, and Isabella refills his cup.

"Anything more?" Isabella asks.

"No, please leave us alone. I'm talking to my husband."

Isabella darts out of the room.

"You shouldn't be so hard on her," Gerber says. "She's only doing her job."

Eva waves off his comment. "I was about to say when she came into the room, that like many people, we let everything else get in the way of our going to church." She pauses again, her eyes narrow. "I thought if I told you, you would laugh at me ..." Her voice trails off. "Because you're thinking at this moment that she's dying, so now she turns to God."

She's right. It did pop into his mind. Terminally ill patients do turn to God, begging Him for healing, asking friends for healing prayers, but when they become well, they usually forget about Him.

"I never told you," she says, "but I pray every morning. I always have. And sometimes at night." She sips the last of her coffee. "As a little girl, my mother read morning prayer to me."

They were Episcopalians, but he had been a Methodist before they married. Gerber frowns, thinking how little he knows about her childhood. "I didn't know," he says.

Gerber stares at his wife. Death is squeezing the life out of her. "Did you want me to call someone? Maybe a priest?"

She doesn't answer. Instead, she pats her mouth, sets the napkin next to her plate and pushes back from the table. "I'm so very tired," she says. "I'm going to my room."

He jumps up and rushes to her side. "Let me help you."

"I don't want your help," she says, yanking her arm free from his grasp.

"I'll come up and give you your shot."

"No, I said!"

After finishing his dessert and coffee, Gerber goes to his office. He bounds up the staircase with his black bag and canister and hustles into Eva's bedroom. The room is painted white with carpet and drapes to match, prompting him to wonder if the many rooms Jesus said his Father had in heaven were like this one.

Eva is resting in her king-sized canopy bed decorated in white, too. The window drapes are closed. The room is illuminated only by a small lamp on the night table. When her health had started to deteriorate, Eva had this guest room renovated and moved into it.

He edges to her bedside, sets the items on the tray, and spreads the canopy drapes. "Just going to insert the morphine drip," he says. He bends over and kisses her on the forehead. Her hands are crossed over her stomach. If he hadn't known better, he'd have thought she was dead. Her long gaunt face and thin pallid skin barely covers her bones. Eva's lips move slightly and she strives to open her eyes to a slit. She says in a whisper, "It's time."

Gerber turns to the morphine pump on the stand. "Your morphine is working fine." He can't do what she is asking.

"No, no," she says, waving her emaciated hand with the inserted I.V. "You know. More so I can go peacefully."

"We've talked about that, sweet. I can't do it."

"You spineless son-of-a-bitch," she tries to shout, but only a whisper leaves her lips. Eva closes her eyes and takes several shallow breaths. "I'd do it for you."

Gerber doesn't have to take her shit any longer. He's now in control. No more the milquetoast husband. Her whining like a dove and the sarcasm she slings at him makes him want to end her life right this moment. Yeah. He could do it. Just shoot the morphine to her. No one would know. He would be free of her. He reaches for the morphine bottle in his bag. Holds it for a few seconds and drops it back into the bag. He can't do it. *He's still the weak sister.* What irony—he still loves the bitch.

"I have something that will cure you, Eva. Trust me."

Her hands are shaking. "Damn you. I don't want it."

Gerber opens the medical bag, removes a glass syringe, attaches a needle and sets it on the tray. He takes the small vial out of the canister.

"Please, Karl, please. I'm begging you. Give me something so I can go."

Your cure is in this vial. He holds it out for her to see—one milliliter, one dose. "Your cure. I promise."

She whacks his hand. "I said no." The vial shoots through the air, hits the wall and explodes into pieces and falls on the white carpet.

"You bitch! Look what you've done. This could have saved your life."

"No more!" she says.

Gerber darts out, runs down the stairs to his office, lifts the phone, and calls Morelli.

"Morelli."

"This is Karl Gerber. I need another sample right away. Belofsky told me to call you."

"It'll be a few days. He's out of town."

"Shit! I need it now."

"Not without his okay. I'll see what I can do."

"Please. Tell him it's life or death."

"Yeah, yeah."

Click.

CHAPTER EIGHTEEN

After the breakup of the Soviet Union, the U.S. media reports that the Russian people now are happy. Belofsky flies into a rage every time he read these lies. The Mafia boss Vladimir Sokolov has a plan that will release their anger on those who helped to crumble their beloved country. Their U.S. enemies are the members of the Senate Committee on Foreign Relations, and particularly their chairman, Senator Barry Plummer. The committee published many articles exposing what they called the evils of Communism in the Soviet Union, and their chairman called for severe sanctions against their country.

This Wednesday morning Belofsky removes a box of small darts and a test tube stand from the kitchen cabinet in his apartment, and sets them on the table.

Russians are known for their unique instruments used in surreptitious killings—one such device is an umbrella, whose sharp point, filled with just a minute amount of deadly toxin, can be rammed into a leg, dropping the victim before he takes two steps.

Belofsky feels elated. He has been sent the latest invention, the minidart. This device is an inch in total length with a needle one-fourth of the span. It's been designed aerodynamically to be shot out of a blowgun. The minidart's tiny barrel holds the toxin, and when the needle penetrates the skin, the barrel drops away after delivering its lethal payload, so the victim is aware of an insect sting, nothing more.

The unseasonable snow that landed on Atlanta brought the temperature below freezing and Belofsky can see his breath in his basement apartment as he removes two refrigerated cylinders and a two-inch glass vial of Tican from his freezer. He places them in the rack on the table. Two hours later, he has finished filling twenty-four minidarts with Tican and inserts twelve of them into each of the two cylinders, packing them into a gym bag along with the last remaining vial of Tican.

He glances around his quarters. *He'll not sleep here again.*

According to the Alliance *Times-Herald* that Belofsky read on the Internet, Nebraskan Senator Barry Plummer, is scheduled to speak in his hometown on Saturday afternoon at a fund-raiser, but will be arriving on Thursday evening to spend time with his family.

Belofsky slips on his hooded jacket, heads out the door, and climbs into the packed Mercedes. He drops the bag on the passenger seat and glances at his watch. Two o'clock. He has two days.

————— ◆ —————

A few minutes before noon on that Friday, Belofsky is a few miles from Alliance, a town in the Sand Hills of western Nebraska. The sky is clear and the sun bright, but the cold wind blows hard and sand whirls like small tornados over the barren plains. A sign at the city limits declares Alliance to be the *Hometown of Senator Barry Plummer*, population 8,595. Belofsky slows the Mercedes to 25 mph when a cop car heads his way. A Best Western looms ahead on the right, and he wheels in under the canopy and reserves a room for the night. On his way out, he picks up a copy of the *Times-Herald* and drives into town. A red, white and blue banner extends over Box Butte, the main street, welcoming their hero, Senator Plummer. At the top of each lamp post on both sides of the street are red, white and blue banners as far as he can see. He approaches a McDonalds, but decides he'll go to the café on the corner and stops in front of Johnnie's Egg House.

The place has six booths, six tables and six stools across the front of the counter.

Belofsky chooses a seat at the counter and removes his overcoat, laying it on the stool next to him. A woman in her early forties with an attractive hairdo and dangling earrings, wearing a white uniform, is arguing with the cook at the service window. She turns and frowns; apparently she caught Belofsky glancing at her rear.

"Coffee, mister?" she says, holding the pot out in front of him.

Belofsky nods as he looks over the menu. She fills his cup and pushes a bowl of creamer and a canister of sugar his way. "What'll you have?"

There's a wedding band on her finger. He looks back at the menu.

"I haven't got all day," she says.

He turns around. The place is empty. What the hell's the hurry? Her old man should beat the shit out of her more often, or maybe he'll do it. "Ham, eggs scrambled, biscuits, gravy."

She goes to the window and shouts, "Coronary blockers for one."

The cook grunts.

Belofsky sips his black coffee and opens the *Times-Herald*. A lot of things are scheduled in town for tomorrow: a calf-roping event, a rifle match, and the senator's speech at the American Legion Hall. Cattle prices are up and so are jobs. Loitering is not allowed along Box Butte, and the homeless are warned not to sleep on the sidewalk benches. Belofsky wonders how anyone could sleep outside in this sub-zero weather. And do the homeless read newspapers? *These people must be tough like the Russian people.* There is an article about people breaking the cigarette urns next to the benches. It costs the city $100 to replace one.

"Where you from, mister?" the waitress asks.

Belofsky hesitates for a moment. The police may be looking for him in Atlanta.

"Oklahoma," he says.

"Oh," she says, sounding disappointed. The cook's bell clatters. She leaves.

Belofsky jerks around when the frigid air hits his back. An elderly couple dressed in parkas moves in and ambles over to a booth in the back.

The waitress returns and shoves two plates in front of Belofsky and asks, "What part of Oklahoma?"

Nosy bitch. He splits a biscuit and spoons up the thick pasty stuff.

"Cat got your tongue, mister? I asked what part of Oklahoma?"

With his mouth full, he says, "Norman."

She frowns. "Did you say Norman?"

He nods, chewing. He had heard something on the radio about a football team in Norman.

"You one of them Sooners?" she asks in disgust. She doesn't wait for him to answer. "You must be here for another reason. We don't play you suckers until next week."

He doesn't look up. *What the hell is a Sooner?* She finally takes the hint and leaves. When she returns from taking the orders from the couple in the booth, Belofsky undresses her with his eyes as she stands at the kitchen window.

Ten minutes later, she slides a check in front of him, stares at the tattoos on his fingers, but says nothing. Belofsky twirls the ice pick in his pocket as he asks her to have a drink with him after work.

"I wouldn't be caught dead with a Sooner," she says sauntering away. "Anyway, my husband wouldn't like it."

He rubs his crotch, thinking about what he's going to do to her.

Belofsky drains his coffee, wipes his mouth with the paper napkin, grabs the check and gets up. He glances at the elderly couple; they're staring at him. He reaches for his coat and moseys over to the register. When the waitress appears, he asks if she knows where the Plummers live.

"Oh, you come to see them Plummers?"

He nods.

"Their boy, Barry, is famous. He's a big senator in Washington... friend of the President. He's speaking here tomorrow." She frowns. "You a relative?"

"Friend."

"Where you parked?"

"In front."

"Back out and go to your right. About two miles out of town, you'll see this big ranch with a white fence," she says. "You can't miss it, there's a huge sign over the entrance. Has their name on it."

CHAPTER NINETEEN

Outside, Belofsky raises his collar and bends forward against the bustling wind on the way to his car. Driving away, he keeps an eye on the odometer. A mile out of Alliance the concrete road ends and blacktop takes over. A span of snow covers rich farmland that has yielded its harvest months earlier. Only the strong live here, he thinks.

The *Times-Herald* reported that Chester and Emma Plummer are wealthy ranchers, have lived in Alliance for fifty years. They raised their only child, Barry, on their five-thousand-acre ranch with hundreds of cattle and pigs. They are proud of their son, now a U.S. Senator. The senior Plummer claims that hard work on the ranch has prepared Barry for the Senate.

The large arch over the entrance: *Sand Hills Ranch* is up ahead. He drives past it, amazed that a white fence continues for miles. *Nothing like this in Russia.* He turns the Mercedes around, heads back to the gate and pulls in, keeping an eye out for security guards. Bare sycamores line the sides of the road, and a two-story white frame house with a porch that covers the front, is up ahead. He pulls over to the side behind the trees about fifty yards from the house.

Belofsky fumbles through the gym bag in the passenger seat for his wool cap, opens the door, grabs the bag and clambers out. He reaches into his coat pockets for gloves and trudges like a bear through snow.

Moving to the side of the house, he eases to the window and looks in. A man with white hair, dressed in overalls, is at the kitchen table reading a newspaper, while a gray-haired woman in a house dress and apron is washing dishes at the sink.

Where's the senator?

He sets the bag in the snow, takes out a canister, two sections of the blowgun, places them in his pants' pockets, then heads up the front steps and knocks several times. When the door opens, a tall man in his seventies stands in the doorway smiling.

"Howdy," he says.

Belofsky fakes a smile. "Out of gas. Can you help me?"

"Sure. Don't stand out there in the cold," the old man says, pulling Belofsky in by his arm, slamming the door shut. He leads Belofsky into the kitchen. "We just finished eating, but mother will fix you something. We have fresh coffee brewing. This is my wife, Emma. I'm Chester."

Belofsky nods. "I'm Tom."

The wrinkled-faced woman wipes her hands on the apron. "Have a seat, Tom, and warm yourself," she says pointing to a chair.

Belofsky throws his jacket on the chair next to him.

"Thought you were a reporter," Chester says. "They hit this house like flies when Barry's here." He shakes his head. "I'm sorry he had to go back to Washington. Folks here won't be too happy about that."

Belofsky's fists tighten and he fights off his rage.

"You're shaking," the woman says. "I'll pour you some coffee. That'll warm you up."

His fury is building and he needs a minute to himself. "I need to wash my hands," Belofsky says.

"Of course," the old man says. "I'll show you to the bathroom."

Bathroom? No bath. He's digging his fingernails into his palms.

Chester opens the door and turns on the light. "Help yourself," he says. "Come to the kitchen when you're done."

"Okay," Belofsky says. He looks around, closes the door. His blood pressure is sky high and he's fuming, ready to kill. He listens to the man's footfalls.

When he can no longer hear anything outside the door, he reaches into his pocket, pulls out the cylinder, opens it, takes out two darts, closes the lid and replaces it in his pocket. He reaches for the blowgun parts and assembles the two pieces. Easing the door open, Belofsky tiptoes through the living room and listens. The Plummers are talking about warmed over chicken fried steak, mashed potatoes and gravy, and something called rhubarb pie.

Belofsky has a good sight on them. The woman is at the stove, and her old man is at the table drinking coffee. Belofsky inserts a minidart into the blowgun, inhales deeply, and takes aim. With a burst of his breath, the dart hits the woman below the left ear. She slaps at it and turns to look at her husband. Belofsky reloads, and shoots Chester below his right ear. "Jesus!" he shouts.

His wife scolds him. "Father, you know better. The Lord's listening."

"Felt like something stung me in the neck."

"Me too. What could it be? Can't be mosquitoes."

He shrugs. "I wonder what's taking Tom so long. Hope he's okay. He was really shaking."

Belofsky appears from around the corner and takes his seat.

"Oh, there you are," Chester says. "We were getting worried about you."

Emma sets a plate in front of Belofsky filled with steak, mashed potatoes and gravy and a large piece of buttered bread. She returns with a cup of coffee and a slice of pie.

The wall phone rings. Emma lifts the receiver. "We'll be there," she says, and turns to Chester. "That was Louise at the church, reminding us about the potluck Sunday night."

Chester nods. "Where you headed, Tom?"

"Oklahoma."

"That so? Where in Oklahoma?"

Emma interrupts. "We've got a daughter in Tulsa."

"Norman," Belofsky says.

"Home of the Sooners," the old man says, slapping the table. "They got a damn"—he looks at his wife—"good football team. They play us next week. Big game for us, Tom."

With an occasional grunt, Belofsky finishes his food, takes a gulp of coffee and reaches for the pie.

"You a football fan?" he asks.

"Soccer."

The fridge cycles on.

The old man shakes his head, "Don't know much about soccer. Not a man's game. Got to make contact." He slams a fist into the palm of his hand and says, "Got to knock the other guy on his... off his feet."

Belofsky finishes his pie and coffee.

"Want more?" the woman asks.

"Have another piece of mama's pie, Tom."

Belofsky raises his hands. "Done."

These old people are fools. Why do they care so much about me? They don't know me. His own mother spit on him, beat him, and wished him dead. He wonders if all Americans are this weak. "Must go," he says.

"Sure," the old man says, pushing himself up from the table, goes into the next room, returns wearing a parka. Belofsky puts on his coat. They go out the back.

"I've got a couple of cans of gasoline I keep in the shed for my tractor." The icy wind threatens to knock them off their feet.

"I'll only be a minute," Chester says, opening the shed and goes in.

The wind catches the door and bangs it shut. Belofsky bolts around the house, grabs his bag and races through the field to his car. He arrives at the Mercedes out of breath, jumps in and speeds off towards town.

He swings around the American Legion Hall, where people are gathering for the senator's talk. The blacktop parking lot is filled and cars are lined up in the streets. *Fools, they don't know the bastard's gone back to Washington.* Belofsky decides to head to Johnnie's Egg House and put the make on that waitress.

Inside, Johnnie's is packed. People are mostly standing and talking above each other. Belofsky finds an empty booth near the door and slips into it and cranes his neck to see if she is on duty. A girl in her late teens hurries round the counter. He orders coffee. When she returns with a cup and the pot, he asks about the other waitress.

"Velma? She took off to hear Senator Plummer." The teenager takes a few napkins from her apron and places them on the table. "Cream and sugar is there," she says pointing.

Belofsky reaches for the cream and stirs it in his coffee. After a couple of swallows, the door flies open, and in charges Velma, throwing her purse down on the counter and removing her coat. She shouts, angrily. "Damn! That Barry was called back to Washington. Of all things, when he promised. This was suppose to be a special day."

The room is filled with groans and shuffling of feet.

The old man was right. People are mad as hell. Belofsky's eyes lock on Velma's body as he twirls the pick in his coat pocket.

CHAPTER TWENTY

Susan arrives in Mystic for the Thanksgiving holidays and is sitting in a leather chair in her father's home office, drinking white wine that he has given her before he went to answer the phone at his desk. His briefcase is to his right and stacks of papers in front of him are so high she can barely see his salt and pepper hair. A bookcase filled with law books is next to him. She can't remember the last time they sat and talked. He rises, rounds the desk and takes a seat in the mirror-image leather chair and reaches for his glass that he placed on the coffee table between them when he went to answer the phone.

Susan has been home only a couple of times since graduating from Yale. Too many heartrending memories are in this place, and now she dreads this holiday season. Even after all these years she senses the emptiness and loneliness left by her mother's passing and her brother's absence.

"Would you like some more?" her father says, noticing that she's swallowed the last of her wine. He reaches for her glass.

"Maybe a little, Dad," she says, thinking maybe it will help her to relax and ease the painful memories.

He returns from the kitchen and she reaches for her drink. The spring in his step before losing his wife and daughter still hasn't returned. There are more gray hairs in his head and his narrow shoulders are sagging more on his six foot frame. He was a devoted husband and a great provider, and Susan knew he loved his children, yet he wasn't one to express his feelings. He neither told them he loved them, nor did he ever hug them, except maybe at Christmas when they were very young. And that was because the kids were so excited over their presents that he had to react to their hugs.

Susan takes another drink and wonders what he's thinking. She blames him for not being there for Michael when he needed his father the most, but she figures her father had been struggling with too much pain and didn't realize his children were suffering, too. He has not remarried, and probably never will. Michael's outward defiance all these years, especially now that his drinking is at a new level, has contributed to a troubled, aging father. She loves her dad and feels sorry for him, but it's time to have their talk.

Mr. Prescott, staring into his glass, which appears small in his large hands, takes a drink and begins telling Susan that Michael borrowed three hundred dollars from a guy who had him thrown into a jail when he couldn't repay it. Mr. Prescott got Michael released, but now he's roaming the streets, a drunk. He has received an anonymous tip, probably from one of Michael's old drinking buddies, who said he has seen Michael sleeping in an abandoned apartment building on the east side of town. Mr. Prescott went there, watched from his car as Michael stumbled into the building with a brown bag in his hand.

"I want Michael here for Thanksgiving, Dad," Susan says.

"He won't come. I've even gone as far as to beg him to come and live with me." He shakes his head. "Michael doesn't want anything to do with me."

The telephone rings. He goes to his desk.

Susan's hoping it's Michael. He could have had a change of heart. Holidays had been an important time in their lives when growing up.

"It's a client," her father says, returning to his chair. "Not important." He sighs. "I don't know what I've done to cause Michael to hate me so."

"Did you ask him?"

"Every time I open my mouth, he walks away and says it's nothing."

"Dad... did you ever stop to think that maybe Michael needed your love and support when mom died?"

His expression is one of hurt. His eyes lock on hers. "I thought I was there for you guys."

"No Dad, you weren't. You never sat down and talked with us about the loss of our mother and how we were going to support each other. At times like those, fathers have conversations with their children and eventually do fun things together to get them through it. We got none of that."

He drops his head again and is silent, a portrait of a man defeated. *Is he crying? Did I go too far?* She had to say it, wanted to for years.

When he looks up, his eyes are glassy, and he sighs. "I'm afraid saying 'I'm sorry' is much too late, but I didn't realize it, and I am truly sorry, Susan. Your mother and I..." He doesn't finish the sentence. Seconds later, he says, "I had a hard time dealing with her death." He pauses again. "I was mad at God and even cried out to him, asking him why he took her from me. She was the best person I've ever known."

Tears flow down Susan's face. She reaches for her purse and retrieves a tissue. *He needs to tell this to Michael.* "You need to tell Michael how you were hurting and that you're sorry you weren't there for him."

"If he would only let me. I never realized that my failure as a father has affected him so."

Susan finishes her wine, sets the glass on the coffee table and jumps up. "I'm going after him, Dad."

"That's not a good idea. You know that part of town."

"But he's out there hurting."

"Then you'll have to go it alone. If I am with you, he'll never come." Mr. Prescott gets up and goes to his desk, writes something, and hands it to her. "You'll need directions."

Susan leaves the house and the northeast cold wind blasts her. She gets into his Cadillac, notices the new smell, and drives to the edge of town. She eases the car along the curb, surveying the two-story brick buildings with boarded windows. She spots the building without a door and pulls to the curb. Susan gets out, hurries to the entrance. Inside, she steps over paper bags and broken bottles, gags at the smell of whisky and vomit. She breathes through her mouth, switches on the flashlight she found in the glove compartment, and roams through the rooms, stepping over flattened cardboard boxes. Burnt sticks and charred newspaper are piled in the center of what was the living room. *It's a wonder the place hasn't caught on fire.*

She rubs her cold nose with a gloved hand.

A moan comes from upstairs. She takes the steps two at a time. "Michael?"

At the second landing, she wanders through the hall, shining light into each room. No doors, no beds, and no life. In the last room, a man is lying on the floor. She eases closer. *Is it Michael?* The guy is on his side, cuddling a bottle of Jack Daniels. His face is filthy, hair matted, and he stinks. But it's Michael. *Thank God.*

Somewhere outside a dog barks. *He'd better not come in here.*

Michael's breath condenses in the freezing air. At least he's alive. She nudges him with her foot. "Michael. Wake up."

He turns over on his back, opens his eyes. "Oh-h-h, no-o-o," he moans, turning his face away. "Not you."

"Get up; we're going home." She pokes him again with her boot.

"Go away," he says, arms flailing. The bottle rolls across the room. Rats are scratching inside the walls.

Susan sits beside him, zips up his jacket, and turns her head to let loose a dry heave. She inhales through her mouth to steady herself.

She pulls back his collar. "How'd you get these bruises on your face?"

"None of your damn business."

She gets to her knees and yanks on his arms. "Come on, help me. Push!"

Miraculously, she's able to pull him up on trembling feet, grabs him around his waist, and they stagger to the stairs. She grasps the handrail as they descend the stairs, one step at a time, still breathing through her mouth. Halfway down, Michael's body shakes like he's having a seizure. He misses a step and they tumble down. He lands on top of her.

"Son-of-a-bitch! Get off of me," she shouts, pushing him over on his back. "You smell like shit."

"Go away. Why can't you let me alone?"

"You're going with me, so shut the fuck up!"

They make it to the car and she opens the passenger side, pushes him in and attaches the seat belt.

Behind the wheel, she powers away, wondering if Michael's odor would linger in their father's new Cadillac. Michael's head is curved backwards on the seat, and he's snoring. When they arrive home, Susan leads Michael straight to the bathroom. Her father watches, shaking his head.

"Put on some coffee, Dad."

"I poured some when I heard the car door slam. I'll get it."

Inside the bathroom, Michael slides down the wall, butt hitting the floor. Susan reaches for the coffee her dad had brought, and takes it to her brother.

"Drink this. All of it," she says.

He pushes her hand away. "I don't want it."

"I said drink it, dammit!"

He reaches for the cup and takes several drinks. She waits until he finishes it. "Now, take off those filthy rags and get your ass in the shower."

He frowns at her. "You going to stand there and watch me?"

"I've seen your naked ass before. Hop in the shower and hurry up."

Reluctantly, he stands, turns his back to her, kicks out of his grubby clothes, steps into the shower, and pulls the curtain shut.

"You can turn on the water now."

"I am. Criminy sakes, give me a break."

Dad brings a trash bag. "You'll need this," he says.

Holding her breath, she bags Michael's things and heads to his room. She returns with fresh clothes as he is drying off.

"Put these on," she says.

"I'm not staying."

"The hell you aren't. I didn't come all this way for nothing. It's time we had our talk."

"Oh, more wisdom from the family."

"You damn right. Especially since you can't seem to face your demons alone."

"I'll stay until you go back to Atlanta."

Susan stomps out.

Fully dressed and looking more like the brother she had known, Michael enters the kitchen, pours himself coffee and sits at the table facing his sister. "What are you doing?"

"What does it look like?"

"A turkey."

"In case you've forgotten, tomorrow's Thanksgiving."

"I did forget." He stares at her over the cup. "You're really pissed at me, aren't you, sis?"

"Now that's wisdom."

"Where's Dad?"

"He went to the store." She shoves the turkey into the oven.

"You cook it the day before?"

"You questioning my culinary skills?"

He throws his hands up. "Don't get your dander up. I'm just curious."

"I'm curious too," she says, wiping her hands on a towel, and sitting across from him. "What's wrong, Michael?"

He shrugs, drinks more of his coffee. "Nothing."

She can see the scowl on his face and knows what Michael is thinking at this moment—*she's going to kill me*. She inhales a deep breath. "Let me explain *nothing* to you. You did poorly in high school, which I think was deliberate, ran away from home several times, told lies, intimidated our friends like you were some mobster, flunked out of college, and held minimum wage jobs no longer than six months because of your drinking." She slams her empty coffee cup on the table. "You even traveled the country for a while, and still nothing came out of it. Dad got you a job and you flubbed that. Then you left Dad, started drinking more, hanging out with your misfit friends, and ended up in jail, twice." She catches her breath. "Did I leave anything out?"

She gets up to fill her cup.

"How about breaking my poor daddy's heart?"

"Didn't forget it. Just haven't gotten to it," she says, taking her seat back at the table.

"You're getting a lot of pleasure telling me all this shit, aren't you?"

"Do I look like I'm having fun?" She rises, goes to the stove and opens the oven door and glances at the turkey, and then returns to the table.

"My, aren't we jumpy," he says.

"Wonder why?" she says.

Silence while she thinks about digging into his psyche.

"Michael, I know that you were only six when mom died and you took it hard, very hard."

He frowns and she sees the hurt in his eyes. "You remember those tantrums I threw, huh?"

She nods. "Sabrina and I missed mom, too," she says. "We tried to take her place, but I knew at the time we could never do that for you. And that seems to be the time when your trouble started."

He says nothing, just stares at his cup.

Seconds later, he says "Where was our dad at the time?" He shakes his head. "I didn't know how to deal with Dad."

"Dad and I had a long talk before I came for you. He told me he was having a hell of a time with mom's passing and hadn't realized he neglected us. And that he's sorry."

"That's all bullshit."

Susan was surprised to see the harshness in Michael's eyes.

"Dad says you won't let him tell you he's sorry that he failed at a time when we all needed him."

Michael doesn't say a word, appearing as if he's in deep thought.

"Are you on drugs?" she asks.

He gnashes his teeth. "I don't do drugs. Alcohol is my only sin."

"What's bothering you Michael? Please tell me. You have to face whatever's bothering you."

"I don't know."

"You do know. If it's not Dad, does it have to do with Mom?"

"Don't go there," he says. He couldn't hide the pain in his face.

"Michael, we all were affected by Mom's death."

He jumps up and goes to the cabinet. "I don't want to talk about it." He opens the doors.

"What are you looking for?"

"Is there any wine around here? I know Dad drinks it."

"We ran out. He's buying some. Drink your coffee. Have a slice of that cherry pie on the counter," she says. "I hear that sweets help."

He cuts a piece of pie and sits at the table.

"Tell me about those bruises on your face and neck."

"I gotta have a drink."

"There isn't any. I'm waiting for you to tell me."

He takes a bite of his dessert. "Happened during my five-day stay in our hospitable Mystic jail. Some bastard worked me over because he didn't like my looks, and the jailer didn't stop him. He called me the rich kid with a big shot lawyer for a father."

"I'm sorry—"

He looks up. "And if that isn't enough, another prisoner vomits on me."

"Michael, listen. How hard would it be for you to be nice to Dad? Move back in here and let him help you. He loves you."

"Loves me? That's a laugh. And stop trying to get into my brain like some psychotherapist."

"Get off it. I only want to help." A car door slams.

"I can take care of myself."

"I see how you're doing that." She gets up and looks out the window. "Dad's here."

"Sis, I know you mean well," he says in a whisper. "But face it. We've grown apart, Dad and me."

"You're really going out of your way to punish Dad, aren't you?"

"I just had to leave this place. How else could I learn who I am?"

"And did you?"

He doesn't answer.

Apparently not.

"You need the courage to dig out of your hole," she says. "Think about it, you can overcome whatever it is that's hurting you. Let me help you."

"I'll think about it."

"You need to embrace the truth," she says, "and work through your pain."

CHAPTER TWENTY-ONE

Gerber rounds the drive in his silver Infinity and stops in front of his home. He looks at the dashboard clock. Nearly ten o'clock. Belofsky had called at eight-thirty and told him he had left a dose of Tican with Morelli before leaving town. Gerber had feared he'd never hear from him again, but that is naïve. Belofsky loves money too much.

Gerber doesn't open his car door; instead he gazes at the box next to him for a few seconds, wondering if he's gotten the real stuff. *He wouldn't put it past the immoral son-of-a-bitch to substitute some placebo for the real thing.* Gerber pauses. *What am I thinking? Am I less immoral than Belofsky in what I am doing, buying this stuff and injecting it into my wife?*

He sighs. Grabs the box and hurries into the house. In his office, Gerber rips open the box, pulls out the cylinder, opens it, and removes the vial and holds it up. He gazes at it for a few seconds. *This will make Eva well, if it's really Tican.* Hopefully, she's still asleep.

This time he'll be ready with the shot, and she won't know he's even in the room until after the injection. He opens his doctor's bag, removes a syringe, and attaches the needle to it, takes out the vial and inspects it. It looks like the previous dose. He removes the cap, inserts the needle, withdraws one milliliter of the miracle drug and drops the empty vial into his bag.

He bounds up the stairs and stops outside Eva's door and listens. No movement. He eases the door open and steps inside. She is breathing hard with her back to him. He slips deeper into the room and edges over to the bed. He spreads the curtain, stabs the needle through her gown into her hip, and forces the plunger all the way into the syringe.

It's done.

"What did you do?" she shouts.

"The cure, my love."

"Damn you! I've made my peace with the Lord and was ready to go." She cries, "I hate you."

CHAPTER TWENTY-TWO

Dressed in jeans, a turtleneck sweater, and red high heels, Susan hurries from the Jetway into the Atlanta airport this evening and follows a stream of passengers toward the main exit. For several days she has cooked for Dad and Michael, but now she's glad to be home and eager to get back into the lab. Nick Hunter had called and offered her a ride. *Maybe he's going to apologize for his rudeness. God knows they haven't hit it off.*

Susan is now living with a secret that Nick would find amusing. But she isn't going to tell him. In Mystic her mind played tricks on her. Thoughts of him and Alec Sutherland kept popping into her mind. She could understand Alec, who she misses greatly, and her heart wrenches every time she thinks about his murder. But Nick? Now that perplexes her. They never got along from the start—since his investigation of Alec's crime scene. She didn't like the pompous ass then, and she doesn't like him now. Or does she? Is there some subconscious feeling for him? *Oh, God, no. Not a detective.*

The electronic doors open and a number of travelers push their way in past her. She steps aside as she makes her way to the curb. It is nearly December, winter is approaching. The wind is beginning to have an edge. Looks like rain.

Nick pulls up in an unmarked black Chevy sedan. She opens the back door, throws in her luggage, and hops in the passenger's seat. "Where's your Firebird?"

"It's in the shop." He doesn't smile. "Do you always wear high heels when traveling?"

"I like them," she says in a voice that suggests it is none of your damn business. *Maybe he doesn't like her jeans and turtleneck either. Tough!*

He drives off, moving into a stream of cars, and takes the ramp on I-

85 N. Nothing is said between them for a few minutes. He's the first to speak. "You look rested."

"Yes, I am. But now it's time for me to get back to work. Do you think I can get my computer back?"

In a monotone, he says, "Gerber had someone put it back in your office. I didn't understand any of that gobbledygook."

"Complicated, huh?" she says, patronizingly. She knew he couldn't decipher her stuff, but he had insisted her notes were part of the investigation.

Nick doesn't respond. He keeps his eyes on the road, and heads for Freedom Parkway.

"Someone's been smoking in here?" she says, not knowing what else to say to break the ice.

"Uh-huh. A. Jaye used it for a few hours. He smokes cigars."

"You don't smoke?" Why in the heck did she ask such a stupid question? Who cares if he smokes? If he wants to kill himself, let him.

"I drink scotch."

She glances at the line of lights in the traffic backed up in the southbound lane, and wonders what drinking scotch has to do with smoking. Maybe he thinks they go together, and if you don't do one, you must do the other.

"I guess if you don't do one, you more than likely must do the other?"

"I've been told you are very bright. Now I can see it's true."

Is he patronizing me? Well, yeah. Didn't I just put him down?

She thinks it's time to stop the verbal fighting. "I am glad you called," she says.

"You are?" he says with raised brows. "I got the impression that you don't think too highly of me."

He looks at her. Now he's smiling as if he is expecting her to say she missed him. *Oh, don't get your hopes up.*

"I just think it was very nice of you to offer to pick me up. Anyway, I was about to call you to check on whether you were getting any closer to finding Alec's killer."

He reaches down and flips on the headlights. "Your tech, Tony Seymour, has been cleared."

From his facial expression, Susan knows she isn't going to like what he's about to say next.

"Ms. McCulley, however, remains a person of interest in the murder of Dr. Sutherland."

"Robin? Why?"

"Failed the polygraph twice."

Susan grits her teeth. "You're mistaken about her. Robin sleeps around, but she wouldn't kill anyone."

"So you're a detective now? Your tech had means and opportunity."

"I may not be a detective, but how hard is it to figure out that everyone in the lab had means and opportunity."

"The difference is motive." He says.

Several horns blast in the southbound lane, and tires squeal.

"You must be thinking she stole the virus, too," Susan says. "And why would she?"

"Do you realize what people would pay for a cancer cure?"

She doesn't answer.

"They'd go so far as mortgage their homes," he says. "She could make millions. Poor Dr. Sutherland was just in the wrong place at the wrong time."

Nick has zeroed in on Robin from the start, Susan thinks, and he probably hasn't searched for anyone else.

He pulls round a white van and speeds away. "On the night of the murder, Ms. McCulley left the lab around nine, and went to the administration building."

"How do you know that?"

"The security guard, Phil Corben, saw her, and when he went off duty around midnight, he saw her again heading back to your building."

Susan is holding her breath. That means Robin had been with Karl Gerber. She wonders if she should tell Nick. "What does that prove?" she says. "Robin was probably going home when Corben saw her. She'd have to pass our building to get to her car."

"Mr. Corben didn't see her leave the Center. She must have gone into your building."

Nick turned off Freedom Parkway onto Ponce de Leon Avenue.

"What was she doing in the administration building at that hour?" he says.

Thinking it would convince Nick that Robin was only sleeping around, she tells him about Robin's involvement with Gerber.

"How come you didn't tell me that the day of the murder?"

"You didn't ask."

"No secret lies dead forever," he mutters.

Is he accusing me of something?

"Gerber could be her accomplice," he says.

"Gerber and Alec didn't get along, but Karl would never be party to a murder."

"You said that about Ms. McCulley."

"Turn left at the next corner," she says, "my apartment is two blocks down on the right."

They are within a block of her apartment when she spots something. The streetlights leave plenty of shadows. She stares hard into the partial darkness. The silhouettes of two large men are in the front seat of a car. "Ohmigod, there's that Mercedes with the two thugs! They must be watching my apartment."

Nick turns off his headlights, lets up on the accelerator, coasts the car along the curb, and eases up behind them. While the car is rolling, Susan opens her door and shoots out of the car like a bird escaping from its cage.

"What the hell are you doing? Get back in here!" he shouts.

Her heels click on the sidewalk as she runs, catching up to the passenger side, grabs the car handle and pulls the door open. The Mercedes' headlights blink on. Its wheels peel rubber as it takes off like a rocket. Susan is dragged, losing her shoes, stockings ripped off her, until the passenger's fist shoots out and whacks her in the face. Cars screech to a halt to avoid colliding with the Mercedes. She flies backwards, tumbling onto a strip of grass by the curb. The last thing she remembers is a flashing red light on top of Nick's car.

When Susan opens her eyes, Nick is looking down at her. She struggles to rise up.

"Stay down," he says. "The paramedics are on their way."

She touches her cheek. "The bone is broken. Just help me up." She pushes hard against his hands. "I said, let me up. It's cold."

He lays a hand on her.

She looks around. "Are they gone?"

"Yeah, they took out of here like a bat out of hell."

"Why didn't you go after them?" she asks.

"You were hurt," he says.

"But I saw your light flashing before I blacked out."

"I slapped it on the roof when I thought they were going to pull you into the car."

A crowd has gathered by the curb. Someone mentions her name. Must be one of her neighbors.

"The paramedics are here," Nick says.

A man and woman jump out of the ambulance, remove a cot with equipment on it from the back of the truck and rush over.

Susan's hands goes up. "I'm okay. Just help me to my feet and get me up to my apartment."

"Lay still, ma'am," the EMT says. "We need to do a primary."

The paramedic says, "ABC is okay." They examined her from head to toe.

"What hurts?" the EMT partner asks.

"Just my cheekbone."

They ask her a bunch of questions.

"I'm a doctor," she says, "and I'm lucid. Stop treating me like a child."

"Doctor, you have a bad bruise on your cheekbone, could be broken, your knees and hands are all skinned up. We need to get you off this cold ground and onto a C-spine and transport you to the hospital."

Susan scowls at her. "I said no. Get me up."

They take her by the arms. "Ouch! My shoulder," she cried. "Okay, let me sit a few minutes."

"Doctor, you'll probably need that shoulder X-rayed."

"If I feel like I do in the morning, I will."

They gather up their equipment and move away. She hears the ambulance doors slam shut and the roar of their engine as they take off.

Nick eases her up.

She watches as a police cruiser with flashing lights and siren blasting careens to a halt beside Nick's car. Out jumps A. Jaye. "Whatta we have, Nick?" When Susan turns around he cringes. "Man, it's Dr. Prescott. She okay?"

"She's banged up a little," Nick says. "Get her purse from my car and shut off the light."

When A. Jaye returns, Susan opens her purse and removes her keys. Nick picks her up in his arms and carries her toward her apartment building. His partner follows.

"What the hell do you think you're doing? Put me down!"

"Carrying a heavy sack of stupidity."

"Stupidity? Who let those guys get away? And who's heavy?"

Nick doesn't respond. Inside, he carries her into the living room, deposits her on the sofa, and goes to A. Jaye. He says something to him, and A. Jaye takes off.

"I can take care of myself," Susan says when Nick returns. She eases up, heads into the kitchen barefooted and opens the fridge. "I need some wine." She reaches into the cabinet for a glass.

"Is that a good idea?" he says.

"I'm the doctor. I guess you're off duty. Care for some?"

Susan jumps as a flash of light shoots through the apartment and rain slams against the windows. The glass falls from her hand. "Wow! A storm's moving in," she says, bending down to pick it up. "If you like, you can have some wine and wait it out."

"I prefer scotch," he says. "But that'll do."

"Good, because I don't have any scotch," she says, filling two glasses with Pinot Gris.

Nick is sitting in a chair next to the sofa. She hands him his drink and takes a seat near him. They swirl their glasses, sniff the liquid, and stare at each other. She wonders if he's going to spill his drink on her white furniture.

"You don't talk much, do you?" she says. "Except when you're interrogating someone."

"Only when necessary."

"What does that mean?"

He shrugs. "When I have something to say."

She drinks her wine and remembers with a shudder what had happened outside. She realizes that the man in the Mercedes could have grabbed her and pulled her in. Nick's strobe light must have scared them off.

A flash of lightning brightens the room.

"I guess I should thank you," she says.

"For what?"

"If you hadn't turned on your red light, I might have been killed."

"That's true." He sets his glass on the end table and looks at his watch. "It's nearly ten. I guess I should let you get some rest. Your jaw looks swollen. Better put some ice on it."

"Do you think they were going to shoot me?"

"Probably, but as you say, the strobe light may have scared them off."

"That means I could still be in danger."

"Probably."

"Is that all you know, 'probably.'"

"I'm not a psychic. If you like I could put someone on you, but it would only be for twenty-four hours."

"Forget it." I can't let them control my life, nor the police."

"A. Jaye's working the plate, but you can bet it's stolen."

She takes a drink and sets the glass on the table. "Have one more," she says. "It's still raining cats and dogs out there." She stands and goes into the kitchen. When she returns, he is standing by the piano looking at her family pictures.

He reaches for his drink. "Good-looking family. I see you have a twin, and a brother," he says, as they move to their seats. "Do they live in Mystic?"

"Only my brother, Michael."

"What does he do?"

"Not much of anything. Can't keep a job and can't stay away from the bottle."

"I see. We had a cop who hit the sauce more than he should have, and the counselor at our precinct got him into an inpatient alcohol treatment center."

"I don't think—"

He interrupts her. "The guy was in there for a couple of months and then as an outpatient he attended AA and got a sponsor. That really helped him. I've heard that there are a lot of good treatment centers here in Atlanta."

"We'll see," she says.

"Your mother is very beautiful. I notice you have a larger picture of her in front of the family picture."

"Mom was special."

"Was?"

She wonders if Nick is really interested, or is he merely attempting to get into her head. "My mother and sister are both dead."

"Sorry. That must have been tough." He steps back and takes a drink.

"Mother died when we were twelve and Sabrina died twelve years later. Now there's only dad in the home. Michael has moved out."

Nick stares at her as he drinks from his glass, but doesn't say a word. She wonders what he is thinking.

"You seem burdened by it all," he says, setting his glass down.

She shrugs. "Nothing I can't handle." She certainly isn't going to tell him anything more. She had said enough already.

"What does your father do?"

"He has a very successful law practice in New Haven."

"Like father, like daughter."

"Meaning what?"

He shrugs. "Type A personalities: successful, strong-willed, independent."

"Never thought of it like that, but you're right. I *am* like my father."

The thunderstorm has abated.

"I'm not very good at this," she says, "but here goes. I'm sorry about tonight. I wasn't thinking clearly when I took off after that Mercedes."

"Is that an apology or is that the wine talking?" he says.

"Why do you question everything I say? Don't you think I'm being truthful?"

"Goes with the job."

"Too bad!" she says. "You should trust people more."

"I did once."

"Should we stop playing games, Detective Hunter?"

"What happened to calling me Nick?"

"Ever since you came to my lab, we've been at each other, and it's time we buried the hatchet, as they say, and start over."

"Sounds good to me."

She holds up her glass. "Truce."

"Truce," he says.

Two bottles of wine later Nick is sitting next to her on the sofa. She looks at the clock on the piano, and says, "It's nearly five-thirty. We've talked most of the night away."

Nick gets up. "The rain has stopped, and it's time I go."

She stands and stares at his glassy eyes. "But first you'll need some coffee. I'll make some. Then you should go."

CHAPTER TWENTY-THREE

The December wind blows hard in D.C. The Russian Embassy has helped Belofsky locate the members of the Foreign Relations Committee, and now he's tailing his last victim.

An hour ago, he had followed the SFRC Chairman, Barry Plummer, and his girlfriend to The Crazy Horse Saloon, a replica of the Parisian Club. Known for its erotic dancers and loud music, it is a hangout for members of Congress and their staff.

Away from the street lights, Belofsky sits in his Buick Century, glances at his watch: eight o'clock. The senator should be coming out soon. Belofsky opens the door, steps out, and slams it. The snow has stopped. He makes his way across the street and waits behind the senator's black Lexus. The crowded sidewalk makes it impossible for him to dart Plummer now. Belofsky gets the urge to abduct the spry redhead coming toward him, but he has his orders, so he squats, removes the ice pick from his pocket, pushes the button on the handle. A six-inch, pointed metal shaft shoots out. He stabs it deep into the senator's tire, a technique he used in Russia to corner club owners who refused to pay the Bear protection. Once out of their cars, he would ram the pick up one of their nostrils and swivel it to sever their brain arteries.

Two pushes on the button and the pick zooms back into the handle. He slips it into his pocket and moves away.

In his Buick, Belofsky watches.

Around nine o'clock, the senator and his date come out, slip into the Lexus and drive off on Georgia Ave. Belofsky is behind them. The Lexus turns on K Street and travels to North Arlington Rd. A few miles later, tail lights flicker in the distance, and the Lexus pulls over, its emergency lights flashing. Belofsky stops two car-lengths behind it, leaving on his headlights. He assembles the blowgun and sets it on the seat, jumps out, and ambles over to Plummer, who is gawking at the flat with his hands on his hips.

Belofsky asks if he can help, but Plummer has already called someone. Belofsky strolls back to his car, reaches in for the canister, opens it and removes a minidart. He slips it into the blowgun. In the shadows, he brings the blow gun to his lips, inhales deeply, takes aim, and blows with such force that the dart shoots out like a bullet. He knows he has hit his mark when Plummer slaps his neck.

Belofsky drives out on the road and after a couple of miles stops on the shoulder and waits. Forty minutes later, the Lexus passes. Belofsky pulls out, staying fifty yards behind them. He follows them through the streets of Arlington. The senator wheels into the driveway of a two-story white frame house, setting back twenty yards from the road. Belofsky has learned that Plummer brings his women to this Arlington hideout.

Belofsky turns off his headlights and watches. The street light provides enough illumination for him to see the driveway. Plummer and the beautiful blonde get out. She slips her arm into his and they amble up the private road along tall bushes standing like sentries, which make it difficult for Belofsky to see the front of the house. The lovers disappear behind the evergreens.

Belofsky starts his car. He will be back when the senator gets sick.

CHAPTER TWENTY-FOUR

In the library, next to the fireplace, Gerber is reading Dante's *Inferno* in a high-back leather chair, *The Loving Chair*. Eva gave it that name after they had sex in it. He reads there often, but trusts that at any moment she will burst into the room, sashaying around in her sheer negligee, giving him that leer of invitation, and then makes her move, dropping to her knees and working her way up his body. *It will be like old times.*

The fire sizzles in the hearth and he slams the book shut. He's read the same page four times. The improvement in Eva's health has been demonstrable. Tican is working. That's good, isn't it? So why isn't he happy? Is this a conscience thing?

Purchasing the drug was illegal, but who would know outside of Belofsky and that wench Robin McCulley. She's involved, too. Eva's illness has taught him that his love for her is much stronger than he had imagined. He can't let her die; he'll do anything for her. He sighs. But even so, the guilt keeps piling on. The euphoria he felt while waiting on her was refreshing because he felt needed for once. Also, he loved it that he was in control. Now that she's better, she'll forget all about him.

The door flings open. The grand dame of entertainment whirls barefoot across the room dressed in a sheer silk gown, puffing out at the bottom, bare underneath. Her dark brown hair is up off the neck, displaying the finest of diamonds. Her rejuvenated face and spectacular jewels reflect the flickering light from the fireplace, as she circles her husband twice, flailing her arms in synchronization with an imaginary symphony. Suddenly, she flops on his lap, laying her head in his shoulder, feigning shame.

The drama exhilarates him. She's her old self again. Her warm body excites him. It's been ages since he had her. He lifts her chin and looks into her sparkling eyes. "You're so beautiful," he says, running his fingers along her bare shoulder. "I need you."

She smiles and whispers in his ear, "I wanted to die, but you cared, and you saved me. Thank you."

"That's biblical love, my sweet."

———— ✦ ————

Week Two—Eva continues to make marked improvement. The guests arrive in tuxedos and evening gowns. The music from the orchestra is soft and pleasant. Gerber crosses the room and asks the bartender for a glass of Merlot. He takes a couple of sips and raises his glass at Lance Sterling and his wife, who are caught up in the spiraling throng of dancers. They wave back.

Lance and his wife are good people. These others are phonies.

Eva, in all her splendor—her eyes sparkling as much as her jewelry—flutters through the room like a butterfly. With a drink in one hand, she hugs some guests and pats others on their shoulders. Gerber thinks of Shakespeare words: *The appurtenances of welcome are fashion and ceremony.*

Gerber spots Harry Wentworth coming into the ballroom, who stops long enough to peck Eva's cheek. Her brother wasn't the hugging type. Unfortunately, she had to invite the bastard. Gerber hurries away, but only makes it as far as the library door before Harry accosts him.

"Karl. I'm happy about Eva. She looks great. Two weeks ago, she was on her deathbed."

"As if you cared."

"Now, Karl. Let's not go there." Harry leans in closer, and says in a whisper, "What did you give her?"

Gerber remains silent.

"I asked you a question."

Gerber takes a sip from his drink.

Go to hell.

"I'm talking to you."

"It's a miracle."

"Bullshit. Nothing was working. You must have found something."

"Lower your voice."

Harry grabs Gerber's lapels. His eyes are blazing. "I don't give a shit. Answer me."

Eva hurries over. "What's going on? You both are acting like children. The guests are looking."

Harry releases Gerber.

Gerber stands his ground. Eva lays a hand on his shoulder. "Honey, come, let's dance."

"Not now, sweet. Later."

She turns to her brother. "Harry, you're becoming a nuisance. Don't make me ask you to leave."

"We just had a little disagreement, sis. That's all."

"Well, go into the library and finish your talk. Keep your voices down."

She whispers in her husband's ear: "Don't let him get the best of you, darling."

Gerber is amazed at the change in his wife. Before Tican, she'd never have taken his side.

"I'll expect that dance when you're finished," she says.

Gerber nods and heads into the library, elated that Eva cares.

"Come on, Karl. You can tell me," Harry says, as the door slams shut. "Whatever it is, we can make a fortune with it."

"It's all about money, isn't it?"

Silence fell over the room while Harry appears to be in deep thought.

"Why didn't I think of this before?" he says. "Yeah, yeah. That's it. Someone is murdered in one of your labs and Tican is stolen. You had to be part of it."

"Don't be ridiculous," Gerber says, moving to the large leather chair.

Harry paces across the room, stops, and points a finger at him, as Gerber sits. "You, yes, you," he says, moving closer to Gerber. "You wanted Tican to cure your Eva. You certainly had means and opportunity. You're the boss over that division." He pauses. "Yeah, that's it. You gave Eva Tican."

"You're crazy. You don't know what the hell you're talking about. Next thing you'll say is that I killed Dr. Sutherland."

"I don't give a shit about him; just get me a vial. We can reproduce it. You know damn well I almost own Tican. I gave that Russian bastard a million for it." Harry paces across the room. "You know your director is one of Eva's dearest friends. Don't make me call him." Harry's face turns fire red. "I must have a sample!"

Gerber doesn't respond.

"When law enforcement tracks down the killers, they'll spill their guts and when they do, they'll confess that you're involved. With my testimony, you'll lose your medical license, the director will fire your ass, and you'll spend years in prison."

"Harry, you got it all wrong—"

"Don't tell me. I don't want to know anything about anything. Just do it!"

———— ◆ ————

The next morning, a passing car flings wet snow on the windshield of Gerber's silver Infinity as he drives around town struggling to clear his mind. Harry Wentworth has turned into a madman, won't listen to reason, and could implicate Gerber if he goes to the police or the CDC Director. Would Harry really do that? Gerber can't take a chance. His pulse races when he thinks about getting involved with the Russian for the third time.

Gerber spots a pay phone outside a Quick Stop and pulls into the parking spot. The lot is covered with wet snow. He scrambles out and waits behind a young man who's on the phone arguing with his *Pumpkin*. The guy slams the receiver on its hook, rushes away, slipping in the slush on his way to a beat-up Ford, and fishtails out of the parking lot.

Gerber lifts the receiver and calls Leopold's, assuming that Belofsky's back in town, not caring whether he is or not.

"Need to talk with Morelli," he says in a rough tone.

"This is Morelli."

Gerber moves in closer to the phone. "This is Gerber. I need another sample."

"What are you doing with the stuff, drinking it?"

"None of your fuckin' business, that's between me and Belofsky."

"Man, I don't know," Morelli says.

"Don't give me that crap. I know you can get it."

Morelli doesn't respond.

"Well, what about it?"

"I'll tell him."

Morelli hangs up on him.

A car pulls up next to Gerber. Teens pop open the doors, jump out, music blaring as they hurry inside. Gerber gets behind the wheel of his car and heads home. Maybe Belofsky won't have another sample, but Gerber figures he does.

The next morning around eleven, Belofsky calls him. Gerber is surprised when Belofsky asks him why he wants it. Never before has he done that. Gerber tells Belofsky that his brother-in-law at Kraft Pharmaceutical actually owns Tican, has an agreement with Sokolov, and wants a sample as agreed. Belofsky asks for two million.

"What?! You must be crazy. Didn't you hear what I just said? Kraft has a contract with Sokolov. You can check with him."

Check with him? Whoa. Did that come from me? Gerber has now connected Sokolov to Belofsky. They have to be in this together.

"Not much money to kill cancer in America," Belofsky says.

"Why don't you check with Sokolov and come up with a price."

"I'm boss. Two million."

"And how do we know you won't screw us," Gerber says, not

really caring and wondering why he even asks.

"You don't."

"How about one million now and another after we test it?"

"No!"

"Okay." Gerber says. He knew Harry would pay it after seeing Eva. "Leopold's?"

"Yah, two o'clock."

Click.

The next day, Gerber picks up the money from Kraft and makes the exchange at Leopold's. Thirty minutes later he returns, pulling into Kraft's parking garage, chooses a spot near the entrance and turns off the engine. He reaches for the package, but hesitates before opening the door. His brother-in-law has made arrangements with Lance Sterling to treat his patients with Tican, but not performing additional testing on Tican before using it is criminal. A jury would probably be sympathetic towards Gerber for injecting his dying wife, but not if Tican kills patients at Sterling's Clinic.

Shit. How in the world did he get himself into this mess? He sighs and pops open the door and goes into the building.

"We're going to be rich," Harry says, standing by his desk, holding the cylinder. "Let's get this to the micro lab."

Gerber follows him to the elevator. They ride down to the second floor, step out and stroll into a well-lit lab with benches, droning instruments, and people in white lab coats. Gerber recognizes the smell of culture media used in Petri dishes and test tube slants.

Harry hands the container to the researcher. "Here's what we've been waiting for."

"We'll get on it right away, sir."

As they leave, Harry says, "Lance's waiting for the samples."

Dr. Lance Sterling, the renowned oncologist, has agreed to test Tican on his terminally-ill cancer patients.

"We're banking on Tican doing its job so we can influence the FDA to approve it for fast-track production. We'll make millions, maybe billions."

"Are you sure about moving Tican into human testing this soon, Harry?"

"Never been more certain in my life."

"It could kill them," Gerber says.

They stop by the coffee stand. Harry pours two cups and hands one to Gerber.

"Tican cured Eva," he says.

"Too many things could go wrong," Gerber says. "We're moving too fast."

"I know what you're getting at, Karl, and I'm not going there. All that animal testing is too costly." He takes a drink of coffee. "What's the big deal? Lance's patients are going to die anyway. Think of it this way: Tican might cure them like it did Eva."

"Be reasonable," Gerber says.

They proceed to the elevator. Harry presses the down button. "Were you reasonable when you injected Eva? You just want more testing to ease your conscience."

Gerber throws his Styrofoam cup into the trash receptacle. "I did it because I love her. She would have been dead in 24 hours. I'm asking you not to go forward with this just yet. That's all."

Harry is in his face. "You just made my case. Lance's patients are dying too. You're gutless. Always were and always will be. That's why you never had a practice like Lance. I don't see how Eva stood you all these years."

"You've never cared one bit about Eva. You're no better than your father." Gerber inhales. "All you cared about was using her to get those rich bastards to invest in your company."

Harry's face turns beet red. "Don't bring my father into this."

Gerber's in his face. "Like father, like son. The old bastard hated Eva and loved only you and himself and his money, and you're just like him."

The elevator door opens, and Harry pushes him in. "Fuck you!"

"You're an immoral son-of-a-bitch," Gerber says.

"Look who's talking. Anyway, it's out of your fuckin' hands."

As the doors closed, Gerber shouts "Rot in hell!"

CHAPTER TWENTY-FIVE

The sun gleams off the hood of the red Ferrari as Harry Wentworth waits for the light to change at the edge of Buckhead District—known as the Beverly Hills of the South. He shoots through the intersection and drives past Lenox Square, a shopping mall with over 350 shops, then wheels into the lot of the Sterling Cancer Clinic, a single-story brick building that covers half a block. He gets out carrying a package and a folder.

Tican's going to make me a billionaire.

The glass doors hiss as they open. Harry hurries into a spacious red-carpeted lobby filled with expensive furnishings and gold-framed pictures. Lance Sterling is in them surrounded by bald, smiling children holding stuffed toys, and others with adults gathered around him. They are smiling.

Apparently the survivors, Harry thinks.

Sterling is famous for the exceptional survival rate of his cancer patients. Harry crosses to the reception booth, furnishes his name to the attractive blonde and tells her that Dr. Sterling is expecting him.

She smiles and lifts the phone.

Seconds later, a tall, physically fit man with sandy colored hair, a nice tan, and a Bel Air smile walks toward him.

"Let's go to my office, Harry," Lance says.

They move into a hub from which six corridors extend out through the buildings like tentacles. Seated behind the circular counter is a man dressed in white. A nurse is in front of the counter thumbing through a loose-leaf notebook. Sterling leads the way past them to the administration corridor and into his office.

"Have a seat," Sterling says, gesturing, and goes to his chair behind the desk.

"Here are the data," Harry says, handing him the folder, and he sets the box on the desk.

Sterling skims through the folder. His brows rise.

Harry gets up and glances out the window. The sun is bright. Nurses are pushing patients in wheelchairs, and some seniors are sitting on the benches in their overcoats

Sterling reaches for the package. "These are the samples?" he asks.

Harry nods. Thank you, Eva.

Lance opens the box and lifts out a cylinder, opens its top and lifts out one of the vials.

Harry's pulse races as he thinks about the money he's going to make.

"I'm amazed at how good Eva looks," Lance says.

"We can expect the same results in your patients," Harry says, returning to his seat.

Lance places the vial back into its container with the others. "Harry, I don't know what's going on. I called Karl several times, but he won't return my calls. We were going to discuss the protocol."

Harry felt his neck pulsate as he leans forward. "Anything related to Tican, you will now discuss with me. Karl is no longer involved in this project."

"Does it have anything to do with the argument you guys had at Eva's party?"

"It had nothing to do with this project."

Lance looks away. "The Kraft virus will be tested in four of my terminals: one with colon cancer, another with liver cancer, a third with lung cancer and the fourth with metastatic breast cancer." His face tenses. "They haven't responded to any of my protocols, and there's nothing more I can do for the poor souls."

Harry straightens in his chair. "Not to worry. Tican's the greatest discovery since the polio vaccine."

"I'm counting on it," Lance says. He leans in to the desk. "My fee will be one mil."

What a bargain.

Lance rises and Harry follows him to the door. "Now I need to attend to my patients."

They move out into the hall and past the nurses' station and into the reception area.

"Your fee is acceptable. How soon can you start?"

"Tomorrow."

"You'll have your money tomorrow afternoon."

CHAPTER TWENTY-SIX

Robin's cough keeps her up most the night, and at four a.m. she rolls out of bed burning with a high fever. Two hours later she's retches up blood in a towel sitting at the kitchen table. She struggles to the sink, fills a glass with water. Blood drips on her hand, she staggers back to her chair, feeling faint. "Where in the hell is Dmitry?" she moans, holding her head back. "I called him two goddamn hours ago." Blood saturates the towel.

I feel like shit. Why did Dmitry go to Washington, anyway? The bastard better not screw me out of my money.

She lurches to the phone, coughs hard. Blood spatters the counter. She falls to the floor.

———◆———

At four in the morning, Belofsky is two hours outside of Atlanta when he gets a call from Robin. She tells him she's sick as hell, and he must hurry. She threatened him earlier with going to the police if he doesn't bring the money, too. He has driven all night and is too tired to listen to her shit. The bitch should be dead by the time he gets there. If not, he'll have to kill her.

Arriving at the Atlanta city limits, Belofsky pulls into a gas station, fills the Buick, and goes into the store for a cup of coffee. Inside, a customer is at the counter paying for coffee and donuts. A middle-aged brunette behind the counter watches Belofsky. He feels her eyes tracking him. He fills a cup, walks around to loosen his leg muscles, sipping coffee, and ends up close to a storeroom in the back.

"Where you goin'?" the woman says. "That's private."

At the candy section he selects a chocolate bar and sets it and the coffee on the counter.

"Anything else?" she asks sarcastically.

He throws the money at her and slips a hand into his pocket as he locks on her gaze.

"What's your problem?" she says. "You one of them skinheads? I don't want no trouble."

It's still dark, and the last customer is gone. No one is at the pumps. Belofsky jumps over the counter and punches the woman in the face, knocking her out on the floor. He drags her into the back room.

Outside, a car pulls up. Belofsky makes sure the driver doesn't see his face as he slips into his car and takes off down the road.

Ninety minutes later, Belofsky breaks into Robin's apartment. She's face down on the kitchen floor in a puddle of blood. He kicks her over. Both eyes roll out of their sockets and spin across the floor like a pair of dice. He knows the signs—Tican's mutant. He isn't concerned about becoming infected—the virus isn't contagious—unless he punctures himself. He has the antiserum.

Belofsky cleans the mess in the kitchen, but can't remove all of the stains. In the living room, he yanks the area rug from under the coffee table, rolls her body up in it, and ties it with a cord taken from the drapes.

At the landfill, outside the city limits, he backs the Buick up to the crater, gets out and looks around before yanking the body out of the trunk. He releases the human enchilada at the edge, laughs as it rolls down the steep slope at super speed, slamming into a pile of garbage.

CHAPTER TWENTY-SEVEN

Susan strolls into the Level-3 feeling a little uneasy as she shoots a furtive glance at the spot where she found Alec's body. Her heart is beginning to race. *Alec, I'm sorry. I really miss you.*

Tony is wiping out a biosafety cabinet. "I see you got my message about cleaning the cabinets," she says.

"Sure did." His brows meet each other in a straight line. "How are you doing, Dr. Prescott?"

"Better, thank you."

"Good."

"I've got work to do in Four so I'll be out for a while," she says.

He nods and turns back to his cleaning.

In the locker room, she sits on the bench and glances at Alec's Blue Suit that hangs on the rack next to hers. She twists the friendship ring he had given her around her finger, a surge of melancholy overtaking her. Too many reminders of him are at the apartment. She has to dispose of his things or she'll never get past him.

She showers, dresses in fresh scrubs, and takes her suit off the rack. She steps into it, pulls the helmet over her head, and advances to the chemical shower. In the Hot Zone she plugs an air hose into her suit and shuffles along the narrow hall. On the right down a connecting hall, the caretaker is in the animal room cleaning cages. He waves. The lab across the way is occupied with two of her team members busy at the instruments. She navigates through the narrow space like being in a submarine, and enters the lab where she and Alec had worked. She plugs into another hose.

Her pulse quickens when she sees Alec's notebook in a niche near the stainless steel compartment where Petri dishes are stored. She takes the journal to the desk. *Times have changed,* she thought. Researchers now enter experiments into computers, but not Alec. He liked to add diagrams and remarks in the margins of the notebook. This he couldn't do in a computer. That slowed him down, but he eventually got the data transferred.

She rubs her gloved hand over his notebook, not being in a hurry to open it. Her heart wrenches and tears form in her eyes. The room swirls and she becomes disoriented. Alec's presence is strong, and his silhouette rises before her in a haze. She must be hallucinating. Susan reaches out to the figure. *Alec?*

"Are you all right, Dr. Prescott?" The words crackle in her helmet.

Her mind clears. She looks up with crushing disappointment. It is one of her team members. "I'm fine, Jim," she says.

"I didn't want to bother you, but Tony called. Says it's urgent."

"I'll handle it. Thank you."

He leaves, and she goes to the phone.

"What's so pressing?" she asks.

"Mr. O'Leary called, looking for Robin," Tony says.

Susan didn't know anyone by that name. "O'Leary?"

"Yeah. He owns the Irish Pub where she hangs out."

"How'd he know where to call?" she says.

"He knew she worked here. Must have called the Center's switchboard. Said he called her apartment several times, but couldn't reach her."

"What did he want?"

"He said the Russian skinhead Robin is dating bragged about getting rid of some redhead. O'Leary's afraid it's Robin."

"Ohmigod. Did he call the police?"

"No. He wanted to make sure she's missing first. I told him I'd call you."

What has Robin gotten herself into?

"I'm coming out," Susan says.

She goes to the containment door after carrying Alec's notebook to the box. She'll remove it once outside. When she arrives in Level-3, Tony mentions that he has called Robin's place several times, too. No answer.

"I'm going over there." She rushes out, stopping off at her office, sets Alec's notebook on the desk and reaches for the phone. Robin doesn't answer. The last time they talked, Robin had a high fever and sounded pretty bad. Maybe she's in a coma, or dead.

Thirty minutes later she's at Robin's door ringing the bell. Placing her ear against the door, she raps and calls out Robin's name. No sounds come from inside. She charges down the stairs to unit 101 and knocks. The door opens, and a woman in her thirties with dark hair smiles at her.

"I'm a friend of Robin McCulley, who lives in apartment 201. I can't seem to raise her or anyone else on her floor. Have you seen her today?"

The Hispanic woman's accent is thick. She says she and Robin had gone to the store two days ago, but Robin wasn't feeling well and they came home early. The neighbor hasn't seen her since. "Go to manager," the woman says, pointing toward the parking lot.

Susan finds the office in the center of the complex. The manager is behind the counter reading a Janet Evanovich novel. Susan introduces herself and explains that Robin McCulley in 201 has been sick for a couple of days with a high fever and chills, and now she doesn't answer her phone or the door. Susan asks if they could go into the apartment in case Robin needed the paramedics.

The manager drops the novel on the counter, lifts the master key from the wallboard and they rush out. When she opens Robin's door, an offensive odor attacks their nostrils. Susan rushes into the bedroom. Robin isn't in here.

The manager is in the kitchen staring at the floor. "Here's where the smell's coming from," she says.

Susan kneels and stares at a dark stain, which extends to the counter. "Does that look like blood to you?"

"Can't tell," the manager says.

"I don't like this," Susan says. She goes to the phone. "I'm calling the police."

"If you need me, I'll be in my office," the manager says.

---·✦·---

Nick and A. Jaye arrive twenty minutes later. The second Nick walks through the door Susan feels a quiver down her spine. Why hadn't she noticed before? He's so handsome. Tall and strong, rough exterior, dark hair and eyes. As he passes her, she smells the clean musky scent of his maleness mixed with a faint odor of soap. Her instincts turn primitive, and she is furious with herself for the way her body is responding. She wants him, but the urge makes mockery of her intellect and self-control. *Dammit. I can't let my guard down.*

A. Jaye makes his walk through wearing gloves, and goes into the living room. While casing the place, Nick says, "Did you touch anything?"

"I know better," Susan says. "But you may want to check that spot on the kitchen floor."

He snaps on gloves over strong hands, and kneels on the floor.

"Did you notice the odd smell when you came in?" she asks.

"Yeah, and this is definitely where it's coming from."

"Aren't you going to scoop up something and put it in a vial or bag?"

119

she says in a commanding tone. His scowl is understood. If only she could take it back. *Big mouth.*

"You've been watching too much TV," he says. "We detectives look for bodies, witnesses, weapons, shell casings, means, opportunity, motives and sometimes we even take notes. The rest we leave to the Crime Scene Processing people."

He's putting her in her place, and she's about to say touché, but decides to let it drop.

"They'll tear this place apart and remove some of it for you."

He steps over the stain, advances to the counter, pulls open the cabinet doors and reaches for a prescription vial. "*Paxil.* Robin must be depressed." He reaches for another bottle. "Only aspirin." He checks under the sink, and takes out a damp rag that is on top of a Clorox bottle. "Whew! This is definitely Clorox." He pauses, looking at Susan. "Robin used this for a reason. I mean there might be a connection, besides using it to clean house."

"Clorox contains sodium hypochlorite solution. We use it in the lab to kill germs," she says to be helpful and in an attempt to mend the broken fence between them.

Two officers arrive, whisper something to Nick, and stand out by the door.

A. Jaye drifts out of the bedroom, holding up an evidence bag. "Got a few red and brown hairs off the bed," he says. He glances at the open door. "I better make sure the uniforms are interviewing the neighbors."

Two individuals wearing jackets with CSU on their backs come in. "Whatta we have, detective?" one of them asks.

"No body, no weapon. Need you guys to tear this place apart and we'll need help from DNA," he says. "Detective Chandler has found some hairs on the bed that could be from two different people. And over in the kitchen, there's blood on the floor."

The investigator nods, and his partner begins snapping pictures.

A. Jaye appears. "Neighbors didn't see anything." He shakes his head. "No one wants to get involved these days. Afraid some shyster lawyer will take everything they've got."

Nick is right about the forensics people, Susan thinks. They moved through the apartment with resolve and thoroughness.

"Over here," A. Jaye says. "Looks like someone removed a rug. You can see the outline."

Susan and Nick move into the living room. "Is that important?" she asks.

"Could have been used to wrap a body," Nick says.

Susan's hand shoots to her mouth. "Robin murdered? Don't tell me we now have two murders."

"Don't jump to any conclusions just yet," Nick says. He picks up a picture from the table behind the sofa and shows it to Susan. "The redhead's with some older woman. You recognize them?"

"The redhead is Robin and that lady could be her mother."

A. Jaye is at the computer on the desk in the corner, looking through the drawers. He unplugs the wires and ties them around the computer. "We'll see what she's been up to."

Nick removes the photograph from its frame and slips it into his pocket. "This may be a tough one to solve, with no body, no weapon, and no witnesses."

Susan climbs out of the Explorer around seven thirty, slams the car door shut with her foot, and lugs two bags of groceries to the entrance of her first floor apartment. This hadn't been a good day. Robin's disappearance has her on edge. Every muscle in her body aches. She is looking forward to a bubble bath, glass of wine, and listening to Henry Mancini entertain her. She steps into the hall and heads to the back. Suddenly, she stops, grabbing the bags as they slip down to her knees. Her gut tightens and her blood pressure must be at 300. Michael lies asleep in front of her door, reeking of alcohol, wearing grubby jeans and jacket.

CHAPTER TWENTY-EIGHT

It didn't take much to get into Robin McCulley's computer. A. Jaye discovers that she had a couple of messages from a girlfriend back home. In her old mail folder, she hadn't trashed her list in months. He scrolls through the messages, opens the earliest ones, and works his way to the most recent. They are from Dmitry Belofsky. He prints them along with Robin's *sent* e-mails.

"You gotta see these," A. Jaye shouts to Nick from across the room, as he removes sheets of paper from the printer.

Nick steps out of his office, and grabs a chair. "Whatcha got?"

"Ms. McCulley's e-mails," he says, handing them to Nick.

"Lemme see," he says as he shuffles through them.

"She's corresponding with some guy named Dmitry Belofsky," A. Jaye says. "In this one she tells him she likes to go every Friday night to O'Leary's Pub and have a drink. If he's interested, she'll be the blonde at the bar."

"That's an invite," Nick says. He stands and throws the sheets on the desk. "Let's go."

———— ♦ ————

Minutes later they make their way into O'Leary's Pub. Behind the bar, a short thin guy with wavy brown hair and narrow face is wiping down the surface in front of a female patron smoking and taking swigs of beer from a bottle. On the jukebox, Whitney Houston is singing, "I Will Always Love You." The place smells of onions.

Eleven-thirty in the morning is too early to be drinking, Nick thinks.

"You the owner?" he asks the bartender.

"Yeah, Regan O'Leary. You guys cops?"

Nick lays the picture on the bar. "Atlanta P.D., homicide. You ever see this redhead come in here?" He pushes the photo in front of him.

O'Leary glances at it, and pushes it back. "Yeah, she's a regular. Robin McCulley's her name. Been some time since I've seen her last."

A middle-aged guy in work clothes at the end of the bar calls out and raises his empty glass. O'Leary heads over, fills it and returns.

"Does Ms. McCulley always come alone?" Nick asks.

"Until recently, she came by herself. Liked to sit here at the bar and talk. She's pretty friendly with my night guy."

"Lovers?" A. Jaye asks.

O'Leary shakes his head. "Nah, he's married. They just talk. But now she's always with this foreign guy."

"Gotta name?" Nick asks.

"She calls him Dimmy—"

"Dmitry?" Nick says.

"Yeah, that's it. Don't know his last name. He may be Russian."

"Can you describe him?"

"A skinhead, big like those wrestlers you see on TV, rough looking." O'Leary ran a finger down his face. "Has a scar here on his right cheek."

"Anything else?"

"Yeah. He came in here one evening with another monster. I don't mind telling you, detective, those guys scared the shit out of me." He pauses to dunk an empty glass into a water bath under the bar, reaches for a towel.

"Whatta they do?"

"They downed a quart of vodka without batting an eye, and boy did they get mean. They danced around, pushing and shoving customers, singing songs in their language. The guy called Dmitry is bragging about snuffing out some redhead. I immediately called Robin's boss at the CDC, talked with one of her people and told them, but never heard anything back."

"I know. That's why we're here, checking things out."

O'Leary nods. "That's good, 'cause I don't want to see anything happen to her."

Nick pulls out his card and lays it on the bar. "If Dmitry or his friend shows up again, will you call me? Any time. My pager number is listed there."

O'Leary picks up the card and nods. "Yeah, but I hope I never see 'em again."

Outside, Nick turns up his collar. "Dmitry's our man. McCulley's definitely involved with him."

"I'll run Belofsky through the FBI database," A. Jaye says, frowning. "Whatcha thinking?

"He may have done her," Nick says, opening the passenger's door to the police cruiser. "Better run Vladimir Sokolov, too."

"Think they're connected?" A. Jaye says.

"Yeah."

A. Jaye climbs behind the wheel. There's crackling on the car radio as Nick gets comfortable in the passenger seat. "Detective Hunter here. Got it, we're on our way." He turns to his partner. "Hit it. Bulldozer operator found a body in the dump outside of town."

———— • ————

A. Jaye wheels past three blue cruisers and the M.E.'s wagon before stomping on the brake, sliding to a stop near the yellow crime-scene tape. Nick jumps out, hurries to the officer at the edge of the landfill.

"Howya doin', detective?" the officer says.

"You the one secured the area?"

"Officer James and I. He's down there with the M.E. You'll need Haz-mats to go down there." He shrugs. "M.E.'s orders."

"Got it," Nick says. Behind the M.E.'s wagon, he and A. Jaye don the white protective suits, adjust their masks and rush to the edge of the pit. They lock arms as they slide in the muck, descending the sharp slope.

"What do we have?" Nick says to the sergeant who is standing five yards from the body.

"The bulldozer was pushing a load around when an arm shot into the air. The Vic is in pretty bad shape. M.E.'s been going over the body."

"Thanks," Nick says.

Doc McCormick and his assistant, Marty look up when they hear Nick and A. Jaye tramping through the crap.

"We've got to stop meeting like this," Doc says. He isn't wearing a mask.

"You'd miss us," A. Jaye says.

"You won't need those masks unless you can't stand the stench."

"Oh, man, this place stinks," A. Jaye says, removing his mask.

"Smells like vomit," Nick says.

"More like shit," his partner says.

Doc pointed to the victim. "Got one here with lots of trauma, afraid the bulldozer didn't see her." He shook his head. "Vic's a white woman. Can't tell much out here."

Nick squatted by the bludgeoned corpse. One arm is still attached. The face is unrecognizable. The upper torso in places looks like ground hamburger meat. The legs and thighs are blue. When Nick was on the force in D.C., he'd written up such cases as *GBH*, grievous bodily harm.

Back at the station, A. Jaye calls out, "Looky here."

"Whattayu got?"

"Dmitry's wanted by the FBI for killing two brothers in the New Jersey mob."

"What about Sokolov?"

"Nothing."

"Damn! I know they're connected in some way," Nick says.

"If so, it'll turn up sooner or later."

CHAPTER TWENTY-NINE

At ten o'clock that morning, Susan makes her way down to the dressing room in the medical examiner's building. Alone in the locker room, she changes into scrubs, pulls a cap over her hair, and slips into gloves. The dissection had started an hour earlier, and she planned it so her time in the pit would be short. She had assisted in postmortems during her rotation in pathology, but viewing this corpse would be difficult. Nick had called her about the body found in the landfill. It was Robin.

She slips on a mask, walks out, and stops for a second to inhale before pushing into the autopsy suite.

Nick is beside the cart, obstructing her view of the corpse. He slides over and she steps in. A large skylight provides illumination for examining the body. In a gown, cap and gloves, Doc faces them. Behind him are two metal tables fifteen feet apart from each other, each joined at one end to metal sinks against the wall. Doc's azure eyes stare at her over his mask. He raises a gloved hand.

"Almost done," he says. "Sure you want to be here, Dr. Prescott?"

Susan nods, but isn't being honest. She really doesn't. Marty had sewed up the Y-incision on Robin with twine like that used in the stitch to cover baseballs.

The brain has been removed and is in a pan next to the body. The scalp is pulled back over the skull, has strands of red hair. Couldn't tell from the face that it's Robin. The legs and thighs are blue, and patches of the trunk look chewed up. Her right arm is bone from elbow to fingers.

"So far, Doc, what have you determined?" she asks.

"Wasn't stabbed or shot," he says. "The bulldozer beat her up pretty bad, but didn't kill her. She was dead about eight, maybe ten hours before being dumped."

The freezer blowers roar.

"Could you tell if she was battered to death?" Nick says.

Doc shook his head. "The skull shows no trauma." He goes to the dissecting table against the wall, brings back a pan, sets it on a tray, swings it over the body, and lifts up amorphous tissue.

"At one time this pink pulp was her lungs," he says. "The brain is in the same condition. I'm thinking some microbe might have gotten her." He looks at Susan. "We'll need your help on this one, Dr. Prescott."

She nods.

Silence falls over the room.

A microbe?

"You're saying some bug did her in, Doc?" Nick says.

"Simply put, yes."

"Shouldn't we be in protective gear?" Nick says.

"If the bug were contagious, the guy who dumped her would be one of them over there," he says, hitching his head toward several carts with covered bodies. "By the way, detective, you need to know that we've got a serial killer on the loose in this town."

"Whatta you mean?"

"That's my third Vic lying over there with a frontal lobe hemorrhage. Had two a couple of weeks ago. When the first female arrived, I thought she had a hypertensive crisis, but ruled that out when the other two females came in with the same condition. Some killer is using something like an ice pick to ram up his victim's nostril and wriggles the tip in a circle, severing the arteries in the frontal lobe." He shakes his head. "And the killer rapes them, too."

"Horrible," Susan says.

"Whoever it is, he's getting more aggressive," Doc says.

"Thanks for the heads-up, Doc," Nick says. "We'll keep an eye out."

"I'll need Robin's tissue and blood samples before I leave," Susan says.

"Got 'em," Marty says, hurrying over to the counter. He returns with a tray of tubes and jars.

———— ♦ ————

Susan steps outside the M.E.'s building carrying the container with Robin's samples. Susan looks around for Nick. *Where in the hell did he go?* The weather has turned colder, and it's sleeting. A sheet of ice has formed in the parking lot and on the cars.

As she walks flat-footed to her SUV, images of Robin's body haunt her. What type of microbe could have killed her? Susan opens the car door and places the box on the passenger-side floor, reaches in the glove box for the scraper. When she finishes the windshield, she slides behind the wheel and maneuvers out of the parking lot. It is twelve-thirty. No time for lunch, she's eager to take Robin's tissues to the lab.

Ten minutes on the road, sleet pounds the windows. The defroster and heater strain. Chunks of ice form on the wipers. Susan wishes someone else were driving.

This must be the worst weather ever to hit Atlanta.

She glances into the rearview mirror. A white sedan is behind her. "Don't get too close," she murmurs.

She's doing thirty now, staying in the flow of the traffic, keeping an eye on the cars in front and in back. Thank God, no sudden stops. She looks for the white car. It must have gone off.

Her pulse quickens. "Ohmigod, is it them?" The black Mercedes with the two men now is behind her. It inches up, moving in close and rams her.

"What the hell?!" she shouts. "Stop it!" She struggles with the steering wheel.

Emergency lights are flashing up ahead. She taps the brake pedal, afraid the car will skid and she'll lose control if she hits it too hard. The Mercedes smacks her again—harder—much harder, this time.

Susan screams. Out of control, the SUV speeds toward a pileup in her lane—three cars, four, and then five. Blood pounds in her throat. Her car accelerates onto the shoulder past the smashed cars and sails off into the trees.

"Oh, no!" she screams. "I'm going to die."

Susan doesn't know how long she has been out. But the sleet has stopped. Her feet are freezing and her chest hurts. She turns her head. *Ouch! That hurts.* She tries to unbuckle her seatbelt, but there is too much pain in her wrist. She lifts her left leg, then the right one. They seemed okay. She rubs her face—blood is on her glove. She is having trouble breathing. She uses her good hand to release her seatbelt.

The door flies open.

"Lady, you okay?" a voice says.

She turns. A young man is looking in at her.

"I'm hurt," she says.

"I've called 911. Sit tight. You're on top of a picnic table. Your car seems pretty stable, and I don't smell any gas. Wow! You've got a gash on your forehead." He reached into his pocket. "Here's my handkerchief; you'll need to put some pressure on it."

"Thanks." Shit. The pain in her wrist is worse, and she probably broke a rib.

"I saw that Mercedes hit you. You shot off the road like a flying saucer, and ended up here."

A police cruiser is racing down the side road with its siren blasting and strobe lights flashing. It comes to a sliding stop about ten yards away. The door flips open, and an officer jumps out, makes his way over to them, slipping on the ice.

"The lady is hurt," the young man says.

And the lady needs to get the hell out of here.

The officer helps him down and asks if anyone else is in the car. "Only the lady," the guy says. She has a bad cut on her head. Looks pretty deep."

The officer hoists himself up on the table and looks in. "How you doin', ma'am?"

"I'm freezing my ass off, and I'm in lots of pain. Get me out of here."

"An ambulance is on its way. We need to wait for the paramedics."

"Do you need any help, sir?" the young man shouts.

"I can manage."

The radio in the police car crackles.

"The EMTs have arrived, ma'am," the officer says.

Good. The paramedics rush over pushing a gurney, lower Susan to the ground, and place her on it.

Susan asks for her purse and the box on the floor.

"I'll get 'em," the officer says.

"I'm a doctor," Susan tells one of the attendants.

"I know, Dr. Prescott," she says, wrapping Susan in blankets. "We came the other night when you were injured in front of your apartment."

"Oh, yeah. I recognize you now." She forces a smile. "I'm not accident prone..."

They shove Susan into the ambulance.

"Ma'am, I hope you're okay," says the young man at the back door. "I gave the license number of the Mercedes to the cop. I gotta go."

Susan tries to lift her head.

"Don't move, doctor."

"What's your name, son?" Susan shouts.

"Sorry. He's gone," the medic says.

"I wanted to thank him."

The officer returns with Susan's things. "I've called in the Mercedes."

"I'll keep them for her," the attendant says.

"I'll need to get a statement," the officer says.

"You can get it at the hospital."

The medics measure Susan's vital signs, attach a neck brace, check the cut on her forehead, and examine her ribs. "You'll need stitches, x-rays and some tests. They may keep you overnight, doctor."

Susan nods. No use arguing. She'll wait until they get to the hospital to squabble over that.

"I can't leave you alone for a minute," Nick says, sticking his head in from the rear of the ambulance.

"Where in the hell did you go after we left the ME building?" she says. "I looked all over for you."

His brow puckers. "What do you mean?"

"I looked for you in the parking lot and you left without saying anything."

"Hey, I looked for you, but thought you were in a hurry to get to the lab."

"You could have waited," she muttered. "Didn't you see my Explorer?"

He shrugs. "I heard your friends in the Mercedes did this to you," he says. He turns to the paramedic. "How is she?"

"Banged up and a deep cut on her forehead. We'll know more when we get her to the hospital."

"I'm beginning to think the bastards are afraid I'm onto something," Susan says, "and I wish I knew what that is."

"A philosopher I know by the name of A. Jaye Chandler always reminds me that it'll turn up sooner or later.'"

"Yeah, well, it better be sooner," she says.

Nick pauses as if he wants to say something, but decides against it.

"Okay, come out with it. What are you keeping from me?"

"I'm sorry we didn't catch the thugs before they did this to you. The plate we checked was stolen, as I thought, but I want you to know I have people on it."

"We gotta go, detective," the paramedic says, grabbing hold of the back door handle.

"I'll meet you at the hospital, Susan," Nick says.

CHAPTER THIRTY

A Camry rental is delivered around mid-morning to replace the damaged Explorer and Susan takes off for work, still feeling like she got pounded in a boxing match. The hospital released her after the ER doctor closed her forehead with twelve stitches, ran some tests, x-rayed her chest, taped a bruised rib, and wrapped her wrist. Nick took her home around eight that evening.

On her way to work Susan stops for a latte and arrives at her office around eleven. Inside, she sets the cup on her desk and eases into her chair, holding her breath. Mission accomplished, she takes a deep breath. *Ouch*! The ER doc has taped her ribcage too tightly. She flashes on the unfortunate incident in the ER where she made a fool of herself, ranting at Nick for not waiting for her outside the ME's office. She couldn't help it. The spirit of fear had overtaken her and screwed up her thinking. If he had waited for her, maybe none of this would have happened, and she wouldn't have embarrassed herself in front of the nurses. Their scowls made her feel guilty and she immediately apologized to Nick. Instead of accepting it gracefully, he lectured her about controlling her temper. That hit her between the eyes like a ninety-eight-mile-an-hour baseball. That was it. She didn't talk to him the rest of the evening.

She reaches across the desk for her coffee and a sharp pain shoots across her ribs, taking her breath away. She reaches in her purse for two Lortabs, washes them down with some coffee, inches her body up in her chair, and takes several small breaths. Maybe Nick's forgiven her by now. One thing in her favor, he didn't seem mad when he left her at the apartment last night. There was even a moment when she thought he was going to kiss her. He might be right. She can be a bitch at times.

The phone on her desk rings. *That's Nick. He's forgiven me.* She lifts the receiver, but is disappointed to hear Karl Gerber's voice on the other end.

"I heard about your accident," Gerber says. "How are you feeling?"

"Bruised, stiff, but I'll live. I am trying to get up enough energy to go into Four once the pain leaves me."

"Good, then you're okay."

Where's he going with this? "I didn't say I was okay, Karl."

"I need you to gather up you equipment. You're going to Nebraska."

"Nebraska?"

"Yeah, you must be okay if you were going to work in Four."

"I said if my pain subsides. I had to take two hydrocodone tabs. But I don't believe I'm up to flying anywhere just yet."

"You're going to Nebraska," he repeated with an edge to his tone.

"Karl, you gotta send someone else." She could probably make the trip, but there's something she's never told anyone. She hates flying in those small prop planes. They scare the hell out of her.

"No. They've specifically asked for you. Take painkillers with you."

"Who wants me?"

"Dr. Tom Overstreet at the Nebraska Public Health Department," Gerber says. "I didn't know you knew anyone out there."

"I met Overstreet at a meeting."

Gerber becomes silent. He's probably thinking she'd gone to bed with Overstreet. "I mean professionally," she says. Tom is a good looking guy, but not her type. Nick is her type. *Why hasn't he called me?*

"They have two dead bodies that are very strange," Gerber says, "and Overstreet needs you in Alliance ASAP."

"Where's Alliance?"

"In the Sand Hills of western Nebraska."

"Never heard of it."

The mechanical air handler in the corridor roared louder than usual.

"Beautiful country. But cold as hell this time of year."

"That's an oxymoron," she says.

"You must be feeling better."

"Karl, I don't know if I'm up to it. Anyway, I really need to stay and work on Robin's samples. The M.E. thinks she might have died from some deadly microbe."

"I heard about the poor soul from detective Hunter, but her samples will have to wait for now."

Poor soul? Jeez, you slept with her more times than I can count, and that's all you can come up with? You stinking rat.

"Have I made myself clear, Susan?"

Dammit! I'm not getting into some small plane.

"You'll be picked up in an hour. Be ready."

Click.

Shit. She dials Nick.

"Gerber's sending me to Nebraska. They got two dead bodies and there's something of a mystery about them, I think."

"What about Ms. McCulley's tissue samples? If Doc's right, that microbe can be deadly and contagious." She heard him breathing heavily in the phone. "Can't that trip wait? Those dead bodies aren't going anywhere."

Her mind flashes on Robin's mushy lungs. "I argued with him, but Gerber won't send anyone else."

"Did you tell him about the microbe?"

"Sure did, but he doesn't care."

Nick says nothing.

"Did you get anything on that Mercedes?"

"Another stolen vehicle. Call me when you get back."

Hmmm. He didn't ask how I was feeling.

———— ♦ ————

The four-passenger plane descends through the turbulent clouds. Seated next to Susan behind the co-pilot is her tech Tony Seymour, and stored in the back are two field cases. The plane bounces from side to side a few times, then straightens out. Susan hasn't said a word since the descent. Her knuckles are white from holding on to the arm rests.

They are approaching a small airfield and the turbulence has settled down. She removes two pain pills from her pocket and pops them into her mouth, uncaps a bottle of water and takes several swallows. The ground is covered with snow and is moving up fast towards them, but the runway is clear. The pilot lands the plane perfectly and guides the aircraft off the runway to a yellow hanger and cuts the power. They deplane, and Susan feels like kissing the ground. She raises the hood on her coat, reaches into her pockets for gloves, and follows Tony, who's carrying two black cases to the man in a parka standing next to a white van.

"Glad you're here, Susan," Overstreet says.

"This is Tony Seymour, Tom."

They shake hands, and Overstreet leads the way to the Health Department van parked next to the hanger, and opens the side door. Tony slides in the cases and hops in. Susan slips into the passenger seat and Overstreet gets behind the wheel and drives off through the wet snow.

"What happened to you?" he asks, gazing at her bandaged forehead.

"A little accident."

He nods as if he knew she didn't want to discuss it. "We've got a dilemma here," he says. "I'm sure you've heard of Senator Barry Plummer."

"Isn't he the chair of the Foreign Relations Committee?"

He looked surprised. "Yeah, and he's from here, born and raised. His folks were found dead at their ranch outside of town."

Overstreet wipes the windshield with his gloved hand and increases the blower speed.

"Emma was found in the kitchen, and Chester in the bedroom, still in bed—no forced entry, and nothing was taken."

He wheels the van around the corner and proceeds on Box Butte Street.

"The M.E.'s puzzled about what bled them out and why their lungs and brains turned to mush."

Mush? Just like Robin's?

"And another thing"—he pauses long enough to glance at her and then back at the road—"their eyeballs were found on the floor."

"What?" Susan says, inching up off the seat. "You gotta be kidding me. Never heard of such a thing."

"I wish I were," he says. "Something scary is going on here."

Susan thinks about Robin's autopsy. Both her brain and lungs had turned into a pulpy mass, but she had so many traumas that Doc probably didn't think anything about her missing eyeballs.

"The M.E. thinks some microbe from outer space got into the Plummers," Overstreet says. "But there have been no other deaths. I told him I'd better call you guys."

"Anything else?"

"No trauma to their heads, no bruises on the arms, and there wasn't any skin or hair under their fingernails. Both were in good health for folks in their late seventies."

Overstreet turns at the stoplight, drives two blocks, and pulls in next to a small concrete block building. "We've stored the bodies in this old meat market."

Meat market?

Apparently he sees the frown on her face. "Oh, they've been out of business for five years, but the freezer still works."

She feels like laughing but decides it would be ill-mannered of her. "I was wondering when you said meat market."

"The M.E. didn't want to release the bodies to the funeral home until we figured out what killed them."

"Were the autopsies done here?" Susan says.

He nods. "The hospital didn't want the bodies brought there."

"We brought hazmats," Tony says.

Susan opens her door and gets out. The sun reflects bright off the snow. She thinks about building snowballs and throwing them at Tony and Overstreet, but Overstreet doesn't seem the playful type. The snow crackles under her feet as she follows Overstreet.

Inside, the room has yellow streaks down the plastered walls and the place smells musty. Two large windows face the street, and a half-roll of butcher paper is still in its holder on one end of the wooden counter. In the wall behind it is a huge metal door that still shines.

Tony sets the supply cases on the counter and opens one. They remove their coats and place them on the counter, don the protective gear, adjust their masks, and Tony picks up the unopened case.

"Ready?" Overstreet asks.

They nod.

At the locker door, Overstreet pulls on the chrome handle, a wave of condensation floats out into their faces, he flips on the lights. Inside, two bodies on carts are covered with sheets. Folders lay on top of the corpses—tags are attached to their big toes.

Susan steps in and turns to Overstreet, who looks like a ghost dressed in the white Haz-mat suit. "You're right. The freezer works."

His eyes seem to smile over the mask.

"Hope we're not in here for too long," Tony says. "I hate the dang cold."

The nearest toe tag reads: *Emma Plummer*. Susan opens the folder and reads the M.E.'s report. Overstreet pulls the white cover down to the Emma's pubic area, exposing the stitched Y-incision from the autopsy. The victim had been a pretty lady with lots of gray hair, and skin that had very few wrinkles. Susan hands the file to Overstreet and uses a penlight to examine her nose, ears and looks into the eye sockets.

"Sure enough, her eyes are gone," Susan says.

At the next table, Susan reviews Mr. Plummer's file. Once again, Overstreet pulls the sheet down to Chester's groin area. His hair is whiter than his wife's and his skin has more wrinkles than hers. Susan closes the file and places it on the old man's chest, begins examining the head. When about finished, Susan turns his head to one side, and shouts, "Got something here. Can you get me a larger light?"

Overstreet grabs one from the kit on the floor and hands it to her.

Overstreet leans in. "Whaddayu see?"

"There's a tiny hole in Chester's neck. Let's check the wife."

"Do you think it's significant?" Overstreet asks, as they shuffle over to Emma's body.

"Don't know for sure, but I'm developing a theory." She turns Emma's head. "Look," she says, pointing with a gloved finger, "She has one, too. It's amazing I even noticed them as small as they are."

Susan glances at the head diagrams in the files. The M.E. made no notation of a puncture wound on either body.

"Apparently Doc can't see as well as he used to," Overstreet says. "He missed it on both of them."

"Don't be too hard on him. Remember, I missed it on Emma. I just got lucky."

"What's your theory about these holes?" the Public Health officer asks.

"I'd bet a ten spot that these holes were made by something that attacked the victims' internal organs and their eyes." She glances down at his kit. "Did you save any blood and tissue samples for me?"

He nods. "They're in there packed and ready to go."

"Good. We'll run some tox screens. Now, would you call the M.E. for me? I'd like to get his permission to incise the holes on both bodies."

"Do you think it's necessary?" he asks. "I mean... you being with the CDC and all."

"We do it as a courtesy measure."

"I'll be back in a minute." He leaves.

"I'm freezing," Tony says. "Are you going to be much longer? I may never walk again."

"Not too much longer. And I'm betting you'll walk out of here."

His eyes smile back and he nods. "I'm surprised you are able to work," Tony says.

"The pain killers help."

Overstreet returns five minutes later adjusting his mask. "Doc says you should feel free to do whatever you need to, just add your findings to the report and sign it."

"Good," she says, and turns to Tony. "Let's do it."

He takes pictures of the hole in Emma's neck, and reaches for a scalpel from the kit and hands it to Susan. She makes an incision.

"The hole isn't very deep," Overstreet says.

"A quarter-of-an-inch," Susan says. "I expected it to be deeper."

Susan performs the same procedure on Chester while Tony snaps pictures.

"Same depth," Overstreet says.

Susan doesn't respond as she writes something on each of the Plummers' reports.

Tony gathers the tools and drops them into a biohazard bag.

136

"Done," she says. "Let's get out of here before Tony freezes to death."

In the outer room, Tony sets the black case on the counter. "Sure is nice out here."

"I see you're walking again," Susan says.

"Barely."

"Do you think something stung the Plummers?" Overstreet asks while he removing his protective gear.

"I doubt if any insect would hit them both in the same place," Susan says. "Those punctures were deliberate."

"You mean someone snuck up behind them and jabbed them with some kind of needle?" Overstreet says, slipping into his sport coat.

"My guess is someone wanted them dead. During my pathology rounds in med school, I assisted in an autopsy on a middle-aged guy who had a hole similar to these old folks, but it was in the hip, and much deeper."

"Made by an injection, I bet," Overstreet says.

"Great deduction," Susan says. "While in the hospital, the patient was administered a shot and the site got infected. It was incised, and the abscess cultured. They tried everything, but the patient died from a resistant strain of bacterium. I forget now which one it was. Probably staph."

"So you're thinking some resistant bacterium was injected into them?" Overstreet says, as he hands her the box of samples.

"I don't know," she says, reaching for the container. "The holes being so tiny have me puzzled. She holds up the samples. "These tissues will unlock the mystery."

CHAPTER THIRTY-ONE

Nick scans the house numbers as A. Jaye drives the black and white through an area of abandoned cars, boarded-up windows and dogs roaming the streets. He edges the cruiser along the curb.

"Some neighborhood," Nick says. "Stop here, this is it."

They climb out and go through a gate. A rusted Chevy without tires is up on blocks. As they make their way to the stairs, they step over toys scattered on the sidewalk covered with chalk markings. Nick knocks on the manager's door. A dog next door on the left barks and its owner peeks out through the curtains. There's an acre of space to the right of the apartment building.

"What's that smell?" A. Jaye says.

"Rotten eggs."

"Smells like baby shit," A. Jaye says. He looks around. A diaper is on the ground next to the porch. "There it is," he says.

A husky woman in a cotton dress opens the door. She is wiping her hands on her apron and doesn't smile. Her hair is fixed into a bun on top.

"Yah?" she says.

"Detectives with the Atlanta Police," Nick says, holding up his ID. "Does Dmitry Belofsky live here?"

"Yah." She points down. "Him gone."

"Could you let us into the apartment?" Nick says. "We have a warrant."

He holds it up in front of her, but doesn't tell her it's a telephonic warrant. Judge Berringer had authorized it.

She reaches for it and looks at it, frowning. "What'd he do?"

"Police business," A. Jaye says. "We just need to go through his apartment."

"Come." She waddles down the stairs, sandals thwacking her feet, and trots around the building to the basement apartment. She hurries down the stairs, fumbles in her pocket for the keys and opens the door. His partner pushes past her and Nick follows. She's right behind them.

"Ma'am, you need to step outside," Nick says.

They slip into latex gloves. Nick flips on the lights and they do their walk through. Nick wanders into the kitchen and A. Jaye moves into the bedroom.

Nick opens the fridge. Empty. He looks in the freezer above, nothing. He rummages through the trash can next to the stove, and finds a small object at the bottom of the can.

"He flew the coop," A. Jaye says, coming out of the utility room, "and he's emptied the place."

"Look at this," Nick says, holding up a small barrel with a tiny needle attached to it.

A. Jaye hurries over and reaches for it.

"Be careful. The point is sharp," Nick says. "There could still be something left on it."

"What the hell is this?" his partner asks as he examines it.

"Don't know. Haven't seen anything like it." Nick glances around the kitchen, opens drawers. "Help me look for a narrow tube."

"You mean like a blowgun?"

"Yeah."

It takes them ten minutes to take the kitchen apart. No blowgun.

"This must be some new kind of dart the Russians have invented," Nick says. "They're good at finding ways to drop victims in their tracks."

"Yeah," A. Jaye says. "Like using umbrellas with sharp points filled with some toxic shit, to jab into some poor sap's leg. By the time he realizes what's hit him; he falls dead."

Nick drops the dart into an evidence bag. When he was on the Metro PD in Washington, he played dart games with his detective buddies, but no one could ever beat him. He's never seen one this small.

"Wonder what Belofsky uses in these things?" Nick says.

"Got me," A. Jaye says. "You can bet it's nothing healthy."

"We'd better find out. And fast."

CHAPTER THIRTY-TWO

Susan Prescott returns from Alliance around six o'clock that evening and hurries to the lab to store the samples. Since she left Nebraska, Susan has been haunted with the feeling that Robin and the Plummers' deaths are related. The condition of their brains and lungs would suggest it, except, unlike the Plummers, Robin had no puncture wounds behind the ear or on the neck that Doc could see. Analyzing their tissues, however, would reveal if there's a connection.

Who's the killer? That's the sixty-four thousand dollar question.

Robin and the Plummers lived a thousand miles apart. Maybe there were two killers. But it would be unlikely they'd used the same toxin, unless... they were working together. She decides to stick to the lab and let Nick do the detective work.

He had asked her to call when she got back. Maybe she'll wait until morning. It's been a tiring day. She leaves the building, heads to her car, and as she opens the door, her pager whines. She climbs in and reaches for the car phone.

"I was about to call you," she says. Telling a little white lie isn't a sin, is it?

"How about coming by my place?" he says.

He doesn't sound mad.

She checks her watch. Seven o'clock. "I've had an exhausting day—"

"We should meet," he says.

She holds the phone in the curve of her neck, backs out of her parking space, and heads toward the gate. "Can't it wait until tomorrow?"

"No. Come when you can." He hangs up.

Well, I guess I got my orders.

She arrives at her apartment, showers, changes into jeans and sweat shirt. It's close to eight-thirty when Nick greets her at the door, escorts her into the living room, and takes her coat. She glances out the large glass doors. A deck extends out to a lake, which is shimmering in the moonlight.

The room has a high ceiling, a bar and dining area off to the side. On the wall behind the bar are framed photos of officers and detectives. In the center is a large picture of a boy in a soccer uniform.

"My son," Nick says.

"I see the likeness."

She hears the sound of a motor boat passing by. Too late to be out on the water, she thinks as she moves in front of the bar. "No picture of your—"

"I burned 'em."

"Bad divorce?"

"You could say that. She took everything. And part of me."

"Your son?"

He nods, and reaches for a glass. "Can I fix you something?"

"What are you having?"

"Scotch... neat."

"On the rocks," she says.

"I thought you only liked wine."

"Not tonight." It's been a while since she took her last pain tablet.

He pours her drink over ice and hands it to her. She looks out on the deck.

"How's your rib and wrist?" he asks.

"Just a tiny bit sore, but otherwise okay." She swallows some of her drink.

"I see your head wound is much better."

She nods. "It seems peaceful here," she says.

He works his way next to her. "It is," he says, gulping his scotch.

"Why did you come to Atlanta?" she asks.

He's quiet for a moment. "The politics got heavy, and DC wasn't fun anymore."

"Too many dipsticks," she says.

He smiles and holds up his glass. "And judges who let criminals off too easily."

"And here?" she asks, finishing her drink, surprised it is gone.

"Not as much. They seem to be the same, wherever I go."

He reaches for her glass and makes her another scotch, brings it to her, and takes a drink of his.

"And how about your life at the CDC? All work and no love life?"

None of your damn business.

She's beginning to feel uncomfortable. Is he fishing about her lovers? Well, she isn't about to get into that.

"How's yours?" she asks.

"Not good."

"Mine either." She wishes she could take that back.

"You never married," he says. "Is work the reason?"

She drifts down the bar. "Not really."

Nick grins. He has a charismatic air about him that she finds attractive.

"My work broke up my marriage," he says.

Somewhere she hears a fridge cycle on.

He finishes off his drink, takes hers and sets them on the bar. He looks at her for a moment. She stiffens. He pulls her into his arms.

"No, don't," she says, but she doesn't mean it.

Nick's warm chest is pressed against her. She hadn't realized how much she'd needed to be held. She feels the heat from his body and smells the scent of his cologne. His strength is wonderful. He bends his head down and presses his lips hard against hers. A tingling sensation travels through her spine. She wants him.

He takes her hand and leads the way into his bedroom.

He unbuttons his shirt and slips out of his jeans, stands in his briefs watching her. She slips out of her clothes down to a red bra and panties.

"I like red," he says.

She says nothing. To some comments there are no good answers.

Out of his briefs, Nick is ready. His body is lean and muscular. Susan unsnaps her bra and lets it fall. Then she runs her thumbs inside the elastic of her panties, pushes them to the floor, and kicks them aside.

They sit on the edge of the bed and he kisses and touches her. He awakens things in her. They make their way under the sheets and hold each other for a while, exploring. She loves the smell of his body.

She feels him ease up on her, his eyes full of desire. She had never wanted Alec this much. In taking her body, Nick possesses her. Afterward, they lay together feeling damp, tangled in the sheets, getting their breath back. She has never been so satisfied.

Nick is on his side, now, facing her with his arm around her waist.

Looking into his eyes, she says, "Did you plan this?"

"I did."

He rolls on his back, and Susan lays her head on his chest.

"Your heart has quieted," she says.

"At one point it was about to burst," he says.

They remain quiet. Outside, a car door slams.

"Something wrong?" she asks, noticing a change in his demeanor.

Staring at the ceiling, he takes a few seconds before answering.

"Everything points to Robin McCulley," he says.

"What are you talking about?" She pushes up on one elbow, and locks her eyes on his. "What's going on?"

"My investigation... you won't like it."

"Try me."

"Robin McCulley killed Sutherland."

Susan swings her legs over the edge and gathers her clothes. "You didn't know Robin like I did."

"The crime-scene techs found the thirty-eight special that killed Sutherland under the seat in Robin's car. Her fingerprints were on it. The bullet taken out of Sutherland matches the weapon."

Susan pulls the sweatshirt over her head. "I am shocked."

Nick moves to the edge of the bed and reaches for his briefs. "Robin and a Russian named Belofsky were lovers. O'Leary saw them together in his place several times."

Nick zips up his jeans.

"The DNA from the semen collected in Robin's apartment confirmed it is Belofsky's, and his fingerprints and hair were all over the place. I think he seduced her into killing Sutherland and stealing Tican."

"But why?"

"Money," Nick says. "Think about it. How much do you think people would pay for a cancer cure?"

"And you think Belofsky killed her."

"I do. He wanted all the money for himself." Nick slipped into his shirt. "Remember the blood in the kitchen? The Luminal also picked up the Clorox. The Clorox didn't destroy all her DNA. Belofsky's the bastard that dumped her in the landfill."

He follows Susan into the living room.

"But how did he kill her?" she says, standing at the bar.

"That we don't know yet," he says. "Want a drink?"

"No." She sighs. "In Alliance I found something that may interest you. Have you ever heard of Senator Barry Plummer?"

"Hasn't everyone," he says. "He's the Senate's playboy."

"His parents were the victims of some mysterious bug. The M.E. there thinks it came from outer space."

"Doubt that," he says.

"Their autopsies revealed pasty brains and lungs, eyes that popped out, and blood that oozed from sockets."

They move to the couch and sit.

"Sound familiar?" she asks.

"Except for the eyes that sounds like Robin," Nick says. "That suggests they were infected with the same thing."

"There's something else," Susan says. "The Plummers had puncture wounds in their necks, but Doc couldn't find any holes in Robin's neck."

"I think Belofsky may have shot something into her," Nick says.

"What about another killer for the Plummers?" she says.

"Nope, I'm going with only one."

"Are you sure it's Belofsky?"

"We found evidence that he is making minidarts. Got one out of his trash."

"Minidarts?" she says.

"That's how the forensic guys described it. A tiny dart. They didn't find any substance in it or on the needle, so we don't know what he uses in the minidart."

"Maybe he doesn't fill it," Susan says.

"That could be."

"Is the needle about a quarter-inch long?" she asks.

"Yeah, and very sharp," Nick says. "The needle is hooked to a barrel that has a thin capillary center like in thermometers." He pauses, rubbing his chin. "It probably can only take in a couple of drops."

"It appears that Belofsky used them on the Plummers," Susan says.

"I'm curious," Nick says. "Could anything still remain on the needle after the dart falls off the victim?" Nick says.

"That depends on the substance."

"Such as?" Nick asks.

"Well, Doc thinks it's a microbe. So let's go there."

"Okay, let's," he says.

"Upon impact, the victim would become inoculated with the microbe, and only a microscopic amount would be needed to infect a person. Let's assume it's a virus. Unlike bacteria, they can't live very long outside the host, which means they'd live for about a week on moist surfaces, but in dry areas, most viruses would live for only a few hours."

He nods as if he understands. "So, if a dart falls on the floor or ground—assuming it isn't wet—the virus would only live for a few hours.

"I'd say so."

"Since nothing was found on or in the minidart by the forensic people, can we assume that it's a virus?" he asks.

Silence.

"That would be a safe bet."

"You're frowning," he says. "What's bugging you?"

"I'm still puzzled about Robin's death," Susan says, rising. "I must go."

He goes for her coat.

"I'm meeting very early in the morning with my research group," she says. "We should know something soon."

She slips into her coat, and he pecks her cheek. She hurries to the door and turns to face Nick. "I'll let you know what we find."

———◆———

The next morning, Nick strolls into his office carrying a cup of latte and sets it on his desk. He pushes a stack of papers to one side, sweeps several empty paper cups into the trash, and sits. He reaches for his coffee, leans back in his chair, savoring the whiff of cinnamon that tops the white foam. As he drinks it, he thinks about his feelings for Susan.

What's happened to that vow he made to himself, never to get involved with another woman? But his feelings are real. He's never felt this way about anyone, not even when he thought he loved Margaret. Susan is on his mind constantly, and he feels good when he's with her. He sips more coffee. She's a great looker, intelligent, and is good in bed. While those are high on his list, they aren't the things that seem to draw him to her. He rocks in his chair. Susan was really upset over Robin. While Susan puts on a show of toughness, she's really a softy, cares for people, and is a warm person. He likes that.

Nick blinks hard and sighs. Susan's interfering with my work.

He reaches for the phone and places a call to Alliance. The sheriff isn't in, but he talks with the deputy.

"This is Detective Hunter, Atlanta PD, homicide, calling about a person of interest in a murder case here who could also be involved in the Plummers' murder."

"The Plummers?" the officer says. "The sheriff'll really be interested. Do you have a name?"

"Yeah. Dmitry Belofsky."

"Sounds foreign."

"He's Russian. I can fax all I have, and his picture."

"I'll have Sheriff Driscoll call you. Go ahead and send everything. Here's the number."

CHAPTER THIRTY-THREE

Susan enters the Hot Zone, reaches for a coiled air hose, plugs in, and courses through the narrow corridor. In the lab lined with biosafety cabinets are suited figures waiting for her. She carefully lifts blood and tissue samples from their refrigerated containers.

She presses the button on her wrist, and speaks over the intercom to her researchers. "Extract the genetic material from these samples labeled Robin, Ernest and Emma," she says, distributing them. "Add restriction enzymes and PCR the fragments. Prepare gels, stain the frags, and measure their lengths."

They nod and move into the next lab.

Susan prepares samples for the electron microscope. For the next eighteen hours, she and her team go without food or sleep.

One of her associates appears at the door, hooks up to an air hose, and shuffles in, handing her the surveys. Susan studies them. The DNA measurements from the samples taken from Ernest & Emma Plummer and Robin are the same, but to make certain the DNA is a match in all three victims, the composition fragments—the arrangement of bases—has to be identified. These analyses would have to wait for now. Her researchers need their rest.

Susan enters the air lock and, after decontamination, goes into the staging area. There she removes her helmet and steps out of the blue suit, changes into fresh scrubs, and lies on a cot in her office. She stares at the ceiling. *Does Nick really think Tican is a biological rather than a cancer drug? Her intuition tells her Nick is suspicious of Tican because he's a detective and not a scientist.* She flips on her side and falls asleep.

Two hours later, she awakes, gets a bottle of water from the small fridge, opens the desk drawer, removes the aspirin bottle and swallows two tablets. Occasionally, she gets a headache when wearing the suit for long periods of time. She leaves her office and heads to the Level-3. The electron micrographs should now be ready. Susan goes to the keyboard and punches in the file name. Minutes later she watches as images from Robin's and the Plummers' tissue preparations flash on the screen. They are the same—a virus with spaghetti-shaped nuclear material encased in a coating.

She scrolls the national databank searching for comparisons. None exist.

What the hell is this thing?

———— ◆ ————

Around nine o'clock, Nick passes through the doors of Headquarters, wandering down the hall, carrying a folder under his arm. He steps into the open area filled with cubicles. Detectives are working at computers, Gladys isn't at her desk. He unlocks his office door, drops the file on his desk, and heads out for coffee.

Gladys has returned. She looks up from her desk. "Did you see the message from your ex I left on your desk?"

"Not yet," he says.

"She's upset."

"Really mad, huh?"

"'Fraid so. And she says if you don't return her calls, you'll be hearing from her lawyer."

"Good. Let her stew," he says, filling a cup with coffee and taking a Krispy Kreme from the box, and heads to his office. The phone rings as he sets the cup and donut on the napkin. He reaches for it and sits. "Nick Hunter."

"Detective Hunter, this is Sheriff Driscoll."

"Yes, sheriff," Nick says, and imbibes his coffee.

"Got somethin' forya," he says. "An elderly couple who was in Johnnie's Egg House identified the Russian from his picture, and said they saw him in there about three weeks ago."

"That's great news," Nick says. "Any sign of a break-in at the Plummers?"

"Nope. No robbery, either. Plenty of cash around the house. Wilma didn't have much jewelry... just plain, down-to-earth folks."

Then why kill them? Nick dunks the donut into his coffee and crunches into it.

Sheriff coughs.

"Where were the bodies?" Nick asks.

"Wilma was in the kitchen and Ernest in bed."

"Anything unusual about them?"

"Darndest thing," the sheriff says wheezing.

"What?"

"Their eyes were gone... lots of blood around the bodies." He paused. "Doc here thinks it is some kind of bug from outer space. Thought that woman doctor from the CDC might help us on this."

"She's working on it," Nick says. "Anything going on in your town when the murders took place?" Nick chomps on the donut and quaffs his coffee.

Driscoll has a coughing spell. "Sorry. Got this cold," he says, clearing his throat. "We had a big celebration that day. Our favorite son, Barry Plummer—a senator you know—came to speak at a fundraiser for the new Community Center. Had to leave before he spoke, though, called back to Washington, unexpected like."

"Guess you didn't find any darts in any of the rooms?"

"Darts? Wasn't looking for anything like that, detective." He sniffs. "You're thinking they were killed with darts?"

"Don't know yet."

"We'll go back and vacuum the place," Driscoll says.

"That'd be helpful."

"Are they poisonous? Don't want my men coming up dead."

"Only if you prick yourself, but I wouldn't worry. I'm told no organism could live in it at this late date. Just be careful."

"We'll play it safe," the sheriff says.

"Anything else you can tell me, sheriff?" Nick can hear someone talking in the background. Sounds like that deputy he had talked to the day before. The sheriff is breathing hard.

"Yeah. One of Johnnie's waitresses was found dead in the woods. The M.E. first thought she died from a stroke. We couldn't figure out what she was doing in the woods. When we learned that your Russian was with her, the M.E. re-examined her, and determined the cause of death was from some instrument like a pick, jabbed up her nostril. Poor thing must have suffered." He paused to blow his nose. "One other thing, detective. She was raped."

"We've had several of those murders and rapes here."

"Could be your man," the sheriff says, wheezing. "Probably his trademark."

Belofsky's our man all right.

"That's about it... Oh, one last thing," the sheriff says. "The FBI was here."

"They volunteer anything?"

"Naw just looked over the Plummers' place. They said something about protecting members of Congress. They wasn't interested in

Ernest or Wilma. A local matter, they called it."

Nick doesn't respond, but he now knows why Belofsky was in Alliance.

"Hope you catch that bastard."

"We will," Nick says. "We will." He pauses to finish off his coffee. "And sheriff... take care of that cold."

Nick hangs up.

He calls out to Gladys. "Get Deputy Director Harlan Kennedy on the phone." He reaches for Belofsky's folder, opens it and skims though the pages, stops at his picture. You're an ugly bastard. We're coming after your ass.

Gladys buzzes him.

"Harlan?"

Kennedy answers. "Nick? How in the hell are you, and how are things down there in the South?"

"Better now."

"How's Margaret?"

The mere mention of her name caused the acid to spurt up into his throat. He reached in the drawer for antacid. "She's in D.C."

"I... I didn't know."

"Need some information, Harlan."

"What are you working on?"

"Senator Barry Plummer's folks in Alliance, Nebraska were found dead several days ago, and your guys paid them a visit. What did the AIC find?"

"How are you connected to the case?"

"We've been tracking the guy who killed them."

"The agent in charge determined there is no threat to the senator, so we're no longer interested."

"I'm afraid our guy was after the senator."

"Whatta you got?"

"Nothing now, but I will."

"Can't help you unless I have more."

"I might need some help on this one," Nick says.

"Sure thing. By the way, my offer still stands."

When Nick was a detective at Metro PD, homicide division, Harlan had been the agent in charge in the D.C. area. They worked together on several cases. Six years ago, Nick's wife decided she'd had enough of his late nights and time away from her. After the divorce, he left D.C. to become Chief of Detectives at Atlanta PD, and Kennedy moved into the J. Edgar Hoover Building as Deputy Director of Criminal Investigations. He had asked Nick to join him.

"Still not interested," Nick says. He hangs up, reaches for his cup and goes into the outer office.

"Chief, your ex called, *again*," Gladys says. "Give me a break and call her. *Willya?*"

"I've already paid the bitch this month's child support."

He walks away. *Don't I have enough problems without her hounding me? I lived with one woman and it didn't work, and now I'm falling for another. When will I learn?*

"A. Jaye," Nick shouts, standing in his doorway.

"Yeah," he says, rotating his chair out of the cubicle.

"Waitress in Alliance ID'd Belofsky. FBI doesn't want any part of that mess."

"Good. He's ours," A. Jaye says.

"Don't think Belofsky was after the parents," Nick says.

"You're thinking the senator?"

"Yep. But why kill the old folks?"

"You know the Russkies. They're mean son-of-a-bitches."

Gladys called out. "Chief, better get this one."

"I'll take it in my office."

"What do you want now, Margaret?"

"Kenny needs clothes for school."

Bullshit. "You already got this month's check."

"I know, but he's better than those other boys and he needs to look the part."

"Stop treating him like your doll. And don't spend every damn nickel you get your hands on. He'll need it when he goes to college."

"You're so damn stubborn," she says, and then she murmurs "You don't care about your son—"

"Margaret, don't go there." Nick is breathing hard. "Have Kenny call me."

He hangs up on her.

CHAPTER THIRTY-FOUR

Susan tosses and turns most of the night, finally hauling herself out of bed around ten, and slips into her robe. She goes into the kitchen and opens the fridge and finds she's out of orange juice. *Damn!* She puts on a pot of coffee and sits. *What the hell is this new virus and how did it get into both Robin and the Plummers?* She rises, reaches for a cup in the cabinet and pours some coffee and goes back to the table. She sighs and takes several sips of coffee. *It can't be Tican. It's sausage-shaped.*

The message light on her recorder is blinking. Maybe Nick has called about their luncheon date.

She sets her glass on the counter and presses the button. The message is from her doctor's nurse.

A cold fist tightens around her heart, and her mouth is dry as cotton. The test results must be in from her physical.

Something's wrong. I feel it.

Susan inhales deeply to regain her composure, and then punches in the number. The receptionist answers.

"This is Susan Prescott. Can I talk to Rebecca? She called me."

"One moment."

Susan paces across the kitchen floor, stops and stares out the window. Her neighbor is backing out of her driveway.

Come on, come on. Answer the phone.

"Dr. Prescott, this is Rebecca. Dr. Bellman would like to see you Monday morning at eleven."

"Is there something in my mammogram?"

"You'll have to ask the doctor. Can you come in then?"

This is only Thursday. I can't wait.

"Can I see him this afternoon or maybe tomorrow? I couldn't

151

make it through the weekend without knowing."

"I'll check and call you back."

Susan clicks off. Dammit! They never tell you anything. She presses fingers to her breast. *There's a mass in there. I know it. That's why he wants to see me.*

The trash truck rumbles through the neighborhood.

The phone hums. She grabs it. "Susan here."

"Dr. Bellman will see you tomorrow at two."

"Thanks," she says. Her hands are shaking.

Eleven fifteen on the wall clock. In less than an hour she'll meet Nick for lunch. She showers, dresses, and on her way out she glances at the hall mirror. *Woman, you look like shit.*

Outside, the sun is high in the sky, but it doesn't raise her spirits. She rushes to her car. The drive downtown to the Peachtree Bistro takes twenty minutes. She wheels into a parking space, leaves the Camry and charges through the door. People are waiting in line, and the place is packed. She looks for Nick. All the booths are taken. The waiter shows her to a table in the back. She tosses her coat over a chair and watches the front. There is a tap on her shoulder. Her body jerks.

Nick smiles. "A little jumpy, are you?"

She glances around, searching for other entrances. "Where did you come from?"

"The little boy's room." He opens his sport coat and eases his large frame into the chair opposite her.

"Hope you washed your hands," she says.

He laughs. "Mother taught me good."

A man in his thirties, thin and tall comes to their table with menus. They order unsweetened iced tea.

"I'm glad you came," he says.

"Why wouldn't I?"

Nick shrugs. "The other night... you seemed a little pissed when you left me." He glimpses at the lunch items on the menu. "Grilled tuna is good here."

"Just salad for me," she says, and moves the napkin off her plate. "Sorry, that's the way I am when I'm in a hurry to get into the lab. I was going to call you yesterday, but it was such a hectic day."

"About... the other night," he says. "I—"

"That was entirely mutual. I found it pleasurable."

"Yes it was... and me, too," he says, "mutual, I mean."

The waiter brings their drinks. Nick selects tuna on rye, and she orders house salad with vinaigrette dressing on the side. He sips his tea, and then gently places his hand on top of hers. "Hello. Come back to earth."

"Sorry. My mind is somewhere else."

"I can see that."

She leans forward. "I have prelims on Robin and the Plummers," she says. "A virus is definitely responsible for their deaths, just like Doc says."

"So, it is a bug?"

"I'm afraid so."

She looks at the coed at the next table working the keys on her laptop, wondering if anyone in her family has had breast cancer.

"It's an unknown virus that looks like spaghetti," Susan says.

Lunch arrives. Nick picks off the tomatoes from his sandwich.

"Unknown?" he says.

"It's not in the national database."

He frowns. "Meaning—?"

"It's been re-engineered. We've measured its DNA fragments in both Robin and the Plummers and they are the same. But we need to determine what's in those fragments. It could tell us a lot."

"God, it's noisy in this place," he says, looking around. He leans in. "You're gonna have to keep the science stuff simple."

She sighs. "The fragments have bases that we label with letters—a-c-g-t." Susan reaches for a napkin and retrieves a pen from her purse. "The "a" joins with "t" like so, to yield the "a-t" pair, and "c" with "g" to provide the "c-g" pair, and these exist in different arrangements in the DNA chain. Got that?"

He took a bite of his sandwich, and shrugs. "All I know about DNA is what the forensic guys tell me. But what you're saying makes sense."

She pours a smidgen of dressing over her salad and takes a bite. "The important thing is that the arrangement of these base-pairs identifies the virus. They should be the same in Robin and the Plummers."

"But to be certain," he says, reaching for the other half of his sandwich, "you have to identify those base-pairs."

"Bingo." She takes another bite of salad. "That's pretty good. See, you're better than you think."

"Lemme ask you somethin' else," he says, apparently feeling more confident. "Mutation... that means a change in the bug's DNA. Right?"

She nods. "It means that something has caused the base-pairs in the parent organism to change their arrangement; thus, a mutant bug."

"Whoa!" he says, raising a hand. "What if your spaghetti virus isn't the original bug, but its mutant?"

His question surprises her, as do his reasoning skills. "You bring up a good point." She glances at the napkin. "In that case we'd have to search for the original virus. Without it, we'd have a difficult time determining where the mutant came from."

A young man bumps into Susan's chair as he heads to the front.

"What?" Nick asks. "You're frowning."

"Don't you think it's beyond coincidence that Vladimir and Belofsky show up at the same time?"

Nick finishes his tea. "So you think they know each other."

"Don't you?"

Nick wipes his mouth and drops the napkin on his plate. "The thought has crossed my mind."

"So? What are the pieces?" she asks.

"Belofsky doesn't strike me as the brainy type. Vladimir has to be the brains, and I think they're involved in something related to Senator Plummer. What? I don't know yet."

"This is getting more complicated by the minute," she says, pushing her salad aside.

It's time she told him about what's bothering her.

CHAPTER THIRTY-FIVE

Two o'clock the next afternoon, Susan sits opposite the handsome doctor, who is skimming through her file. He has fair skin, thick brown hair combed back like a TV evangelist.

She is holding her breath.

"Susan, there's a small mass in your left breast," he says. "I don't see anything in your file where you've had any cysts or masses before." He removes his glasses. "Is that correct?"

"Never."

"We'll need an ultrasound," he says, more to himself, frowning. "I'd like to have you go with Rebecca and let me examine you first." Rebecca appears a few seconds later.

"Get Dr. Prescott ready, I want to examine that left breast."

That left breast? That left breast is part of a human being... me.

Susan follows the nurse into the next room. Behind a closed curtain, she takes off her clothes and dresses in a gown that is folded on the seat. When she pulls back the curtain, Rebecca is there to help her onto the examining table. Susan lies under a sheet.

The doctor appears. "You've been through this before," he says. "It won't take long."

She turns her head and closes her eyes as he slides the sheet down to her waist. She can't look into his eyes while he touches her breast. He raises her arm above her head, and begins by moving his fingers in a circular motion covering the entire breast from top to bottom, side to side. He then guides his fingers up and down vertically in rows, as if he were mowing a lawn. He palpates an area she figures contains the mass.

God! Why doesn't he say something?

"Yes, there's something there," he says, squeezing harder this time. He ends by squeezing her nipple. She wants to scream, but bites

155

her lip.

Come on. I need some good news.

He glances at his nurse. "Let's do the ultrasound."

She nods, reaches for something that looks like a tube of tooth paste, and drips the cool gel on Susan's breast, guiding the transducer around the area. When done, she wipes off the liquid and pulls the sheet up over Susan's chest.

"Just lie there, dear," she says. "We'll be with you in a few minutes."

"Can't I sit up?" She looks around. No one is in the room. Susan sits up, holding the sheet against her.

The doctor returns. "Susan, you'll need a needle biopsy. The mass appears to be a cyst and it feels soft, and that's a good sign. Usually, if liquid is drawn from the biopsy it's more likely a cyst. But if they find cells, it could be a tumor."

"Level with me, doctor. Do you think it's malignant?"

"Let's not go there just yet, Susan. Let's stay positive." He leaves.

She falls back, shaking so hard she finds it hard to breathe.

I have cancer, dammit. I know it. Mom, Sabrina, I'm not ready to join you.

Susan has never been this scared. Never. She wasn't this scared when the thugs in the Mercedes shot at her. The past twenty years, she's been losing herself in her work, but expecting this day since she has the same gene that killed her mother and Sabrina.

The nurse enters carrying an envelope and helps Susan down from the table. "These are your instructions," she says, ushering Susan out of the room. "Dr. Abernathy, the surgeon, will perform the biopsy on Monday at nine. Be there at eight, you'll need someone to drive you home."

CHAPTER THIRTY-SIX

Nick is standing by the magazine rack, paging through an issue of *Country Life* that is six months old. He hasn't read a word, just looking at the pictures. He glances at his watch.

Susan should be out by now. It's been over two hours.

The waiting room door swings open and Susan heads to the reception window.

Nick throws the magazine on the table and meets her at the exit.

Outside, she holds his arm as they make it to his red Firebird under a sky loaded with roiling clouds and the rumble of thunder. He opens the passenger door for her. Light rain hits the windshield as he drives off.

When Susan told him about a possible lump in her breast during lunch yesterday, he had remembered his aunt's battle with cancer; especially how his mother had lived with the fear of her sister dying. They tried not to treat his aunt any differently after they got the word, but they couldn't. Women he had met during her chemo told him that the mere thought of breast cancer scared them to death. When they were told they had it, all life jetted from their bodies like water from a fire hose. They walked around for days stunned. His aunt reacted the same way. She thought they'd made a mistake. Maybe they got her tests mixed up with someone else's. God wouldn't let this happen to her. She overcame her denial and battled the cancer with all her strength and through her faith, recited thirty scripture passages every day. She knew she would whip it. And she did.

Nick turns on the wipers and glances over at Susan. She's staring out the window. A few miles down the road, he realizes she's scared to death. Unless he misses his guess, she really wants to talk about

157

it—just like his aunt did when she was facing her fears.

"You okay?" he asks.

"My body's numb and I'm scared to death."

"Care to talk about it?"

A garbage truck grinds past him.

"There's definitely a lump. Could be a cyst or tumor, the doctor said. He's scheduled me for a biopsy on Monday."

Nick doesn't like the sound of that.

Turning back to the window, she says, "My mother and Sabrina had breast cancer."

"Sabrina?"

"My sister—"

"That twin in the picture?"

She nods. "They died."

Whoa. Now he knew the depth of her fear. High risk. "Can we look at the bright side?"

"I'm trying."

"I'd like to go with you on Monday, if you don't mind," he says.

She nods. "I'd really like that."

"How about some place for dinner tonight?"

She shakes her head. "My place? I have steaks. You haven't been there since I tried to tackle that Mercedes."

"I'll cook 'em," he says.

"I'll do the salad."

"Agreed." He pulls the Trans Am next to the curb in front of her complex and turns off the engine.

On the stoop is a man, maybe in his early thirties, dressed in jeans and a jacket to match.

"Who's that?" Nick asks.

"That's my kid brother, Michael," she says. "He showed up at my door a few days ago."

"So that's Michael—the guy who likes the sauce."

"We're working on that. I got him into an alcohol treatment program thanks to you," she says, not getting out of the car. "He's trying real hard."

Nick can relate to family problems. "I have some baggage, too."

"I bet I can guess what that might be."

He smiles. "Forget her. I'm hungry."

They get out. Michael frowns at them.

"Who's this, sis?" Michael asks.

"This is Nick Hunter."

"So you're the cop?" he says.

Nick nods. "I'm guilty."

"Don't like cops."

Nick smiles. "I don't have much of a fan club."

"Let's go inside," Susan says, yanking on Michael's arm. "We need to talk."

Inside, Susan takes Michael down the hall. She whispers something, but Nick can't make out what she's saying. Susan returns, takes some money from her purse, and hands it to Michael. He glances at Nick as he goes past and out the door.

Nick follows Susan into the kitchen. "He's still got a chip on his shoulder."

"He's working on that, too, I think," she says shaking her head, "and he's got his orders to turn his life around, and soon."

"That's a start. Hope he keeps going to that treatment center. They really help."

"I've got rules. If he breaks even one, he's outta here and he knows it."

"Good."

She opens the fridge, takes out the steaks and red wine and hands them to Nick.

"Michael doesn't know about my doctor's appointment, and I don't plan on telling him. Not yet."

"Okay by me." Nick's pager vibrates. "Got a page from my office. Can I use your phone?"

"On the counter."

"What's up, Gladys? He did? That's great."

"Something important?" Susan asks as she's cutting tomatoes for the salad.

"Alliance sheriff found minidarts at the Plummers' place. They were under the fridge."

"That proves—"

Nick interrupts. "Belofsky killed them." He pours their drinks and hands her a glass only a quarter full. "Let's drink to Sheriff Driscoll."

Outside, the rain has picked up. He hopes it isn't a downpour like the last time he was here. Not a word is said between them as he prepares the steaks. Susan seems to have slipped into deep thought again.

Nick breaks the silence. "More wine? It'll take your mind off whatever you're thinking."

She nods. He refills their glasses. Her color is returning, and there's a sparkle in her eye. "Hey, the news could be good," he says as he pulls her to him.

She sets her drink on the counter, and lays her head in the hollow of his shoulder. "I'm working on being brave, and the wine is helping a little."

Nick lifts her chin and kisses her on the lips. They part. It was a good kiss. She kisses him back. Her saucer-size, brown eyes melt his heart. He embraces her again.

She whispers, "I think I'm in love with you."

———— ♦ ————

When Nick gets home there's a message from Kenny on his recorder. Nick glances at his watch. It's only eight o'clock. He should be up.

Margaret answers. He asks for Kenny. She doesn't say a word; instead she calls out to their son.

"Your dad's on the phone."

Nick could hear Kenny running down the steps. "Dad? I was just going to bed. Big game tomorrow, we're playing Cleveland and I'm starting."

"That's really great, son. You take 'em down."

"Wish you could be here, Dad."

"I know. Say, I was thinking about sending you a basketball. It was going to be a surprise, but thought maybe you might want something else—"

"No, Dad. A basketball would be great."

"Okay then."

"Dad? I'd like to come visit you some time."

"Okay. Let me work it out with your mother."

"Gotta go. Love you, Dad."

"Love you, too, son."

CHAPTER THIRTY-SEVEN

Monday morning doesn't arrive fast enough to suit Susan. She arrives at the surgeon's outpatient clinic with Nick around eight to fill out insurance and medical history forms. When she scans down to the living will question on the form, her hand begins to shake. She can't think about death now. Sure the thought has flashed into her mind, but it isn't her time, she keeps telling herself.

The door to the reception area opens, and Susan's name is called. A nurse ushers her into a suite of stalls, tells her to undress and slip on the gown and skid-proof socks. She is tying the strings on the back of the gown when the curtain is pulled back.

"My name is Heather. I'll be taking care of you, Susan," she says, closing the curtain. Please lay down on the recliner." She slaps a cuff on Susan's arm, records her blood pressure, takes her temperature, and fastens a name band around her wrist. She examines Susan's arm for a vein, turns her palm down and presses on the veins in the back of her hand, swabs it with antiseptic solution, opens a packet and removes a needle. "This may sting a little," she says, as she inserts it into Susan's vein. It does more than sting, it hurts.

Susan hears some woman in the next stall crying and wonders if it's fear or bad news. She has the urge to ask Heather about that person, but knows with all the privacy stuff, she wouldn't tell her.

"We're done here," Heather says, as she tapes the needle to her hand. Susan follows her into the surgical suite and is helped onto the table. Two other women are working at the counter. One is reaching for something from the overhead glass cabinet. Next to Susan is a stand with an IV bottle hooked up to a tube. One of the women covers Susan with a warm blanket while the other one connects the IV

161

to the needle in her hand.

Heather injects something into the tubing.

"What's that?"

"Something to make you relax."

The first woman cleans Susan's breast with gauze soaked in a red antiseptic. The sedative is taking effect now, and Susan feels like she has finished off a half-bottle of wine.

The door opens. A tall man in a white jacket moves to her. "Dr. Prescott, I'm Dr. Abernathy. I'll be doing the biopsy."

She fixes her eyes on his stubby fingers, and wonders how he could handle something as delicate as a biopsy needle. She's drunk now, and doesn't care.

Heather hands him a syringe.

"I'm going to deaden the area," he says.

"L-o-c-a-l," she spurts.

He smiles. "I see the sedative's working. You'll feel a little prick."

Yeah, sure, she thinks. *Probably more like a hot poker.* She turns her head and closes her eyes. Barely feels the sting.

"There," he says, dropping the syringe on the tray. "While the local's taking hold, I'll go remove some stitches."

The sedative is making her sleepy. Susan opens her eyes. She must have dozed off. Looking at the ceiling, she listens to the footfalls of the women working across the room. *What time is it?* She turns her head but can't see any wall clock on either side of the room. The door opens and Abernathy ambles over. "Before I begin, I'd like to explain the procedure."

Susan receives some encouraging news. Abernathy tells her that most breast biopsies reveal no signs of cancer, and that this procedure is the least invasive. He will direct a very thin needle into the lump and draw out a sample. Abernathy adds that it will help him to distinguish between a liquid-filled sac—a cyst—and a tumor.

"We're expecting the best," he says. He nods to the nurse, who hands him the instrument.

His soft voice puts her at ease. She closes her eyes. *Go to it.* Her head is pleasantly spinning, and the way she feels now, he could take her arm off and she wouldn't care.

Think about the time Alec and I flew to Maui—swimming in water clear as champagne. Best week of my life—nothing but peace and quiet—so spiritual. I had that experience only once before, when Sabrina and I were in church with Mom and Dad during a Christmas Eve service.

"We're done," the doctor says. "Just lie there for a few minutes."

Maybe Nick and I could go to Maui.

One of the women helps Susan up and Heather takes her back to the pre-op room. "You can sit in the chair, and wait until you feel like it, then get dressed. Can I bring you something to drink?"

"I'm good."

After dressing, Susan is ushered into the next room, where Dr. Abernathy is sitting at his desk.

Susan settles into a chair facing him, and Heather stands nearby.

"How are you feeling?" Abernathy asks.

"Dizzy," she says.

"I want you to rest for the next twenty-four hours." His eyes go to the ceiling. "This is Monday. I'll call you Friday morning. The results should be in from path."

Four days!

She has to ask, "How does it look, doctor?"

"Hard to say."

"Oh, come on. You've seen my mammogram and ultrasound. From your experience, what are my odds?" she says, voice rising.

He frowns. "Better than fifty-fifty."

"I could have guessed that myself, Doctor," she says.

Abernathy leans in to his desk. "There isn't much more I can tell you. You're a doctor. You know that."

Bullshit. You know more than you're telling me.

Heather takes Susan to the waiting room and leaves her at the front desk. The receptionist smiles, "Dr. Prescott, your friend over there," she nods in the direction where Nick is, "has been pacing the floor for over an hour. I think that's sweet."

Susan drifts over to Nick. He is sitting down now, rapidly turning pages in a magazine.

He jumps up. "How'd it go?"

"Won't know anything until Friday."

"Your eyes look glassy."

"Sedative. It's starting to wear off."

Nick takes her by the arm and escorts her outside. The sun is behind the clouds. She's got a knot in her stomach. They drive off.

On the way home, she watches the road, trees passing swiftly, just like her life. What's in her future? She's in love with the man sitting behind the wheel, driving her home like they were already married. What if she has cancer and needs a mastectomy—maybe both breasts—would he still want her?

Dammit, Mom and Sabrina, tell me it's not my time.

Nick doesn't say a word until he guides the Firebird into a spot in front of her apartment.

"Once I get you to the door, I'll head to the station," he says. "You'll need to rest."

"Doc says that I need to take it easy for the next twenty four." She reaches for the door handle, and is half-way out when she turns to him.

"I've been thinking," she says. "If the results turn out bad, I'll need my dad."

CHAPTER THIRTY-EIGHT

After resting for twenty-four hours, Susan is eager this Wednesday morning to get back into the lab. She believes it will be the best way to keep her mind off this Friday. In the passenger seat is Michael, and they haven't said a word. She guides the Camry into her parking space and turns off the ignition.

"Here are the keys," she says, turning to her brother. "Make that meeting with your counselor and look for a job, and don't wreck this car. I don't own it. Be back at the apartment by five, and call and leave me a message the minute you get there. I'll let you know when to pick me up. Okay?"

He nods.

She climbs out. The early morning wind blows through her hair as she heads to the Path building. Inside, she hurries to the staging area. Her team is already in the Hot Zone, sequencing the DNA base-pair fragments from the spaghetti virus taken from Robin and the Plummers. Susan wriggles into the Blue Suit, pulls the helmet over her head, and after seven minutes in the chemical shower dries off and steps into the Level-4. She plugs into an air hose, and shuffles past the animal room, carrying Alec's journal. She never thought about it before, but today she feels claustrophobic.

She had planned to read the rabbit experiment Alec had been working on, but forgot about it when she'd had her cancer scare. She lumbers into the lab and sits with his notebook on her lap, stares at it for a few minutes, feeling the sadness returning. *He's gone. Really gone.*

She opens Alec's journal to the last entry—the day Alec was killed. He had injected Tican into rabbits three weeks before and was waiting to determine if there were any ill effects from the virus. She reads the methodology and turns to the results section. In the middle of the page is an unfinished sentence.

After 21 days Tican....

Alec was beginning this sentence when he was shot. She quickly turns back and rereads his entries. What was he going to write about Tican? Did it kill the rabbits? And where are they? She shuffles into the necropsy room, opens the freezer. A wisp of condensation curls out. She waves to scatter the fog. On the shelf are three rabbits wrapped in plastic with Alec's markings. She can barely see them, takes the top one to the autopsy table, removes the covering, and places the animal under a heat lamp. Thick gloves make it difficult for her to work. An incision is made down the abdominal wall, the opening is stretched, and the organs removed. Liver, pancreas and kidneys look good, and the intestines and heart are unaffected. The skull is split and the brain examined. Adrenaline courses through Susan's veins and her pulse begins racing. The rabbit's brain and lungs look like glue. And the eyes are gone.

For the next ten hours, she sections muscle tissue for the electron microscope while her co-workers separate the virus from the rabbit's blood for genetic analysis.

Back in the Level-3, sitting in scrubs at the main computer, Susan opens the micrograph file for Tican to compare it with the new virus. Tican appears on a split screen as a sausage-shaped virus. She punches another key and the photograph of the spaghetti-shaped virus taken from Robin and the Plummers appears next to it. She taps several keys and waits for the latest picture of the virus taken from the rabbit, and wonders what shape it will have.

Here it comes.

A horizontal line first appears and begins expanding vertically. Susan's breath catches as the image of the virus taken from the rabbit inches its way up the screen.

It's a replica of that spaghetti virus taken from Robin and the Plummers.

Oh, no. Her fingers race on the keyboard to bring up the spaghetti virus' DNA base-pairs and those of Tican.

A band of pain shoots around her head as she stares at both images.

Ohmigod, Ohmigod! What have I done?

She jumps up and darts out of the room.

CHAPTER THIRTY-NINE

Susan rushes to her office, throws the file on her desk, and flops in her chair. What a mess she has made with her life. Shameful. She has allowed herself to become so entwined with the fear of cancer that she became vulnerable. How could she be so naive? Her heart is breaking. She can't go into rewind and correct for past mistakes, but now she can make things right by finding a way to neutralize her nemesis, Tican.

She glances at the desk clock. Nine p.m. She has forgotten about Michael. She reaches for the phone and calls him. No answer. She breaks the circuit and dials Gerber.

Please be there, Karl.

"Gerber," he says.

"I have to see you right away."

"I was just heading out the door," he says, sounding irritated.

"It's urgent. I must see you, now!"

"Make it fast," he says.

Telling Gerber is the last thing she wants to do. She slams the phone on its base, reaches for her coat, and steps out of her building with the research file under her arm. She races through the shadows to the admin building.

Gerber is at his desk when she enters. The file is shaking in her hand.

"Sit down, you're jumpy," he says. He pushes his chair back and rounds the desk and sits next to her. "Now, what's this all about?"

"Bad news, Karl. Bad news." Her head is throbbing.

His eyes widen. "Cancer? You've got breast cancer?"

She held up a hand. "No, no, not that," she says in frustration.

They had talked about her family history of breast cancer, but he couldn't have known about her recent tests.

"Then what?"

"Tican turns deadly."

His body jerks forward. "What the hell do you mean, *deadly*?"

"It mutates into a biological."

Gerber looks as though someone had kicked him in the stomach. "There was no hint of mutation in your data."

"I know. I know." She hands him the file, jumps up and paces across the room like a tiger in its cage. "Just discovered it in Alec's work. Look for yourself." She stops in front of him, waiting for the shoe to drop.

He studies the photographs and the genetic data.

"Alec had injected Tican into rabbits," she says. "After twenty-one days, it mutates into a virus that looks like spaghetti. I've labeled it M for mutant, and X for unknown." She sighs. "It's identical to the virus found in Robin and the Plummers. Tican's the original virus!"

He hurls the folder across the room. Papers land everywhere. "Son-of-a-bitch."

"The autopsy confirms that MX attacks the brain and lungs," she says. "Even the eyes."

Karl shoots to his feet, brushes by her and stares at the picture of himself on the wall shaking hands with CDC bigwigs, accepting an award for his work on the Ebola virus a decade ago.

He turns and scowls at her. "You know what you've done?"

She nods. "I've helped Vladimir bring a biological into this country. I'm sorry."

He throws up his hands. "I mean, do you know what you've done to *me*? I supported you and that damn Russian." He shakes his head. "The Director will have my ass. And what about Harry? He'll kill me."

"I'm sorry, Karl."

"Stop saying you're sorry. You're like everyone else in this fuckin' place—only think of yourselves." He paces, arms crossed in front of him.

As if you are any different, you narcissistic jerk.

His face turns crimson, and his eyes shoot darts at her. She has never seen him this angry.

"God knows what Vladimir's going to do with his virus." he says. "Many lives could be at stake."

"I know, that's what's haunting me."

"Did Vladimir at any time ever mention an antiserum?" Gerber asks, heading to his desk.

"No. Why would he? He promoted Tican as a cancer drug."

"I thought maybe I could appease the Director if we had one." Gerber flops in his chair.

"Not a bad idea, Karl. Whatta you think about me reassigning my projects, and working full-time on the antidote?"

He nods, seemingly taking some comfort in the idea. "That would help, wouldn't it?"

"So you approve?"

"Yeah, yeah. That'd be okay. Go to it."

"Great. I'll begin tomorrow. Are you going to report my finding to the Director?" she says, moving to her seat.

Gerber's face turns ashen. His eyes are glued to the floor.

"Are you—?"

"I'll handle it."

She jumps up. "Karl?"

"I said I'd take care of it. Now leave me alone."

At the door, she hesitates before opening it. "I know you don't want to hear it, but I'm really sorry, Karl." She leaves. Back in her office, Susan tries to reach Michael again. No answer. She calls a cab.

--------◆--------

Gerber waits until Susan has closed the door. He frantically dials the number for Leopold's lounge. Surely Vladimir wouldn't have developed such a horrible thing without an antiserum.

Morelli answers.

"This is Gerber. Get a message to him. It's urgent. Have him call me."

"Not in town."

"If I don't reach him someone close to me is going to die." Gerber's heart nearly explodes in his chest when he thinks about Eva. "Tell him I need the antiserum. I'll pay whatever he wants." His hand is shaking so hard he nearly drops the phone.

Morelli hangs up.

Gerber dials his brother-in-law, Harry Wentworth.

"Hello."

"This is Karl. It's urgent we talk."

"I have nothing to say to you."

"I'd reconsider if I were you. There's a good chance your ass could end up in prison."

169

CHAPTER FORTY

Nick is chugging a beer, watching the Colts battle the New England Patriots when Susan calls. He mutes the TV.

"Glad you're up," she says in a whimper. "I've got bad news."

She's crying.

Nick is holding his breath. Surely she couldn't have received any bad news from the doctor this soon. "You haven't heard from the doctor, have you?" he asks.

"No, no. It's about Tican. An hour ago, I discovered... it... it mutates into a deadly biological."

A car door slams somewhere outside.

"You mean it changes just sitting around?" Nick asks.

"No, no."

Nick realizes he's frustrating her with his questions.

"It has to invade the body first, and in twenty-one days it changes."

"Is the damn thing contagious?"

"No, but you saw what it did to Robin."

"So that's why the guys in the Mercedes were after you? They wanted you dead before you learned about the mutation."

"'Fraid so," she says.

"So, Tican killed the Plummers, too," he says.

"Yeah, but I'm going nuts wondering what Vladimir's going to do with it."

"It won't be good. I can tell you that much," Nick says.

"There could be hundreds of victims out there," she says. Susan clears her nose with a loud sniff. "I'll be responsible for their deaths, and it scares the hell out of me."

"Belofsky's our man. Vladimir's ego is too big to do the dirty work.

What are your plans now?"

"I've cleared my desk and Gerber's authorized me to work on the antidote, but it'll be a challenge with all my samples gone."

"Have any theories?"

"I'm concentrating on the mutant, which I'm calling MX."

"I'll get the FBI in this and we'll go after Belofsky. I'll be in touch," he says, and hangs up. He releases the remote, watches the last few seconds of the game, and finishes his beer. Then he calls his FBI friend, Harlan Kennedy.

"I know it's late, but I got something," Nick says. "Remember our conversation about the elderly couple in Nebraska—the Plummers?"

"Sure," Harlan says.

"Vladimir Sokolov. Does that name ring a bell?"

He didn't answer.

A. Jaye's FBI's database search has revealed that Belofsky is wanted for killing two New Jersey mobsters, and Sokolov's file is marked for FBI eyes only.

"Belofsky killed the old couple," Nick says. "And Sokolov's the brains. I just wish I knew what they're up to."

"Got evidence that ties them together?" Harlan asks.

"Sure do. Susan Prescott at the CDC just called me. She's discovered that Sokolov's drug turns out to be deadly. A biological. Takes twenty-one days, though. That ties Sokolov to Belofsky, who used the virus to kill the Plummers."

"Is it contagious?"

"The Plummers lived with it in 'em for three weeks, and no other deaths were reported."

"Then there's no immediate danger to the American public."

Nicks pager vibrates. "Oh, shit." *Margaret's paging me.*

"What?" Harlan says.

"Nothing. Go on."

Harlan explains. During their efforts to dismantle the organized crime enterprises, the FBI has uncovered a Russian plot to move in on the mob's drug and prostitution rings in the east and then in the central U.S.

"They're probably going to use the virus to kill them," Harlan says.

"Maybe. But I'm not totally sold on that."

"Lemme have it?"

"Belofsky wasn't after the senator's parents."

"Who then?"

"Makes sense that Belofsky wanted to knock off their son, the senator," Nick says. "The Russian's interest in the mob's business has to be a cover. The Plummers weren't part of the mob."

"Sounds good. But I must have something hot to go to the Director. Find out more and get back to me."

Click.

Nick calls Susan. "Sorry, were you asleep?"

"Nope," she said, "too much on my mind."

"I have news from Harlan about Tican. He's got evidence that Sokolov's going to use the virus on the mob. So the danger may not be as bad as you think."

"You don't sound convinced," she says.

"I don't quite buy it, but Harlan seems pretty confident." Nick fills her in on the details, but the whole time he's talking, he realizes Susan hasn't said a word.

"What's wrong?"

"It's after eleven, and Michael hasn't come home, and he has my car."

Double trouble. "You want me to come over?

"No."

CHAPTER FORTY-ONE

Susan is sipping a low fat, half-caff in Starbucks this cold December morning. When she got home two nights ago, the Camry and Michael were gone, and he had taken sixty dollars from her dresser drawer.

The past two days have been rough, even without the Michael drama. She can't shake the anxiety and the thoughts of her mother and Sabrina since the biopsy. Sabrina had gotten sick and fallen into a deep sleep and never awoke. She looked so peaceful lying there. Death could be a truly blissful state where the soul begins its journey to the other side. Someday she'd find out, but not now.

Today she will get her results. *Mom, I'm scared.*

A screaming child at the next table rouses Susan from her thoughts. She drinks the last of her coffee and turns to the entrance, wondering if the man who'd just walked in is married, and if his wife is healthy.

Get hold of yourself.

She heads out to the rented Ford Taurus. Her pager vibrates. She grabs the car phone and punches in the numbers. Her throat tightens.

"This is Susan Prescott," she says.

"Hold for Dr. Abernathy."

She stops at the light. Her heart thuds against her ribs.

"Dr. Prescott, this is Dr. Abernathy."

It's spread all through me....

The light changes, and she speeds through the intersection.

I'll need chemo and will die in the end.

"Your mass is benign."

She hears his voice as if it came through a tunnel.

"Susan! Did you hear me? It's *benign*. You're okay."

"Are you sure?"

Oh, how dumb. Dumb. And alive.

"Trust me! You're fine. Your primary care doc wants to see you in six months."

Click.

It rolls over her like a tsunami.

She pulls over to the curb.

And bawls.

———— ◆ ————

Nick arrives at headquarters and strolls towards his office. Two officers are at the elevator with a man in his thirties in handcuffs between them. It's Michael. He's pretty banged up.

One of the officers says, "How you doin', Nick?"

"Morning, Stone," Nick says.

Michael's shirt is ripped and hanging over his belt, his eye is purple and swollen shut. He has scratches on one cheek, and his arm is in a sling.

"What happened to this guy?"

"Dipshit's name is Michael Prescott," the second cop says. "He's drunk, totaled a Camry he says is his sister's rental. Hit a tree."

Michael's eyes are fixed on the floor. Blood has streaked and caked on his forehead.

"I know him," Nick says.

Stone frowns. "Friend of yours?"

"I know his sister. She's Dr. Susan Prescott at the CDC."

Stone's brow rises. "Sounds like an important person."

"She's been worried about him. Didn't come home last night."

The other cop says, "He's been in the ER. We're booking him on DUI, resisting arrest and assaulting an officer. Me."

Nick smells booze on Michael.

The elevator doors open and Michael is escorted inside.

"Seeya," Nick says, hurrying to his office.

Gladys calls out. "Your son's called twice."

"I'll get to him. Don't worry."

"Please do. The poor kid seemed pretty upset."

Nick closes his door and flops at his desk. He studies the phone, wondering what Margaret has put Kenny up to this time. He makes the call.

Kenny answers.

"You okay, son?"

"You forgot again, Dad."

"What?"

"The basketball? You promised."

Damn! "I'm really sorry. I've been so busy—"

"You're always busy. You don't care about me."

Nick hears Margaret in the background urging Kenny to ask for money. After two years of marriage, the snooty bitch had thought Nick was nothing but a dumb cop. She turned lazy on him and spent money like he was the commissioner.

"I do care, Kenny. I'll put it in the mail this weekend."

There's silence.

Through the closed door, Nick can hear phones ringing and detectives' voices in the homicide unit.

"Kenny?"

"You always say that, Dad."

"I'm doing my best, son. I promise I'll send it."

"Can I come and live with you, Dad? Please. Mom doesn't make pancakes."

"You know I'd like nothing better, but I'm gone a lot. For now you need to stay with your mother."

"But, Dad, she won't let me hang out with the guys. My friends are makin' fun of me."

"I'll talk to her."

Silence on the other end. "Son?"

Nick hears muffled crying. "Kenny, listen to me. Maybe you can come in a week or so. Okay?"

No response.

"I know you can hear me. I love you."

Click.

Nick stares at the wall. Good fathers don't forget about their sons the way he does. Maybe he isn't cut out to be a dad. Margaret would certainly agree. He should have never married.

Nick glances at the door. He's lucky to have Gladys and A. Jaye. They are his family. And now Susan means more to him than anyone, except maybe Kenny. He had promised himself after Margaret left he wouldn't get involved again with another woman. But his heart has betrayed him. *I love her. There, I said it.*

He's been worrying about Susan. They'd beat the cancer together if she has it. He's read where there are better treatments today. Even if she had to have her breasts removed, he'd still love her.

He sighs. The phone rings and he answers it on the third ring.

It's Susan. He feels his heart racing and he's holding his breath.

"Good news," Susan says.

Nick's muscles relax.

"My tumor is benign."

"Benign. That means good, right?"

"Yeah, of course. Isn't that great?"

"The best news I've heard in a long time. I've really been worried about you."

"You're sweet."

"We'll have to celebrate," he says, "but right now I hate to dampen your spirits, but—"

She interrupts him. "It's about Michael, isn't it?"

"Two cops brought him in thirty minutes ago."

"Oh, no." He could hear her strong sigh. "Is he okay?"

"He's drunk, banged up from hitting a tree... your Camry's totaled. He was treated in the ER, but he's okay."

"Thank God! I'm on my way."

"Do you have transportation?"

"I've got another rental."

Nick waits thirty minutes, then heads to the lobby. Susan rushes through the door and meets him at the elevator.

"Where's that no good son-of-a-bitch?"

"Upstairs."

They ride to the second floor. Nick steps out first. An officer with a round face and crew cut is sitting behind a desk in the middle of the room.

"Hey, Nick," the sergeant says.

"What's up, Sarge?"

He shrugs. "Same-old, same-old."

"We're here to see Michael Prescott," Nick says. "This is his sister, Susan."

"Uniforms brought him in an hour ago," Sarge says. "Cap wants to see ya first. You know the way," he says, hitching his head to the right.

"What's this about?" Nick says.

Sarge shrugs. "Beats me. Just told me to tell ya."

Nick and Susan stop at the first door on the left. He taps on it. A voice calls out for them to come in.

The big man behind the desk doesn't get up. Captain Duffy looks like a wrestler, has muscular arms and no neck to speak off, big chest. He's mean as hell, but Nick heard from Sarge that the Cap likes Nick because he isn't intimidated by anyone.

"You wanted to see me, Cap? This is Dr. Prescott."

Duffy nods. "Take a seat."

"I understand Prescott hasn't been booked yet," Nick says.

"That's right." He frowns at Susan. "Seems your father has friends in high places."

He turns to Nick. "Got a call from the Chief who got a call from the Commish."

"Does that mean Michael won't be charged?" Susan says.

"That's exactly what it means, Doctor." He reaches for the phone. "Detective Hunter and Dr. Prescott are coming to take Prescott." He stands up and looks at Nick. "You know the drill."

Nick nods his thanks.

Susan rises. "Thank you, sir."

"Another thing," Duffy says, scowling at Susan, "I don't want to see your brother in here again."

Cap is pissed. Nick doesn't blame him. Nick wouldn't like anyone going over his head, either.

"You won't," Susan says.

Susan storms out of police headquarter and darts into the parking lot with Nick and Michael in tow. She hasn't said a word since Michael's release. Somehow this thirty-two-year-old child has become her responsibility. *Sweet Dumplin*—the name their Mother had called him—has turned into a monster. Through the years, Susan has tried to talk to him. He just keeps saying she'd never understand. He's right. She doesn't.

When they arrive at the parked Ford Taurus, she asks Nick to drive.

Susan opens the back door, socks and kicks and shoves Michael into the back seat.

"Don't say a word," she says and slams the door shut. She gets in next to Nick. His frown tells her he wants to know, what next? She tells him to head to the bus station downtown.

Susan turns and faces Michael. "Empty your pockets. I want to see how much you have left of the sixty dollars you stole from me."

Ten dollar bills fall on the seat. "I got fifty."

"Well you're going to need it. I'm buying you a ticket home. I want you on that bus, and I never want to see your face here again."

CHAPTER FORTY-TWO

Dr. Lance Sterling carries Agatha's chart into her room. Agatha Boxer, an eighty-year-old with terminal breast cancer, was inoculated with the Kraft virus eighteen days earlier and now shows marked improvement.

"You're cheerful today, Agatha," Sterling says.

In a hospital gown, her thin frame turns away from the nurse who is seating her in a leather chair, and Agatha smiles. "You bet. I'm going to watch Days of Our Lives. Want to join me?"

"Thank you. I'll pass."

Sterling pages through her chart.

"She's doing very well," the nurse says. "It's amazing."

"That's what we want to hear." .

"Oh, doctor. I nearly forgot. Mrs. Boxer has been complaining about a little pain in her chest and a cough."

"How about the others?"

"No, just her."

"I'd like to listen to your chest, Agatha." The nurse mutes the TV, opens Agatha's robe, and unties her gown. Sterling pulls the stethoscope from around his neck and listens to her chest.

Agatha, focuses on the TV, says, "Hurry, doctor, this's the best part. That hunk's going to hop her."

"Take several deep breaths and exhale slowly. Again. Thank you, everything sounds good. We'll keep an eye on you, Agatha."

She nods.

"She's got a little congestion, nurse. Give her some Tylenol and Sterling's cocktail."

"Yes, doctor."

He leaves and meets the head nurse hurrying towards him. "You have an urgent call from Mr. Wentworth, doctor. Line one."

"I'll take it in my office."

Sterling settles in behind his desk, lifts the phone and pushes the blinking button. "Got good news for you, Harry, the patients on Tican are doing great." He moves a stale cup of coffee to one side. Sterling hears Harry's heavy breathing. "Harry? Did you hear what I said? Tican's working."

"Terrible news," Harry says. "Terrible." He snorts. "We're about to be crushed by an avalanche."

"What the hell are you talking about?"

"Not on the phone. I'll be there in fifteen minutes. Meet me outside."

"I have patients—"

"The hell with them! Do you want to go to prison?"

Click.

Sterling sighs. It has to be about Tican.

Outside, Sterling watches as Harry's Ferrari squeals to a stop next to him. He darts around the front, opens the passenger door and slides into the seat.

"What the hell's going on?" he says.

Harry tears out of the parking lot without answering, face blazing with anger. Two blocks down, he stops for the light, reaches for a tissue and wipes his forehead. "Tican's a hoax."

"What? Didn't you hear me on the phone? My patients are doing well."

"Got the news a few minutes ago from Karl. Susan Prescott has found that Tican mutates after twenty-one days." Harry burns rubber when the light changes. "Karl's sending Prescott's data to my office for us to examine. It should be there by now." He pauses to catch his breath. "The mutant attacks the brain, lungs and eyes in minutes. Minutes!"

"Hold on. I don't believe this."

Harry swerves to avoid a pedestrian.

"Slow down! You're going to kill someone."

"It's been what, sixteen days since the injections?" Harry asks.

"Eighteen."

Harry shakes his head. "We've only got three days."

"For what?"

"What the hell do you think? To get rid of the patients before they die horrible deaths."

"Are you crazy?"

Sterling remembers Agatha's slight cough and the hurting in her chest.

Harry zooms around the corner. "How else are we going to get out of this?"

"Being rattled won't help," Sterling says. "Let me think for a moment."

Harry races past two cars, swings into Kraft's parking lot and into his space.

"I have an idea," Sterling says.

"It better be good." Harry kills the engine.

"If the patients do die, we'll say they didn't respond to the treatment... happens all the time. Remember, they're terminal."

"But Karl says they'd vomit blood, eyes will pop out, and brains will come out of their noses."

"If we see any of that happening, we'll clean them up and cremate them."

A grin crosses Harry's face. "Now that's a plan. What about their families and your staff?"

"I can handle them." He notices the dubious look on Harry's face. "Hey, *you* worry too much. If someone reports us, I'll tell the authorities we followed protocol using data provided by the renowned CDC. Dr. Prescott's studies would confirm that Tican has anticancer properties."

"Would they buy it?"

"Who would question the CDC?"

"Thank, God!" Harry says. "You're a genius."

Karl Gerber tosses most of the night. At dawn he bolts out of bed. Guilt weighs on him like an anvil. He dresses and rushes through the hallway. Gold-framed pictures of the Kraft dynasty—his wife's treasures—hang on the walls.

Gerber glances at Eva's door. If he doesn't hear from Belofsky soon, Eva will be dead in twenty-four hours. He darts down the curved stairs and dashes into the kitchen where Isabella pours him hazelnut coffee. Gerber grabs the cup, hurries to his study, and sits at his desk, willing the phone to ring. It's nine o'clock.

He takes several drinks, sets the cup on his desk. Lays his head down. Ten minutes later, the phone rings. He grabs it.

"Yes."

"Morelli said you want antiserum."

Gerber knew the voice. "I must have it. My wife is dying."

"Five hundred thousand."

"Okay. When?"

"When you get money?"

"I can have it in a few hours."

"Good," Belofsky says.

"And don't fuck with me, Belofsky. I want the real thing." A pain shoots across Gerber's chest.

"Take it or leave it."

"Where do we meet?" Gerber asks.

"Morelli's. Deliver the money to him."

"What time?"

"Twelve."

Click.

Gerber takes a drive to clear his head. He has to get the money, but there is something he has to do first. He spots a telephone booth outside a supermarket and wheels the Silver Infinity up to it. He can't use his car phone. The cops can trace his calls.

A security car with its yellow light blinking goes past.

Gerber lifts the phone. "Atlanta PD," answers the man on the other end.

Gerber hesitated.

"This *is* Atlanta PD," the officer says again.

"Detective Hunter, please." His voice cracks.

There is silence. "I'll transfer you to homicide."

"Homicide."

"Detective Hunter, please."

"He's not in yet."

"Can I leave a message?"

"What is it?"

There would be no way this call could be traced, but Gerber isn't sure. Must hurry.

"Tell him that Belofsky—the man he's looking for—may be at Leopold's lounge at noon today."

"Spell that name," the detective says.

"That's B-e-l-o-f-s-k-y."

"Your name?"

"Just make sure he gets it." Gerber hangs up.

CHAPTER FORTY-THREE

Nick Hunter is behind the wheel of the unmarked cruiser drinking a vanilla latte, the only guy in homicide who likes gourmet coffee. The late-morning December sun is high in the sky, shimmering off the hood. Nick has received an anonymous tip that Belofsky might be coming to Leopold's at noon. A. Jaye is sitting next to Nick. They watch from across the street.

"There's somethin'," Nick says. They lean back in their seats so not to be noticed. A white Honda Civic stops in front. Big guy gets out clutching a package, opens the doors for two cuties, a blonde and a redhead.

"That's not Belofsky," Nick says.

"Probably one of his goons," A. Jaye says. "Ready?"

"Give 'em a minute." Nick says.

"Oh-oh, looky there," his partner says. "There's Gerber."

"What the hell is he doing here?" Nick says. He consumes the last of his coffee. "Gerber has that package the goon carried in." Gerber hustles to his car and speeds off.

"Sure is in a rush."

"Something's gone down. Let's go," Nick says.

They dart across the street.

Inside, the big guy is at the bar with the babes.

The swarthy man, large around the middle and bald, sets two beers in front of the gals and ambles over to Nick. "Can I help you guys?"

"Detective Hunter," Nick says, holding up his ID, "and that's Detective Chandler. We're Atlanta P.D., Homicide."

"Whattayu want?"

"What's your name?" Nick asks.

"Morelli, I own the joint."

Nick moves to the big Russian sitting next to the redhead, and A. Jaye lingers behind the ladies, who are drinking beer from tall glasses. Morelli drifts down the bar.

The blonde swivels on the stool, spilling her drink. The redhead is puffing on a cig, watching TV. Their escort downs the last of his vodka. Morelli hurries over to refill it.

"What you want?" the big guy says to Nick.

"To ask you a couple of questions," Nick says, staring into his blue eyes. The Russian's wearing a black turtle-neck sweater and slacks to match, and he makes two of Nick. "What's your name?"

"Stanislavski."

At the end of the bar, Morelli switches channels and stops on the news.

"Let's see some ID," Nick says.

The big man pulls out his wallet, takes out a card and hands it to Nick.

"International driver's license?"

Stanislavski nods.

"You're a Russian citizen?"

"Yah."

Nick shouts to Morelli. "Are you deaf? Turn the sound down."

"Let me see your passport." Nick says to the Russian.

"Back in the room," he says.

A. Jaye raises his brow, indicating that Stanislavski's lying.

"You know Dmitry Belofsky?" Nick says.

"Yah."

"You his bodyguard?"

"His driver. You going to take me to station and kick shit out of me?"

"Don't tempt me. You came in with a box and a man walked out with it. What was in it?"

He shrugs as he drinks his vodka.

"Drugs?" Nick asks.

"Don't know."

"You sweethearts know anything about that box?" A. Jaye says.

The redhead says, "We don't know nut'in." She blows smoke in his face. The blonde swallows a mouthful of beer and keeps her eyes fixed on the TV.

"I'll need your names and addresses," A. Jaye says. "You ladies need a ride?"

"That's my Honda out there," the blonde says. "We're staying."

"Suit yourself," he says.

Nick nods to his partner, reaches for the Russian's arm. "You're going with us."

He stands and Nick steps back.

They lead the giant outside to the patrol car.

At the Peachtree Station, Nick guides Stanislavski into an interrogation room. Once he's seated at the table, Nick sits across from him and A. Jaye leans against the wall.

"You know Vladimir Sokolov?" Nick asks.

The big guy's eyes widens, he shakes his head.

You're a lying bastard.

"Where's Belofsky?" Nick flips open his notebook, takes a pen from his shirt pocket.

The Russian says nothing.

"One more time. Where'd Belofsky go, and what was in that box?"

Nick leans over the table, locks on his stare. "Either you talk or your ass rots in jail."

"I got all time in world. You don't know Russians."

Nick consulted his notebook. "Let's see: fake ID, dealing in drugs, no passport, resisting arrest, assaulting an officer, refusing to answer questions. You'll be with us a long time." Nick is stretching it, but he's banking on the Russian not knowing anything about police procedures.

"Okay. Have it your way." Nick gets up.

A. Jaye says, "I'll take the tub of shit and put him in a cell."

———— ◆ ————

Five the next morning, Nick is awakened out of a deep sleep. He reaches for the phone by the bed. "What is it?"

The officer on the other end says: "That Russian wants to see you right away. He says it's important."

Maybe the big guy's had a change of heart.

Nick parks the Firebird, hops out and goes into the precinct. On the first floor, he stops for coffee, fills it with milk, drinks half of it, and calls A. Jaye at home. "Stanislavski's going to sing."

"I'm on my way."

Nick finishes his coffee. What is it the goon said: *You don't know Russians?* He sure the hell is wrong about that. Nick has hated them since the Cold War. And now he hates them even more since the fall of Communism. Some things haven't changed. The murderous KGB/Mafia is ruthless, and they still fill many unmarked graves. *I know you damn Russians.*

Nick fills his cup again and waits at the elevator for A. Jaye. He shows up ten minutes later and they take the elevator to the second floor. Nick tells the guard to open the cell. Inside Stanislavski is covered with yellow light, bent over on the edge of a metal-framed bed with his hands between his legs. The only other things inside the cell are a stainless steel commode and a bulb hanging from a single cord.

He looks up.

"This better be good," Nick says. "Whaddayu want?"

"Talk now."

"Let's have it."

"Belofsky went to Washington."

"Why?"

"To meet Bear."

"Who's the Bear?"

"Sokolov."

"Vladimir Sokolov?"

"Yah."

"No surprise there," A. Jaye says.

Outside, thunder crackles.

"What are they doing in DC?"

"Business."

"What kind of business?"

"Bear brings Russian girls to America, little ones, big ones."

Telling Mafia secrets means the Bear would have Stanislavski's head.

"How about drugs?" Nick could barely see him nod.

"Yah."

Snoring comes from the next cell.

"What's Belofsky going to do with those darts?"

"Bad." Then he jabs at his neck.

"Does he use darts to kill people?"

He nods. "Yah, kill."

Nick thinks about the holes in the Plummers.

"So, who are they going to kill?"

"Big people."

"You mean government people?"

"Yah."

"Got some names?"

"Don't have names."

Nick stares at him, thinking Belofsky is smart enough not to tell his driver.

"Anything else I should know?"

Stanislavski sighs and shakes his head.

"Don't forget, Nick, Belofsky is wanted for killing two Mafia brothers in New Jersey," A. Jaye says.

"Thanks." Nick turns to the Russian. "Are they going to kill Mafiosi, too?"

"He no tell me."

"You took a box into Leopold's. Who is the man you gave it to?"

"Belofsky say give package to Morelli."

Nick wonders about Gerber. Is he in organized crime? And were the Plummers dealing drugs? Something isn't kosher.

"Why are you telling me all this now?" Nick asks.

"You help me stay in U.S. where Belofsky no find me."

"I'll think about it. But you know the Mafia will track you down sooner or later."

His eyes widened and he sits back down on the bed, head lowered.

Nick calls out to the guard. "Open her up, we're done here."

Back on the first floor, he and A. Jaye stroll down the hall to the cubicles.

"Did you notice that one of his fingers was clipped off at the first joint?" A. Jaye says.

"Yeah," Nick says. "You screw up in the Mafia and a finger is lopped off. Screw up again and you could lose an ear, or end up in an unmarked grave."

"I'll check out Morelli in our database," his partner says. "The guy says Sokolov's selling girls to the mob. He's probably into drugs, too."

"They go together," Nick says.

Gladys shouted, "Nick? Guess what?"

"What?"

"Your ex is on the line!"

"She never calls me this early. Tell you what; send it to my voice mail." He turns back to his partner. "They could be planning to muscle in on the mob, but my gut's telling me that's not the reason they're in D.C.," Nick says.

"Got something here on Morelli," A. Jaye says scrolling in the computer. "He has a couple of arrests for bookmaking. Just a small-time crook."

"We'll pay him a visit after lunch," Nick says.

———◆———

Nick and A. Jaye enter Leopold's around two in the afternoon. Morelli, the owner, is working the register receipts behind the bar. A middle-aged man and woman are at a table watching the football game, eating nuts and drinking beer.

Morelli's taking money from the register then puts it in a bag and places it in the drawer. He hurries, but not before he turns and scowls at Nick and A. Jaye. "Whatta you dicks want?" he says. "You guys aren't going to be a thorn in my side, are you?"

"That depends on how much you cooperate with us," Nick says.

A. Jaye goes to the back, opens the corner door and disappears.

"On what?" Morelli asks.

"Whatta you got in the back?"

Morelli's hand shakes as he takes a Camel and lights it.

He's definitely hiding something, Nick thinks.

A. Jaye returns, and says to Nick. "There's a big lock on a room behind the partition in the back." Both men turn to Morelli. "You taking bets, Morelli?" Nick asks.

Morelli looks like he's seen a ghost.

"Well," Nick says. "Guess we'll have to call that in."

"Listen," Morelli says. "Give me a break, detectives. I haven't taken a bet in months."

"We're homicide," Nick says. "Don't care about your business in the back. We'll let it ride if you tell us what we want to know."

"Sure. Whatta you want?" He looks at A. Jaye and back to Nick. "See, I'm ready to cooperate."

"Tell us why Dmitry Belofsky uses this place," A. Jaye says.

Morelli takes a drag on his cig, blows the smoke, and sets the butt in the ash tray on the bar. "The big guy is in here a lot. One of my best. Uses the place like his office. Doesn't cause any trouble. I just let him be."

"Is he your partner in what goes on back there?" Nick says, nodding his head to the back.

Morelli's hands go up. "No way, man. I've been here forty years. Just me. I have no partners."

"We know he's Russian Mafia, so maybe you're paying him some kind of protection," A. Jaye says.

"Man. I'm telling you. He doesn't bother me and I certainly don't bother him. He does his business, drinks, and goes. That's all."

"What kind of business?" Nick says.

"He has something people want. I never asked what it is."

"You must have an idea what it is," A. Jaye says.

"Some kind of special drug, I think," Morelli says.

"Tell us about Karl Gerber," Nick asks.

"You mean the pain in the ass?"

"Why's that?"

"He's always calling for somethin'."

"You bullshitting us?" A. Jaye asks. "Like what?"

A middle-aged couple comes in and sits at the bar. Morelli gets their drinks and hurries back.

"I asked you a question," A. Jaye says.

"Look. These Mafia boys play rough. If they find out I talked to you, they may chop me up and throw me to the wolves."

"Either they get a piece of you, or we do," A. Jaye says. "Which is it?"

"Now, one more time," Nick says. "Why is Gerber a pain in the ass?"

"Okay, okay," Morelli says. "He met Dmitry here once, over three weeks ago and they did some exchange. Like I said, I believe it was some kind of drug. Then a couple of days later he called again for more of it." He takes another drag on his cigarette and the smoke shoots out his nose. "He said it was a matter of life or death."

"So he would pick up the stuff here, is that correct?" A. Jaye says.

"Yeah, that's it.

"How'd you get this drug each time?" Nick asks.

"Dmitry drops it off, or he'd send it with his bodyguard."

"How come he didn't meet with Gerber at noon?" A. Jaye says.

"He's out of town."

"Dmitry's driver said he was told to bring the package to you, and I'm guessing you gave it to Gerber," Nick says. "Is that right?"

Morelli blinks hard. "Yeah."

"Know what's in it?" Nick asks.

Morelli shrugs. "I've told you, I don't know, and I didn't ask. I'm only the middle guy." He shakes his head. "Whatever it is, the guy said he now needed it to save someone close to him that's going to die. That's what he always says."

"So, it's been about three weeks since he got the first package from Belofsky?" Nick asks.

"Yeah," Morelli says. About three weeks."

Outside Leopold's, Nick turns to A. Jaye. "Wonder how Belofsky got that box to his driver if he's out of town?"

A. Jaye shrugs. "That's a good question."

"Maybe he left it with him because he knew Gerber would be needing it for his wife," Nick says. "Ms. McCulley told me Gerber's wife had colon cancer."

"What do you think he gave her?" A. Jaye asks.

"Tican. But I'm wondering why he needed a second dose?"

"Maybe it takes more than one," A. Jaye says.

"I don't think so," Nick says, rubbing his chin. "Now three weeks later, Gerber needs what Stanislavski brought in the box. It has to be some kind of antidote because Susan Prescott found that Tican mutates into a deadly bug after three weeks."

"You the man, boss."

CHAPTER FORTY-FOUR

Gerber climbs out of the Infinity caressing the package like a mother holding her infant. He hurries into the house and heads into the library. Eva's in there waiting for him. He calls out. "Eva, I'm back." He opens the box and sets the canister on the desk. She doesn't know it's the antidote. He told her she needed just one more dose to finish the treatment. She hadn't been feeling well the last few days and was eager to take the last treatment.

This will save her.

Logs are glowing in the fireplace. He loosens his collar.

Suddenly, he turns. *What's that god-awful smell?* A pungent odor is traveling from the *Loving Chair.* Blood is spreading across the carpet like an oil spill, streaming a path toward his feet. "Lord Have Mercy!" He rushes over to the chair.

Eva is slumped over like a wilted flower—robe and nightgown are soaked in blood. He raises her chin and her head falls backward. He jumps back, can't catch his breath. *Jesus, what... what—?* Eva's eyeballs lie in her lap, blood's frothing from their sockets. A putrid smell rises from liquefied brain that is oozing from her nose.

Gerber's stomach flip-flops. He races out and bounds up the stairs, vomits in the toilet, and crouches over the sink to splash water in his face. Lifting his head, he stares into the mirror and says, "You killed her."

Gerber straightens his shoulders and stands erect. After a couple of deep breaths, he goes into his bedroom, sits on the edge of the bed with his head in his hands. Minutes later, he jumps up and goes to his closet, opens the doors. He reaches in for his tux and throws it on the bed. It takes him ten minutes to put it on. He stands in front of the mirror tying his tie.

Eva will be proud to see me in my tux. She always says I looked handsome in this monkey suit.

Opening the dresser drawer, he takes out a nine millimeter P-35 hand gun and a box of shells, slides one into the chamber, and sits on the bed. Eva smiles at him in the mirror.

The early years of their marriage were blissful. They hadn't been able to keep their hands off each other. Nightly, they'd rendezvous by the fireplace in the *Loving Chair*. But then she became infatuated with her flamboyant parties and two-faced friends. She discarded him like a rotten apple. He resented her after that, and especially hated her narcissistic brother, Harry, who had turned Eva against him. But lately she has loved him more than ever and now he has killed her. Soon they will be together again.

Will God forgive him for what he's about to do, commit another sin? What does the Bible say about suicide? That he'll live in darkness for all eternity.

Lord, have mercy on me. I don't want to go to hell. I want to see my Eva again.

He raises the gun to his temple, and closes his eyes.

CHAPTER FORTY-FIVE

Nick snaps on gloves, makes his way to the uniformed officer near the library door. The maid had called in the death of Karl and Eva Gerber.

"Where are the bodies?" Nick asks.

"The wife's in there," the cop says, shaking his head, "Never seen anything like it. Her husband's upstairs in the bedroom." He looks at his notebook. "Name's Dr. Karl Gerber and hers is Eva."

"Got it," Nick says. "Who's in there with her?"

"Assistant M.E."

"Has forensics finished?"

"Five minutes ago."

"Who's up there with the body?"

"One of our guys and the techs."

A. Jaye comes over, "I'll go up and check it out."

In the library, Nick finds a bushy-headed guy in a green lab coat bent over the high-back chair.

"Where's Doc?" Nick asks.

Marty looks up. "Hello to you, too, Detective Hunter. Doc's on another case." Marty is holding Eva's head in his blood-spattered hands. "She's a mess."

"Holy mackerel. What in the hell—"

"No idea, Detective." He shakes his head. "Only thing I can tellya she has no bullet holes, no knife wounds, been dead ten or twelve hours." Marty pauses while he eases Eva's head onto the arm rest. "Man, she's a mess."

"You've already said that," Nick says.

"I did, didn't I?" Marty yanks off his gloves. "I'm done. Can we have her?"

"Did the techs take pictures?"

"Zillions."

"There's not much left for me to look at. She's all yours. Tell Doc I want his report yesterday."

"It won't do any good, but I'll tell him."

"Also, remind him we'll need samples for Dr. Prescott."

"Will do," he says picking up his bag.

Nick glances around the room. "Any struggle?"

"No defense marks on the body," Marty says.

Nick spots something on the desk. He reaches for the cylinder. If this's what I think it is, Susan would want to test it. He bags it. Bet ten bucks it was in that package Gerber carried out of Leopold's.

Marty follows Nick out. Two men wearing scrubs wheel a gurney into the library. The uniform at the library door tells Nick the maid is in the next room. Her name is Isabella Dobbin.

"Jesus Christ!" someone shouts from in the library.

"I thought they'd react that way," Marty says. "I'm heading upstairs."

In the next room, a slender woman with red eyes and silver-streaked dark hair sits on the couch, holding crumpled tissue in her lap.

"I'm Detective Hunter, Ms. Dobbin."

She tries to smile.

"Did you touch anything in the library?"

She shakes her head. "I ran out as soon as I saw her. Horrible, horrible." She wipes her eyes. "The doctor's upstairs."

"What time did you leave yesterday?"

She twists the tissue in her hands. "I've been with them for ten years."

"Were they home when you left?"

"Yesterday was my day off."

A. Jaye appears, tells Nick that there is a suicide note next to Gerber, and the M.E. and techs are working the scene. "You were right," he says, "looks like Gerber gave his wife Tican."

Nick nods and asks him to get a statement from the maid, and then join him. He climbs the stairs and heads into the bedroom. Gerber is on his back. The left side of his head is splattered over the silk bedspread. The techs are shooting pictures.

"He must of gone berserk when he saw his wife," Marty says.

"Yeah, and *she's a mess*," Nick says.

"You liked that, didn't you, Detective?"

"Made my day."

"Well, he's a *mess* too."

"Touché," Nick says, staring at the remains.

Suicide victims are never pretty. Nick has seen more than his share in D.C. He remembers a case involving a middle-aged attorney who had shot herself in the chest. Her husband was a big-shit CEO. They had no children. Too busy. This shapely brunette with porcelain skin, shiny hair, and long sexy legs was sprawled on the floor in her office. Her husband had ditched her for a twenty-something brainless bitch. He found it interesting that women more than men lie down to commit suicide. More often than not, they leave suicide notes, and she was no different. It was one of those, *nobody-loves-me; I gave him my life, the-ungrateful-bastard* type of notes.

Gerber's is similar, sorry-for-what-I-did to Eva. I tried to save her, had-no-other-choice.

Nick bags the note. A. Jaye comes into the room. "Look what Gerber left on his desk," Nick says.

"Don't tell me. It was in the package he got from Morelli."

"Yep. It's the antidote," Nick says, holding up the bagged canister in front of him. "Remember, Morelli told us that Gerber said he needed it to save someone's life? And here it is."

"But unfortunately, he was too late," A. Jaye says.

———— ✦ ————

Nick is on his way out of the precinct when Gladys hands him a note.

"Chief, your ex says she'd like for you to take Kenny."

"Wow! That's a new one. Wonder what brought this on?"

"And since you don't understand women, you wouldn't know what that is."

"You're too smart for your own good," he says.

"That's why I run this place."

"You got it."

"Just don't forget that boy while you two are battling each other. He's vulnerable."

"Thanks for the tidbit."

"You need all the help you can get."

He rushes out of the station into the bright afternoon sun, drives to the CDC with the CSU file and the canister beside him. It takes him twenty minutes to get to Path Building 15. He gets out with the stuff and meets Susan inside the door. She escorts him to her office, where he chooses a chair facing her.

"Now, what's so important that you dragged me out of the lab?" she says, sitting behind her desk.

"Sorry to be the one to tellya," he says, pausing for a second as

Eva Gerber's body flashes in his mind. "Karl Gerber committed suicide, and his wife is dead, too."

She jumps up, her brown eyes widen. "What?"

"It happened sometime yesterday in their home. Gerber left a note. He was depressed."

"But why take his life? He's known for months Eva was dying of colon cancer."

"Wasn't that. It was what he did to her."

The air-handlers kick on and roar.

"Whaddayu mean, 'did to her'?"

Nick opens the file, slides out the photos and spreads them on the desk.

She reaches into the fridge for two bottles of water, hands him one, takes a drink, and glances at the pictures. "Ohmigod! Poor Eva." Susan looks away and takes another drink, probably to keep from vomiting.

"Blood is everywhere. Her brains turned to custard," Nick says. He swallows some of his water as if none of the gruesome scene bothers him. "Doc called before I left the station. Eva's lungs were mushy and all but gone. Sound familiar?"

She blinks hard. "MX," she says, keeping her eyes fixed on Nick.

"Uh-huh. Doc will be sending you Eva's samples."

Susan nods, rises, and stands next to the bookcase. Nick wonders what she's thinking. Has Eva's death affected her that much?

Nick glances at the framed picture of Susan's mother on the desk. He finds it curious there isn't one of the family, like the one on the piano in her apartment.

"How's Michael?" he asks, hoping to get her mind on something else.

She frowns. "Are you a psychic?"

"Doubt it."

"I got a call from him last night. He's still here in Atlanta. Never boarded that bus, turned the ticket in for a refund, and went to the treatment center and is back with his counselor. It's the first time he's taken any action on his own. I'm really encouraged."

"Guess he decided it was time to turn loose of the booze," Nick says. "See, you did have an influence on him."

"I don't want to get my hopes up." She retakes her position behind the desk. "Do you think Karl got Tican from—?"

Nick interrupts her. "You're thinking someone in your lab?"

"I was going to say Robin."

He leans forward. "Remember how pissed you were when I told you she was my prime suspect?"

"I just couldn't believe it then."

"Remember those spots on the kitchen floor? They contained her DNA."

"Think she cut herself?" Susan says.

"Doc found a scar on her knee."

"Then Belofsky didn't kill her. He just dumped her," she says.

"I believe she murdered Sutherland, stole all the samples, and along with Belofsky sold one to Gerber," Nick says. He reaches for the bag, removes the canister and sets it on her desk. "Here's the antiserum Gerber got from Belofsky. We saw him carrying it out of Leopold's."

"So, Eva died before Karl could administer it?" she says, reaching for it.

Nick nods. "And he blamed himself for her death."

Susan appears upset. "I'm to blame," she says. "Poor Karl was acting on my data." She glances at the photos on the desk. "I don't blame him. I would have administered Tican to my dying mother or sister, too. That's how much confidence I had in it. If only he had given this to Eva in time."

"It wasn't meant to be," Nick says.

"I'll get on this right away." She sighs "I was so naive to trust Vladimir."

"Learned something, did you?"

"Yeah, don't believe everything you're told."

Nick can relate to that. He never trusts eye witness accounts, or what suspects say. They never tell the truth until he drills them with the evidence.

"I lost my objectivity," she says. "I wanted a cancer cure so badly that I never once suspected Vladimir." Tears welled in her eyes. "He knew I was vulnerable, and he treated me like I was nothing."

"You have to get past it." Nick says, drinking more of his water.

"If only we had more time," Susan says. "Maybe a few months."

"For what? The antidote?"

"No. To genetically re-engineer Tican into a cancer drug."

He jumped up. "You gotta be kidding me."

"No, I'm serious. I really believe it's possible."

"I'd forget that if I were you."

"I guess you're right."

"I know I'm right. Now, how's your work on the antidote?"

"Nothing yet."

"Will Belofsky's antiserum help, you think?"

She shrugs. "Won't know until I analyze it. I'm sure Vladimir produced it, and he was a good scientist even though he turned out to be a monster."

CHAPTER FORTY-SIX

Nick is in his office leaning back in his chair with his feet on the desk. He has just finished talking with Harlan about recruiting the FBI to help in the capture of the Russian mobsters, Vladimir Sokolov and Dmitry Belofsky. Nick plans to fly out early tomorrow for their afternoon meeting.

He leans in to his desk and glances at Belofsky's folder. Something about him has been bothering Nick for some time—why did Belofsky used a handgun to kill two New Jersey mobsters? Why didn't he use Tican on them, too? Could it be that he didn't have it or the minidarts at that time? That could be it. But the question now is: Who is Belofsky going to kill with it, if not the mob? Nick doesn't agree with Harlan that it's the mob. He jumps up and races off to the second floor, telling the guard to open Stanislavski's cell.

The prisoner leaps up.

Nick rushes in, grabs him by the collar. "Belofsky isn't after the mob, is he?"

"Yah. I told you."

"If you don't talk, it may be time to turn you over to the Russian Mafia. Now, who's Belofsky planning to kill?"

"I told you—"

Nick slaps him across the face. "I'll ask you one more time. Who?"

"Senator Plummer!" he shouts.

Just as I thought. "Anyone else?"

"Many senators."

———— ◆ ————

Arriving at home this night, Nick eases the Firebird into the garage, hits the remote to close the door, and goes into the den. He tosses the keys on the bar, reaches for a glass hanging overhead, dumps in some ice and three jiggers of Chivas Regal. He takes a swig, savors it, moseys over to the glass doors and looks out over the lake. Light from the full moon sparkles on the water. A boat passes. He doesn't understand people who drive their boats on the lake in the winter months. He goes to his easy chair, flops in it, and drinks his scotch, thinking about Senator Plummer. Stanislavski has confirmed Nick's hunch, but what is the connection between Plummer and Belofsky? The mystery haunts Nick.

He sets the drink on the coffee table, opens his computer and enters the Internet.

The phone rings.

Not now.

The answering machine kicks on. It's Margaret. "You haven't called me. I want you to take Kenny. Call me, dammit!"

Gladly, sweetheart.

Nick's search on the Net leads to over thirteen hundred items on Barry Plummer. He opens the senator's biography. Plummer is a fifth-term Republican senator, an expert on foreign policy, had a close relationship with the 40th President, Ronald Reagan, and now with the current President, George H.W. Bush. Plummer's values seem to be rooted in the plains of Nebraska, where he was born in February, 1940.

Nick reads several of Plummer's speeches on foreign policy. Most pound the Russians, and last year, in 1991, as the Chairman of SFRC, he called for the downfall of Communism.

Every word of Reagan's 1987 "Tear Down This Wall" speech delivered at the Brandenburg Gate in West Berlin is there, too. A local newspaper had a front page editorial on the speech, and on the second page is a short paragraph about an incident that had taken place between someone in the President's entourage and a Russian woman that day in Berlin. Apparently pressure had been brought to bear on the newspaper not to print names and details.

Outside, a car backfires. Nick winces. He reaches for the phone.

"What is it?" Harlan says.

"Are you still in contact with your CIA guy?"

"If I need to be."

"You need to be," Nick says. He told Harlan about what he'd found. "Could your friend dig out the details on those two?"

"Where are you going with this, Nick?"

"A gut feeling."

"Care to enlighten me?"

"Not until you get me what I want."

"Tomorrow."

Click.

Nick gets up and at the bar he refreshes his drink, gulping it while watching the news for the next thirty minutes. The phone rings. *Margaret again?*

Nick finishes his drink. He picks up.

"Bad news," A. Jaye says.

"Let's have it."

"The big guy hung himself in his cell."

"Shows you how much they fear the Russian Mafia," Nick says.

CHAPTER FORTY-SEVEN

In D.C. a Lincoln limo pulls out of the Russian Embassy onto Tunlaw Road and heads for Wisconsin Ave. Belofsky is in the passenger seat beside the chauffeur. In the back are Sokolov and his two bodyguards, Petrovich and Nenasheva. It has been raining for two days.

A white utility van, which is moved every morning, appeared across the street from the Embassy the day after Belofsky and Sokolov had met with the D.C. mob. Today, two men in white coveralls are on utility poles. When the limo goes past, the driver says, "FBI." They laugh.

Several miles down the road, they turn on M Street. Belofsky watches as the driver keeps checking the rearview mirror, and seconds later pulls over and stops behind a green Ford Explorer XLT. Nenasheva hops out before Belofsky, holds the door for the Bear and takes the car keys from the driver, opens the Explorer for the Bear. Petrovich and Nenasheva transfer the luggage. The Embassy driver takes off. Belofsky looks around, slips a hand behind his back under his jacket, and touches the gun inside his belt. This is not a good place, he thinks.

Nenasheva slips in behind the wheel; Belofsky slides in next to him. Petrovich and Sokolov are in the back. The rain is turning into sleet. Nenasheva switches on the wipers and the headlights and drives off. They cross the Francis Scott Key Bridge and pick up the Custis Memorial Parkway. Fourteen miles from Dulles International Airport, the roads are now covered with a glaze.

"Be careful," Belofsky says, "the roads are getting slippery."

"Yah, "Nenasheva says.

Cars in the left lane are slowing, and dozens of tail lights are flashing like fireflies. The right lane is beginning to slow. A gasoline tanker in the left lane, going twenty miles over the speed limit is skidding in an attempt to stop. The rear end begins to fishtail.

"Watch him!" Belofsky shouts

"Holy shit!" Nenasheva says as the tanker strikes their front, spinning them around like a cup in a carnival ride.

"I can't control it!" Nenasheva screams.

Belofsky shouts, "Turn the wheel in the opposite direction!"

Nothing works.

They spin off the road and overturn several times. The doors fly open. Belofsky is thrown clear. The Explorer ends upside down, thirty yards away, exploding into flames.

Belofsky is lying face down in the mud. He turns on his side, wondering how badly he's hurt. His left wrist and ankle are killing him. He's bleeding from the nose. He eases up into a sitting position. Headlights from the vehicles above brighten the area. He's in a clearing close to a park filled with evergreens. His heavy jacket probably protected him from more cuts. He tastes blood and his teeth feel loose. He climbs to his feet and takes a few seconds to steady himself. He tests his ankle. Not broken, but it hurts like hell. He doesn't know about his wrist. People are rushing to the Explorer. His comrades could not have survived that fiery crash. Belofsky has to get away before someone checks on him. He heads toward the trees, but hears moaning, then a cry.

"Help, help...."

Belofsky slides in the mud as he trudges a few yards over to see which comrade is lying there. Blue eyes show through a face covered in mud. It's the man that has ordered him around like a fuckin' slave and threatened him hundreds of times about burying him in an unmarked grave.

"Is that you, Dmitry?" he says.

"Yeah."

"My legs...."

Belofsky kneels beside his boss, reaches in his pocket, pulls out the pick, presses the button on the shaft, lowers his head and whispers, "We Russians like to inflict pain," then rams the pick up the Bear's nostril, twisting the tip in a circle, enjoying every scream.

Now, I'm Mafia boss.

The medics arrive at the top of the road.

Belofsky shuffles into the park.

CHAPTER FORTY-EIGHT

Nick arrives at the Deputy Director's outer office in the J. Edgar Hoover Building in D.C. A slender brunette with a pleasant smile ushers him into Harlan's office and says, "Mr. Kennedy will be with you shortly." She leaves the door open.

The room is larger than Nick remembers. A couch is now against the wall, and more books are on the shelves. He sits in the chair in front of the desk, reaches for a People magazine, and scans through it. His pager vibrates. It's Susan.

He hears Harlan outside the door talking to another agent about some criminal investigation. Harlan steps in and closes the door. He has on a white shirt with sleeves rolled up and a dark tie.

"Good to see you, Nick."

Nick stands and grips his hand and smiles. "You're still trim, I see."

"I try." He gestures for Nick to sit.

"I need to call Dr. Prescott at the CDC," Nick says. "I just got her page."

"Sure. Use the phone next to you. No need to dial nine."

Susan answers on the third ring. "No, I'm in D.C. with Harlan Kennedy. Yeah, I'm sitting down." He listens. "Yes, I'm here. I heard you the first time." He hangs up.

"Everything okay?" Harlan says.

"Nope."

Harlan reaches for the folder on top of a stack, opens it, and rifles through some papers. The murmur of voices can be heard in the next room.

"I have the information," Harlan says.

"That was quick."

"We're the FBI." He smiles. "The Russian woman is Tonya Lukashova and... the man..." He stopped in mid-sentence. "This is top secret stuff."

"When did that ever stop you?"

"Depends on what you're going to do with it."

"How about the guy's name and I'll tell you."

"Senator Barry Plummer."

Outside the window, a pigeon landed on the ledge.

"You don't seem surprised," Harlan says.

"What is Tonya's connection to Plummer?"

"You won't believe it."

"Try me," Nick says.

"She's Belofsky's sister."

"No way!" Nick laughed.

"'Fraid so. She was the journalist covering Reagan's visit."

"A journalist? How in the hell did she accomplish that? You know Belofsky's background."

Harlan didn't respond. He's reading something in the file.

The pigeon sidles across the ledge and glances in.

"Come on. What did you get?" Nick says.

"Photos." Harlan hands them to Nick.

Nick studies them for a minute or so. The senator and Tonya are naked. Her ankles and wrists are chained to the bed, and the senator is on top of her.

"He treated her rough," Harlan says.

"I can see that. Think she set him up?"

"We thought so at first, but there were other trysts." He pauses. "How much do you know about the senator?"

"Nothing about his sex life."

"Mean to his women," Harlan says.

"Appears you don't like him."

"Not high on my list."

A blower rumbles. Warm air flows into the room.

"Anything else?"

Harlan leans forward. "After being in Berlin with Reagan, Plummer never stopped hammering the Soviet Union."

"I know. His speeches on the Internet are filled with vitriol," Nick says. "Toss that in with the senator's affair with Tonya, and Belofsky's in a helluva frenzy."

"That's why you wanted this information, isn't it?"

"Uh-huh. To prove my hunch. The driver Stanislavski confessed that Belofsky's going to dart the senator. Now we know the *why*."

"Holy crap." Harlan reached for the phone. "Stop the surveillance.

Bring in the Russians, now!"

A jet flies over the building and scares the pigeon off the ledge.

"I have men stationed outside the Russian Embassy. Vladimir and Belofsky are in there."

"Too late," Nick says. "He's probably finished."

"Whaddayu mean?"

Nick leans forward in his chair. "Belofsky wouldn't steal Tican just to infect Plummer."

Harlan's body jerks. "Who else?"

"Plummer's committee members, too."

"What evidence do you have?"

"His driver told me that Belofsky was going to kill many senators, and Belofsky left Atlanta sixteen days ago with twenty-four darts. Ask yourself, why so many?"

Harlan lifts a sheet of paper from the folder. "According to your fax, the virus mutates after three weeks into a hemorrhagic one."

"Yep."

"That means... the senators could be dead five days from now," Harlan says.

"You got it."

"Is there any treatment?"

"I thought there was an antiserum."

"Whaddayu mean, was?"

"That call I just made to Susan?"

"Yeah?"

"She's finished analyzing a sample."

"And?"

"It's snake oil."

"Jesus!" Harlan jumps up, and rushes out the door. "Gotta see the Director. Be right back."

Nick goes behind Harlan's desk and stares out the window. The traffic on Pennsylvania Avenue is heavy and dark clouds are gathering in the eastern sky. *Shit.* He'd hoped the antiserum was for real and Susan could reproduce it. Now they are faced with losing all nineteen senators.

Harlan returns. He's disheveled.

"What's happening?" Nick says.

"Director Kincaid's on his way to the White House."

"And you?" Nick asks.

"I'll work in our command center at SIOC."

"SIOC?"

"Strategic Information and Operations Center. It's where we manage crises twenty-four/seven. All field agents and law enforcement agencies will be on alert."

"Quite an elaborate scheme for a bug that doesn't seem to spread, and we're talking only about nineteen senators"

"Can't take any chances. They could have infected most of Congress."

"Belofsky wouldn't have had time to infect more than the SFRC members."

"Are you sure it doesn't spread?"

"Susan assures me."

"Okay."

"Like to make a suggestion," Nick says.

"Good. I want you in on this."

"I'd like you to get the CDC to transfer Susan Prescott up here to their satellite lab."

"Why?"

"Prescott's a doctor besides being a scientist. She can draw blood and work on an antidote."

"Done," he says. "You think she can find a cure in time?"

"I hope so."

Harlan looks at his calendar. "Damn! The 102nd Congress is out for Christmas." He grabs the phone, tells his secretary he has an emergency. Instructs her to track down the members of the SFRC, and tell them the Director would like to talk with them.

"I know it's Christmas break, dammit! Call their homes, page them, do whatever it takes."

Nick waits. "That could create quite a stir," he says.

"I know, but Kincaid can handle them. He'll order our field agents to bring the senators to Walter Reed. Won't be told the truth until after their arrival."

"What about their families?" Nick says. "They'll panic."

"Agents will be instructed to tell them threats were made against their lives."

Harlan's phone rings. "Yes. Son-of-a-bitch." He turns to Nick. "Vladimir and Belofsky snuck out of the Embassy in the Ambassador's Lincoln hours ago. When our men stopped the car, only the driver was in it."

"Shit!" Nick says.

"You know this town better than anyone, Nick. I'll call Atlanta and Metro and tell them you're on this case."

CHAPTER FORTY-NINE

The shrill ring of the phone startles Susan. She raises her head, groaning from the stiffness in her neck. She blinks hard at her wristwatch: Six o'clock.

She grabs the phone. "This better be good."

"You up?" Nick says.

"Do I have to be?"

Harlan has arranged for them to stay in a hotel close to the CDC satellite lab in D.C. Susan's staff is housed in apartments three blocks away.

"Meet you in the lobby in ten minutes for coffee," he says.

"Not too swift before my first cup. Make it thirty."

Susan showers, dresses and takes the stairs to the first floor. Nick is at one of the tables in the breakfast room nursing orange juice. Senior couples occupy two tables in the back, eating waffles and watching the news on the overhead monitor.

"What, no caffeine?" she asks. "You must be made of steel."

He raises his glass. "First my picker-upper. Then the java."

She goes to the coffee urn on the counter and fills two mugs, returns and sets one in front of him, and she sits, takes a couple of sips and gazes into Nick's eyes over the rim of her cup.

"Do you miss your partner?" she asks.

"A. Jaye?"

She nods.

"He's busy on another case. Anyway, I got you."

"The strangest thing," she says.

"What?"

"I got a call from Michael late last night."

"He's still in Atlanta, isn't he?"

"Yeah, and I was wondering how in the world he got my number here."

"What did he want?"

She takes a swallow of her coffee. "He's been trying to reach me at my apartment in Atlanta and was worried when I never answered. That's a switch. Now he's checking up on me."

"Man, that's great. That shows the counseling is working." Nick gets up to fill his cup and returns.

"Did you give him my number?"

"Me? Not me."

"You look guilty," she says.

He raises his hands, smiling. "I'm innocent."

"I don't believe you."

A woman and a girl of nine years pass their table, carrying plates stacked with waffles.

"Enjoyed last night," she says. "I like it when you take advantage of me. Don't stop, okay?"

Nick smiles. "You guys ready in the lab?" He swallows some coffee.

"All set to go."

"Anything new?"

"Doc sent me Eva's samples. Now we'll look for her antibodies."

"Think you'll find any?" Nick says.

"I'm expecting the titer to be low."

"Titer?"

"The amount of antibodies in the serum. If Eva had survived MX, then the titer would have been elevated."

Nick frowns. "If you had gotten her blood before she bled to death, would it have made any difference?"

"No. The mutant works so fast the immune system can't react in time."

"That's unfortunate," he says.

Susan takes a drink of her coffee and explains that when foreign substances, called antigens, enter the body, the immune system reacts: Beta cells and T cells launch into action and plasma cells are formed that produce antibodies. The process takes time.

"What I still don't understand is why the senators' immune systems don't wipe out Tican before it mutates?" Nick asks.

"Because Tican, like the AIDS virus, has a mind of its own. You may have heard that the AIDS virus hides in lymphocytes for years making it invisible to the immune system."

He nods.

She continues. "Well, Tican is similar. It hides in the lymphocytes too, but for only twenty-one days."

Nick frowns. "Then for those twenty-one days Tican becomes invisible to the immune system, too, right?" he says.

"Yes, and after that time it mutates into MX and is released into the bloodstream where it acts very fast. The immune system can't build up a sufficient number of antibodies in time to kill it off."

Nick moves forward in his chair. "So, what you're saying is that the senators are going to die because you can't get the right kind of antibodies."

"You got it." She pauses to finish off her coffee. "Do you really think the senators are infected?"

"I do for a couple of reasons. Belofsky's driver told me under great duress that his boss was going to kill Plummer and many senators, which I took him to mean the members of Plummer's committee. Also, you know about the minidart that A. Jaye and I found in Belofsky's apartment. He must have brought some with him here along with the samples of Tican. That also makes me believe that he's infected more than just Barry Plummer. I can't say with certainty that all of his committee members are infected, but that's where you come in. You'll determine that."

"Okay, but I guess I was hoping he was going after the mob— wishful thinking on my part."

"What now?" he asks.

"Pray for a miracle." She looks down at her empty cup for a few seconds and doesn't say a word.

"What's wrong?" he asks.

"If I can't come up with an antidote, they'll all die and their blood will be on my hands."

Nick squeezes her hand. "You were just doing what you thought would cure millions of women with breast cancer. Remember that." He wipes his mouth, gets up and looks at his watch. "I gotta go. It's nearly seven, and I have a meeting with Harlan in an hour."

They head out of the hotel and stop at the curb. A sanitation truck drops an empty Dumpster on a concrete slab at the edge of the hotel. Heads turn. Nick depresses the button on his remote. The doors click open on one of the black Suburbans the FBI has provided for them. He slips in and drives off.

Susan climbs in behind the wheel of the second Suburban and glances at the dashboard clock. Seven a.m. *Three days before Christmas.*

She waits for an instant before starting the car, thinking about how difficult it might be to save all the senators. If Nick's information is correct, some were darted on the fifth of December at the earliest. All nineteen senators couldn't have been infected on the same day. That would have been virtually impossible. She figures it would be Christmas morning before any one of them would die without the antidote.

She turns the ignition, steps on the gas, and enters the traffic.
Seven a.m. Seventy-two hours and counting.

———•———

Nick steps into the SIOC conference room. Assembled around the table are eight of Harlan's top investigators and Metro Police Chief Tom Doocy. Nick chooses a chair facing the Chief, his old boss. They exchange smiles. They got along okay when Nick was on the force.

Harlan introduces Nick as a former Metro Homicide detective who will be working closely with him and Doocy. Harlan's secretary arrives carrying a stack of folders, and sits at the opposite end of the table.

Harlan instructs the group that they will be searching for Senator Barry Plummer, Chairman of the SFRC, and two Russian mobsters— Vladimir Sokolov and Dmitry Belofsky. He tells them that detective Hunter has convinced him that Belofsky has darted the committee with a virus that will turn deadly after days in their bodies. Agents are now bringing the senators to Walter Reed for blood work and to confirm Hunter's suspicions. Those infected will be treated with an antidote as soon as it's available. And Plummer is missing.

Harlan nods at Nick, who takes his cue.

He stands and begins by describing Sokolov as former KGB. In Russia, no one crossed him. They knew the price would be severe pain and death if they did. Belofsky is his henchman, a cold-blooded killer who enjoys watching his victims suffer. He has sold phony antiserum to one of the docs at the CDC, but Nick thinks Belofsky has the real stuff, and is waiting to sell it for megabucks. Nick has no proof, just a hunch that the buyer is Senator Barry Plummer.

Harlan interrupts. "You can bet Belofsky will be contacting him. Find Plummer and we grab the Russian and the antidote. If we don't get it, the senators will die in a few days." He nods to his secretary. "My secretary will pass out profiles on these three persons. Memorize everything in those folders, and pay special attention to the photographs."

A hand goes up. "Sir, how much time did you say the senators have?"

"Seventy-two hours, we think."

Feet scraped the floor.

Another hand. "When was Senator Plummer last seen?"

"Over two weeks ago."

Nick adds. "He was spotted with his mistress coming out of the Crazy Horse Club. We'll be watching the place."

CHAPTER FIFTY

Susan watches as the black Suburbans stream towards the heavily guarded entrance of Walter Reed where she and Nick are standing. Senators mutter as they clamber out and file past her. Harlan Kennedy escorts them inside to a room with rows of chairs, and a dais with a podium and six chairs. The senators huddle around a coffee bar, talking over each other. Susan follows the aroma of fresh coffee and fills a cup, takes a drink and returns to the front.

"What the hell's going on?" Senator Cartwright asks. He is the Democrat from Massachusetts.

Another shrugs. "Who knows?"

Susan doesn't know him; only knows a couple of them.

"Something about a threat on our lives," another says. "Came into my home and carted me out like a piece of furniture."

Their voices raise an octave higher.

A door in the front opens. The room falls silent.

The Surgeon General marches out with FBI Director Kincaid and Dr. Austin Tremont, Chief of the Hospital Medical Staff. They move up on the dais.

Susan is behind Harlan. They stroll to the podium. Nick is one step behind her.

Director Kincaid advances to the microphone and taps it lightly.

He motions for everyone to sit.

"Good morning, Senators," he says.

Loud groaning and foot-shuffling resonate throughout the place.

Kincaid begins by introducing everyone on the platform.

Senator Cartwright jumps up. "We demand to know about this threat on our lives."

"Please, Senator. Take your seat. We're going to tell you everything."

Cartwright throws up his hands in frustration and sits back down.

Kincaid looks over the group, then walks back to Harlan. Susan hears him whisper, "I don't see Senator Plummer."

"Still looking for him, sir," Harlan says

Susan wonders if they'll find him in time.

Kincaid speaks into the mike. "Gentlemen, we have a situation."

The complaining is louder. Cartwright rises, again. "Where's our Chairman, Senator Plummer? And why isn't he here?"

"He hasn't arrived yet, sir. Please. I have much to cover." He waits until the room is quiet. "We believe that you all have been infected with... with an organism." He pauses, apparently to let this announcement sink in.

Several senators jump up, shouting that they feel fine.

Cartwright shouts, "How do you know we have this thing? No one has run any tests on me." He turns around, apparently looking for other colleagues to attest to the same thing, and several do.

"That's why you were brought here," Kincaid says. "Tests must be performed to confirm our suspicions." He turns and looks at those on the dais. "Detective Hunter from the Atlanta PD, homicide, is here," Kincaid says, pointing to Nick, who makes his way to the podium.

Nick adjusts the mike and explains that he found darts in a Russian mobster's apartment. This thug, whose name is Dmitry Belofsky, has a driver who confessed that Belofsky was going to infect Senator Plummer with some deadly virus. Nick also reports that his investigation has revealed that Belofsky came to Washington to infect all of the senators on the Foreign Relations Committee.

Dead silence.

Cartwright is on his feet again, saying, "You're taking the word of a thug. I don't believe it."

Kincaid takes the microphone. "We can't take any chances with your lives. If the doctors find that you aren't infected, then we've won."

"Say he darted us," Cartwright says, "I didn't feel anything."

"Something stung me in the neck,'" Senator Girard from Louisiana says.

"Are we the only ones—?"

"We don't have confirmation that any other members of Congress were infected."

"—Why us?"

"Russian Mafia is convinced that your committee contributed to the collapse of the Soviet Union."

"—That's bullshit. I want to know more about the bug that's in me. Why couldn't I have gotten antibiotics from my family physician and avoided all this shit?"

"The Surgeon General has a few words," Kincaid says.

"Senators... I'm afraid there's no other way to say this, so I'm going to lay it on the line. As you know, antibiotics aren't effective against viruses. You're feeling fine now because the virus won't make you sick until it's been in your body for three weeks. Then it attacks with a vengeance."

"How long do we have?"

"Seventy-two hours."

"—Son of a bitch. What's the treatment?"

"Maybe an antidote."

"—Whaddayu mean *maybe*?"

"Dr. Prescott of the CDC is working on it. She's identified the virus." The Surgeon General turned to Susan, "I'll ask her to come forward at this time."

Standing at the podium, Susan reaches for a bottle of water, opens it, and takes a swig. God, she hates what she's about to tell them. "Senators," she says, "the Russian scientists who engineered this virus used what we call enzymes to introduce a few changes in it to make it deadly—"

"We don't give a damn about that scientific crap."

"—Can you make an antidote?"

Susan takes another drink, looks over faces pelted with fear. Without the antidote, they'd be dead in three days. Tican has become her nemesis.

"Dr. Prescott, we're waiting." Cartwright says.

She sighs, and speaks into the microphone. "The Russian scientists probably isolated the gene that produced the mutant's antibodies and cloned it. We don't have time to do it. We're working on another approach."

Cartwright shouts. "Maybe that Russian... what's his name...?"

"Belofsky," she says.

"So, maybe this Belofsky has the antidote."

"He might," she says.

"—Make him an offer he can't refuse."

Nick stood. "Even if we find him today, there won't be enough time to test it."

"For Chrissake. Test it on me." Susan recognizes Senator Williamson, a Republican from Kentucky.

The Surgeon General raises a hand. "Gentlemen, I know how you feel—"

"The hell you do," Cartwright says. "You stand there feeding us bullshit while we're running out of time. Pay the man what he wants.

We'll take our chances." He looks around at the other senators for affirmation. They nod.

FBI Director Kincaid turns to Harlan. Susan leans in to hear him say, "Think you could cut a deal with Belofsky if you find him?"

You can't deal with the devil, she thinks.

"Not a chance," Harlan says.

"Any word on Plummer?"

"None."

The Surgeon General says, "We're doing our best."

He nods to Dr. Austin Tremont, Medical Officer, who addresses the group. He informs them that they'll be housed two to a room, blood work and other laboratory tests will be performed and that Dr. Prescott is in charge and she'll analyze their blood. "She and her staff are working around the clock to develop an antidote."

Tremont asks the senators to stand and follow the medical personnel to Building 14.

CHAPTER FIFTY-ONE

In hospital scrubs, Susan walks beside the metal cart filled with medical paraphernalia and a leak-proof box containing tubes, sixteen of them, filled with blood taken from the senators over the past two hours. Harriet, her tech, guides the cart as they move down the hall on the second floor past the nurses' station, and Austin Tremont follows on the opposite side. Only two more senators to go and the emotional roller coaster will be over for today.

Earlier, Susan had met with the family members packed in the waiting room at the other end of the hall. The fear on their faces and the crying children haunt Susan. Because of her, some will soon be wearing black. She takes a deep breath before pushing into the room.

Senator Frederick Cartwright, the Democrat from Massachusetts, occupies the bed near the wall. Daemon Girard, a Republican from Louisiana, in the bed nearer to the door, is sorting through wallet-sized pictures. The room is painted a light cream, as are the others. Two leather chairs are at the other end of the room.

Susan guides on latex gloves, reaches for the blue plastic tray and sets it on Cartwright's bed. "I'm Dr. Prescott," she says. "This is my associate, Harriet, and you know Dr. Tremont. We're here to draw blood, sir." Susan cleans the site with antiseptic and tightens the tourniquet around his arm, twists off the cap from the needle. Harriet and Austin are at Girard's bedside drawing blood.

"I remember you," Cartwright says. "You were in the meeting this morning. Go to it, young lady." His eyes are moist and shiny from the sedative given to him earlier. "Let's get it done."

Susan inserts the needle and fills three tubes. She caps, labels, and places them in the leak-proof box, along with the others.

"What will my blood tell you?"

"To see if you're infected with the virus."

Austin sets Senator Girard's samples in the box. "I'll check on the others," he says, and leaves. Harriet moves next to Susan.

"But isn't that why we were brought here?"

"We want to make sure."

"When will you know?" he asks.

"By morning," she says.

"What if... I'm infected?" he says.

"We'll treat you," she says.

"But you don't have anything, do you?"

"No, sir, we don't, but we're working on it."

The toilet in the next room flushes, and a door slams.

Cartwright's hands are shaking. "What if you don't find a cure in time? What can I expect? And don't spare the details."

Susan doesn't want to scare him, but she knows he won't let up until he hears the truth. "You will start coughing up blood, a little at a time, and then profusely. You will bleed out of your eyes and nose. Your lungs will collapse, and there's the possibility your eyes could pop out."

Cartwright grasps her hand. "That's horrible. I don't want to die, doctor," he says.

"We won't let that happen. We're working twenty-four/seven."

"Do either of you remember being stung?" Susan says. "Some senators say they felt something like a bee sting."

Harriet moves the cart towards the door.

Girard's hand goes up. "I do, doctor. It was December the third. I remember because I had an important meeting that day, and I was going to my car in the Capitol garage. Noticed this wrestler-type standing by the car next to mine dressed in a black uniform and cap, but didn't think much about it. Figured he was one of the drivers. I remember him because he had a long scar down his face. When I opened my car door, that's when I felt the sting in my neck. I thought I twisted it getting in the car." He pauses. "He's the guy, isn't he?"

Susan knew it was Belofsky. "It is," she says. "You say it was on the third?"

"Yeah."

"A couple of your colleagues remember theirs happening around that time."

"Mine is definitely the third," Girard says.

"I'll be damned if I remember anything like a bee sting," Cartwright says, laying his head back on the pillow. He sighs and whispers, "Maybe he didn't get me."

Maybe he got you earlier.

Susan notices that the younger lawmaker in the other bed is shaking under the covers. Susan reaches for a syringe and a small bottle with a rubber cap from the cart, withdraws liquid and injects Girard. "You'll feel better in a second," she says. "I've given you a sedative."

"I'm worried about my wife and children," he says.

Harriet pushes the cart out the door.

"I met your two daughters," Susan says, thinking about how scared they were, which reminded her of the time she and Sabrina said goodbye to their mother.

"They're seven and nine," he says.

"Sweet ages." She makes her way between the beds.

Girard looks at her with sad eyes. "I wish I could see my wife and children," he says, turning his head, and then mumbles, "Before I die."

"You can. They're in the waiting room. I'll have them come in."

"Ask my family, too, willya, doctor?" Cartwright says.

"Sure."

CHAPTER FIFTY-TWO

The CDC research satellite in Washington is located in the northwest part of the city, with three buildings surrounded by tall sycamores inside a stone wall perimeter, looking much like a small college campus.

It is three days before Christmas and Susan, Tony, and the new techs, Harriet and Ryan, have been working in the Biosafety Level-2 lab since late afternoon processing the senators' blood. Susan leaves at ten that night and heads to her new office.

In the admin building, she leans back in her chair, closes her eyes and hums as she breathes. The office is as still as being in a vacuum. Her eyelids flutter and her heart rate slows. Images of Eva's body ravaged by the virus swirl in Susan's mind—blood-soaked gown, green vomit mixed with blood flowing out of Eva's mouth and down her neck, sockets filled with blood, eyes in her lap. Susan sighs. Now she pictures Senator Cartwright bleeding from every orifice, eyeballs rolling from their sockets, landing on the bed, and staring up at him. Since her youth, she has believed that evil roams the world, and now she knows Belofsky is evil incarnate.

And what about me? What am I?

There's a knock at the door. Susan bolts upright.

"Dr. Prescott. We've finished the work on the senators," Tony says. "Tican's in all of 'em, but no antibodies. Sorry."

She glances at her mother's photograph on the desk. *I'm sorry, too.*

"What now?" he says.

"Stick their samples in the fridge, and you guys get some rest. Tomorrow morning I want everyone in the conference room down the hall at seven sharp."

"Got it," he says.

On her desk are stacks of journal articles that she has reviewed the last several days. From her readings, she's come up with an idea on how to make the antidote. She sighs, feeling a little better; maybe even a tiny bit happier. Most of the senators will be saved, including future generations, especially, if someone in Russia is hiding samples of Tican.

She glances at the wall clock.

Eleven p.m. Fifty-six hours and counting.

At five o'clock the next morning, Susan slips into the Level-2, opens the fridge, takes out all the vials of Tican, and for the next hour, combines their contents into a black tube, caps it, and shoves it in the back of the fridge. She cleans the glassware, the counters, and heads for her office around six forty-five.

She steps into the conference room at seven on the dot, carrying copies of a handout. Tony and Ryan are by the window, drinking coffee and eating fruit. They take their seats when they see her. She places copies of the handout in front of them.

Susan looks around. "Where's Harriet?"

The guys shrug and pick up their copies.

The door opens and Harriet shoots in and takes a seat. "Sorry, overslept."

"There's a copy on the table," Susan says.

Harriet nods and reaches for it.

"What you have is the outline of what we'll be doing," Susan says. "We'll begin by removing the mutant virus MX from Eva Gerber's blood, applying the same procedure used to isolate Tican from the senators' blood. MX had a dreadful effect on Mrs. Gerber because it acted so fast her immune system couldn't react in time. Tican, like the AIDS virus, hid in her lymphocytes, and consequently no antibodies could be stimulated to neutralize it."

A noise outside the door attracts their attention. Someone is pushing a squeaky cart down the hall.

Susan continues: "After three weeks, Tican mutated into MX, which killed poor Mrs. Gerber. Vaccine researchers have shown that viruses have some of their population without DNA, called *empty particles*. I'm counting on MX having these particles," she says. "Without their DNA machinery, MX particles are nonvirulent, cannot hide anywhere, and their surface proteins, acting as antigens would stimulate the production of antibodies. Empty MX particles could serve as our antidote."

"That would be great," Harriet says. She looks around, seemingly thinking she was accused of brown-nosing her boss. "Well, wouldn't it?"

The men shrug.

"Certainly," Susan says.

Ryan rises to refill his coffee mug.

"Tony, you'll recall that in Atlanta Dr. Sutherland tested Tican in rabbits," she says.

"I do."

"Once we separate the particles, we're going to inject them into the animals," she says. "If we're lucky, the particles will produce antibodies."

She looks at her watch. "It's eight o'clock. We have forty-seven hours"—she pauses long enough to emphasize the timeline—"to isolate, purify and test the particles before the senators start dying. That means we'll be working around the clock. Hope you have your cots in the lab."

CHAPTER FIFTY-THREE

Belofsky, wet and bleeding, clothes torn, makes it back to his D.C. apartment four hours after the accident. He hobbles into the bathroom and looks in the mirror. Cuts are on his face, blood is caked around his nose and mouth. He washes away the blood, plucks a towel off the rack with his good hand—the other one seems broken—and presses the towel hard against his face. He had a hard time breathing earlier, but the agony in his chest is about gone.

He removes a bottle of Advil out of the medicine cabinet and goes into the kitchen, where he pours vodka into a glass, washes down four tablets in one swig, emptying the glass. The liquor eases his pain. He pulls on the wrist that is out of joint until it pops into place and wraps it tightly. He fills another glass with drink, takes it into the living room to the recliner, and flips on the TV to the news. He's feeling good now. He's the new Mafia boss.

He takes several swallows of vodka as he watches the anchor covering a story about the "Ice Pick" murders. Belofsky laughs. The victims' pictures flash on the screen. His heart races and he shouts at the screen. "I did that." Maybe he'll get him a woman tonight. He downs the last of his drink.

Suddenly, his body shoots forward, eyes glued to the TV. Belofsky's mug fills half the screen and the anchor is delivering a profile on him. Viewers are asked to call the FBI at the number on the screen if they see him.

He jumps up, groans when he sees Nick Hunter. Nenasheva told Belofsky that Hunter had captured Stanislavski. Hunter must know now that the senators have Tican in them. It's time to get the hell out of D.C., but Belofsky has something to do first. He goes to the window and looks

out on the street and at the park across the way. No cops.
It's time.

CHAPTER FIFTY-FOUR

Nick swings the Suburban around the circular drive and stops under the canopy supported by three white columns in front of the Plummers' mansion. Harlan and Doocy pull up behind him and get out.

The three-story white frame colonial house with Gothic windows sits on a hill with two cottages and three garages. A Mercedes and Lexus are in two of them.

These folks have money.

Nick waits at the door for Harlan and Doocy, then rings the bell. He's surprised when this tall beauty with blonde hair and slender built opens the door. He's expecting a butler in tails, wearing white gloves, or maybe an older woman, more rounded and not so damn good looking. She's wearing a red dress that comes above her knees, and looks younger than her fifty years. Chief Doocy steps in front of Nick.

"Thank you for seeing us, Veronica," the Chief says.

"Hello, Chief Doocy. Good to see you again," she says.

"Let's go into the sitting room," Veronica says. She smiles, and ushers them through a circular foyer that a giraffe could fit in, gleaming with Italian marble and opening into a large area with hardwood floors, and a wide staircase with incredible woodwork that leads up to heaven. She takes them around the stairs, down a hall wide enough for an elephant and into a room filled with white furniture, fireplace, grand piano, and walls with gold-framed paintings. Nick thinks he recognizes a Monet, probably an original. The furniture appears new. Probably rarely used.

They wait until she takes her seat and the three men sit. The hem of her dress is much above her knees. Nick eyes her muscular legs and smooth, milky skin. He likes what he sees.

"Now, what's this all about, Chief?" she says.

"Thank you for seeing us," he says, again. "This is FBI Deputy Director of Criminal Investigations, Harlan Kennedy," the Chief says, pointing to his left. Harlan nods and produces his ID.

Her face brightens. "Thank you, that's not necessary," she says in a warm, smooth voice, sounding more like Marilyn Monroe.

"And that is Nick Hunter, a homicide detective," Harlan says, turning to his left. Nick grins. "Pleased to meet you, ma'am."

She produces another friendly smile that makes Nick feel warm all over.

"We'd like to ask you a couple of questions," Harlan says, leaning forward.

Nick thinks Harlan sounds apologetic. The attractive blonde is probably flustering him.

A maid dressed in a neatly pressed uniform appears.

"Care for anything to drink, gentlemen?" Mrs. Plummer asks.

They decline and the maid makes her exit.

"So you haven't located him yet?" she says.

Harlan's eyes widened, apparently surprised at her directness. "Not yet," he says. "We learned from Chief Doocy that you last heard from the senator the day Congress went on vacation. Is that correct?"

"Yes. He called to tell me he'd be going away a few days on a trip with friends."

Yeah, probably some floozy, Nick thinks.

"Do you know who he went with?" Harlan asks.

"Gentlemen, let me be frank. My husband and I... well, we aren't on the best of terms. He seldom tells me anything."

"So, you don't know where he went or who he's with?" Nick asks.

Her shoulder-length blonde hair swayed as she shook her head. "I'm sorry."

"Does he usually go off on these trips?" Nick says.

"I'm afraid so."

"How do you stay in touch?"

"He calls when he wants to."

Nick realizes she never calls her husband by his first name.

"What if you have an emergency?" Harlan says.

"I have a sister. We stay in touch. If I forget to call, she checks on me."

"Mrs. Plummer—"

"Please... Veronica."

"Veronica, your husband is in great danger," Harlan says. He tells her about the virus, and he doesn't sugar-coat its lethality. "If there's anything that could help us find him, anything at all, no matter how insignificant you may think it is, please tell us."

Is Harlan hinting at a girlfriend?

She eases out of her chair and walks to the mantel without saying a word, rubs a hand over a picture in which she's standing between two good-looking teenagers. She doesn't appear to be upset over the news about the senator. "I'm afraid my feelings for my husband changed when my boys were in middle school," she says. "You see, I'm an embarrassment—no, a disappointment to him."

"Oh, no, Veronica," Doocy says.

"Oh, yes, Chief. I became a model right out of high school, and was flying around the world doing shoots. I don't have the level of education my husband would be proud of. A Ph.D. would make him happy, or maybe a master's degree." She sighs. "You're probably wondering why he married me… easy to explain, gentlemen. He uses me as a showpiece for when we entertain his friends, and to sit with him on platforms while he makes those awful political speeches of his. He loves the D.C. life, but I hate it."

She could have had any guy she wanted, Nick thinks. Why does she put up with his bullshit? The reason has to be money. Lots of money. This home has to be worth millions. *It's always the money, isn't it?* And a roof over her head—security for a woman who no longer has a career. She's too old now to model again.

"There is one thing… a strange man called last night," she says, returning to her seat. "He wanted to talk to 'Senator Plummer.' Said he had something that would save his life."

"Did he say what it was?" Nick asks.

"No, he hung up when I told him the senator wasn't here."

Nick looks at Harlan and Doocy.

"Was there anything unusual about his voice?" Nick asks. "Did he have an accent?"

"A strong one. He sounded like he could be Russian." She sighs. "How much time… I mean when will the senator get sick?"

She still didn't call him by his name.

"A couple of days," Nick says.

———— ◆ ————

Kenny drops his backpack on the floor in the den, takes off his jacket and throws it on the couch.

"Let me show you around," Nick says. Kenny stays close to him, going through the rooms, but not seeming too interested. They end up at the bar, where Nick reaches into the fridge for a Bud and a Coke. He hands the soft drink to Kenny, who gulps half of it.

"Thirsty?"

"Yeah, didn't get much to drink on the plane." He moseys behind the bar, looking at the photos on the wall. "Dad! Here's a picture of me with my soccer team."

"I took that after you guys beat North Central. Remember?" Nick swallows some of his Bud.

Kenny shifts from behind the bar. "I remember." He looks out the glass doors on the lake. "That's when you left us."

A hammer slams into Nick's chest. He didn't expect his twelve-year-old son to be so honest. "Come sit."

Kenny collapses in the chair across from the TV.

"Figured someday you'd want an explanation. I guess this is as good a time as any." Nick finishes his beer and sets the bottle down.

"Understand one thing, Kenny. You weren't the reason your mother and I split up. Don't ever think that. Okay? It was me."

"I wanted a dad," Kenny says. "Why did you leave us?"

"Work came between your mother and me. I was gone a lot."

Somewhere outside a truck horn blasts.

"We just couldn't get along."

"Sometimes I got scared and hid in the closet," Kenny says. "You guys fought all the time."

"That's why I left. I'm really sorry. I want to make it up to you."

Kenny jumps up, throws his drink can into the trash and lingers by the doors. "Can I go out on the deck?"

"Sure."

There is overcast this late afternoon, and the wind is blowing. "You may need your jacket," Nick says.

"I'm okay." He's at the edge of the landing, watching a speedboat buzz by on the choppy waters.

"I like it here."

A dozen birds land in a tall oak. They screech and discharge droppings.

"Mom says I could come and live with you, Dad."

"I'm surprised your mother said that." He remembered the way she lied to the judge to get Kenny. Nick thought she'd never give him up. But he's twelve now, and the judge should be okay with it.

"She doesn't want me anymore."

What did the mean bitch say to his boy? He'd like to wring her fuckin' neck. "Did she scream at you?"

"No, Dad. She's got a boyfriend. They go a lot." He glances at the boat returning. "I'm in the way."

So that's it.

"Mom's not Mom anymore," Kenny says, turning back to face his dad. Tears well in his eyes. "Nobody wants me."

"That's not true, son. I want you. You're going to live with me from now on." Nick grabs Kenny and pulls him into his arms. "I love you, son."

"Loveya, too, Dad."

CHAPTER FIFTY-FIVE

Susan and her techs head out of the conference room and stride through a glass walkway to the Path building. Inside, they enter a room filled with computers, electron microscopes, DNA sequencers, and the world's most advanced instrument technology. Susan steers them through the back door, where they end up in the locker room. The women remove their clothes in a separate area from the men, don green scrubs, and snap on latex gloves. They slip into disposable gowns and a second set of gloves, seal them at the wrists with tape, and pull on face shields. When done, Susan walks them down a hall and pulls hard on the lab door marked *Biosafety Level-2*. The CDC had opted for inward air flow into this lab, creating a negative pressure that prevented the release of odor or any microorganisms to the outside.

The M.E. in Atlanta had expressed Eva's tissue and blood samples to Susan. Tony and Ryan carry them from the freezer to the biosafety cabinets and set them inside under the glass door to thaw. Harriet joins them. Looking through glass panels, the techs reach for the flasks and begin extracting MX particles while Susan prepares tissue samples for the scanning electron microscope. Eleven hours later they finish. Tony and Ryan head to the electron microscope in the instrument room.

Harriet brings the vial of purified particles to the counter for Susan to check her results. Susan's heart sinks.

"Doesn't look like much, Doc," Harriet says.

Susan nods. "Enough to test in the rabbits, but we'll need more. A lot more." Where in the hell could she get more M-X particles?

"Can we call Atlanta for more blood?" Harriet says.

"'Fraid Mrs. Gerber bled out too fast. The M.E. sent all he had."

"What are we going to do?" Harriet says. "Even if Eva's particles work in the rabbits, we can't use their antibodies to treat humans."

Susan doesn't answer. Instead, she moves to the window and looks out into the corridor. *Dear God, I need a miracle.* A minute passes. The miracle hits her between the eyes. She shudders at the thought. *It's the only way.*

"You okay, Doc?" Harriet says.

Susan turns to Harriet. "I know how we are going to get more particles."

"How?"

It's gruesome, but Susan doesn't know of any other way.

"From here on out it's going to be gruesome," Susan says.

Harriet's eyes widen. "What do you mean?"

Tony and Ryan come in. "How'd it go?" Susan asks.

"The micrographs should be streaming in shortly," Tony says.

"I want you two to bring up four rabbits," Susan says. "We'll test the particles in two hours. That should allow the rabbits enough time to acclimate. I want all of you to get some rest. You're going to need it."

Harriet says, "Wait, Doc. You haven't told me what it is that's going to be so terrible."

"Not now. I got some figuring to do." Susan pushes through the door, removes her face shield, and pulls off her gloves and gown.

Back in the admin building, she steps into her office, flops in her chair, and sighs.

Eight p.m., December 23rd. Thirty-five hours left until some senators start keeling over.

From the desk drawer, she removes a pad, reaches for a pen and begins calculating the number of particles needed to save nineteen senators. Using the amount of particles taken from Eva's blood, and the number of liters of blood in the human body, Susan determines the number of particles needed that might cure one person. Next she calculates the number that could be gotten if they drew blood from all nineteen as soon as they showed signs from Tican mutation. Her fear is coming true. There wouldn't be enough to save all the senators. Additional blood will be needed to get more particles, and that can only come from blood taken from some of them as they approach death. She looks at her figures and recalculates, hoping she's made a mistake. Seconds later, she realizes she's made no mistake. Staring at her figures, her pulse begins to speed up. *Five must die.* She'll need their blood to save the others.

Susan glances at the picture on the desk. *Mom, I gotta do this. There's no other way.*

She lifts the phone and dials a number. Lets it ring ten times. Finally, a nurse answers. Susan hears screaming and shouting in the background.

"This is Dr. Prescott. What's going on?"

"We're in a crisis, Doctor."

"Let me talk to Dr. Tremont."

"He's wrestling a patient. I'll tell him you called. I gotta go."

"Don't hang up!"

Click.

Susan redials.

"Tremont."

"What's all that commotion?"

He doesn't answer, instead he's shouting at someone. "Mercedes, take Senator Weldon back to his room."

"Tremont?" Susan says. "What the hell's going on?"

"Son-of-a-bitch, you've created a mess here," he says. "Did you tell Cartwright his eyes were going to pop out?"

"He asked me what he could expect if we didn't find the antidote. I told him the truth and that the eye thing was possible."

"After I got your message I told the senators they were infected. Man, they went bananas," he says. "Cartwright told everyone there was no treatment and you'd never find an antidote in time. That they'd all bleed to death and their eyes would pop out. It's been total hell." He sighs. "We've had senators running up and down the hall screaming they were going to bleed to death, others were shouting that their eyes were about to pop out, and a few tried to escape down the stairs. One even tried to jump out a window in the men's room. We've restrained them and they're sedated. Their families are with them now, praying."

"Is anyone bleeding or coughing up blood?"

"Not yet, but Cartwright and Girard are complaining of pain in their heads and chests," he says, "and lots of them are coughing. We're running out of time. You don't have the antidote, do you?"

"That's why I'm calling. We're ready to test it, and if it works, we're going to need their blood." She hesitates, but has to say it. "The way I figure it five senators must die, but their blood will save the others."

There is silence.

Shit! Come on, Tremont.

"It's crucial that you monitor them closely," Susan says. "Call me the minute someone coughs up some crap or bleeds... a sign that the virus is mutating. Call me then, not a minute later! We'll come and take blood before... and after they expire."

"Susan? They're not guinea pigs," he says.

"Dammit, Tremont, I need you on board with me. We've gotta have their blood. You want to save some of them, don't you?"

She hears voices in the background. "Tremont? Are you there?"

"Okay, okay. I'm with you on this."
Click.

———◆———

Four hours later, dressed for the Level-2 lab, Susan opens the door and goes in. It's nearly midnight. The team joins her at the rabbit cages. Harriet heads to the fridge for the vial.

"Usually, antigens are injected ever twelve hours," she says, "and antibodies appear in a week. But that's not always the case. We're going to inject every two hours, and take blood until we find antibodies. Any questions?" Hearing none, she says, "Let's go do it."

The first round of injections were administered around one a.m.

"We have less than thirty-one hours. Let's hope this works."

"What about it, Doc?" Harriet says. "Were ya gonna get more particles?"

"Later," Susan says, turning to Ryan. "Are the EM pictures in?"

"Got 'em," he says. At the computer, he fingers the keyboard. Images of MX and Tican appear on a split screen.

"Their protein envelopes appear identical," Susan says, staring at the pictures. "Now bring up the brain and kidney."

"Sure thing."

"Wow! The cells are full of MX," Harriet says.

"Doc is lucky he was able to get samples," Susan says.

She fought off the mental images of Eva's last minutes on this earth.

"How come there weren't any lung samples?" Tony says.

"The virus releases enzymes that dissolve the lungs," Susan says.

The rabbits rustle in their cages and chew on the metal doors.

"Did she suffer?" Tony asks.

"The pain in her lungs must have been excruciating until the virus attacked her brain."

"Time to inject the rabbits again," Harriet says.

Blood is drawn and taken to the cabinets. The second round of injections is completed at three a.m. The process is repeated at five and seven a.m. No antibodies are found in the sera of the one, three or five o'clock samples. Susan hides her disappointment. Maybe we're going to see more eyes popping out. Dammit! These particles have to work. Blood is drawn and the last injections are made at nine a.m.

Christmas Eve. Twenty-two hours.

The phone rings. Susan's heart sinks. *Please, God, not yet.* "This is Dr. Prescott," she says.

"I've missed you," Nick says.

It is so good to hear his voice. She has been sleeping at the lab. Couldn't leave… so much to do. "Missed you, too." She could use a hug right now.

"I know. Any luck with the antidote?"

Why is everyone riding her? *Get hold of yourself.* "Not yet, but getting close."

"You don't sound like yourself."

It's because she thought it was Tremont calling. Her heart is still thumping. "Just tired," she says. "Did you find the senator?"

"Not yet."

She wonders if Plummer is dead.

"Antibodies in the seven o'clock!" Tony shouts. Ryan hurries to his side.

"Gotta go, Nick."

"Loveya."

"Me, too," she says.

Click.

Susan hurries to Tony. "Let me check it." She feels giddy and senses the tide of joy washing over her. "The particles are doing their stuff."

"Antibodies in the nine o'clock, too," Harriet says.

"Alleluia! Alleluia," the techs shout in unison.

The titers were high.

Eleven a.m. Twenty hours.

Susan sits on the edge of the desk and tells her techs to grab a seat. It's time to let them in on the gruesome story. "Now that we know the particles work, I can tell you where we're going to get more particles." She stares at their narrow eyes.

They know.

"From the senators," Harriet says.

"Right. We'll get a call the second one of them coughs up blood or bleeds from the nose or eyes."

"Does that mean they're dying?" Ryan says.

"Means the virus is mutating and attacking their cells."

"But they'll die, right?"

She detects sorrow in his voice. "I'm sorry. They must."

"Sweet, Jesus. You planned this all along," Harriet says.

They're staring at Susan, probably thinking she's a cold-hearted soul. Thank God they don't know she is responsible for this tragedy. Saving most of the senators should count for something.

"Know a better way?" Susan says.

Silence is their answer.

Finally, Tony says, "How much blood?"

They're not going to like this.

"How much? Harriet asks in a defiant tone.

"Five liters."

"Wow!" Tony says.

"—Sweet, Jesus."

"Our job is to save as many as we can. When the hospital calls, Harriet and I will rush over there and draw blood. Tony, you and Ryan will get ready for the extractions. When we return, we're going to be damn busy."

Susan wished that no one had to die. The fear and pale faces of the senators' families still linger in her mind. She has experienced those same emotions when she lost her mother and sister. The senators' families will learn, as she did, that their loved ones who pass will always be with them.

The phone rings. Susan grabs the phone.

"We're on our way."

Twelve noon, December 24th. Nineteen hours.

———◆———

Susan and Harriet dart out of the admin building with leak-proof boxes and hop in the Suburban. They race north on Georgia Avenue, turn right on Elder Street, and pull up to the guard shack. Susan holds out her ID. "I'm Dr. Prescott from the CDC to see Dr. Austin Tremont."

"Pass through, ma'am," the soldier says.

In the underground garage of Building 14 she swings into a spot by the entrance. They spring out, reach for the boxes and take the elevator to the fourth floor. Tremont is talking to a nurse outside the doctors' lounge.

"What do we have?" Susan says, almost out of breath.

"Let me help you with those things," he says, placing the boxes on a cart against the wall. "Four senators: Cartwright, Girard, Muller and Simon."

"I remember Cartwright and Girard."

"The other two are the women on the committee."

"Any bleeding?" Susan asks.

"They're coughing up mucus with streaks of blood, and complaining of sharp pains when they breathe. One has a nose bleed."

"Where can we dress?"

He guides them through a door. They slip into gowns and gloves. After fastening on face shields, they follow Tremont into the hall. He pulls the cart away from the wall.

"We need to hurry," Susan says.

When they come to the waiting area, Susan's heart feels heavy as iron. The senators' families are talking nervously, wiping tears, while others stare at the floor. The Girard girls are sleeping with their heads in their mother's lap. Susan steels herself.

"Holy Moses. Are those family members?" Harriet says.

"They won't go home," Tremont says.

"That's so sad," Harriet says.

"Shut it out of your mind," Susan says. "We've got work to do." She hurries past the grieving relatives, trusting that the protective clothing has disguised her.

"We have the senators in a special critical care unit," Tremont says. "Nurses have been instructed to watch for any signs of bleeding."

"Good," Susan says.

The glass doors hiss open. There is a circular nurses' station in the center of the room, ten private units are around the periphery. Each has a glass door and a curtain behind blocking the view inside.

Two senators in hospital gowns and gray ankle socks stumble out shouting. Nurses jump up and hurry to them. "I'm not going to die in bed," the woman senator says, restraints dangling from her wrists. A nurse grabs her. "Let's get you back in bed, dear," she says.

The elder senator is holding his eyes, crying, "My eyes are hurting, they're going to pop out."

"Senator Cartwright, you must get back in bed," Susan says, helping the nurse guide him into his room.

"You're the bitch!" he shouts. "You fuckin' lied to us. Where's my antidote?"

Please," Susan says, "we're doing all we can."

"Lies, all lies. Lord, God, I don't want to die," he cries. One side bar on his bed is down, and the restraints are still tied to both sides. They get him back in the bed and tie him down. "Give him 2 mgs of lorazepam, nurse," Susan says.

Tremont hurries out of Senator Mullen's room. "How is she?" Susan asks.

"She's resting."

Harriet is by the cart in front of the nurses' station. "They knocked out the other two senators and tied them to the bed," Harriet says. "They look like ghosts."

"There's a couch over in the corner." Tremont says. "You can wait there and I'll get some coffee." He leaves and returns minutes later with cups and a pot. Susan has swallowed half of her coffee when a nurse rushes over. "Cartwright and Mullen are bleeding!"

"I'll take Cartwright," Susan says.

"I'll do Mullen," Tremont says.

"Harriet wait by the cart and be careful storing the bags," Susan says.

"All right, all ready," Harriet says.

The nurse grabs supplies and follows Susan.

Cartwright is unconscious. Blood is oozing out of his eyes and nose, more from his mouth. Susan inserts a needle and fills bags with his blood. Cartwright coughs—blood shoots over her face shield. "Whoa," Susan shouts, backing away. The nurse brings her a towel and Susan cleans her shield, then goes out to Harriet. Are you marking these bags pre-death?"

"Is the Pope Catholic?

"No time for funny business. Did Dr. Tremont finish with Mullen?"

"Holy Moses," Harriet says. "You should of seen him. He was soaked in blood."

"Quick! Simon and Girard." Tremont shouts.

"I'll handle Simon," Susan says, darting into her room.

The nurse is holding a bowl under Simon's chin. "She's coughing up a lot of blood."

The senator appears to be in her late fifties, slender, and has a few streaks of gray.

"Blood's coming from her eyes now," the nurse says. "I've never seen this before."

"It's going to get worse," Susan says. "Wait until her brain oozes out of her nose."

"Oh, the poor thing," the nurse says.

Susan draws blood and takes the bags to Harriet.

That makes four senators.

A screeching noise at the entrance catches Susan's attention. Two medics rush in wheeling a gurney.

"Got another one from the second floor, doc. He's bleeding pretty bad."

"Put him in the room down on the right," Tremont says. He turns to Susan. "That's Senator Bannister. I'll attend to him."

That makes five.

Thirty minutes later, Tremont shuffles out looking exhausted. He and Susan end up in the doctor's lounge at the end of the hall.

Two p.m. Christmas Eve. Seventeen hours.

"Coffee or Coke?"

"Water. Thank you."

"Haven't been in such a rat race since my residency days," Tremont says. He hands her a bottle. "That was some time ago."

"Me, too," she says, removing the cap and taking a drink.

"You look beat," he says.

"I am, but we have to keep going."

"I nearly forgot… it's Christmas Eve."

"Never gave it a thought until I saw the decorations at the nurses' station."

"Do you really think your particles will work?" he asks, swallowing his Coke.

"I do," she says, thinking Tremont is more clinician than scientist. "You seem skeptical."

"It's just that I don't know. But you're the scientist."

"That I am," she says.

The door flies open. The nurse shouts, "Cartwright and Muller have expired."

Susan drops the bottle and water gurgles out as it rolls across the floor.

They bolt out.

Susan runs to Cartwright. No longer can she be shocked at what she'll see. The senator's worst fear has happened—his eyes lie on his chest. The sockets are filled with blood and pieces of brain flow out of his nostrils. She stares at him for a few seconds.

You're going to save the others, senator.

She inserts the needle and fills bags with his blood.

Tremont sticks his head in the doorway. "Hurry, the other three have just died."

"I'm done here," she says, and stumbles out of the room.

Three p.m. Sixteen and counting.

CHAPTER FIFTY-SIX

Jessica Winters ambles into the den and flips on the twelve o'clock news. The last few days with Barry have been heavenly. He cooks and waits on her, and she is thrilled that he hasn't run off to the Capitol.

With a blast of music, a news alert flashes on the screen. The anchor says, "We've just got word that the FBI has taken senators from their homes and rushed them to Walter Reed Army Hospital. We don't have all the details, but we're working on it." He presses a finger to the button in his ear. "We've also learned that the Chairman, Senator Plummer, is not among them.

"Oh, my God!" Jessica shouts. "Walter Reed? That means something terrible has happened to them."

The anchor continues. "The senators are members of the Foreign Relations Committee. We're attempting to find out *why* they were taken to the hospital. Once we get that information, we'll bring it to you."

Jessica dashes into the kitchen, opens the door leading to the backyard and calls out: "Baby, come quick."

Instantly, he hurries in carrying a tray of grilled steaks. "You must really be hungry," he says.

"They mentioned you on TV."

He shoves the meat into the oven and turns to her, frowning. "You sure you heard it right?"

"Of course." She moves to him. "FBI took senators to Walter Reed. The guy on TV said you were missing from the group. Oh, Baby, I'm scared. Someone probably poisoned them. Do you feel okay?"

"I feel fine," he says, hurrying to the den and glancing at the TV screen. He watches. Nothing is mentioned again about him or his committee. He hurries to the phone in his office, lifts the receiver and starting at the top, he pushes each of the buttons arranged in a vertical line next to the last names of his committee members, one at a time, and waits. Minutes go by and no one answers. "Shit."

"What are you doing?" Jessica asks.

"Trying to reach my committee."

She stomps her foot. "I told you, they're all at the hospital."

Another alert explodes on the screen. Jessica and the senator rush into the den.

Their eyes are fixed on the screen. The announcer repeats the earlier information, and adds: "It's believed the senators are infected with a virus. If Senator Plummer is watching, he should call the FBI immediately at the number on the screen. It's most urgent." The anchor touches his ear, again. "I'm being told that the FBI is going to have a press conference in a few minutes. Please stand by."

Jessica mutes the sound. "Baby? You gotta call 'em."

He doesn't respond.

"Dammit. You got a freakin' bug in you. Call 'em."

The clock marks the passing of time with a steady beat. Tick, tick, tick.

"They're not telling us everything," he says.

"Look. The FBI's coming on." She releases the mute button.

A man at the microphone pulls out a sheet of paper from his coat pocket, introduces himself as FBI Deputy Director Harlan Kennedy and the man in hospital whites standing next to him as Dr. Austin Tremont, Chief of the Medical Staff at Walter Reed. Harlan tells the press he'll not be taking questions, but additional information will be distributed. He pauses again, looking at his notes. A mug shot of Dmitri Belofsky appears on half-screen. Harlan takes his time pronouncing the name.

"Look at the freakin' scar on that Neanderthal's face," Jessica says. "I'd hate to meet him in a dark alley."

"What would you be doing in an alley anyway," Plummer says, smiling, apparently wishing to release some tension by inferring that she might be there having sex.

She waves a hand, "Oh, you. Get it out of the gutter. You know what I mean."

Harlan continues. "This man you see on your screen is responsible for infecting senators on the Foreign Relations Committee with a virus. If anyone has seen him, or knows of his whereabouts, please call us at this number. If you spot him, do not, I repeat, *do not* try to apprehend him. He is extremely dangerous." Harlan glances at Tremont. "Dr. Tremont has something to say."

Is my baby going to die? Jessica wonders.

Tremont steps up to the microphone and lowers it. "We're doing everything we can for the senators," he says. "We've learned from the CDC that the virus is new, but fortunately it does not go airborne. So it isn't contagious, and there's no reason to panic. The CDC has it under control, and the senators will be treated with an antidote."

"They're covering it up," Barry says. "Look at his eyes and his body language. They don't have shit."

"You don't know that."

"What did I just say?"

She shoots a death stare at him. "You think you know everything."

"Hell, I've been a politician all my life. I know when a person is lying. I'll get some antibiotics from my own physician and I'll be fine."

"It's a damn virus!" she shouts. "My doc told me antibiotics don't work on them."

"Well, I'm not going to Reed. I could die in that prison."

"You'll die if you don't go there." She gets up, goes to the phone and reaches for the receiver and holds it out to him. "Please. At least call them?"

He yanks the phone out of her hand and slams it down on its base, pushes her aside.

Baby, you're so damn stubborn.

"For all we know my entire committee could be dead." The phone rings. His body jerks.

Jessica yanks the phone away and looks at the caller ID. "It's Veronica."

"Don't answer it," he says.

She shoves the phone into his chest. "Dammit, she's probably freaking out over your ass."

He shoots a scorched look at her.

She mutes the TV. Because of his stubbornness, he's going to die.

"I told you never to call me," he says into the phone. "I'm fine... I'm not lying. I said I'm fine." He shifts the phone to the other ear. "Okay. I will. Okay, okay, I said, I would." He reaches for a pen. "Let's have it." He writes on the pad by the phone. "Yeah, yeah, I got it."

The clock strikes one... tick, tick, tick.

Jessica asks him what Veronica said.

"Some guy's got a cure for sale."

"What guy?"

"Veronica says he sounds foreign."

"You think it's that Belofsky guy?"

"Probably some crackpot. Besides, how did he get my home phone number?"

She shrugs. "How in the hell do I know?"

"The bastard says he shot me with somethin' that's going to kill me."

"Shot you? He must be crazy."

Barry appears in deep thought. "Wait a minute. Remember that night we had the flat tire after leaving Crazy Horse?"

"Yeah. You thought you pinched a nerve in your neck."

"That could be the time this bastard shot me with the virus."

"Baby, how much is he asking for the cure?"

"A mil."

"You gotta be kidding. You gonna pay it?"

"It's my life we're talking about."

Tick, tick, tick.

Barry dials the number on the pad.

"What about me? I might be infected, too?" she says.

"Didn't you hear what that doc at Walter Reed said? It isn't contagious." He raises a hand. "It's ringing... You the one who called my home about some cure? Who are you? I'd like to know who I'm dealing with. Okay, okay. Will my girlfriend need it, too?" Barry places a hand over the mouth piece. "He says you weren't infected, just me." He removes his hand. "Why do you care what happens to me? Yes, money is important... how do I know the antidote will work?" There's a pause.

Jessica doesn't trust the guy. He could screw Barry.

"When and where do you want to meet?" Plummer asks. "An hour? Here? I'll need more time to get the money. Okay." He hung up the phone. "This guy knows everything about us. He says you're a hot piece, and... uh, a good looker."

"Call the FBI. Let them get the son-of-a-bitch," she says.

"No feds. If he sees them, he'll take off like a gazelle running from a starving lion, and I'll be a dead man." He drops the phone, and falls to his knees.

Jessica rushes to him. "Baby, what's wrong?"

"A little dizzy," he says, sitting on the floor.

"I'll call 911."

"No!"

"Baby, I'm scared."

"No! I said." He rubs his head. "Haven't eaten since last night."

"How about some water?"

"Shit, no." He reaches for her hand. "Help me up."

"Let me take you to the emergency room."

"I said no!" He paces across the room. "See. I'm okay."

"Are you sure?"

"I'll be in my office talking to my banker. Bring me a steak sandwich and a beer."

Tick, tick, tick.

———•◆•———

Belofsky knocks on the door. The big woman in the next apartment answers. "Haven't seen you in a while, man."

"Been gone."

Her little boy comes running from the kitchen with jelly on his hands and face. Belofsky skirts him. *Fuckin' kid.*

"You come for your stuff?" she says.

"Yeah."

He follows her to the fridge. "It's still where you put it," she says."

Belofsky grabs the small Styrofoam cooler from the freezer, heads towards the door, and stops. He reaches into his pocket for the tool. Maybe he'll take her now. But she never called the cops. He decides to let her live.

She opens the door, not knowing how close she came to dying.

Back in his apartment, Belofsky sets the cooler on the counter and opens it. *Lots of ice. Good.* When he hands the cylinder over, it has to be cold. He goes into the bedroom and dresses in his new suit, reaches for his Makarov on the dresser and shoves it inside the belt at the hollow of his back. In the bathroom, he covers his scar with makeup, pulls on a brown wig and slips in blue contacts. He stares into the mirror. Now he's a blue-eyed man with brown hair in a dark business suit. Not bad.

Belofsky grabs the cooler and leaves.

CHAPTER FIFTY-SEVEN

Nick drives away in the Suburban from his D.C. hotel around eight that morning and enters the traffic. His pager vibrates. He reaches for the car phone and dials the Deputy Director. A car cuts in front of Nick, nearly hitting his front fender.

"Damn D.C. drivers!" he shouts. "They don't know what *yield* means."

Harlan answers, tells Nick to meet him on New Jersey, north of L Street. They've gotten a tip on Belofsky. It's a bad area in the Southeast. It's 1992, and Washington is still the most violent urban region in the U.S. and a cesspool for criminals.

When Nick arrives, he wheels in behind Chief Doocy's squad car. Across the street are five black Suburbans. Harlan is talking to an agent by the lead vehicle. The street is empty, except for two dogs that race past. Folks in this part of town stay in when they see the cops and remain pretty tight-lipped. That's why Nick is surprised someone ratted on Belofsky. Whoever it is must have gotten the shit kicked out of him.

A team of FBI agents, dressed in blue jackets with large FBI letters on their backs, fall in behind Harlan with their nine millimeter Glocks in hand.

Nick joins Harlan and Doocy in the middle of the street.

"Belofsky's apartment is in the next block, second floor, front," Harlan says. "Follow me."

Several agents dash behind the building and others flow in and up the stairs like a tsunami, with the triumvirate bringing up the rear. The agents line up with their backs against the wall outside Belofsky's apartment. Eyes appear out of the apartment next door. A woman's stare is locked on Harlan's Glock. A four-year-old boy wraps his arms around his mother's leg.

Nick knows he has to play it cool if he wants to get anything out of this mother. He rubs the little guy's head.

"What's his name?"

"Jordan," she says.

Another one named after Michael. "Like Michael Jordan?" he asks.

"Yeah. The Man." she says, and smiles.

Jordan runs back into the room.

"Do you know Mr. Belofsky next door?"

"Sorta. Whatta him do?"

He's a killer and you'd better not confront him. "Is he home now?"

Her face turns serious. "Him gone."

"When did he leave?"

"Don't know. Ain't seen him."

"How long has he lived here?"

Jordan returns, screaming for candy.

"Maybe six months."

"Anyone stay with him?"

"Him always alone."

"Thank you ma'am. You take care of Jordan."

"Nick always had a way with people," Chief Doocy says, turning to Harlan.

"Are we going in or what?" Nick says, not liking the attention.

"Damn right," Harlan says, signaling to the squad leader.

They knock the door off its hinges with a ram rod and rush in with stiff arms stretched out, swinging their weapons from left to right.

"Clear," an agent says coming out of the bedroom.

"Clear in the bathroom and utility room," another says.

"All clear, sir," the leader says.

A bed and a chair are in the bedroom. A recliner is in front of a small TV in the living room. Nick opens the fridge. "Nothing in here but bottled water."

Harlan and Doocy rummage through the cabinets.

"Half-bottle of vodka and an empty glass on the counter," Doocy says.

Harlan slides the glass into an evidence bag.

"Got something here," Nick says, pulling a piece of Styrofoam from the freezer at the top of the fridge.

"What's the Styrofoam for?" Harlan asks.

"My guess is a cooler to keep the antidote cold."

"One thing I don't understand," Harlan says. "Why bring antidote with them if their mission is to kill senators?"

"I got a theory," Nick says. "Belofsky's not only a sociopath, but he's a greedy guy. He knows he can get big bucks for the antidote, and probably snuck it in without Sokolov knowing it. Belofsky's going to charge Plummer a bundle."

"Why does he need money?"

"He's bodyguard told us Belofsky's going to move in on organized crime," Nick says. "He'll need lots of money to buy some people off to become the big guy, a Mafia boss."

Harlan's pager vibrates. He looks around. "Where the hell is the phone?"

"There isn't one," Doocy says.

"Let's get out of here."

In his car, Harlan calls his office. "Put her through." He looks at Nick and Doocy. "It's Senator Plummer's girlfriend, Jessica Winters."

"Think I know why she's calling," Nick whispers to Doocy. "Belofsky."

Doocy shoots him a thumbs-up.

"This is Deputy Director Harlan Kennedy," he says. "Yes, I'm in charge." He listens for about thirty seconds. "That can be arranged." He pulls out his notebook. "What's that address? Got it. We're on our way."

"Where's the senator?" Nick asks.

"We got a break," Harlan says. "They're in Arlington and Belofsky's meeting them in thirty minutes with the antidote." He slides into the car. "Here's the address. The senator doesn't want the FBI near the place. He's afraid Belofsky will take off if he sees us, and he won't get his antidote. So, Nick, you'll handle the surveillance."

CHAPTER FIFTY-EIGHT

Susan and Harriet rush the two leak-proof containers out of the Army hospital to the Suburban. They drive out of the complex and speed south on Georgia Avenue under the roar of thunder and flash of lightning. Susan calls Tony from the car phone. "Get ready, we're on our way."

Four p.m. Christmas Eve. Fifteen hours.

A storm has moved in as Susan pulls the SUV into her space next to the admin building.

"Jesus, it's raining cats and dogs," Harriet says. "Hellava way to spend Christmas Eve."

"Sorry," Susan says. "We've got work to do. Let's go."

They hurry into the building with the boxes. After changing into fresh scrubs, they step into the lab. Tony and Ryan take the containers, Susan instructs them to keep the bags marked *pre-* and *post-death* separate and when they collect serum to label the containers with those same names. They immediately go to work. The phone rings. She wonders if more are dying.

It's Tremont. "How long will it be before you know?" he asks. Not being a researcher, she knows he isn't convinced her particles are going to work. He's a negative person, and she is right not to expect any encouragement from him.

"Any changes in the other senators?" she says, holding her breath.

"No. I've been a little jumpy since we lost the five."

The centrifuges are humming.

"Dammit, Tremont, get off my back. I'll call you when we're done."

Click and he's gone.

She's probably made him mad, but that's tough. He's acting like a teenager.

It takes them two hours to remove the serum.

Seven p.m. Twelve hours left.

Outside, lightning pops. Did it strike the roof?

Susan paces. Her synapses are on fire. So much is riding on these particles. They worked in the rabbits, but will they in humans?

"Doc? The serum from those sick guys had particles," Harriet says. "Now, we'll do the dead guys' serum."

"Senators, Harriet, Senators, not *guys*."

"Okay already."

Eight p.m. Eleven hours.

Susan heaves a sigh wondering where Nick is and if he's found Senator Plummer. No time to call him. Once this is over, they'll spend more time together—one relationship she prays is going to last a lifetime.

"Doc, as you said, there's lot more particles in the dead *senators'* serum," Harriet says.

"Great! Wonderful!" Susan shouts, feeling exhausted, like she's won a race. "Hurry, let's get these vials packed. Now we're going to learn the truth." She lifts the phone.

"Tremont, we're on our way."

Ten p.m. Christmas Eve. Nine hours and counting.

CHAPTER FIFTY-NINE

Barry Plummer is heading out the front door.

"Where are you going?" Jessica asks. "Stay put."

"Where the hell do you think? The guy'll be here any minute." The senator hurries down the stairs and rounds the hedges to the driveway and looks around. *Where's that detective? He better not blow this or I'm a dead man.*

———— ◆ ————

The December sun is peeking through the clouds when Belofsky drives the white van into Arlington. He checks the mirrors for cops. Twenty minutes from Plummer's street, he pulls into a Quick Stop, gets out and checks himself in the window's reflection. A business professional looked back at him. *Good.* The cops will never recognize him. He walks away with confidence.

He gets a coffee. The dark-haired beauty with alluring breasts behind the counter glances at him and smiles as she waits on the customer in front of him. Good piece, he thinks. He has his hand around the shaft of the pick in his pocket, fantasizing. *Pull up your skirt, baby. Roll down your panties while I shove it in you. Then I'll kill you.*

He hesitates. She looks too much like his sister, but younger. He leaves with his coffee and drives off. The fuckin' cops may think he's stupid, but they'll never get him. He's the big boss now. He passes Plummer's place, circles the block twice. No FBI vans, no agents on telephone poles and no police cars. Tall hedges in the front yard block his view. He pulls next to the curb, gets out and crosses the street,

247

moving up the driveway past the Lexus, watching his back.

Plummer is on the lawn, face down. Belofsky kicks him in the ribs. Plummer moans. He kicks him again, harder. Plummer shoots over onto his back. "What the hell," he says, opening his eyes. "I feel like shit. You trying to kill me? Where's my antidote?"

A jet flies over.

"I need my cure." Plummer says.

"You got money?"

Plummer sits up, runs a hand through his hair. "The bank needed more time."

Belofsky grabs him by the shirt and pulls him up. "Get money. Now!"

"Give me the antidote. I need it now!"

"No! First, get money."

"You'll get it, big guy." Plummer coughs. "We'll have to go to my office to get it."

Jessica appears at the door. "What's wrong? What's he doing to you, Baby?"

"Nothing."

"Baby, you don't look so good."

"Get your purse, that big one, and hurry," he says, pushing her into the house. Belofsky watches from the door. A few minutes pass and they rush out. Plummer holds on to Jessica's arm as she clutches a bag and he brings a satchel. "Let's go," he says to Belofsky.

They head to the van. "Hurry," the Russian says, shoving them as they cross the street. The senator stumbles and falls, Jessica pulls him along. "You're sick," she says.

"I have to do this," Plummer says. "It's the only way."

Belofsky opens the side door and they throw in the bags. Jessica jumps in, and the senator joins Belofsky up front, but can't seem to hold up his head. They speed off.

Ten minutes later they are heading into D.C., and Jessica is giving directions. Belofsky checks the mirrors again, turns left at 30th Street and stops in front of a six-story office building on the corner. They hop out. Plummer struggles to hurry to the entrance.

Inside, they take the elevator to the sixth floor. Belofsky pushes Jessica and Plummer out. The senator falls and instantly, Belofsky has him back on his feet. It is the weekend and no one is in the three-suite office. Plummer points to the wet bar in the corner of his office and Jessica leads him to it. He drops the satchel. "We'll have to push this bar to one side," he says to Belofsky. All three shove it to one side, exposing a large metal plate in the tiled floor. Plummer fumbles to open a desk drawer, snatches a ring of keys. His hands shake as he fumbles through them to select the one he wants. He kneels and opens the door in the floor.

"Wow!" Jessica shouts, "Crisp twenties. Did you make them?"

"Don't be a wise ass. There's a hundred in each pack. We'll need five hundred. Start counting." He begins throwing bundles on the floor next to Jessica. She and Belofsky stuff them into the bags as they hit the floor.

"Why are you hiding money in the floor?" she says.

Plummer doesn't answer; he's shaking.

"Well?" she says.

Finally he says, "This's campaign money."

"You mean payoffs?" she says.

"Hurry," Belofsky says. "No talking."

CHAPTER SIXTY

Susan and Harriet rush into Building 14 at Reed. They ride the elevator to the second floor. As they step out, Tremont and two nurses approach them. "We're ready," he says.

"Got to hurry." Susan sets the box on the cart and looks at her watch. **Eleven p.m., Christmas Eve. Eight hours left.**

The nurse helps Susan with the gloves. Susan looks at the clipboard. The senators in 201 are Blair Radford and Carlos Sanchez. She opens the box and finds vials #1 and #2. "I'll take these." She reads the nurses badge. "Jonna, follow me. Harriet, you man the cart and mark off the names as we come out."

Tremont reached for vials #3 and #4 and goes into 202 with nurse Mercedes.

Susan pushes through the door. "Senators Radford and Sanchez, we've got good news. I have the antidote."

Radford is in the bed next to the wall. He is in his sixties, but looks younger. Jonna cleans his arm with an antiseptic.

"Will it work?" he asks.

"I'm counting on it," Susan says.

"I've got seven grandchildren who need me."

She inserts the needle and pushes on the plunger, delivering 1 cc of antidote. "I'm done," she says, handing the syringe to Jonna.

"How long before we know?" he asks.

She wants to tell them they'll be okay. But she doesn't know. Maybe she's thinking it'll work to convince herself. If the antidote doesn't work, by morning they'll all be dead.

"By morning," she says, moving to Sanchez, who is in the bed near the door. The dark skinned senator has glassy eyes and a pleasant smile

250

that takes up most of his face. He sticks out his arm. "How about you, Senator Sanchez, do you have a big family?" Susan says.

"Many. I hope to see all of them back in New Mexico."

She is praying he will. "We'll be back to check on you later." In the hall, she looks at the wall clock. That took four minutes. Tremont and Mercedes come out of 202.

"Any problems?" she asks.

"None."

"Let's keep it going."

Minutes later they meet at the nurses' station. Harriet pushes the cart down a few doors.

Susan inspects the list. "Just about done. We'll take Larsen and Watts in 206. Tremont, you treat the last one, Justin Weldon, in 207."

"Gee, thanks. He's a mean son-of-a-bitch." Tremont reaches for the vial marked *13*, and turns and walks towards 207. A phlebotomist carrying a tray full of supplies rushes round the corner and rams into Tremont. The vial flies from his hand, bounces off the cart, hits the wall and explodes into pieces as it hits the floor. Tremont's knees buckle and he lands on the floor, shaking.

Susan turns. *My God, that's Senator Weldon's dose.*

"You idiot!" she shouts, adrenaline shooting through her veins. "You realize what you've done?"

Tremont sits up, head on his knees. "God... I'm sorry."

"Sorry, hell," Susan says. She turns to Mercedes. "Give four milligrams of lorazepam to Senator Weldon, stat. And don't tell him a thing."

She nods.

Susan and Joanna head to 206. "Be careful with those vials," Susan says.

"Don't worry."

When Susan shuffles out, the wall clock above the nurses' station registers twelve midnight. "Merry Christmas," she says to Harriet.

"Gee, thanks."

Seven hours until life or death.

The elevator doors open and Michael stands there in the hall, surprisingly well dressed in a blue sport jacket and navy blue pants with a light-blue shirt open at the collar and shiny loafers. His hair is neat and he's shaven.

Wow! Is that my brother? Susan thinks.

He must have seen the surprised look on her face. He moves slowly towards her with his hand out. "Hi, Sis," he says. "I'm clean."

"Yes you are," Susan says, following with a big smile. "You look great."

"I've come to finish that talk we had at Thanksgiving."

"How did you find me?"

"I got a little help," he says.

"Nick?"

Michael smiles, but says nothing.

"There's nothing I'd like better than to have our talk, but this isn't the time, Michael," Susan says. She takes him by the arm and moves to the waiting room. In a whisper, she says, "Michael, I've screwed up badly, but I've been able to fix it, and now people's lives are in my hands for the next seven hours." She glances at the empty chair nearest to the hall.

"How about waiting for me here? I know it's a lot to ask. There's a cafeteria on one."

"Sure thing. Don't worry about me. You go do your thing and I'll be around."

———— ♦ ————

At seven Christmas morning, Michael pushes through the lounge door with a cup of coffee.

"Time to get up," he says.

Susan opens her eyes. "What? What's wrong?"

"It's seven. Dr. Tremont told me to wake you. I thought you could use this." He hands her the cup.

The last thing Susan remembers is lying down after making rounds at four a.m..

"Gosh, I forgot all about you, Michael. I'm sorry."

"Don't fret; I'm proud of what you are doing. The nurses took good care of me. While I don't know what happened, Dr. Tremont told me you saved many lives."

Susan rises, stretches her muscles, and takes the coffee. "My head hurts. I need this." She swallows half of it, sets it on the table. "Let's go."

Tremont meets them in the hall. "Weldon died a horrible death thirty minutes ago," he says, apologetically.

"We have to check on the other senators," she says to Michael. "I won't be long."

He smiled, seemingly proud of his sister. "I know."

As they move down the hall, Susan looks closely at Tremont. He appears tired and his face is drawn. *I know what you're going through. I've been there.*

"You start at the other end and I'll meet you at the nurses' station," Susan says.

He nods.

Susan heads into 206. Larsen is near the door. The curtain has been drawn between the two beds. He is staring at the ceiling, holding the sheet under his chin, eyes wide as saucers. No signs of blood.

"You okay, sir?" she says.

"Am I going to make it?"

"Sit up and let me check you. Anything hurting?"

"No."

She slides the stethoscope over his chest and his back, looks into eyes, ears, nose and mouth. "Everything seems normal."

"So, am I going to be all right?"

"Yes, you are."

"Thank you, doctor. Thank you, thank you. You're a saint."

He wouldn't say that if he knew the truth.

Susan shuffles to the other side of the curtain. Senator Watts' wife is sitting in a chair reading a Nora Robert's novel. She looks up. "Jeremy hasn't said a word for two hours."

"Let's see how he's doing." He's shaking, but no bleeding. "Senator, how are you feeling?"

"Scared to death. With each breath I've wondered if it was literally my last."

"Well, you don't have to wonder any longer. How about sitting up for me?"

After checking him over, she tells them that the senator will be fine.

"We want to thank you for saving his life," Mrs. Watts says.

"They've certainly kept us pretty busy," Susan says.

Watts grabs her hand. "Thanks," he says. "None of us would have made it, if it weren't for you."

"You're welcome."

"Doctor..."

"Yes?"

"Merry Christmas."

"Merry Christmas, Senator."

Susan leaves the room and meets Tremont as he approaches from down the hall.

"Gotta hand it to you, Susan," he says, "they're all doing great."

"I'm glad it's over." She sighs, feeling relieved. "Now, I've got to spend some time with my brother."

'I understand," he says.

———— ◆ ————

Michael is in the waiting room reading a novel when Susan approaches him. "I'm free now," she says, "How about something to eat?"

"I've eaten, but I'll come with you."

"How's the novel?"

"I enjoy reading about James Patterson's detective, Alex Cross."

"Wish I had more time to read other things beside scientific journals." She shrugs, "Probably an excuse on my part."

They take the elevator to the first floor, step out and walk around the corner to the back.

Inside the cafeteria, Michael finds an empty table and Susan goes through the line for egg substitute with unbuttered whole wheat toast and black coffee.

Moving through a number of half-occupied tables and carrying a tray, Susan goes to Michael, removes her plates of food and sets the tray on an empty table.

"Michael, you really look great." She sits in the chair facing him. "I can't get over it."

"Thanks. I'm determined to stay with therapy for as long as it takes."

"Good."

"My counselor back in Atlanta says we're really making headway. I like her. Her name is Angela"

"It's so good to hear that from you, Michael," Susan says, as she takes a bite of her eggs and breaks off a piece of toast.

Michael leans in to the table; his gaze is fixed on Susan, and says, "Sis, Angela has helped me to see that my behavior and my drinking were tied in to my running from my pain."

"Because of Mom's death?" Susan adds.

He nods. "Mostly because I thought Mom left me, but it also has to do with my feelings towards Dad."

"I'm not surprised," she says.

"I hadn't realized that I transferred my anger to him. I just knew I hated him. It was all due to Dad not taking Mom's place when I needed him."

Susan remembers her conversation with her father at Thanksgiving. Fathers have conversations with their children during those times and do fun things together to get their children through their hurting.

Susan reminds him, "You were only six years old."

"I know, but Angela says that I still haven't grieved Mom's death properly, and if I do, it will help me to connect my sadness and confusion and anger to her leaving me, and I'll begin healing."

Susan drinks some of her coffee and listens with great interest.

"There's something else," he says. "I'm working on building my confidence. Angela's given me exercises to overcome my fears, so I can go digging for the facts about my life that I've buried because of the pain."

"Remember," Susan says, "that 'perfect love casts out fear.'"
Maybe he'll learn to love Dad again.

"I have faith that I can now overcome my demons and be transformed into a good person."

"Oh, Michael," Susan says, reaching across the table and placing her hand on his. "You've always been a good person. It's just that a tragedy knocked you off the beaten path of love, but now you're back."

"I'm on my way to see Dad before returning to Atlanta, but I wanted to come by and talk to you first. I want us to be close again."

"We will, Michael, always." She rises and they hug. "Dad's waiting for you."

CHAPTER SIXTY-ONE

Nick drives past a white van that just pulled away from the curb across from Plummer's Arlington home. At the corner, he makes a U and follows it. Harlan and Doocy are waiting a couple of miles away.

Nick reaches for the car phone. "I'm tailing a white van on I-66 heading to D.C. Belofsky and Plummer are in the front seat, but I don't see the girlfriend."

"On our way," Harlan says. "Keep the line open."

Nick speaks again. "The van's turned on 30th Street and has stopped in front of an office building."

"We're close," Harlan says.

The building has six floors and lots of glass.

"They're leaving the van, the woman's carrying a big purse, and Plummer has a satchel," Nick says. "They're going into the building."

"Plummer's law firm is on the sixth floor," Harlan says. "Don't go in until we get there."

"Roger that," Nick says. No way he's going to wait. He hurries to the glass door. It's locked. He cups his hands and looks in. A security guard walks past a bank of elevators. Nick raps a coin on the glass. The guard stops and looks his way.

"Police!" Nick shouts, holding his ID against the glass. Maybe the guy won't notice he's with *Atlanta* PD. "I'm working with the FBI on a case," he shouts. "They're on their way right now. I need to come in."

The man looks puzzled.

"Come on, come on," Nick says.

The guard opens the door.

"Senator Plummer came in here with a woman and another man. Did you see them?"

"Yeah. They went up to his office."

"Plummer's been taken hostage," Nick says. "The FBI is pulling up now. Wait here and let them in." Nick takes off and rides the elevator to the top.

The elevator chimes as the doors open, and Nick rushes out.

"There's that detective," Jessica shouts as they are coming out of the office.

Belofsky pushes them across the hall, through the exit door and down the steps.

Nick is on their heels.

When they reach the fourth level, Belofsky drops the bags, knocks Jessica over the railing, and kicks Plummer down the steps. He turns and fires two rounds, hitting Nick. Before he goes down, Nick empties his Glock. Belofsky's riddled body sails over the banister.

FBI agents burst in around Nick, and Harlan flies through the door on the main floor and races up the stairs. He helps Nick sit up against the banister.

"Hold this cloth against your neck," Harlan tells him. "You've been nicked."

"He got me in the shoulder, too."

"Let's get that shirt off."

"Jesus! Take it easy," Nick says as he slips out of the shirt. "I believe the bullet's still in there."

"I thought I told you to wait for us," Harlan says.

Nick doesn't answer.

"Yeah, you got a hole in you a little smaller than a dime. We'll get the medics to look at this."

Harlan helps Nick to the ground floor. As the paramedics are wheeling Plummer out, Harlan asks them to look at Nick's wounds.

The M.E. waves to Harlan.

"You got here in a hurry, Doc," Harlan says.

"Yeah, you're lucky I was close by when I got the call." He bends over and examines Belofsky. "Someone got this big fellow good," he says. He turns and heads to Jessica.

The paramedics bandage Nick and put his arm in a sling. "You'll have to go to the hospital," the medic says.

"We're headed there now," Harlan says.

"Wait up," Nick says. Harlan follows him over to Belofsky's body. "Want to take one last look at the cruel bastard," Nick says.

"Didn't you tell me he jammed an ice pick up victims' noses?" Harlan says.

"Nostrils," Nick says.

"Well, you blew off the front of his face."

"That's payback for all the women he tortured. I hope he rots in hell."

"This young lady died from a broken neck and head trauma," the M.E. says. "I can't do much more here. Can we move 'em?"

"All yours, Doc," Harlan says.

Outside, the paramedics have shoved Plummer into the ambulance and are racing off to Reed with their siren blaring.

Nick asks one of the agents to check in the white van for a package. He returns seconds later with a Styrofoam container.

"What's in that?" Harlan asks as he opens the driver's door and gets behind the wheel of the Suburban.

"It's Belofsky's antiserum," Nick says, as he eases in. "Hurry. We gotta get this to Susan."

Harlan flips on the strobe lights and siren and races off to Walter Reed.

CHAPTER SIXTY-TWO

Susan waits for Nick outside the examining room. The paramedics have brought Plummer into the ER, and Austin Tremont is in with him.

Nick better hurry with the antiserum, or Plummer's not going to make it.

The black Suburban pulls up to the entrance. Nick clambers out and rushes to her.

"That the antiserum?" she asks.

"Yeah." He hands her the cylinder."

"What happened to you?"

"Belofsky shot me," he says.

"I'll check you when we're done here." She darts into the room.

Five minutes later, Susan comes out with a sad look. "The cylinder's empty."

"Holy Moses. That scum bag. Belofsky was going to rip Plummer off and let him die. Guess you were right not to trust him."

She holds back from saying, *I told you so.*

"What about *your* antidote?" he says.

"Used it all."

"What shitty luck for Plummer," he says. "Are the others okay?"

"We lost six and maybe soon it will be seven, but twelve are going to make it." Susan didn't have to tell Nick it was her fault some senators died; he already knew it.

"Let's go into this examination room," she says, escorting him into the next room. She helps him out of the sling and removes his shirt.

"You look tired," he says, as he holds his arm close and pushes himself up on the table.

"I haven't slept in thirty-six hours." She lowers the overhead lamp and unravels the bandage on his neck. Touching his neck stirs her.

259

Quivers flow down her spine. She and Nick haven't been together for days and now she wants him.

"Just a flesh wound. Doesn't need any stitches." She tells him to lie back so she can examine his shoulder wound.

"The bullet's still in there," he says.

Susan palpates around the wound with her gloved fingers. "You're right. I'll have to remove it." She leaves.

Seconds later, Susan returns with a nurse, and they go to the counter. "When did you have your last tetanus shot?" Susan asks.

"Couple years ago."

"Good."

The nurse wipes the wound with an antiseptic. She reaches for a syringe. "This may hurt a little," she says, as she injects a local anesthetic in and around the wound.

Minutes later, Susan reaches for the probe on the tray. "Does that hurt?" she asks, probing.

"No."

"Good." She drops the probe and takes pointed forceps and noses it into the wound, digging for the bullet.

A couple of minutes later, Susan holds the bullet in the light for Nick to see, and drops it into a pan. "Don't think you'll need the sling. I'll get you some pain pills."

"No narcotics, maybe just ibuprofen," he says.

She nods. "You can dress the wound now, nurse," Susan says, moving to the counter.

The door opens. Tremont enters, looking distressed. "We lost Senator Plummer."

That makes seven.

CHAPTER SIXTY-THREE

Susan and Nick leave Walter Reed around seven that evening, and thirty minutes later she stops in front of their hotel and turns off the engine.

She feels like she hasn't slept in a weeks, but can't succumb to sleep. Not just yet.

"We missed dinner," she says.

"Don't feel much like eating."

"Neither do I."

Inside, they take the stairs up to the second floor, side-stepping the cleaning woman pushing her cart past them.

"Working late?" Susan says.

"Happens sometimes," she says.

Susan reaches in her purse for her key, but before she can insert it into the lock, Nick lifts her chin and plants a soft kiss on her lips. She kisses him back.

"Any pain in that shoulder?"

"None. Anyway, your kisses are easing my pain," he says.

"Corny," she says. They laugh.

In the hall, the ice machine kicks on and ice drops into the bin.

Susan opens the door and pulls Nick in. She unbuttons the top button of her blouse, and then the next. "Are you just going to stand there now that you aren't in any pain?" she says.

"No," he says, helping her. He sheds the blouse off her shoulders. Her skirt drops to the floor and she hurries into the bathroom. Nick gets out of his clothes and hops into bed. Susan sashays into the room wearing a red teddy and slides under the covers.

Susan wakes up with the sun coming through the window that

overlooked the street. She and Nick are lying sideways in the bed with the covers on the floor. She's surprised at the time: ten-thirty.

Nick's back is to her.

"Are you asleep?" she asks.

"Can't you hear me snoring?"

She punches him lightly. "That's not funny."

He moves on top of her.

"Now that's more like it," she says.

An hour later, Susan tells him to get dressed.

"Where we going?" he says, rolling out of bed.

"Breakfast. I have something to tell you," she says, pulling on her jeans and sweat shirt.

He dresses in slacks and shirt.

Outside, the bright sun makes Susan feel fresh and energized. They enter the café two doors down from their hotel. The place reminds her of Starbucks. Free-standing tables are in the center of the room, tables and chairs around the sides, a few overstuffed chairs occupied by students working on their laptops. She chooses a table by the window, facing the street.

"This must be important," Nick says. "You haven't said a word since we left the room."

"It is."

The waiter approaches. They order coffee and toasted bagels.

Susan reaches for Nick's hand. "Nick, Tican has changed my life. Once I got past the shame of being betrayed by Vladimir, I learned something about myself."

The waiter brings their food. She drinks some of her coffee.

"While I worked on the antidote, my subconscious was working overtime to get my attention," she says. "I realize now that the dying senators became a metaphor for cancer, and it hit me what I should be doing with my life."

"And what's that?" he says, spreading grape jelly on his bagel.

"Cancer research," she says. "It's what I really wanted to do all along and I didn't listen to my instincts."

"Deep stuff," he says with brows in a horizontal line.

"Why the sad look?" she says.

"That decision could affect us." He took a bite of his bagel. "And I don't want it to."

She anticipated his reaction. "Nothing will change between us."

"It will if you leave Atlanta." He swallows his coffee. "You know the saying: out of sight, out of mind."

"I don't plan to leave," she says. "I am planning on working for one of the research centers in Atlanta."

"But there's something else," he says.

She's holding her breath. *He's not going to leave me like the others, is he? Not Nick.* She loves him too much to lose him.

"Kenny lives with me now," he says. "Could this affect our relationship?"

She breathes a sigh of relief. "No, of course not. From what you've told me, Kenny will be happier with you."

"I was hoping you'd say that. I want you to meet him. He's a wonderful boy."

"I'd like that very much."

"Great," Nick says. "Then we don't have anything to worry about." He finishes his coffee and looks at his watch. "It's twelve-forty-five. We gotta go. Harlan wants me to meet with him at one-thirty."

They step outside and head back to the hotel.

"Our flight isn't until five," she says. "Got a couple of things I need to do."

Their Suburbans are at the curb.

"By the way, how's Michael doing?" he says.

"You don't know?"

"Know what?"

"That he came here to see me."

He frowns. "How would I know that?"

"Because you told him where to find me. Don't act so innocent. I can tell from your face you did it."

He seemingly can't hold back the smile that covers his face. "Okay. I admit it. I did it because he needs you."

"Thank you. He looks so good and is doing so well. We've made up and he's on his way to make things right with Dad."

"Good. You all need each other. Family is important. That's what I've learned lately." Nick opens his car door. "Meet you back here at three. Harlan can take us to the airport."

"That's the least he can do," she says, "since he has to pick up his SUVs anyway."

———— ◆ ————

Susan swings the Suburban in next to the admin building at the CDC satellite lab, gets out and rushes to the research building. The techs had left early this morning for Atlanta.

Susan steps into the Level 2. At the fridge she reaches in for the black tube she had shoved in the back earlier, drops it into a small refrigerated container and slides it into her purse.

Tican.
She walks out.

THE END

A NOTE TO READERS

Thank you for reading my novel. I hope you've enjoyed reading it as much as I did writing it. If you liked *72 Hours*, I hope you'll look forward to reading *The Watchman* and my latest novel, *You'll Never See Me Again: A Crime to Remember*.

As an author, I greatly appreciate any and all reviews on my books, so if you can take the time to leave one where you purchased the book, I'd be grateful. Reviews help other readers find new books, and they're especially important to newer authors like me. Thank you for sharing your love of reading with others!

Every quarter I hold a drawing for a free, autographed copy of one of my novels. Please go to my website (www.robertamagarian.com) and sign up. In addition, you will receive quarterly newsletters and hear about any new releases.

Website: www.robertamagarian.com

Facebook: www.facebook.com/authorRAM

Twitter: www.twitter.com/authorRAM

LinkedIn: www.linkedin.com/in/robertmagarian

Email: author@robertmagarian.com

Goodreads:
www.goodreads.com/author/show/4019298.Robert_Magarian

ACKNOWLEDGMENTS

To Charmaine, my best fan and love of my life. I couldn't have done this without your support.

To Captain Scott Waldrup, Aton, Illinois Police Department for your help on police matters.

To Craig Manning, CDC, Atlanta, for your invaluable assistance about the Centers for Disease Control and Prevention.

To Cheryl Hampton, Atlanta PD, for your assistance.

To the FBI agent, who wishes to remain anonymous, for your help with FBI matters.

To Dr. Collie Trant, M.D., Chief Medical Examiner, State of Oklahoma, Oklahoma City, for enlightening me on the use of the ice pick in the murders.

To author Carolyn Wall, my teacher and confidant, for your patience in making this novel work better. Your insightful comments helped me immeasurably.

To Nancy Hancock, for carefully reading the manuscript and for a great editing job. You're the best.

To my brother, Dr. Edward Magarian, for reading the manuscript and for your advice. I enjoyed our many discussions.

To my life-long friend, Dr. Joe Allen, for reading the manuscript and for keeping me in line.

To Dr. Brandt Cassidy, Director of Operations, DNA Solutions, Inc., Oklahoma City, for your specialized knowledge and advice on the microbe.

To Kathleen Cassidy (Brandt's wife), for reading the manuscript and for her comments. Miss you Kathleen. You left us too soon.

To Tim Kellogg, paramedic (NREMTP), for your help with the accident-prone Susan Prescott.

ABOUT THE AUTHOR

Robert Magarian is the author of three thriller novels: *The Watchman, 72 Hours,* and *You'll Never See Me Again: A Crime to Remember.* In addition to his fiction, Robert is the author of two nonfiction essays, *Follow Your Dream* and *A Journey into Faith.* He lives with his family in Norman, Oklahoma.

www.robertamagarian.com